G

**Praise for Book One
*Son***

"A very promising sta...
...*enver Post*

Praise for *Song of the Beast*

"A good introduction to this wonderful fantasy author's work because it's a stand alone yet has length, intensity, and themes common with her previously published Rai-kirah trilogy. This new novel has even stronger narrative drive than its powerful predecessors; it's a fantasy I didn't want to put down."
—*Victoria McManus, SFRevu.com*

"Berg's fascinating fantasy is a puzzle story, with a Celtic-flavored setting and a plot as intricate and absorbing as fine Celtic lacework. . . . The characters are memorable, and Berg's intelligence and narrative skill make this stand-alone fantasy most commendable."
—*Booklist*

"The plot keeps twisting right until the end. . . . Entertaining characters."
—*Locus*

"A well-crafted mystery."
—*Kliatt*

"Dragons' voices and one man's sheer, indomitable will blend to produce a powerful story of courage and faith. *Song of the Beast* is this summer's sleeper hit."
—*The Davis Enterprise*

Transformation, Revelation, and *Restoration* The acclaimed Rai-kirah Saga

"Vivid characters and intricate magic combined with a fascinating world and the sure touch of a Real Writer—luscious work!"   —*Melanie Rawn*

"This well-written fantasy grabs the reader by the throat on page one and doesn't let go. . . . Wonderful."
—*Starburst*

"Berg greatly expands her world with surprising insights."
—*The Denver Post*

THE
SOUL WEAVER

Book Three of
The Bridge of D'Arnath

CAROL BERG

A ROC BOOK

ROC

Published by New American Library, a division of
Penguin Group (USA) Inc., 375 Hudson Street,
New York, New York 10014, USA
Penguin Group (Canada), 90 Eglinton Avenue East, Suite 700, Toronto,
Ontario M4P 2Y3, Canada (a division of Pearson Penguin Canada Inc.)
Penguin Books Ltd., 80 Strand, London WC2R 0RL, England
Penguin Ireland, 25 St. Stephen's Green, Dublin 2,
Ireland (a division of Penguin Books Ltd.)
Penguin Group (Australia), 250 Camberwell Road, Camberwell, Victoria 3124,
Australia (a division of Pearson Australia Group Pty. Ltd.)
Penguin Books India Pvt. Ltd., 11 Community Centre, Panchsheel Park,
New Delhi - 110 017, India
Penguin Group (NZ), 67 Apollo Drive, Mairangi Bay,
Auckland 1311, New Zealand (a division of Pearson New Zealand Ltd.)
Penguin Books (South Africa) (Pty.) Ltd., 24 Sturdee Avenue,
Rosebank, Johannesburg 2196, South Africa

Penguin Books Ltd., Registered Offices:
80 Strand, London WC2R 0RL, England

First published by Roc, an imprint of New American Library,
a division of Penguin Group (USA) Inc.

First Printing, February 2005
10 9 8 7 6 5 4 3 2

For Mother

In the Lists of the Dar'Nethi are tallied the full number of the Talents: Singer, Builder, Silver Shaper, Tree Delver . . . They are named without interpretation of their worth and without report of their rarity, for who is to say that the common Builder, who sings his bricks into the harmonious arch that pleases a thousand eyes every morn, is of any less value than the Word Winder, who creates an intricate enchantment that only a few can use to any effect? D'Arnath himself was born to be a Balancer, a most ordinary gift, but it was magnificence of his soul that made him a Balancer of Worlds.

Yet there are three rare Talents that cause a hush to fall among the people when they are named. One is Speaker, for the gift of discernment and truth-telling is rarely welcomed, and those who practice it are never other than alone.

The second is Healer, for of all things, life is the most sacred to the Dar'Nethi, and the youth or maid who accepts the gift of life-giving is both blessed for the glory of the calling and pitied for the burdens of it.

The third is Soul Weaver. Some say there has never been a true Soul Weaver, for who could relinquish his own life so completely, taking unto himself the full body, mind, and spirit of another being—lending strength or courage, skill or knowledge—and then be able to yield the other soul undamaged? Who could do such a thing and himself remain whole? Some say the Soul Weaver should not be entered in the Lists. It could be no part of the Dar'Nethi Way, for it is an impossible calling and only a legend amongst a people who are themselves the stuff of legends.

Ven'Dar yn Cyran
"A Brief History of the Dar'Nethi Way"

PROLOGUE

Karon

My senses were deafened by Jayereth's pain. Desperately I fought to maintain my control, to prevent her agony from confusing my purpose. We were bound by an enchantment of healing, our mingled blood linking our minds in the realm of flesh and spirit. If I shut out the experience of her senses, then I was powerless to heal her, but if I could not quiet her enough to see what I was doing, she was lost just as surely. Dark waves already lapped on the shores of her life.

Jayereth, hear me. . . . Hold fast . . . for your daughter, newly born to grace your house . . . for T'Vero who cherishes you . . . for your Prince who is in such need of your service . . . With everything I knew of Jayereth I commanded her to hold quiet—just for the moment it would take me to see what I needed to see.

She understood me, I think, for there came the briefest ebb in the death tide, an instant's clearing in the red mist of her pain and madness that let me perceive a host of things too terrible to know: ribs smashed, lungs torn, blood . . . everywhere hot, pooling blood and fragments of bone, her belly in shreds . . . Earth and sky, how had they done this? It was as if they knew every possible remedy a Healer could provide and had arranged it so I could do nothing but make things worse.

Another instant and I was awash once more in Jayereth's torment, feeling her struggle to breathe with a chest on fire and a mind blasted with fear. I could not give her strength or endurance, only my healing skill and a few pitiful words of comfort. But even as I fought to knit together the ragged edges of her heart, her last remnants of thought and reason flicked out. Her screams sagged into a low, flat wail . . . and then silence. I had lost her.

Let her go, I told myself, *you can't help her by traveling the only road she has yet to travel. That road is not for you . . . not yet.* Forcing aside the wave of enveloping darkness, I gritted my teeth and spoke the command, "Cut it now."

My companion cut away the strip of linen that bound my forearm to Jayereth's and allowed our mingled blood to feed my sorcery. The cold touch that seared my flesh was not his knife—his hand was too experienced for that—but the sealing of a scar that would forever remind me of my failure in my young counselor's last need.

The red mist vanished and the death tide, and my bleary eyes focused on the ravaged body crumpled on the stone floor of my lectorium. The only sound in the candlelit wreckage of the chamber was my shaking breath as I knelt beside my fallen counselor and grieved for the horror she had known. *Cross swiftly, Jayereth. Do not linger in this realm out of yearning for what is lost. I'll care for T'Vero and your child. On D'Arnath's sword, I swear it.*

I envisioned Jayereth as she had been, short and plain, with brown hair, a liberal dash of freckles across her straight nose and plump cheeks, and the most brilliant young mind in Avonar tucked behind her eccentric humor. When I summoned Jayereth's young husband, T'Vero, I would try to keep this image in mind and not the gruesome reality.

"Was there nothing to be done, my lord?"

Two small, strong hands gripped my right arm and helped me to my feet. Bareil always knew my needs. Unable to speak as yet, I shook my head and leaned on the Dulcé's sturdy shoulder as he led me to a wooden stool he'd set upright. Padding softly through the wreckage, he summoned those who huddled beyond the door.

One by one the four remaining Preceptors of Gondai crept into the chamber, gaping at the devastation. The oak-paneled walls were charred, the worktables in splinters, the shredded books in jumbled heaps. No vessel remained unshattered, no liquid unspilled; every surface was etched by lightnings more violent than those from any storm of nature's making. The acrid smoke of smoldering herbs mingled with blue and green vapors from pooled liquids to sting noses and eyes. Most fearful, of course, was the corpse sprawled in the midst of the destruction—Jayereth and the rictus of horror that had been her glowing face.

"How was it possible, my lord Prince?" one whispered.

"Who could have done this?"

"In the very heart of the palace . . ."

". . . treason . . ."

The word was inevitable, though I didn't want to hear it.

". . . and her work, of course . . ."

"All lost," I said. I had known it in the instant I'd heard the thunderous noise.

Jayereth's discovery should have been secured the previous night. I was her Prince. It had been my responsibility. But selfish desires had lured me into a night's adventure, and so I had put off duty until this morning. Too late. Before I could protect Jayereth or her work, our enemies had ripped her apart and left no place for me to heal.

With a furious sweep of my hand, I cleared the tottering worktable of chips of plaster and broken glass, then kicked the splintered leg and let the slate top crash to the floor. Only when the dust had settled again had I control enough to address my waiting Preceptors. "Search every corner of the palace, every house, ruin, and hovel in the city. No one is to leave Avonar. Ustele, you will watch for any portal opening. We will discover who dares do murder in my house."

Useless orders. Useless anger. No common conspirator had wrought such destruction fifty paces from my bedchamber. The protections on the palace of the Prince of Avonar were the most powerful that could be devised. For a thousand years no enemy had breached these rose-colored walls, and no Dar'Nethi thought-reading was required to understand what every one of the wide-eyed Preceptors saw. No soulless Zhid had slain Jayereth—no lurking stranger. The murderer was one of us.

Bareil went to summon Jayereth's husband. The Preceptor Gar'Dena, a giant of a man resplendent in green silk and a ruby-studded belt, brusquely dispatched the other Preceptors to the duties I had detailed. When Gar'Dena and I were left alone, he looked down at Jayereth. "Has there been any disruption in the Circle? Any sign from Marcus or the others? This event leaves me wary of all our enterprises."

I shook my head. "No ill word from the Circle." As far as we knew the Lords had not yet noticed our most powerful sorcerers taking up positions on the boundaries of the Vales, ready to form an expanding ring of impenetrable enchantment around the healthy lands of my adopted world. "As of yesterday, Ce'Aret had almost two hundred in place. And we've had no news of our agents in Zhev'Na, but, of course, we've no way to know if they've been taken. Maybe that's what this is—the notice of their failure."

We both knew it wasn't so. The elimination of Jayereth and her work was no blind strike of retaliation, but clearly aimed. Someone knew what she had discovered and knew that she'd not yet passed on all of her knowledge. Only six people in the universe knew the secret—and to any one of them I would entrust my life.

Gar'Dena lowered his massive bulk to the floor and with the gentlest of hands straightened Jayereth's tortured limbs. With a plump finger and a soft word, he smoothed her face into peace, masking blood and charred flesh with a delicate tracery of illusion. "She was just the age of my own Arielle and destined to be the greatest Dar'Nethi sorcerer in a thousand years. Ah, my lord, I could not comprehend it when you pulled her from my gem shop and raised her so high in your councils. When you showed us what you'd seen in her, I wept at my lack of vision. Which of us is vile enough to have done it?"

I rested my back on the charred wall and rubbed my

aching head. "If I knew, that one would already lie dead at her feet."

There had been a time when such words coming from my mouth would have caused me an hour of self-reproach, of castigating myself for abandoning the ideals of my youth, the tenets of my people that said there was no gift more sacred and more untouchable than another's life. But justice, too, was an ideal worth serving.

Gar'Dena bore Jayereth from the study in his thick arms, laying her in the palace preparation room as if she'd been brought in from outside. Our custom required us to let the dead lie undisturbed for half a day, lest the departed soul find its way back to its body before it crossed the Verges into the afterlife. But no one could be allowed to know the assault had taken place in the heart of the palace, not before we discovered the culprit. The news of such penetration by our enemies would cause panic. And I already knew that Jayereth wasn't coming back.

I remained in my private sitting room, slumped in a chair doing nothing until Bareil tapped on the door to let me know that T'Vero had arrived. A short, sturdy man, painfully young, his eyes wide and wary at this early summoning, followed the Dulcé into the room. "My lord Prince," he said, bowing halfheartedly. "Where is my wife? She never came home last night."

I did as I had to do, grieving with the young husband at Jayereth's side until he had taken into himself the wholeness of his sorrow. After giving him my promise, as I had Jayereth, that their child would want for nothing I could provide, I left him alone to stand vigil with her. When the time was completed, he would take her away.

My belly sour, my eyes like sandhills, I returned to my study to await the reports of my Preceptors. The Preceptorate was a body of the most talented, most powerful sorcerers in Gondai, charged with teaching and guiding our people, including their sovereign, in matters of sorcery. In effect, the Preceptors served as my council of advisors in everything of true importance. Treachery and cowardice had left four of the seven seats vacant when I had taken up my duties in Avonar four years

ago. Taking the time to learn my way around the politics
and personalities of Gondai, I had filled only two as yet.
Now one of those was vacant again.

Over the next hours each of the remaining four came
to me to report that nothing could be discovered of un-
warranted entry into the palace, of surreptitious enchantments or openings of portals that could allow a villain's
escape. I did not scrutinize the content of the reports so
much as each messenger, looking for the nervous twitch
or the cast of an eye that would tell me where I had
been wrong.

First the acid-tongued Balancer, a woman who had
given ruthlessly in the war against the Lords of Zhev'Na
for seventy years, sacrificing her family and home and
exhausting her physical strength.

Then the irascible old Historian who never took his
piercing eyes from my hands, judging their works by
the exacting standards of Dar'Nethi history and his own
peculiar view of our destiny, whose open distrust and
unyielding criticism dismissed any belief in hidden treachery.

Next the exuberant giant of a Gem Worker whose
meaty hands had held the fragile secret of my safety and
Seri's while I was imprisoned in Zhev'Na, the faithful
steward whose stubborn strength had held Avonar together until I returned.

And last, the newest of my counselors, the unpreten-
tious Word Winder who could create the most complex
enchantments from the nuances of spoken language, the
gentle teacher of the Way, the friend who could challenge me to a debate about the ethics of healing and
then in the next breath set me laughing at a bawdy song.

The door of my private sitting room clicked shut behind Preceptor Ven'Dar, leaving me alone. A breeze
whispered through the open casement, stirring my hair
as I sat staring at the white lights that blossomed through
the city in the deepening blue of the summer evening.
Crowds of people in jewel-colored garb filled the streets,
calling greetings and laughing at the merry enchantments
of street entertainers, laughing, even after a millennium
of war in which nine-tenths of our world had been ru-

ined and three-quarters of our population had perished or been enslaved. Always before, even on the most difficult of days, I had been able to find solace in the beauties of my new home and the strength of my people. Not on this night.

On the mirrorlike surface of a small table next to my chair sat a red lacquered box. Only Bareil and I knew what lay inside the box: a small triangular pyramid of black crystal, set in a plain iron ring. Simple enough. Yet its simplicity belied its history. At the age of thirty-two I had been executed—burned to death, the penalty for being born a sorcerer in the mundane world beyond D'Arnath's Bridge. But before my soul could cross the mysterious boundary we called the Verges, the border between this life and the life that follows, the Dar'Nethi sorcerer Dassine had reached out with his enchantments and ensnared me, binding me to this simple artifact until he could return me to life in the body of his violent, soul-dead prince. Now, my finger's touch upon the black stone's surface would release me from this body I'd been given and transport me to the realm of the dead where I belonged.

Unbidden, my hands took the red lacquered box that held my mortality and turned it over and over, my thumb rubbing the smooth simplicity of its lines. What life I had was a gift, given not to correct the misfortune of my too-early death, but in hopes that I might find some way to heal a universe ripped apart by evil. I already had ample reason to question Dassine's belief that I was capable of such a task. Now, things had grown far worse. Here was a simple dilemma, and I would have given a lifetime of sleep not to have to consider it.

Treason. Murder. I could not attach the words to any of the four Preceptors. Not even a Word Winder as skilled as Ven'Dar could do that. But unknown to my four counselors, I had shared Jayereth's news with two others, and it was the thought of that indiscretion that threw me into such great agitation as I gazed into the failing light of this villainous day. The Preceptors didn't know of my venture across the Bridge the previous night, when loneliness had sent me running to Seri for a brief, sweet hour. Thus they didn't know I had told her of Jayereth's news. Yet their respect for my extraordinary wife was so great that they would never touch her with a trace of suspicion. Even Ustele and Men'Thor, who constantly reproached me for my "unseemly attachment to these uncivilized, untalented mundanes," spoke of Seri with admiration.

But neither did my counselors know that I had spoken to the very person who had allowed Jayereth's talent to take wings. In the heart of the Lords' fortress, he had freed me of my slave collar, and in that single act of redemption made possible the solution that could free every Dar'Nethi slave. But the Preceptors would not understand that I had entrusted Avonar's deepest secrets to my son, he who had been, even for a few hours, Dieste the Destroyer, the Fourth Lord of Zhev'Na.

Unforgivably, irretrievably stupid . . .

CHAPTER 1

"*Ce'na davonet, Giré D'Arnath*! You'll dance at my daughter's naming day. I bring you the key!" Jayereth, late again. She danced into the council chamber, the garish beads that dangled from her hair, her neck, and her waist clacking as she whirled across the stone floor on her toes. I could feel Ustele's hackles rising. Jayereth scandalized many of the elder Dar'Nethi, who had not yet recognized the wisdom beneath her youthful irreverence.

"And what key is that?" I felt unremittingly dull, perhaps because I'd been sitting in this Preceptorate meeting since breakfast. Men'Thor had just left the chamber after sitting all day in the row of six auditors' chairs, here again at his father Ustele's invitation. Between them they had added another six hours to their four years of argument that my plan to defeat the Lords of Zhev'Na without bloodshed could never work.

To successfully counter an eminent Historian and a silken-voiced Effector who could make the most outlandish schemes sound as simple as planning a trip to market required more muscular debating skills than I possessed. Many people urged me to appoint Men'Thor to one of the vacant seats on the Preceptorate. But I suffered nightmares of having the father at one ear and the son at the other.

"You really must attend our meetings on time, Preceptor Jayereth," snapped Ce'Aret. "Happily, we've just begun our regular order of business."

Not so happily. That meant we had at least three hours of minutiae still to discuss. My mind had been wandering across D'Arnath's Bridge for half the day, conjuring the gleaming impertinence of my wife's brown eyes and the throaty richness of her voice. It had been far too long since I'd seen her . . . months. I needed to bury my face in her sweet breast and let her remind me again of who I was and what perverse path of fortune and duty had decreed we must remain so far apart.

Ignoring Ce'Aret's admonition, Ustele's glare, and Gar'Dena's and Ven'Dar's amused stares, Jayereth twirled once more, halting just in front of my chair, teetering on her toes until I thought she must fall into my lap. But she settled to her feet, pushed away the bead-woven brown curls fallen across her eyes, and swept a graceful bow, stirring the stale air of the stone council chamber with the scent of ginger soap. "I've brought the key to unlock the chains of your people, my lord! Is that not what you commanded me? No Dar'Nethi need fear the seal of Zhev'Na ever again."

At last her words penetrated my daydream and caused me to pay attention. "Mordemar . . ."

". . . has no power over any who wear this." She dangled a tiny silver medallion from her fingers on a fine silver chain that chinked lightly as she teased my eye. "It can be embedded into armor, or jewelry, or inset into a boot." The slip of metal she dropped into my fingers might have been a sliver of ice, setting my every hair crackling with frost, every pore stinging with life and health—monumental enchantment.

The key, indeed! I'd sworn that no Dar'Nethi would wear the slave collars of the Zhev'Na one moment longer than I could prevent, and the companion vow was to rob the Lords of the mordemar they used to seal the collars, the vile material that stripped a Dar'Nethi of the substance of his soul and with it all power for sorcery. And against all advice and expectation, I had entrusted the search for an answer to this thoroughly unconventional young woman. "You've found the countering enchantment."

"Give me a fortnight, and I'll refine the working until no metal is required. Let me show you."

Like a whirlwind reshaping the landscape, Jayereth

laid a crucible filled with gray powder and two thin, battered straps of metal side by side on the council table. As the other Preceptors gathered close, a burst of invisible fire from the young woman's hand caused the powder to slump into gray sludge. Even after four years, the stink of it wrenched my gut.

"Now watch. Feel." She poured the molten mordemar from the crucible into the narrow space between the two strips of metal as if to seal the closure of a slave collar. The liquid fell in thick, soft plops, spreading quickly as it touched the surface of the table, dissolving the steel edges of the collar and filling every bit of the space between. In moments it had hardened to a dull gray ridge. I closed my eyes and felt its vile enchantment swell into a dark knot in the path of life, a wretched blight that was the death of power and hope for the unlucky slave.

"Now touch it with the medallion."

Swallowing the memory of despair, I opened my eyes and laid the slip of silver on the hardened seal. As if the chamber walls around us had yielded a great sigh, I felt the dark enchantment unravel, dissolve, and swirl away. The gray seal disintegrated, leaving naught but two ugly strips of metal and a patch of dust.

"Magnificent!" bellowed Gar'Dena over my shoulder. "Great Vasrin's hand, girl, you've done it!"

Ven'Dar fingered the metal and the dust, sniffing it, tasting it. His smile grew slowly and when he looked up, his gaze met mine straight on. "Marvelous." No other words were necessary. He knew what this meant to me.

"We must think carefully about this," said Ustele, hobbling back to his seat, one hand raised in warning. "We can't just— Such a weapon. This news must stay amongst us. Secret. Until we decide how to use it."

"Balderdash!" said Gar'Dena. "Proclaim it to the world. Let the Lords know their time is fading."

"Well done, Preceptor," said Ce'Aret, her withered cheeks flushed, her fist clenched. Ce'Aret had lost three sons, two daughters, and her only grandson to the Lords of Zhev'Na and their warrior Zhid, four of them taken into slavery as she watched from the walls of Avonar. "Of course you can't be babbling the formulation about

the city. We can't have the devils restructure the making
of mordemar to counter your formulation. As Ustele
warns, we must be careful and thoughtful."

"Did anyone assist you?" I asked, awed at the enor-
mity of Jayereth's accomplishment. Yes, caution was certainly in order. "Have you told anyone? Written it
down?"

"No, no, and not yet." Grinning delight danced across
her countenance. "I wanted to surprise you, lord Prince.
You've seemed out of sorts of late."

"No insolence, young woman!" But I grinned back at
her, knowing she spoke truth.

Four years of unrelenting duty had been dragging at
my spirits, leaving me snappish and dull and feeling
sorry for myself. For weeks I had been promising myself
a venture across the D'Arnath's Bridge to steal a few
hours for my own need, and the only thing that had
enabled me to sit through this day's tedium was my vow
to go this very night no matter the Preceptors, the Lords,
or the end of the world.

But this discovery changed things, of course. I ran my
fingers through my hair trying to focus on duty and quell
the resentment rising in my gut. One of Gar'Dena's
daughters was ill. Ven'Dar was due to take the evening
inspection on the city walls, a duty that would take
hours. Neither Ce'Aret nor Ustele had a moment's patience with Jayereth and both were asleep with the pi-
geons on most evenings. We dared not spread the news
to Zhev'Na, but the surest way to secure Jayereth's
knowledge was to share it amongst ourselves. "This
meeting is over. I'll go with Jayereth, so she can show
me her—"

"No need to shepherd me, my lord," said Jayereth,
bundling her materials into her arms. "I've already
started copying my notes. If Mistress Ce'Aret will excuse
me from the rest of the meeting, I'll promise not to leave
the palace tonight until warded transcripts are safely in
each Preceptor's hands."

"Good . . . yes . . . that should do." I grabbed on to
her solution. Of course it was better that she commit

her information to paper so we could all know it. I could be back by the time she finished her transcriptions.

Jayereth bowed to the four Preceptors, and then sank to one knee in front of me, her plain face alight with triumph. "By midsummer every Dar'Nethi in Avonar will know how to make one of these. We'll have them free, my lord. Every slave shall be free."

As she hurried out of the room, Gar'Dena and Ustele continued to argue about how we should handle the news. The debate grew more strident by the moment, its premises all too familiar.

"Just stop!" I shouted. "Enough for today. Go find yourself some dinner, keep the information to yourself, and think carefully about it. Make sure Jayereth knows where you can be found so she can deliver her transcripts. We'll continue this discussion and all our other business tomorrow."

"I would speak with you about this matter as soon as possible, lord Prince."

"No, Ustele. Not tonight . . . I've other things to do."

"Where will you—?"

"It is none of your concern. We'll discuss it tomorrow." I was in no mood to be lectured about the frivolous expenditure of my time or my reckless usage of the Bridge that was "designed to keep the universe in balance, not to enable family visits." I left the old man muttering.

Without stopping to wash, shave, change clothes, or even grab the gifts I had selected months ago for my next visit, I ran down the stairs and passages into the deepest heart of the palace, walked through the warded door that would open only for me, and stepped through the wall of white fire and onto D'Arnath's Bridge. Two hours or so for the crossing, and I would be with Seri.

CHAPTER 2

Seri

Enough! I threw the wilted seedlings into my basket, stood up, and stretched my aching back, brushing away a long-legged spider tickling my grimy hand. The remaining bean plants stood nicely separated in the row of dark earth. My old friend Jonah would have been pleased that I remembered his lesson: Removing healthy seedlings to leave the others room to grow was necessary for a successful crop.

The sun was almost down. The evening damp creeping out from under the heavy leaves bore the rich scents of early summer: thyme and mint, greenness and good soil. I carried my basket to the waste heap at the edge of the garden, dumped the contents onto the pile of damp leaves, weeds, and dirt, and tossed the basket into the wooden barrow. As I rinsed my hands with a scoop of water from the rain barrel, running footsteps crunched the gravel path leading from the stableyard. I spun in the direction of the rosy afterglow just in time to see two long, blue-clad arms reaching for me, just in time to flush with pleasure and call his name. "Karon!"

I couldn't understand his answered greeting, as his head was buried in my neck and my hair, and no more words were forthcoming for a while as he kissed every finger's breadth of my grimy face. "I've only an hour," he said at last, spinning me dizzy in a fierce embrace. "Tomorrow comes quickly, and I've a thousand things pressing. Jayereth just brought us the most marvelous news, and I ought to be with her. But I've decreed this

time ours. Duty shall have no share of it. Only the two
of us . . ."

The two of us: I, a woman of middle years, living on
the charity of an old friend, and my husband, the Prince
of Avonar, ruler of a kingdom that was not of my own
world. To anyone who heard it, our story would sound
absurd. The body my husband wore was not the one I
had embraced in the brief years of our marriage. The
Prince D'Natheil bore little physical resemblance to the
slender, dark-haired Healer with the scarred arm who
had been burned to death sixteen years ago at the behest
of Leiran law. For ten years I had believed myself a
widow.

Yet this tall, fair sorcerer prince with arms like oak
trees and a back like a fortress wall was truly Karon. I
could hear it in his voice as he told me of how he'd
been unable to shake the image of my face while sitting
in a meeting of his counselors that day. I could sense it
in his manner as he paused to catch his breath, backing
away a step and holding my hand, half embarrassed at
his own display of passion. I could see it in his clear
blue eyes that shone with love and good humor and a
sheer, stubborn goodness that insisted on seeing its own
reflection even when gazing on the deepest horrors of
two worlds. Before I'd heard the story of how his salvation had come about, before he had regained his own
memory of his life, death, and return, I had known him.

As his gaze enfolded me like a sheepskin cloak in
winter, his skin thrummed with restless energy. His fingers, warm and wide, twined with my own, asking . . .
hoping . . . needing . . . "Ah, Seri, I miss you so."

I understood. I was not stone. But I held him at arm's
length, pulling him onto the path that led through the
gardens and walking briskly into the surrounding parkland. "First, tell me what thousand things prevent your
staying more than one pitiful hour. It's been three
months this time." Three months, two weeks, and three
days, in fact, since his last visit.

Four years ago Karon had brought our son Gerick,
our young friend Paulo, and me out of the grim fortress
of Zhev'Na, through the horrors of the Breach between

the worlds, and back to the world I once believed was
the only one in the universe. Gerick had repudiated the
Lords of Zhev'Na and cast his lot with us, giving up
immortality and sorcerous power beyond our compre-
hension because he refused to have our blood on his
hands. At that time, we had decided that Gerick could
not risk another crossing of the Breach, even using
D'Arnath's Bridge, until we had built a barrier of time
and love and ordinary life between him and the Lords,
and so Karon had taken up his duties in Avonar without
us. Gerick and I had come to stay with our friend Tennice in this genteel country house, surrounded by cherry
orchards and parkland and the rolling green countryside
of Valleor.

"Nothing different. Work. Traveling everywhere. Trying to get my own people to trust me. Trying to end this
damnable war. Trying to heal what I can. I've given up
thinking life will get simpler or easier. But I swore not
to talk about business. This time is for you. Anything
else—"

He tried to drag me to a stop, but I wrenched my
hand away and kept walking. "No. You must and will
talk about business. I need to know what you do every
day, Karon, what you think about, whom you talk to
and what they're like, the good and the bad of it. Tell
me about the weather, about your palace, and your
horse, and the healings you work. Imagining such things
is the only way I'm allowed to share your life. At least
tell me of reality, so I'll know I'm imagining something
close to it." So I wouldn't keep thinking of him as a
stranger when he was too far away for me to seek the
truth in his eyes or his manner or his voice.

In our first year at Verdillon, Karon had come to us
every few weeks, staying for days at a time. But necessity
ended that luxury. Karon was the Heir of the ancient
sorcerer king, D'Arnath, sovereign of all that remained
of Gondai, the magical world beyond the Breach, the
sole protector and defender of D'Arnath's Bridge, this
singular enchantment designed to counter the Lords and
their evils. Yet he knew almost none of his subjects and
had only a limited understanding of their world. The

Dar'Nethi needed the reassurance of their sovereign's presence. I could accept that. I was a warrior's daughter, raised to understand the obligations of a noble. If Karon was to lead his people, then he and his people had to learn to know and trust each other. Traveling the length and breadth of his realm, visiting every town and village to speak with his subjects, listen to their stories, and heal their ills, and developing his plans for ending the war left him little opportunity to make the time-consuming and difficult passage across D'Arnath's Bridge to this world. And so, as the months passed, his visits had become increasingly rare and far too brief. I felt as if we were going backward.

"All right. If that's what you want . . ." And so we walked in the spring-scented evening, and he gave me what I'd asked for, reining in one passion only to unleash another. He told me of the Preceptors and his plans and the increasing dangers of his war. ". . . The Zhid raiders grow bolder every day. Two farms burned last week, another village destroyed the week before, half its people taken as slaves, half left in madness, and its children . . . Oh, Seri"—his voice shook and his fingers almost crushed my own—"I came very close to heeding Men'Thor and Ustele and their constant harangues."

"They still call your strategy treason—the Circle, everything else?"

"Men'Thor is convinced that the only way to destroy the Zhid is to kill them all. The self-righteous bastard never changes his tone of voice and never changes his mind, no matter how you argue it. Ustele rails that we've lost our nerve, that I violate D'Arnath's oath every day I permit such horrors to continue. And truly, last week when I saw those slaughtered children, I wanted nothing more than to ride for Zhev'Na myself, my sword in hand. But today we had such news. Jayereth has found an answer. . . ."

Our pace increased until I almost had to double-step to keep up with him. His face shone as he explained how, after so long a preparation, months of travel, long, grueling hours of intricate enchantment, meetings and

argument, talking and convincing his hesitant subjects,
his plan was ready to go forward. One might have
thought his magnificent venture engaged already for the
vigor with which he propelled me about the cherry
orchard.

But as the last light faded in the west, his steps slowed
again. He pulled me into his arms, pressing my head to
his shoulder. The fine cambric of his shirt felt soft
against my cheek and warm with the muscled flesh underneath, and I cursed duty and politics and everything
else that conspired to keep us apart. "Ah, love," he said,
"you've let me babble far too long. The time runs . . .
and we've not even spoken of Gerick yet."

I closed my eyes, smothered my unhappiness, and
yielded pleasurably to the hand that stroked my hair. "It
wouldn't break my heart if we had more time with you."

"I've thought so much of him lately, wondering if the
time was any closer. . . . What do you think? Does it go
any better with him? The nightmares? Earth and sky,
how I want to be here with you. I scarcely know the
boy. I don't even know what he studies." His arms
threatened to squeeze the breath out of me.

"He still has nightmares, and he still won't talk about
them. But they seem less frequent of late, and less . . .
disruptive . . . and in every other sense he grows easier,"
I said, pulling away enough to keep breathing, as well
as to keep my mind on our son. "He maintains a more
even temper. He and Tennice get on famously, and the
more intense their work, the better. You'll be proud of
all he's accomplished. He can discuss history and philosophy, mathematics, astronomy, and politics at a level
worthy of Martin's drawing rooms. In only one area does
he lag a bit. . . ."

"Surely it could not be the discipline Leirans call natural science?" Karon stooped until his face was on a level
with mine, his blue eyes wide and teasing. "All those
'nasty plant names and vile animal parts when one
should only care about beauty and usefulness'?"

I slapped him—not hard—and shoved his face away.
"All right. So natural science was never my strength.
And, the bright muses bless him, Tennice knows even

less than I, so we've eased up on Gerick for now. But in everything else Gerick excels. More important"—I dropped my voice a bit and pulled him farther along the path, letting foolery carry us into more serious realms— "he speaks freely of his childhood at Comigor and so many things we thought he might never acknowledge. And a few times—not many yet—he's made a passing reference to his life in Zhev'Na. Just as you hoped he would."

"But as to sorcery . . ."

"He still won't discuss it, and I've seen no evidence he's tried to work any enchantment."

Karon stopped again, leaning his back against the brick wall of the kitchen garden, shaking his head in puzzled disbelief. "He seems to think he can give it up. Does he have any idea . . . ? He's sixteen; he'll be coming into his primary talent any time now, which will make abstaining infinitely more difficult. . . ."

". . . just like all the other tricks nature plays between twelve and eighteen," I said.

He smiled ruefully. "Life can seem quite a jumble in the middle of it."

"You won't believe how he's grown. He's almost as tall as Ka—you . . . were. Before." I almost bit my tongue. *Everlasting curses, you stupid woman . . .*

"You mean the real me."

There it was . . . the false note that would sneak its way into the harmonies of our time together. Why could I not reconcile myself to his change? In everything of importance, this was the man I had married. I couldn't blame him for the traces of sadness and bitterness that lingered long after his words had been spoken. Yet this very response embodied the subtle differences that still bothered me. The sadness was Karon. The bitterness, never.

I tried to shake it off. How could I regret anything? He was with me. "The first you," I said, unable to look him in the eye.

Gently, he took my hand, kissed it, and pressed it to his brow, a gesture of affection that had its origin, not in the magical world of the Dar'Nethi, but here in courtly

Valleor, the country of his youth in the human world. We turned and walked back toward the house, letting comfortable familiarity soothe the awkwardness. The disturbance was not gone, though. How could we ever explore these things when we never had time? Each visit was the same. No sooner had we reintroduced ourselves to each other and laid bare the questions that needed to be answered than it came time for him to go.

"Forgive me, Seri. Soon . . . I promise . . ." Karon had never used his power to read my thoughts uninvited. But then, he had rarely needed to. I seemed to be incapable of hiding what I felt.

Despite my unhappiness, I could not send Karon back to Avonar burdened with my resentments. I took his hand, kissed it, and pressed it to my own brow, trying to absorb the feel of him . . . the smell of him . . . the truth of him. Then I nodded toward the kitchen door. "You'll see Gerick before you go?" Concern for our son was one matter on which our opinions did not diverge.

"If he's willing. I suppose he'll be no easier with me."

"It's true you're not his first topic of conversation, and yet, just yesterday he asked when it was you'd studied here at Verdillon."

"He says so little when we're together. I can't tell what he's feeling. I don't want to push, but with the Circle complete, Marcus and the others in place in Zhev'Na, and now, Jayereth's news . . . I'm giving her a fortnight to refine her working, and then I'll send out scouts for the last reports from the borders. It's one reason I wanted to come tonight. Once we close the Circle, I won't be able to leave until we see how the Lords respond. If anything should happen to me . . . I've so much to tell him, things I've learned about this strange world he's destined to govern. We need to move forward. If only he'd *talk* to me, give me a sign that he's ready to listen."

"Don't fret. He's reserved with all of us, not only you. He just needs more time with you—to learn how different you are from what the Lords taught him. Trust comes only with time and experience."

Karon had given Gerick back his human eyes and restored to our son his mortal life, doing his best to heal the wounds of a childhood lived in fear, loneliness, cruelty, and murder. But even Karon's blessed magic could not undo Gerick's greatest injury. As a child, living in my brother's house, Gerick had isolated himself because he could do things our world called "vile sorcery." And when the Lords had stolen him away to Zhev'Na, they had fostered and nurtured his belief in his own evil, linking it with destiny and power and inevitability. By the time Gerick understood how they had deceived him, he had become so steeped in their hatred and suspicion he scarcely knew how to live in any other way. And the Lords' first, last, and most enduring lesson had been mistrust of his father.

We found Gerick waiting in the library, perched on the back of a chair reading a book. He showed no surprise. He must have spotted Karon and me from a window.

"My lord." Gerick, at sixteen only slightly beyond middle height, tossed his book aside, sprang to his feet, and bowed formally to Karon.

Karon returned the bow and then stepped close, touching Gerick's shoulder and smiling. "You've grown fairly these months, Gerick. How do Tennice and your mother keep you in clothes and boots?"

"I don't need much," said Gerick. Serious. Neutral. Karon's hand might have been a stray leaf fallen on his shirt. "How long can you stay?"

Karon's hand fell back to his side. "Not long, unfortunately. Not long at all. I'd like to tell you— Would you walk with me a bit?"

"Of course."

I watched them as they strolled through the garden in the dusky light, one tall and broad in the shoulder, one slender and wiry, each with his hands clasped carefully behind his back. In their brief times together, Karon tried to explain both the history and the current politics of his realm. Gerick listened, but, as with so many things, offered no opinions of his own and refused to be drawn into conversation. All too soon they were coming back through the library door.

"Seri, love, I've got to go"—an extraordinary bright-ness filled Karon's eyes—"but my plans have changed a little. I'm taking Gerick with me."

Astonishment almost stole my breath. "Across the Bridge. Are you sure? Is he—?"

I looked from one to the other. Gerick's demeanor reflected none of Karon's unspoken joy and excitement, only the same sober reserve he displayed on each of Karon's visits.

"Gerick, are you ready to do this? Has it been long enough? To cross . . . to go to Avonar . . . such a big step . . ." So near Zhev'Na.

"With all that's going on in Avonar this seems like an important time," he said. "I'll be all right."

Such vague reassurance did not soothe my unease in the least. "Karon, shouldn't you prepare him . . . for those he'll meet?"

The Lords had taught Gerick to despise his father's people, and, indeed, almost every Dar'Nethi our son had encountered had tried to deceive, corrupt, or murder him. And the Dar'Nethi knew almost nothing of Gerick—only that he had been stolen by the Lords, brought up in Zhev'Na, and rescued by his father. Intro-ducing them to each other was going to be a task requir-ing the utmost delicacy.

"It's the middle of the night. No one will even know he's there. I need to show him the Bridge and the Gate. Where I live. Where I work. I'll have him back here safely before morning." Karon's eyes begged me to un-derstand why I could not come with them.

Of course I understood; they had to learn to talk, to deal with each other without my serving as intermediary. If this venture was successful, perhaps we could all go next time. Be together . . . Before I could think what other questions to ask or what cautions to give them, they had walked out of the house and vanished into the light of the rising moon.

For an hour I paced the library and drawing rooms, desire and anxiety and long-unspoken hopes and possi-bilities wrestling in my imagination. I imagined the two of them treading the luminous path through the chaotic nightmare visions of the Breach between the worlds, and emerging in the chamber of cold white fire that was the Heir's Gate, deep in the heart of Avonar. From there they would follow winding passages, where the lamps sprang to life to light the way in front of you and faded as you passed, until they came to the graceful, sprawling rooms of the Heir's rose-colored palace, the quiet fortress heart of the most beautiful city one could imagine. The safest place in a world inhabited by the Lords of Zhev'Na.

Hours it would take them to make the passage across the Bridge, hours to make the return journey. If they were to be back before dawn, they would have very little time in Avonar. No time for the Lords to know Gerick was there. For four years Karon had been traveling between Verdillon and the palace, and the Lords had not found us here. Karon knew the risks; he would watch, listen, and be wary.

A tap on the library door brought our housemaid with a supper tray. "Will you be needing anything else, ma'am?"

"No. Thank you, Teriza."

"I'll be off then to Mistress Phyllia's and be back in the morning early. She's got her a grumpy little mite this time, wails half the night, wakes half the village. You must call Kat to do for you till I'm back."

"You're kind to help the woman. Stay as long as you need. We'll manage."

The house was quiet. Tennice was away in Yurevan, visiting friends at the University. From a distance came the echo of a child's laughter—Teriza's niece Kat, most likely enjoying a tease with Paulo while taking him a late supper in the stables. He was sitting with Tennice's bay mare and her two-day-old foal, the first to be born under Paulo's sole care.

I threw a log on the library fire and poked at the smoldering coals until it caught. Then I turned up the lamp beside my chair and pulled needle, thread, and a skirt with a ripped hem from a neglected basket on the floor. Though I detested sewing, stitching helped impose some order on my thoughts. . . .

* * *

A soft kiss on my forehead woke me. Moonlight
streamed through the garden door, outlining the shadowed form with silver.

"Karon . . ." I smiled through my lingering dreams,
knowing he could sense my pleasure even in the dark.

"He's home safely and on his way to bed." His wide
hand brushed away the hair stuck to my cheek. "An
uneventful journey. He can tell you. But a first step.
Soon, love . . . soon."

He lifted me in his arms, carried me up the stairs, and
laid me in my bed, pulling the coverlet over my shoulders. The scents of Verdillon's emerald grasses and the
rustle of ash leaves brushed by soft air drifted through
the open window of my room. The leaves were rimmed
with silver, and their fluttering created dancing patterns
of moonlight on the walls. Another lingering kiss and he
was gone. I smiled and slipped into peaceful slumber. . . .

"No more! I will not!" The agonized cry shattered
the night.

I threw off the coverlet, my sluggish mind struggling
to recall why I was in bed fully dressed. But my feet
knew what was needed and hurried down the softly lit
passage. Gerick huddled in his bed asleep. Fear, revulsion, and denial rolled through the bedchamber like dark
waves, pushing me away even as I pulled his quivering
shoulders into my embrace. "Gerick. Wake up. You're
safe at Verdillon. Nothing can harm you here."

His eyes flew open, but whatever horror they looked
upon was not in the realm of waking. He clung to me
as if he were in the grip of a whirlwind. "No! Stop!"

"Gerick, it's only dreams, just vile, wicked dreams." I
held him tight, stroking his shining hair and rocking him
slowly until his fevered trembling eased and his cries
died away. As had happened on so many other nights,
he blinked and was awake. I knew to let go then. He
would accept no comfort once he was awake.

"What is it, Gerick?" I asked, as he rose from the bed
and stood at the open window, a blanket pulled tightly

about his shoulders despite the warmth of the night. "What frightens you so?"

"It's only dreams. They're nothing. I'm sorry I wake you."

"If only you'd let your father help you." I knew it was wrong as soon as I said it.

"I don't need his help. Please, Mother, I'll be all right."

And so, as always, I kissed his forehead and returned to my room. From my window, I watched him stride across the moonlit courtyard toward the stables, ready to drag Paulo from his bed to join him for a predawn gallop through the neighboring fields and forests. Once again I blessed Paulo, who seemed to be the only person Gerick could turn to in his need. When I returned to my bed, I lay puzzling again at what triggered Gerick's nightmares, the bright hopes of the evening tarnished.

CHAPTER 3

Gerick had already finished breakfast by the time I went downstairs the morning after Karon's visit. I didn't know whether he'd ever gone back to bed, but he always did exercises in the yard before his breakfast, so any sleeping he'd done would have been very short. In late morning I found him in the library, standing next to a small table on which lay an open book. He was running his fingers over the page, and he started when I wished him a good morning.

"Ah, just the person I need." He grabbed my arm and dragged me to the large library worktable, patting a pile of manuscripts and papers. "You *must* rescue me. Tennice set me to read fifty pages on Leiran-Vallorean border disputes by tomorrow, but my Vallorean just isn't good enough to make any sense of it. Do you have time to give me a boost?"

"Of course. But you must pay my fee first. You can guess I'm rabid to know about last night. Your father said the journey was uneventful . . ."

Gerick's face closed down and his whole body tightened, as always happened with any direct questioning. His hand on the stack of papers fell motionless. I would have sworn he had stepped away from me, though his feet had not moved. But then he shrugged his shoulders and glanced up, before quickly averting his eyes. "The Bridge was amazing, the crossing not half so fearful as I expected. Horrible things all around, but not touching me this time. Not inside me. It felt almost . . . familiar."

I shuddered a little, recalling our journey out of Zhev'Na through the chaotic Breach.

"And the Gate . . . I'd never imagined it, the power of the enchantment. But it was a long journey for the short time we spent on the other side—less than an hour. He showed me his apartments, his private library, and a marvelous map of the whole world of Gondai that hangs in the air, so you can see the actual landforms and the mountains rising up from the plains. We walked down the passage to his lectorium, but he heard one of his Preceptors still working in there, so we didn't go in. He hadn't expected anyone to be about. We were out of time, anyway."

He pulled a chair up close to the worktable and drew his papers toward him. "I'd best get to work now."

"Thank you for telling me."

"Mmm." He dug a thick sheaf of papers from the stack. "Here's what I was having trouble with . . ."

We spent a pleasant hour with no further mention of the night's adventure or his nightmare. When he had his task well in hand, I took up the letter I'd come to finish.

As the clock in the hall below us struck the noon hour, Gerick threw down his pen and shoved a rolled manuscript across the table. "That will have to be enough," he said. "My eyes have gone crossways, and the pen's gouged a ridge through my fingers."

"I doubt you'll suffer the ill effects for long," I said. "It's an important subject. Border disputes are blamed for every war between Leire and Valleor, but if you read the histories, you'll see how much more there is to it. Leirans think of Valloreans as soft and corrupt. Valloreans think of Leirans as ignorant barbarians. Both are quite wrong. And someday you'll recognize what a liberal-minded statement that is from your Leiran mother!"

"I don't see what use it is for me to learn such things." He stripped off his coat and threw it on a chair. "I'll finish it later. I need to see what's up in the stables."

Leaving unspoken the motherly platitudes that came to mind, I returned to my own project. Peace, routine, care that did not smother, whatever we could of a normal upbringing in a gentleman's house, that's what we tried to provide for Gerick.

I instructed him in languages, composition, mathematics, "motherly" things like manners, and unmotherly things like the politics of the Four Realms. Tennice tutored him in philosophy, rhetoric, history, and law, and tried to speak with him of matters a sixteen-year-old boy might not wish to discuss with his mother. Paulo was his friend; Teriza, the housemaid, treated him with respectful distance; and thirteen-year-old Kat was his worshipper. He had been uncomfortable, at first, with the serving girl's unremitting devotion, but her innocent charm had worn away enough of his reserve that he could accept her small services with a solemn and gracious demeanor. It seemed to help that Kat worshipped Paulo in exactly the same way.

The only area in which our regimen differed from that of most Leiran households was in its emphasis on the intellect at the expense of military training. As a boy at Comigor, Gerick had been provided with a fencing master, and it had been his childhood ambition to be a master of the sword as my brother Tomas—the man he had once believed to be his father—had been.

But Gerick had not touched a sword since leaving Zhev'Na. He had vowed to forego physical opposition of the Lords when he became one of them, and, to seal his oath, the Three had melted his weapon as it lay on his palms, scarring them horribly. Karon didn't know whether Gerick's refusal to take up the weapon again was based in the belief that using a sword in any way would be a violation of his vow—bearing arms against those he had sworn not—or whether the experiences of Zhev'Na had somehow made the sword repugnant to him. The question remained as yet another mystery Gerick could not or would not explain.

When, in my turn, I was ready to leave the library, I indulged a bit of curiosity. The book that had interested Gerick was a journal belonging to the late Professor Ferrante, a history scholar at the University in Karon's student days and one of the few people in the Four Realms who had known that Karon was a sorcerer. Our friend Tennice had inherited this house when the professor was murdered by the Zhid. On the open page were Ferrante's notes from a time twenty years past, scribblings of students' names and assignments, notations of appointments and tutorials. I could see no item more interesting than the others, until I came to one near the bottom of the page.

K. unable to complete exposition of Cenadian glyphs due to climbing accident. Advanced him twenty diracs to hire a scribe until next funds from M. Warned him the wrist will knit crooked when he refused to have Ren Gordac see to it. Should have thought. It was his left. Unfortunate the boy can't take care of it himself. How strange to have such skill. Stranger still to be unable to take advantage of it.

Gerick must have guessed the passage was about Karon in his student days, as I knew it was. Karon's left arm had already been covered with scars, each one the mark of a healing he'd done and a telltale to anyone hunting evidence of sorcery. As I descended the stairs, I wondered if Karon still felt the ache in his left wrist when winter came, even though the bone was not the same one broken in the fall so long ago. How much of memory resides in the physical body and how much resides in the soul? That was another part of the lingering awkwardness between Karon and me; even after four years neither of us knew exactly how much of him remained. Surely if we had more time together, things would be easier.

The rest of the afternoon passed quietly as was usual at Verdillon. The stream of our life flowed peacefully here. I felt safe and hidden, despite the sullied hopes of the night.

After supper Tennice, back from Yurevan, challenged me to a game of chess. A grumbling Gerick returned upstairs to the library to finish his work, and Paulo headed back outdoors, leaving us alone in the sitting room.

Seri.

I looked up from the chessboard, but Tennice's bald-

ing head was still bent over it. "What's the problem?"
I said. "Can't you find a wicked enough move? You'll
have me in three as it is."

Tennice didn't look up, but twitched a bony hand in
dismissal. "Hush, Seri. I thought you had better
manners."

"But you said—"

Seri, I'm in the garden. Is it safe to come in?

The voice wasn't Tennice's at all. "In the garden . . .
of course . . . Yes, of course, come in! It's just Tennice
here with me."

Tennice looked up this time, his puzzlement quickly
erased. "He's here again so soon?"

Twice in two days? Unheard of. Perhaps the time for
closing the Circle had come sooner than expected. I hurried to the garden door to welcome him, not daring to
hope that this visit meant a longer stay. To my surprise,
Karon wasn't alone.

Awkwardly I folded my arms in front of me instead
of wrapping them around him. "Come in, please. It's a
fine night for company." A slender, light-haired young
man followed us through the back passage.

As soon as we reached the sitting room, Karon nodded formally to me and then to the young man, one
hand extended toward each of us. "Madam, may I introduce Radele, son of Men'Thor yn Ustele? Radele, this
is my wife, Lady Seriana Marguerite of Leire and our
friend, Tennice de Salviet." Karon then dropped his
hands and clasped them behind his back. "I've brought
Radele to stand guard here as I've said for so long I
would."

"Stand guard . . . has something happened?" I asked.
Ever since our Dar'Nethi friend Kellea had returned to
the village of Dunfarrie the previous year, Karon had
wanted to bring in a Dar'Nethi to protect Gerick and
the rest of us in ways only a sorcerer could do. He'd
kept putting it off, saying he wanted to find someone he
knew well enough to entrust with such a mission.
Strange that he hadn't mentioned a word of this last
night. "Have you given the signal already? The war—"

"I just found the right person, someone willing to take

on an exceptionally important duty, where he'll most likely never need to lift a finger." Karon moved across the room to the sideboard, where he began pouring wine. "We'll assume he'll acquire no glory here."

I stared for a moment at his back as if an explanation might be scribed in the silver embroidery adorning his black doublet. Able to read nothing in Karon's posture, I switched my scrutiny to the newcomer. "Welcome to Verdillon, sir. As my husband says, may you have no occasion to find glory at arms here."

The young man made a graceful bow. "I'm a glory-shirker, madam," he said. "Never have decided what rhyme the Singers would put with my name: meal, deal, seal. Very unwarlike, ineloquent rhymes."

The young Dar'Nethi's face was pleasant and open, his fair beard and mustache neatly trimmed. Pale brows and lashes framed eyes of the usual Dar'Nethi blue that sparkled with good humor. But why in the name of sense would Karon choose the kinsman of Men'Thor and Ustele, who in four long years had shown him nothing but hostility?

Tennice excused himself, saying he would summon Gerick and inform Teriza we had guests. Radele accepted a seat on the long couch near the hearth, but Karon remained on the far side of the room, leaning against the sideboard. He seemed exceptionally subdued, especially in contrast to his animation of the previous night. The hospitality of the evening was clearly left to me.

I took a seat beside Radele. "So are you a poet, sir, knowing so much of rhyming?"

"No poet, my lady, certainly not. My mentor was forever berating me for my lack of memory, and offered constant suggestions for my improvement, including setting important reminders into verse . . ." With much animation, Radele began a long story of a rhyming spell he'd made as a boy. ". . . though he at last gave in, for the winter was bitter cold in the western Vales that year. But the master never could wear the hat without breaking into tears at the memory of his cat."

I could not stop laughing at his tale. Even so few

moments' conversation revealed Radele to be as charming in manner as in appearance, entirely unlike Karon's reports of his dour father and grandfather. The young Dar'Nethi promised to be a delightful addition to our household.

The young man's good humor was going to be a necessity, of course. Gerick wasn't going to like having a Dar'Nethi bodyguard. Not at all.

As I was still smiling at Radele's story, Gerick hurtled down the stairs, stopping in the foyer to run his fingers through his hair and pull a tight, rust-colored jacket over his beige cambric shirt. Then he stepped into the sitting room, bowing first to Karon and then to me. "Good evening, my lord. Mother."

Karon nodded to Gerick without speaking and took another sip of his wine.

Radele rose from the couch. Sober, expressionless, Gerick stood waiting by the door, looking first to his father and then to the visitor. Lest the awkward silence grow lengthier, I took up the introductions. "Gerick, may I present Radele yn Men'Thor yn Ustele? Your father has brought him to stay with us for a while. Radele, this is our son, Gerick yn D'Natheil." Dar'Nethi conventions included paternity only through living forebears, else Gerick's lineage would have been a bit more complicated.

"My lord." Radele bowed, his palms extended in the Dar'Nethi custom of greeting. I could find no fault with his respectful address or posture though neither seemed particularly warm. "A pleasure to meet you at last. I glimpsed you last night on your visit to the palace—your first, I think—but the Prince whisked you away before we could be introduced. Everyone in Avonar is anxious to make your acquaintance. I shall be the envy of the city."

That everyone in Avonar was anxious about Gerick was no doubt true. But I didn't think it had to do with making his acquaintance. Gerick was the Prince of Avonar's son and successor, acknowledged by the Preceptorate of the Dar'Nethi. But that acknowledgment had occurred before Gerick had stepped into a spinning, man-high brass ring called an oculus and become the Fourth Lord of Zhev'Na. Despite Gerick's subsequent repudiation of the Lords, I could not imagine that the Dar'Nethi loathing for the Three of Zhev'Na would ever permit Gerick to sit Avonar's throne. But for the moment, Karon chose to proceed as if Gerick were his heir, saying that his own beliefs and deeds must stand as Gerick's advocates with his people.

Gerick did not address Radele, just inclined his head in a minimal politeness and removed himself to the farthest chair available while still remaining in the same room with us.

To my relief, Tennice returned just then, followed by Paulo bringing a tray of refreshments from Teriza. Further introductions and greetings left Radele engaged with Tennice. As I showed the tall, skinny youth where to set the fragrant tea, cold ale, and plates of various sweets, fruit, and cheeses, I whispered. "Stay, Paulo. I think Gerick would appreciate it."

"If you say, ma'am"—he kept his voice low as I had done—"but I'm not dressed for company."

I tugged at the red scarf he wore tied around his neck over his well-worn russet shirt and work breeches. "You very well know that you are welcome in our house at any time whether you're wearing a loincloth or a ball gown." He grinned and snatched a jam tart.

The dusting of freckles across Paulo's thin, ever-sunburned face was almost the only reminder of the lame, illiterate boy from Dunfarrie that fate had embroiled in our adventures six years ago. Karon had healed his twisted body, and in return the shy youth had saved Gerick's soul. His lanky frame now towered over Gerick and me. Paulo had turned eighteen this summer, a young man now.

As I had anticipated, Paulo gravitated to Gerick's side, sitting on the floor beside Gerick's chair and stretching his long legs across the tight-woven carpet. While Radele sat between Tennice and me, listening appreciatively to Tennice's stories of growing up as the studious middle child between two rowdy brothers, the two youths munched on Teriza's cakes and pastries. Gerick murmured a bit to Paulo, even extracted a smile and a few words from him, but he never smiled himself, and he made no effort to speak to any of the rest of us throughout the evening.

Despite Tennice's humorous monologues and Radele's witty ripostes, Karon stayed apart as well. He sat in a chair close to the door, resting his chin on a closed fist. My attempts to involve him in the conversation were met with a monosyllable at most. Yet his attention never wavered in the slightest from the company. Every time the talk slowed, the air felt oppressive.

All too quickly Karon rose. "I need to get back."

His movement drew all of us into activity. While Tennice advised Radele about breakfast and washing water and the other facilities of the house, the two boys crammed the last of Teriza's pie into their mouths, piled up the dishes, and carried them off to the kitchen. I went straight to Karon.

"What's happening here?"

Karon took my arm and drew me farther from the others into a window alcove. "I'm sorry, I can't explain. I've got to go"—he spoke so quietly that no one else could possibly have heard—"and I must speak with the boy for a moment."

"But—"

"Seri, be very careful. Please. Listen well and observe."

I wouldn't let him leave it at that. "Listen to what? Karon, why ever did you bring Men'Thor's son here?"

"Because I need someone honorable, someone capable, and someone whose heart is not engaged with me or my family." I started to protest again, but he pressed one finger to my lips. Then he kissed my hand, pressed it fiercely to his brow, and spoke out over my head. "Gerick, could you walk out with me?" His hand brushed my shoulder as he walked toward the door, giving Radele a stiff, wordless nod at the same time.

"Of course," said Gerick. He set the last cups and plates back onto the table from which he'd just taken them and followed Karon into the front courtyard.

I peered through the window as they stood talking for a few moments. A serious conversation. Brief. Gerick folded his arms across his chest and watched thoughtfully as Karon strode into the distance and vanished.

I wouldn't have been half so worried save that, throughout the entire evening, Karon had never once looked me in the eye. Something terrible had happened. I just didn't know what.

Gerick had nightmares again that night. When I hurried to his bedchamber, I found Radele, sword drawn, examining the windows and doors and flicking the draperies aside as if expecting to find a cowering intruder. But only the moonlight had passed through the diamond-paned windows that overlooked the sleeping orchard . . . only the moonlight and whatever it was that violated a young man's dreaming.

"All seems secure," Radele said, when Gerick's cries were aborted by his waking. "Is there anything I can do for you, young sir?"

"You can remove yourself from my bedchamber." Gerick did not even look at Radele. He grabbed his breeches from the foot of his bed and drew them up over his leggings, tucking in the rumpled shirt he had worn to bed.

Radele didn't move. I smiled halfheartedly at the Dar'Nethi and nodded toward the door. Expressionless, he bowed and left the room.

"Gerick—"

"I'm sorry to have waked everyone," he said, pulling on his boots as if he couldn't accomplish the task fast enough. "But I don't need anything. Certainly not from him." He planted a cold kiss on my cheek and hurried out, taking the stairs two at a time, leaving me alone in the moonlit bedchamber.

I sighed and smoothed his blankets, then followed him into the passage. Before returning to my own bed, I stopped at the stair landing where Radele slouched in a shadowed nook. He had one knee bent, the foot planted on the wall behind him, and was peering out of a small, round window that looked down on the stableyard. "Radele, I must apologize for my son's rudeness. As my husband likely told you—"

"Don't trouble yourself, my lady," he said, straightening his posture at my approach. "It is not my purpose to ingratiate myself with your son or to judge my success by his attentions, only to guard those who live in this house as my prince has commanded me. Watching and listening are my truest talents."

"Your sword was most efficiently drawn," I said.

The young man grinned, his white teeth gleaming in the darkness. "My sword knows no place to be save in my hand. I've lived the sum of four and twenty years, ten of them on the walls of Avonar, watching and listening to prevent the cursed Zhid from slithering over. I'm not one to sit at leisure while others take action."

"Watch well, then. Good night, Radele. And thank you."

"Good night, my lady. Sleep well. You've nothing to fear."

CHAPTER 4

I did not sleep well. Not that night or for many nights after. The weather turned beastly, with hot, heavy air in the mornings that boiled into violent thunderstorms in the afternoons. Neither Gerick nor Radele volunteered to enlighten me as to the concerns that had brought Karon back to us so soon. I was so angry at being left out of the mystery that for days I refused to speak to either of them about Karon or his visit. Then I was furious with myself for being so rock-headed.

After a week I swallowed my pride and mentioned to Gerick that his father had not told me what was bothering him so sorely. Perhaps he had indicated something in those few moments before he left?

Gerick colored a little. "He made me swear not to repeat anything he said . . . even to you. I'm sorry. He said it was for your safety."

I spent that afternoon beating the sitting room rugs that Teriza had hung outdoors to air. Teriza swore the things were only half their original thickness when I was finished with them.

Everyone in the house suffered from ill humor as well. I berated Gerick for his continuing rudeness to Radele and snapped at Teriza over nothing until she threatened to leave us. Gerick threw down his books and stormed out of the library in disgust at a burdensome assignment, and swore that he would start sleeping in the stable if Radele entered his bedchamber one more time. Tennice argued with a sullen Paulo over his late rides with Gerick. And Gerick had nightmares three more times that week, each episode more severe than the last. Soon every voice made me start, every closing of a door demanded investigation. If something didn't change soon, we were going to kill each other.

Only Radele seemed unflappable . . . when one could find him. He kept out of sight in the corners or the shadows. I had thought he would bring new perspectives to our conversations and lend his good humor to our company, but he never joined us at table or lessons or our evening gatherings. Though Teriza swore he came to her table for meals and even lent a hand around the kitchen while there, I could not have vouched for it.

One morning after I stumbled over him lurking in the garden, startling myself out of a year's life, I asked him in exasperation if he wouldn't come out from the shadows a bit. "You're welcome to use the library, eat with us in the dining room, sit with us in the evenings. Tennice is a masterful chess player. Paulo keeps finding broken-down horses that turn out to be race-worthy, and Gerick thinks a day worth getting up for if only someone will race with him whether on horseback or on foot. The two boys know the countryside like their own hands and would enjoy showing you. You've no need to stay apart."

"Though your company is a pleasure, of course, my lady," he answered, "I've no interest in games. And I doubt I would find anything of interest in your library, just as you'd find nothing suitable for you in the libraries of Avonar."

Perhaps it was the course of the week that made his answer so annoying. "I believe I'll find many things of interest in your libraries."

He cocked his head, looking at me quite seriously. "Do you truly think you'll come to Avonar to live?"

"Gondai is my husband's home, Radele. He sits the throne of Avonar, and my son is his successor. Of course I'll come."

He did not comment, just bowed and walked away. What did Karon mean when he said he needed someone whose heart was not engaged with our family? I slammed the wicket gate so hard it bounced back open again.

*   *   *

After a second week of this peevishness, a tentative tap on the study door brought Teriza with news. "A man's come to see you, my lady. He's waiting in the small sitting room."

Visitors at Verdillon were a rarity. Pausing only long enough to wipe my pen and close the inkwell, I followed Teriza down the wide staircase and into the sitting room. Awaiting me was a sturdy man wearing a thin-at-the-elbows coat of dark blue and holding a soft, wide-brimmed hat in his hand. The flame-colored patch on his coat proclaimed him a sheriff, a local magistrate whose first responsibility was the extermination of sorcerers. Fortunately his weathered face proclaimed him a friend—Graeme Rowan, the sheriff of Dunfarrie.

"How wonderful to see you, Sheriff. And Paulo will be delighted."

"It's fine to see you, too, my lady," he said, taking my hand and offering a polite bow.

I didn't lie when I said I was happy to see Rowan. Though I had once despised him for his office, he had shown himself to be a faithful ally and a man of honor and integrity. Yet one close glance at the sandy-haired sheriff made it clear that he was not to be the instrument to relieve the tensions of the household. Deep creases lined his ruddy brow. When I sat on a couch that faced the windows overlooking the overgrown lawn and cherry orchard and motioned him to join me, he perched on the edge of the cushions.

"What brings you so far, Sheriff? Just a visit, I hope." One says the words.

"Free to speak plainly, ma'am?" His soft-spoken manner and country accent did not accurately reflect the capabilities of a man responsible for maintaining the king's law in a sizable district of Leire. Graeme Rowan was easily underestimated.

"I've never known you to do otherwise," I said.

The lines in his brow failed to soften at my meager humor.

"There's no one but me in the house." I said. "Tennice is gone to Yurevan for the day. Teriza and Kat are heading off to market. Gerick is most likely in the sta-

bles with Paulo, and Radele, our new Dar'Nethi bodyguard, is never far from him."

"King Evard wants to see you." He held out a small
folded paper.

"Evard!" The paper was heavy and stiff, of good qual-
ity. Nothing was written on the outside, and the red wax
seal bore no device. I turned it over in my hand. "How
is that possible?" Almost six years had passed since the
day Gerick had been abducted by the Lords, and I had
followed him to Gondai and Zhev'Na. I thought I was
well buried.

Rowan's voice was tight and low. "All I know is that
ten days ago, two gentlemen of the Royal Household
come to Dunfarrie. Their only interest was your whereabouts. I told them the story we agreed on, that I'd
heard naught of you since your nephew's abduction. I
said how I had it straight from the bailiff at Comigor
and the sheriff of the district that no trace of you or the
boy had ever been found. But these two men said the
king believed you alive and that he 'very much wished
to speak with you.' "

Very much wished . . . That didn't sound like Evard
at all. "How could he know I was alive? And what could
he want?"

"I asked them that. They said only that if I was to
'happen to run across you,' then I was to say that your
pardon stands and that this matter is with regard to the
last conversation you had with His Majesty."

"That's when I told him about the other world and
the threat to this world posed by the Lords. I wasn't
even sure he believed me." Once caught up in rescuing
Gerick from Zhev'Na, I had never looked back at my
old nemesis, the King of Leire. Our enmity was too
deep. His boyhood friendship with my brother had
prompted him to issue a pardon for my "crimes" of con-
sorting with sorcerers, but I expected no further favors
from him. "So what did you tell them?"

"That anyone who thought you were alive was an op-
timist, and anyone who thought you'd be living in Dunfarrie again was a fool." Rowan fidgeted with his hat,
his face knotted into a frown. "For certain they didn't

believe me. The whole business smells bad. That's why I thought I should bring this myself."

I broke the seal. The message was brief and to the point.

> *Your counsel is needed. Sunset on the fifteenth day of the Month of Veils. On the arched bridge in your late cousin's famous gardens. E. R.*

"Windham . . . he wants to meet in Martin's gardens at Windham." I wadded the notepaper and threw it to the floor. "Cheeky bastard! How dare he set foot there!"

Martin, Earl of Gault, had been my mother's distant cousin and my dearest friend and mentor when I was a girl. On the same day the king and the Council of Lords had condemned Karon to burn, Evard had executed Martin, his beloved mistress, and Tennice's brother Tanager, accusing them of plotting with sorcerers to topple his throne. Only chance had allowed Tennice to escape death. No matter who claimed Martin's land and titles now, the thought of Evard walking in Martin's gardens was vile. Vile.

"One more thing," said Rowan. "The messenger said, 'Tell her that a search for one missing person may turn up others who should never be found.' "

Cold fear quickly doused my indignation. "Stars of night! Could Evard know about Gerick?"

"They said no more than I've told you. I thought maybe they knew of the three sorcerers living at your place. At least *they're* well away."

On his first venture to save D'Arnath's Bridge, Karon had healed three Zhid, restoring the souls that had been stolen from them centuries before. The three had stayed at my old cottage for a while, but were now back in Gondai on a mission for Karon. Out of Evard's reach, at least. But if the king had any idea about Gerick . . . that he was Karon's son . . . a sorcerer, too . . .

I snatched up the letter from the floor and stared at it again. And then there was the matter of Tennice. . . . Rowan watched me, his thumb rubbing the brim of his hat.

"I can't let Evard start looking for me," I said. "Any questioning of my old associations would lead him to Tennice's father, which could easily point them here. Not only would that endanger Gerick, but Tennice is still condemned." That my old friend had escaped execution sixteen years ago was only a matter of luck.

"Perhaps it's time for you to move on. Away from here."

"Where could we go? We can't hide forever." *Very much wished . . . Your counsel is needed . . .* "Besides, I'm curious. . . ."

Perhaps it was the week's tension that made me so certain I had to answer Evard's summons, anything to get away from Verdillon and the teeth-on-edge days. For myself, I wasn't afraid of the king. Even his not-so-veiled threat could not shake my confidence; I believed it nothing but an indication of urgency, a clumsy effort at persuasion. Evard had always been a bully. But his friendship for my brother, proven over and over again, had prevented him from physically harming me. And somehow, on the day I had told him of Tomas's death and the strange circumstances surrounding it, I had felt that youthful loyalty transferred to me, a gift of grief in a heart that knew little softness.

No, my only concern in such a meeting would be Gerick's safety. I didn't want Evard getting curious about him, yet I couldn't leave him behind, either; the echoes of my son's night terrors still rang in my ears.

"I think I'd best find out what he wants. Gerick will have to come with me. And Radele, too. We'll travel in disguise, so if Evard is planning a trap, it won't work, because we won't arrive in the way he expects. The change will do us good."

I mustered my arguments carefully before approaching the others with my idea. But to my astonishment, Gerick threw himself into planning it right away. "Paulo will have to come, too, don't you think? He's the best of all of us at slipping in and out of places and getting people to say things they never meant to say. We'll want to scout out the situation before you meet King Evard."

The trees were noisy with chattering blackbirds as Gerick and Tennice and I sat on the lawn that evening, discussing the journey to Montevial. Graeme Rowan had already ridden out for Dunfarrie, convinced I should be shut up in a lunatic asylum.

"Don't even think I'll allow you near this meeting, dear boy!" I said. "You and Radele—and Paulo, too, if he has to come—will stay well out of the way."

Though dismayed at the consideration, Tennice agreed that we needed to find out what Evard wanted. ". . . but if you're going to do this, discretion and speed must be of first importance," he said. "Too many together are noticeable. I still say, *both* young men should remain here."

"Gerick and I stay together," I said.

"And I won't go without Paulo." Gerick's lean face was animated and determined. "He can travel separately. As a horse trader perhaps. All the better to watch out and not be one of us. And my mother and I—and I suppose the Dar'Nethi shadow *must* come—we could be . . ."

". . . a family looking for a squire's billet for a son," I said, caught up in Gerick's enthusiasm. "It's the most common reason for a mother and son to be traveling to Montevial. A father dead in the war. The family seeking someone to take the boy under his wing."

"Just what Philomena was trying to do for me after Tomas died, before I went to Zhev'Na," said Gerick.

He said it so casually. *Zhev'Na.* The syllables pricked my heart, evoking horror and hope in a confusing muddle. The name recalled so much of grief and despair, yet for Gerick to speak of the Lords' fortress with equanimity was surely a sign of his healing. He guarded his thoughts so fiercely, I grasped at any sign of progress.

"Exactly," I said. "Radele would be the fencing master who's taught the boy until now. Can we pull it off?"

"Of course we can," said Gerick. "I'll be interested to see Montevial again. My last time there I was eight or nine, when Papa—Tomas—took me to see the ruins at Vaggiere. Actually, I think he wanted to show me his new chambers in the palace more than he wanted to show me the ruins."

"I would imagine he did. Tomas was an inveterate show-off." I smiled at Gerick, and he returned it, a brief, glorious reflection of my brother and Karon all in one. He didn't smile enough.

Tennice, as always, was skeptical, but Gerick's cheerful mood won him over. My old friend unfolded his long legs and got up from the grass, grimacing and stretching his ever-aching back. "I'll speak to Teriza, get her started on your provisioning."

Gerick sprang to his feet. "I'll tell Paulo. He'll think it a lark—riding horses all day for weeks."

During the discussion Radele had remained unobtrusively in the shade of a myrtle hedge, a vantage from which he could see both the lane from the main road and the service road that led from the stableyard deeper into the parkland. The moment Tennice and Gerick were out of earshot, the young Dar'Nethi confronted me, his face quite solemn. "Madam, you cannot be serious about this fey masquerade, traipsing about the countryside . . ."

I stood and brushed the grass from my skirt. "I'm quite serious. And if you've heard so much, then you know you're to accompany us."

"We must wait here for the Prince's return."

"That could be months. King Evard likes getting his way, and if he starts hunting, he could discover this place long before that. I'll not have Gerick's or Tennice's safety compromised. It's too dangerous to wait."

"I don't think it will be months. Probably only a few days. And in any case, my lord's commands to me . . ."

". . . said nothing about preventing a journey to Montevial, I'm sure. He would never set me any such restriction."

"You? Of course not. But he would not have the young Lord . . . put in such a risky position. The boy must not leave here until the Prince returns."

A chill prickled my skin. *The young Lord.* That's what they had called Gerick in Zhev'Na.

"I would never put my son at undue risk, Radele. Our position at Verdillon may not be secure, even now, so Gerick cannot remain here. He needs to be with me. Besides, he needs to get out in the world. He's not a prisoner."

"But the Prince said—" He stopped abruptly.

"*What* did he say?" My fragile patience snapped. "I've been waiting for someone to speak of it. Tell me what he said that might preclude our going."

The young man flushed and clamped his lips firmly.

"Then we'll go. If my husband wishes to find us, he can use the guidestone I wear around my neck, rather than popping in here unexpectedly. If you want to wait for him here, then do so. But if your duty is to protect Gerick, you had best pack your kit." Enough of secrets and hiding.

"My duty, my lady, is to defend my world and this one of yours against the Lords of Zhev'Na. I *never* forget it." Sparks flashed from beneath his deference, as if my words had struck steel. This was a young man who had fought his first battle at fourteen.

"I'm sorry, Radele. I didn't mean to imply otherwise."

He bowed stiffly. "I'm sure that if any extraordinary dangers manifest themselves along the way, your prudence will call an end to the venture."

"You can be certain of it."

Radele made no further argument. He also said nothing more about Karon's orders, though his sidestepping had done nothing to soothe my disquiet.

Two days later, when we set out in the sultry heat of the early morning, the young Dar'Nethi joined in our playacting with his more accustomed good humor, waxing his blond beard and mustache into stiff curls, claiming that his own fencing master had prized his facial glory in that way. But if anything, the young man had increased his vigilance. I don't think he ever took his eyes from Gerick.

CHAPTER 5

Paulo left Verdillon a day ahead of us. He had proposed shyly that if Tennice were to stake him to a few silver pieces, he could come up with a fair-sized string of horses from Valloreans desperate to sell their stock before it was confiscated by the Leiran army. Taking the horses to Montevial would not only be a benefit to our neighbors and an excellent ruse, but could make us a tidy profit as well. Though we lived modestly, Tennice's resources were not unlimited.

Gerick and I rode in Verdillon's old pony trap, a mode of travel slower than riding our own mounts, but more suited to our roles. I wore a widow's headcloth and an old-fashioned velvet gown that I'd dragged out of Tennice's attic. We found Gerick a rakish green cap to hide the color of his hair and outfitted him in threadbare finery suitable for an impoverished youth of gentle family looking to impress someone in the capital. Gerick and I laughed at ourselves when we donned our disguises, and enjoyed our first day on the road as if it were a holiday.

The town of Prydina, where we were to meet Paulo, had grown up at the meeting of the main north-south route through Valleor and the road that crossed the Cerran Brae, the range of low peaks and sharp ridges that defined the Vallorean border with Leire. Prydina boasted a sizable marketplace, an even larger illicit trade in untaxed Leiran goods, and a full complement of pickpockets, thieves, and beggars.

We took a room on the outskirts of town at a modest

inn called the Fire Goat, a suitably respectable accommodation for an impoverished gentlewoman, her son, and his fencing master. Once the cart was unhitched and unloaded, Gerick and I sat down to supper in the inn's common room. Radele did not join us. He seemed uneasy with the press of people, saying he'd prefer to watch the horse, the cart, and the inn from outside.

Despite a long day's traveling from Verdillon, Gerick was not inclined to go upstairs once we'd finished eating. "We've not been anywhere in all these years," he said, leaning across the scrubbed pine table after the barmaid took away our plates. "Don't you want to hear some news of the world?"

He was right. Gerick and I rarely ventured beyond Verdillon's walls and never to a town of any size. Tennice often rode into Yurevan, always returning with much to say of the newest books at his favorite bookseller's or who was teaching philosophy at the University, but little of politics or gossip. Nothing like the news one could get in the common room of a crossroads inn.

I ordered us each a tankard of the local ale. As the daylight faded outside the smoke-grimed windows of the Fire Goat, a potboy threw a fresh log on the smoky fire, poking and fussing until it was crackling. The dancing flames revealed all sorts of folk: a ruddy, broad-faced man with a curling red beard, a solitary woman, pinched and pale, with darting black eyes and bad teeth, a heavyset man, careworn and gray, who slumped over his supper at a table beside three noisy companions. Some eighteen or twenty patrons crowded the little room, and as the ale flowed from the landlord's barrel, the talk grew louder and less cautious.

From the sound of it, Evard had made little progress in his attempts to bring Iskeran under Leire's heel alongside Valleor and Kerotea. The Valloreans in the room, always distinguishable by their fair coloring and somber garb, smiled behind their hands at the stories of the Leiran king's setbacks. A threadbare merchant pronounced unsettling rumors from Montevial of spies and executions and an entire slum quarter of the city that had been burned by a mob. Other travelers nodded their heads, confirming that the capital city of Leire was an uncomfortable place these days.

A bony man, a tinker by trade, told a harrowing and unlikely story of getting caught in a bog and being rescued by a pack of wild dogs. The fantastic tale left the company hungry for more stories.

"Come, let's each offer a tale or a song," said the pale woman with bad teeth. "The company will buy a tankard for the one as tells the best."

A Vallorean tax-clerk, one of the poorly paid local functionaries reviled as traitorous tools of the cruel Leiran governor, volunteered for the competition. He redeemed his unsavory profession for the evening with a hilarious tale of two Leiran tax collectors being chased all over northern Valleor by an outlaw named 'Red Eye.' The pale woman had the landlord refill the man's mug, not waiting for the voting at the end of the evening.

One rawboned farmer, his unshaven face pitted with pockmarks, kept the company in high hilarity with his tale of a Leiran merchant who had been left naked in a tree with two wolves tied to its bole while his entire stock of cloth and leather was divided among the starving populace of a Vallorean village. The company roared with delight.

Gerick listened intently to every word. While the barmaid passed another round and the listeners shouted raucously for the next story, he murmured, half to himself, "Why didn't the villagers kill the merchant? It was stupid to let him go." He might have been speaking of strategy in a game of draughts.

"Perhaps they didn't think the cloth was worth a man's life," I said, "even a stupid man's."

"He'll come back and kill them. That one"—he pointed to the farmer who had told the tale—"that one will lead the soldiers back to the village. Then they'll all be dead."

His conviction sent a shiver racing up my back. Sometimes Gerick seemed like a quiet, reserved boy of sixteen, and sometimes . . . I was relieved when the talk turned back to weather, crops, and the experiences of two hunters who had gotten themselves lost in the mountains over the winter, surviving by holing up in a bandit cave.

When pressed to contribute my own traveler's tale to the evening's entertainment, I told the story of my father pretending to fall ill after he'd taken Tomas and me on a ride into the wild hills near Comigor. Papa had wanted to see us find our own way back home safely while he was there to protect us. It made a good story, but short and simple enough that I could suppress my Leiran accent and keep us unremarked.

The warmth of the smoky room, the long day, and the week's hectic preparations soon laid their tally on my eyelids. But each time I proposed retiring, Gerick would say, "Not yet. The fellow in the corner is going to sing again," or "I want to hear more of the tinker's stories of Vanesta." After several rounds of this, and his failure to look me in the eye as he made his excuse, I began to suspect the reason for his reluctance.

I laid a hand on his arm. "If the dreams come, I'll be right there. No one will hear you."

He flushed and kept his eyes on the company. "Everyone in Prydina will hear me. And my watchdog will come running to make sure I've not fouled my bed . . . or Dar'Nethi honor . . . or whatever it is he's expecting me to corrupt."

"Maybe you won't dream tonight." No use trying to reconcile him to Radele's attentions.

"Please, just one more tale. Then we'll go up." The skin around Gerick's eyes was taut and smudged. When had he last slept more than two hours at a stretch? If I could just convince him to talk to me about the things that were really important . . .

The hour grew late. The grizzled innkeeper propped his massive chin on his hand, and the potboy snoozed in the corner, allowing half the lamps to go out untended. A tired serving maid lugged yet another round of ale to the table of four men. Two were itinerant farriers looking for work among the travelers. The third was the scrawny tinker who apparently arranged to have hu-

morous adventures wherever he went, and the fourth
was the heavyset, gray-bearded man who'd been drinking steadily all evening and saying very little. When the
bearded man reached for another tankard, the tinker
laid a hand on his hairy arm. "You're single-minded in
your cups this night, friend. We've all shared our travels
until our tongues are parched and our heads empty. I
think it's your turn to tell us a tale."

"You don't want to hear no tale of mine."

"And why not?"

"It's not the tale as comfortable folks like to hear."

The few stragglers scattered about the room urged
him on. "Tell it, goodman. The company must judge the
tale. Naught's comfortable about stories of outlaws, nor
naked merchants, nor tax collectors."

"Come, friend," said the tinker, "if you gift us with
an uncomfortable tale, why then we'll buy another round
to smooth our spirits and tell yet another to finish the
night."

When the bearded man began, the words fell from his
tongue reluctantly, as if it was only their ponderous
weight that caused them to be spoken at all. His voice
was a rumbling bass, speaking the soft slurring dialect
of northern Valleor, a rugged land of rocky green hills,
cold blue lakes, and bitter, hungry winters. . . .

"I run sheep near Lach Vristal. I started twenty year
ago with a breeding pair earned as my indenture price.
My full twelve year I worked from dark freezing morning to dark freezing midnight for to earn my freedom
and my sheep. When my debt was paid, I found me a
lay and built a hold for the sheep and me.

"I got me a wife from Vristal town, and in five springs
I had two sons and a daughter living, and only one babe
buried. My eldest Hugh come a fine sheepman and
works shoulder to shoulder with me. My daughter took
all of us in hand since she was ten when her mam died
of lung fever, and she's never missed a day's cooking
nor spinning nor churning.

"My Tom, though, is a wild boy, born with only one
hand. His mam spoilt him young. He spends his days
running the hills and playing his whistle what he made

from tonguegrass. Oh, he'll help as he will with shearing and herding, but his heart ain't in his work, only in his music and the hills. I told him that when he come to manhood, he'd see how he'd have to work twicet as hard as a whole man just to feed himself.

" 'Twas on one night just gone Tom come late to the hold, and the moon was in his eyes. 'Pap,' he said, 'I've seen a road that goes no place you've ever been.'

" 'There's a deal of roads I've never been,' says I, 'but not inside three days' walking. If a sheep can find its way there, I've been on it.'

" 'No, Pap. This road goes into a new land. The sky is purple and black and filled with lightning, and the stars are green, but the land is not. It's a broken place, Pap, and I've got to go there so to see what it may be.'

"I beat my boy, then, for I thought he'd been at the drink in Vristal town, and no matter what you've seen me put down this night, we don't favor hard drink in my hold. But when I beat him, Tom didn't say naught, nor argue, nor cry out as he might on another day, but only looked at me quiet with the moon in his eyes.

"The next night Tom come home late again. 'Pap,' he says, 'I'll take you to the road. The one-eyed man says I belong in that land and not here, but I want you to see it before I go. Mayhap you'll believe me and not think me unfit to be your son.'

" 'Have you gone and tangled yourself with a jongler?' I said. 'Jonglers are thieves and gamblers and liars.'

" 'He's no jongler, Pap. He's a bent man, no taller than your waist, but a beard down to his belt. He's got only one eye what's purple in the center of it, and a growed-together flap of skin where the other eye should be.'

" 'You've been at the drink again, Tom,' says I. 'I've got to beat it out of you.'

" 'I understand, Pap,' was all he said, and he took his beating so like a man, I lost the heart to strike him and dropped the cane after only five strokes.

" 'You'll go out no more these nights,' I said. 'You'll work till you drop, so's you can't go drinkin'.'

" 'Got to go, Pap. Got to see what's down that road where the sky's purple and black.'

"I tied him to his bed with double knots at his arms and his legs, but he was gone at sunrise, the ropes wound neat and laid on his mat. His brother and me followed his tracks till we found his things: his spare shirt, his knife, all but his whistle that he'd made for himself. They was all laid neat in a pile on a flat rock, and no footprint led away from that place. That was eighteen day ago. We've found naught of him since then. I've come here looking for jonglers, especially a one-eyed man what's bent and no taller than my waist. I'm afeared for my Tom, as I think he's been taken to evil purpose. He'd not been in the drink. I see it now. Some jongler put these tales in his head, for my Tom's a good boy, as is only come seventeen. And that's my tale, so if you have a need, pour ale atop it, as that's what I intend to do."

The silence was deep. Only the pop and hiss of the hearth fire convinced me I hadn't suddenly lost all hearing. The story itself carried little weight with me. To lose a son young, whether to disease or drink or to the ever-present Leirans who snatched boys to serve in the army was common among the poor of the Four Realms. And to blame the child's fate on fairies or monsters was the usual practice. But I felt the father's grief vividly. Until those years in Zhev'Na when I had watched the Lords stealing Gerick's soul, I had thought seeing one's newborn infant dead the most grievous of sorrows. But far worse was losing a child nearing adulthood, seeing life's fullest promise dashed so bitterly.

In selfish relief, I reached for Gerick's hand that lay on the scuffed table. His fingers were stone-cold. I glanced up quickly. His skin was chalky, his eyes huge and dark. "Gerick, what is it?"

"Nothing," he whispered, pulling his hand from mine and averting his eyes. "Nothing. It's just a story."

Though the old man was a mesmerizing storyteller, the tale of a drunken sheepherder's son paled in comparison with Gerick's own strange adventures. "I think the boy ran away," I said. "There was violence between him and his father. Perhaps this tale is the man's way to explain it. What do you think?"

Gerick shrugged, color rushing back into his cheeks.

"I suppose I'd run away if I was beaten like that or tied to my bed. Can we go up now?"

I laid down a coin for the landlord, and we climbed the stairs, leaving the laggards draining their mugs and mumbling about getting home before the sun came up.

Sleep would not come. The rope bed and its straw-filled pallet seemed to develop a new lump or sag wherever I settled. I drifted in and out of dreams and worries and plans that seemed important, yet were indistinguishable by morning. Every time my eyes flicked open, I saw Gerick sitting on the floor, leaning against the wall, wide awake. His elbows were propped on his drawn-up knees, his hands clasped and pressed to his mouth.

When I woke from my last fitful nap, just after sunrise, Gerick was not in the room. I gathered up our last pack and hurried downstairs to find him. The Fire Goat's common room was bustling with every sort of person, from tradesmen to officials with ruffled silk doublets and gold neck-chains.

"Two for Vanesta. Anyone here bound for Vanesta?"

"Party of six for Fensbridge, looking for a strong swordsman."

The shouts came from every corner of the room. Concern about the bandits who plagued the mountain roads prompted travelers journeying any distance to join with other groups for mutual protection. Evard's soldiers were off fighting the war in Iskeran or hunting down those who failed to pay their taxes and tributes to support the interminable conflict. None were left to keep the roads safe from highwaymen, and the number of highwaymen increased every day that men got more desperate to feed themselves and their families. Local officials like Graeme Rowan were outmanned, their territories too large to patrol in a year of trying.

"Two women for Yurevan. To accompany a family or larger mixed party. No ruffians. No peasants."

I pushed through the smoky, crowded room toward the door, fending off a disheveled man who smelled of wine and leered broadly at me, saying he'd take me wherever I wanted to go. I pulled my widow's cap down lower and escaped into the yard, searching for Gerick.

The muddy yard was packed with horses, wagons, baggage, and even more people, generally of poorer aspect than those inside. A familiar lanky form moved down a string of eight or ten horses, offering each a private word along with a handful of grain from a canvas bag slung over his shoulder. I would have sworn each beast looked more cheerful after Paulo had stroked its neck and whispered in its ear. One of the string was Gerick's gray gelding, Jasyr, and another was my chestnut mare, Kelty, brought along not to sell, but to be available if Gerick and I should choose to ride.

Across the yard by the fence, Radele was helping a young woman load several heavy boxes into a wagon. He shared a laugh with her, then tugged his soft-brimmed hat down low over his face and slouched against our cart. The rugged little pony was harnessed and ready. I waved to get Radele's attention. He saluted and tipped his head toward a far corner next to the stable, where Gerick was engaged in earnest conversation with the despondent storyteller from the night before. My fists and stomach unclenched.

As I hurried across the courtyard through the people tying baggage onto carts and ponies and bawling mules, a burly drover leaped onto a heavily laden wagon, whistled loudly, and yelled, "Moving out for Montevial! We wait for nobody."

Radele gave me a hand into the pony trap, then swung gracefully into his saddle, nudged his mount forward, and accosted the drover. Gesturing toward my cart, he dropped a few coins into the drover's hand as I had instructed. The drover signaled me to take up the position just behind the lead wagons, and then, with a loud bellow, he headed his own wagon out the gates.

Gerick's seat was still empty. But Radele rode directly across the path of the wagon next to me, causing the driver to pull up sharply and curse when he couldn't squeeze in ahead of me. The young Dar'Nethi gave me a grin and a flourish of his hat. I reciprocated.

Just as I thought I might have to forfeit Radele's advantage and relinquish my desirable place near the head of the caravan, Gerick sprinted across the yard and leaped into the seat beside me. "Sorry," he said, as I snapped the reins, and we rolled through the gates of the innyard.

Once we were past the town walls, most of the sizable party stretched out behind us on the road. "So," I said, keeping my eyes on the road, "has he news of his one-eyed jongler?"

Gerick shifted beside me on the thinly padded seat. "No. I just—I just wanted to tell him I hope he finds his son. I said that I knew someone who'd been stolen away like his boy and had come home again, so that he shouldn't give up looking."

"Any price he has to pay is worth it."

But when I turned to smile at Gerick, his thoughts were very far away, and when I asked what troubled him so about the man's story, he averted his eyes and sat up straight. "Nothing." The set of his face told me not to bother asking more.

Our road wound through the green foothills of the Cerran Brae, sweeping gently upward toward the Leiran border. Some forty people comprised our party. The three principal drovers were Leiran, and six Leiran soldiers, two mounted and four on foot, guarded their three heavy wagons—some Vallorean province's tax levies of money and grain.

Just behind us rode a pair of hunters leading five pack mules heavily loaded with skins to sell in Montevial's market, and a vintner's party hauling a valuable cargo of Vallorean wine to a Leiran baron. The vintner's men had most likely been delighted to hear that a tax-levy shipment was in their party. Either the soldiers and the gruesome penalties for interfering with a tax levy would scare off any bandits, or the bandits would be so intent on the chests of gold and silver buried under the grain sacks that the wine might escape their notice.

Behind the vintner's men rode a delegation of four Vallorean magistrates hoping to gain tax preferences for their towns, a standoffish Leiran man, his wife and two grown sons, and a belligerent Leiran stonemason and his assistant who had been participating in the continuing effort to remove the names and likenesses of Vallorean royalty from the public buildings in Vanesta. The party was filled out with local people traveling to Leire in search of work or missing relatives. Paulo and his string of horses had been relegated so far to the rear, I couldn't even see them.

Scarcely able to keep up with the rest of us were a gaunt Vallorean and his family. The man carried a small boy on his shoulders and pulled a wheeled sledge by a rope tied around his broad chest. His wife carried an infant lashed to her back with straps of cloth, while three other children, none more than ten, trudged along beside their pitifully few household belongings, helping steady the sledge over rough places in the road.

At our first rest stop of the morning, I learned from his weary wife that the man was a master smith. Smiths were prized in every land, but the Leiran governor of Valleor had recently decreed that no Vallorean craftsman could practice his own trade until he had apprenticed to a Leiran master. As we prepared to resume our journey after the horses were rested and watered, I offered to let the children take turns riding in the trap with Gerick and me. When the smith heard my Leiran accent, he bluntly and unequivocally refused.

The first stretch of the afternoon was a short steep pitch over a low ridge. The Vallorean family quickly fell behind. When I slapped the reins harder than necessary to convince our pony to make the climb, Gerick eyed me curiously. "What's wrong?"

"There are more lost souls in the world than just the mad sheepherder's son," I said, relaxing my grip a little. "And I would dearly love to make Evard walk with them a while."

"Is it true you almost married King Evard? No one ever mentioned that at Comigor."

"Has Tennice been telling you stories?"

"Some. When I asked him why you looked like you were going to spit every time you said the king's name, and how you always called him Evard and not King Evard, Tennice said you were going to be queen."

As we rolled through the hazy afternoon, I told Gerick about the beginnings of Evard's and Tomas's friendship, and the understanding between the young King of Leire and my brother about me. And in order to explain how Tennice had used his knowledge of the law so I could choose for myself whom I wanted to marry, I had to tell him about my cousin Martin, Earl of Gault, and his magnificent country house called Windham, and how I'd met Karon there, falling in love with him before I'd known he was a sorcerer.

Gerick listened, but made no comment.

It felt good to be on the move. For all its beauty and comfort, Verdillon was only a temporary home. My home was with Karon, but I wasn't at all sure where. The rose-colored palace in Avonar was D'Natheil's place, not Karon's . . . not *my* Karon's. Despite what I'd said to Radele, I couldn't envision myself living there, and that left me feeling rootless and more uncertain about the future than I had ever been. Yet my unease could be only a small portion of what Gerick must feel. That consideration gave me patience with his silence and his moods when I had patience for nothing else in the world.

The air grew cooler as we moved slowly upward, and for the first time in weeks no storm broke in the afternoon. A breeze rippled the leagues of grass to either side of the road like an emerald sea. Gerick took over driving the cart, and despite the constant jolting, I fell into a drowsy reminiscence of Windham. Telling Gerick about those days had made the memories incredibly vivid. I could almost hear Karon's robust baritone harmonizing with Martin's off-key bass on a particularly bawdy song at a Long Night fete. When I laughed aloud at the memory of it, I felt Gerick's eyes on me. My skin grew hot. Certain that he would ask what amused me so, I tried to decide if telling him the words to the song would be at all proper for a mother to a youthful son.

But his question, when it came, was very odd. "Why do you wear your hair so short?" He was gazing at me with the strangest expression—part curiosity, part wonder, part terror—and had let the reins go slack. The cart was rolling to a stop.

"Here, you'd best keep us moving or the others will pull their wagons around, and we'll have to eat dust." I snatched the reins from his still hands and gave the pony a flick so that we started moving again.

He continued to stare at me, his question hanging in the air like an annoying bee.

"On the day they executed your father, they cut off all my hair," I said at last, trying to shove aside the accompanying images of fire and horror. "It's the Leiran custom for public penance. By the time it grew back again, I was living in circumstances that left me no leisure to take care of it. It was easier to keep it short." I had never let it grow past my shoulders again.

"You wore it very long before they cut it."

I couldn't tell whether that was a statement or a question. "It had been cut off so short only once before, when I was six and Tomas stuck tar in it."

Gerick didn't laugh, nor did he ask any more questions that day. He pulled his cloak around his shoulders and rode in tight silence, jerking himself awake whenever his head nodded. Radele rode just behind us, his eyes fixed on Gerick's back.

Eight days into our journey, our road crested the Cerran Brae. The climb, though not horribly steep, was long and steady, wandering alongside a marshy riverbank between enclosing ridges. Grumbling that the pleasant early days of the journey had left us laggard, the drovers pushed the party hard, as we would find no ground suitable for making camp until we reached the drier Leiran side of the pass. But the failing light forced them to call a halt soon after we'd crossed, rather than farther down the Leiran side as was usual.

We camped in a long, narrow meadow, hemmed in by steep ridges on two sides, and by the pass behind us. The little valley necked down tightly, the lower end of the road and a dribbling stream crowding between the encroaching ridges before passing into the thickly treed forest of Tennebar. Early summer was cold so high on the mountain, and a blustering wind funneled through the pass and the valley, setting shirts and cloaks billowing wildly.

"Pull up there in that hollow," said Sanger, the principal drover, whose neck was as wide as his head. He sat his horse across the road while directing each of the groups of travelers to follow his wagons into the meadow. "The vintner and the trappers will set up between you and my wagons tonight."

Gerick nodded and clucked to the pony, heading for the grassy depression the drover had indicated, just off the road. I wondered why the change in procedure. On other nights Sanger had allowed everyone to set up wherever they pleased.

"You'll be north picket on third watch," the drover said to Radele as the trap jounced across the short, dry tufts of grass. "We'll need your boy, as well. He's not stepped up as yet, but we're using everyone tonight. I've a bad feeling about this place. Too high. Too many notches in them rocks."

"Third watch," said Radele nodding. "I'll try to persuade the boy . . . my student . . . to do his share."

Gerick slapped the reins harder than required to move the pony along.

One by one, the traveling parties passed by us. By the time Paulo and his string of horses scuffed up the dust, following the vintner's wagons and the trappers' mule train toward the center of the camp as Sanger directed him, Gerick and Radele had unhitched the trap. While I unloaded our packs, Gerick rubbed down the pony, and Radele strolled over to the scraggly stand of pine across the road to hunt for firewood. He emerged a short time later dragging a dead sapling.

As I rummaged through our supplies, wishing I had something to cook that was more savory than the barley porridge we'd eaten for three nights running, Radele suddenly dropped his tree in the middle of the road and came racing across the meadow through the dusk, shouting, "Riders!" His tone left no question as to his opinion of the intentions of those approaching.

The word flew through the camp like leaves blown on

the chilly gusts. Men shouted harsh commands and
grabbed the halters of horses left to graze. Women
snatched their pails from the spring and ran back to their
parties. A few people like me stood stupidly peering at
the road where nothing was visible as yet.

"Get back to the wagons, my lady," said Radele, pelting into our grassy depression. "You'll not be safe out
here."

From the back of our little cart he snatched a long
canvas bundle that he threw to the ground at Gerick's
feet. "You've trained with the masters, eh? Time to put
your skills to some *decent* use."

At the same time, Sanger barreled up on his big sorrel.
"What's going on?"

"Riders on the lower road," said Radele, already
buckling the saddle girth under his bay. "At least twenty,
coming fast enough they're up to no good. If we get
your soldiers and the vintner's men down there where
the road narrows, we can stop them before they come
up this far."

"How could you—?"

"I've exceptional hearing," snapped Radele.

Shouts and pointing fingers told me that the sudden
rumbling in my belly was not growing anxiety, but the
drumming of hoofbeats. Radele was in the saddle before
I could blink. He drew his sword and motioned to three
of the Vallorean magistrates and the stonemason and his
assistant, who had ridden up behind Sanger. "Muster
your riders!" shouted Radele. "These fellows and I will
hold until you get there!" And he and the five travelers
took off for the neck of the valley.

Sanger rode back toward the center of camp, but instead of dispatching riders to follow Radele, he shouted
and waved at his soldiers, the vintner's men, and the
trappers to stay right where they were. Now I understood his placement of the camp. Sanger wanted his back
to the solid cliffs on the southwest and his left flank
protected by the little bogs and springs that dotted the
heart of the meadow. And he wanted the most interesting prey such as wine casks and pelts—and their sturdy
defenders—in between his levy wagons and any assault

from the road. Parties like ours and the Valloreans and the Leiran man and wife were left on the outskirts of the camp. Expendable distractions.

For a moment Gerick stared at the bundle Radele had thrown at his feet, making no move to open it. Then, he snapped his head from me to Radele and his riders, streaking down the road, to Sanger and his soldiers, taking up their positions about the heart of the camp.

"Come on," he said, touching my arm. "We need to find Paulo." Before I could question or object or think of what else to do, he took off running for the flat grassy area near a spring where Paulo had hobbled his horses and left them to graze.

I followed. Paulo caught sight of us before we were halfway to the spring. My feet slowed when my boots squelched in a mud hole. My heart slowed when I saw Paulo leading Gerick's Jasyr and his own Molly, already saddled. "Wait," I said. "We need to consider—"

"Take care of my mother," said Gerick, grabbing my arm and shoving it into Paulo's grasp, while snatching Jasyr's bridle.

"What do you think you're doing?" I said. I wasn't used to being handed about by striplings.

"You and Paulo need to get behind the soldiers' line." Gerick was already in Jasyr's saddle. "It's the safest place. If the Dar'Nethi can't hold the neck of the valley, then anyone outside that line is dead."

Faint cries and a rising dust cloud from the eastern end of the road told us that the fight was engaged.

"We'd best warn the rest of the folk, then," said Paulo.

"Just take care of my mother."

A knot of terror caught in my throat as Gerick wheeled the gray and kicked him to a gallop across the meadow. But when he reached the road, he turned, not toward the battle raging at the lower end of the valley, but the opposite way, back toward the pass. My skin flushed with relief that my son was not riding into harm's way, yet at the same time another, more uncomfortable, feeling swelled within me. What was he doing?

"My lady, come along with me." Paulo yanked his

quarterstaff from the straps that lashed it alongside Molly's saddle, then whispered in the mare's ear and slapped her flank, sending her back toward the open pasture. He whistled after her, and she whinnied cheerfully. Then he took my arm and tugged gently. "We'd best hurry."

The two of us herded the Leiran man and wife, the fourth Vallorean magistrate—a gaping, big-bellied man—and the other Vallorean travelers toward Sanger and his levy wagons. The granite ramparts that flanked the meadows eerily amplified the clash of weapons, and the shouts and screams of men and horses from down the valley.

Though the soldiers and guards allowed us to pass through their line, they made no move to aid the panicked travelers. Those travelers unarmed or unfit we situated under the wagons, while setting the better equipped to stand in front of them. I refused to crouch underneath, but climbed atop the roped pyramid of vintner's casks where I could see what was going on. My knife was in my hand.

I was a Leiran warrior's daughter, and I had been taught that refusal to fight was cowardice. After Karon's arrest, when he had invoked the principles of a lifetime and refused to harm another person to save his own life or the lives of his child or his friends, my instincts and upbringing had named him a coward. After long and painful years, I believed that I had come to terms with Karon's convictions. But now it seemed that Gerick, too, had run away, leaving his companions to defend themselves.

As I tried to devise some other explanation—he'd detected some other threat or he was circling around to take the bandits by stealth—Radele and a single rider raced up the valley road, hotly pursued by at least twenty mounted raiders, whooping and yelling. The battle quickly engulfed us. The frenzied bandits on their squat ponies swarmed through the camp, raising a horrific din: thudding boots, pounding hooves, roars and screams of men, grunts and squeals of beasts, the clangor of weapons.

An ax-wielding man on a shaggy, thick-chested pony charged from the choking dust and noise straight toward our position, a ragged green scarf flapping about his head. Paulo stiffened and gripped his staff with both hands. I crouched low just behind him, clutching my knife. But before the outlaw could reach us, a passing soldier in pursuit of another bandit slashed at the charging beast's legs with his great-sword. The pony squealed and skidded. The rider leaped free, twisting in the air, and crashed to the dirt just in front of Paulo.

But the now-vanished soldier had only postponed the assault, for the snarling bandit scrambled away from the fallen beast and leaped to his feet. With a blood-chilling cry, he raised his ax over Paulo's head. Paulo lifted his staff and braced for the blow. Yet in a sudden onslaught of man and horse and flashing silver, the bandit pitched forward before he could strike, his face thudding into the ground as Radele severed his spine with a sweeping blow. Radele's mount reared, and the Dar'Nethi raised his bloody sword in salute before vanishing again into the fray. The bandit's green scarf had been torn away by the trampling hooves.

That was as close as Paulo and I came to harm. Paulo did not stir from my side, and though his staff remained ready, he did not have to wield it in my defense.

The raid faltered quickly. Radele seemed to be everywhere at once, appearing out of the gloom wherever the press was hardest, his fair hair gleaming, his blade shining silver in the torchlight, brighter by far than any other. One after another, he took the bandits down, while the drover and his stolid men held their line.

Night swallowed the ragged remnant of the bandit horde. As the fighters drew harsh breaths and the wounded moaned, travelers crawled slowly out from under the wagons and wandered off through the trampled grass, searching for their companions, picking up scattered belongings, lighting fires and torches. The soldiers invited Radele to join them at their fire, any disagreement about tactics seemingly soothed by victory.

"I'd be better occupied to scout the valley perimeter, I think," said Radele, patting the neck of his panting horse. "And I need to cool this fellow down."

I dressed the slashed hand of the stonemason as he

wept for his dead assistant, his sister's only son, while Paulo bandaged the arm of the fat Vallorean magistrate, who sat rigid with shock and uncertain how to proceed. His three companions had died at the neck of the valley. Only Radele and the stonemason had survived their venture. But everyone agreed that their efforts had weakened the bandits so they could be finished easily.

Sanger set up the watch and appointed parties to bury the dead: two Vallorean travelers and one of the vintner's men in addition to the four lost with Radele. Nineteen dead bandits were left on the rocks for the wolves to find. Two prisoners were bound to the sides of the levy wagons and would remain there until we reached Montevial—if they stayed alive so long.

"Where's the young Lord?" said Radele, slipping from his saddle as I set a pot over the hot little fire Paulo had built for me. Our own camp had remained relatively undisturbed in the raid. I had collected our few ripped and dirty blankets and dented pots scattered as the raiders fled.

"I don't know," I said.

"He had something needed doing," said Paulo, giving a last poke to the coals and standing up. Though anxious to see to his stock, he had refused to leave me until Gerick or Radele returned. "He'll be back."

Radele's gray tunic was splattered with blood, but his face was impassive as he looked around the campsite, his eyes settling on the canvas bundle that lay untouched beside the cart where he had thrown it. The young sorcerer picked up the bundle and unfolded the flaps of cloth, revealing a plain steel hilt protruding from a worn leather sheath. "I noticed he doesn't wear a blade. Evidently my spare sword wasn't suitable."

Paulo bristled. "He don't have to—"

"That's enough, Paulo," I said sharply. I didn't need them arguing. Not tonight. "We've a long journey still to go."

Paulo snatched his quarterstaff from the ground and strode out of the camp.

Radele unsaddled his horse and rubbed him down before allowing him to graze, soothing him with soft words as he worked. When the horse was calmly crunching the dry grass alongside our unrattled pony, he joined me at the fire, a waterskin in his hand. He sat heavily on the ground, downed half the contents of his waterskin, and poured another good measure over his matted hair, rubbing his face and head vigorously.

"Will you eat something?" I had made up our barley porridge, but thrown in a precious lump of sugar, a handful of currents, and a thick glob of butter to make it more appetizing.

He flashed a grin. "I'll eat my boots if there be naught else, but this smells far better."

He took the bowl, devouring its contents before I'd set the pot back on the fire. As we talked of the dead and injured travelers and prospects for the journey ahead, he ate all that was left.

"You fought bravely tonight," I said later, as I cleaned the pot and bowls and packed them away. "You'll likely gain no glory in either world from this battle, but your Prince will hear of your deeds."

Radele was cleaning his sword. "To be honest, my lady, for a Dar'Nethi to brawl with such as we met tonight takes little courage. The only enemies that measure a man are those that come out of Zhev'Na." He ran his oily rag the length of his gleaming blade and did not look up.

Slowly the camp settled into exhausted quiet, the soft voices of men as they traded off the watch joining the shrieks of hunting birds and the distant howls of wolves. Though weary to the bone, I could not sleep. Sometime after the watch changed, I heard the creak of heavy-laden wheels and the slow scuff of boots on the hard road down from the pass. After a quiet exchange with the watch, the smith and his family moved to a patch of open ground a short distance from us. They must have dropped to the bare ground to sleep.

Blanket around my shoulders, I sat up and squinted into the darkness, hoping to see one more rider. Though I waited as long as I could hold my eyes open, he did not come.

When I woke to the drowsy bustle of breaking camp,

Gerick was hitching the pony to the cart. Jasyr was nowhere in sight, back in Paulo's string I guessed.

"So, you're back," I said, throwing my bundled blanket in the cart. "It's jack and ale for breakfast."

"Hmm." He yanked at the buckles on the wither
straps and girth. He didn't look at me.

I kicked dirt over the glowing ashes of our fire, and
then gathered up the rest of our belongings and tucked
them under the seat, leaving the bag of dried meat and
a flask of ale where Gerick could get them when he was
ready. I didn't know what to say to him. Fear, shame,
and frustration had me ready to shake him until his teeth
rattled. And so I decided that until I was in better control of my own feelings, I'd best avoid a confrontation.
I climbed into the cart.

Radele hurried into camp from the direction of the
stream, his hair dripping and face clean, wishing us a
good morning as he swung himself into his saddle. For
Gerick's part, the Dar'Nethi might not have existed. My
son jumped up beside me; I clucked to the pony, and
we rolled out.

In the ensuing days, no matter how I tried to approach
him, Gerick refused to speak of his actions on the night
of the raid. Although concern for his well-being had
quickly shouldered my personal disappointments aside,
I could not avoid one simple fact. Gerick had run away,
while men far less skilled at combat than he had died
fighting to protect us all. He needed to acknowledge that
truth someday. If he was to grow into a man of honor,
he needed to think about it.

Radele's polite deference remained unchanged. I
could see that it rankled Gerick far worse than the
scornful glances and resentful whispers from some of our
traveling companions. One evening a few nights after
the raid, when Radele had gone off to stand watch, I
tried again. "We need to talk about it, Gerick. You've
not spoken ten words these last three days. You've not
looked me in the eye."

His face flamed, and he threw his cup to the dirt. "It's
nobody's business what I do or don't do. Name me cow-

ard or devil, whatever you want. I don't care. Just leave me alone!''

He strode into the darkness, leaving a huge angry hole in the night.

After a while, Paulo spoke up softly from across the fire. "He can't fight, my lady. He just can't. I think he's afraid.''

But Paulo couldn't, and Gerick wouldn't, tell me what my son was afraid of.

CHAPTER 6

Eighteen days after setting out from Prydina, we rolled up to the thick-towered city gates of Montevial, the capital city of Leire, the most powerful city in the world—in the mundane world, that is. *Mundane* . . . so those of us with no power of sorcery were called by the Dar'-Nethi living in the world of Gondai and its royal city Avonar. The word raised my hackles. These "untalented" people were my friends, acquaintances, and kin. Intelligence, wisdom, and wit flourished here along with our many faults.

Yet the number of my people that knew the truth about the world—about the Lords of Zhev'Na who nourished and fed on our troubles or about the glories of Dar'Nethi magic that held steadfast against that wickedness in a half-ruined world far away—could be counted on one hand. After everything I had learned in the past six years, it felt odd and a bit shameful that my friends, acquaintances, and kin bustled about their concerns in such appalling ignorance.

We arrived in late afternoon, approaching the bridge over the wide, sluggish Dun River beneath a thin, gray, overcast sky that did little to alleviate the sultry heat. The red dragon banners hung limp from their standards, swelling occasionally with a vile-smelling breeze off the river. Just upriver the drain channels in the walls dumped the city's sewage into the slow-moving water. Ragged hawkers, selling everything from diseased chickens to temple offering jars to remedies for gout and boils, swarmed out of the ramshackle city that had grown up outside the city walls.

The gates were always crowded at the end of the day, but I'd never seen the mess so bad as this. The roadway was mobbed for half a league west of the city, well beyond the stone bridge, the crowding made worse because as many travelers seemed to be leaving the city as entering it. Anxious travelers, shoving, pushing, and shouting at each other. Animals bawled and dragged at their traces.

Two men hurling curses at each other clogged the center of the stone span, knives drawn in some dispute over tangled wagon wheels. We dismounted and elbowed our own path through the bumping and pushing throng, leading the pony cart. Snippets of complaints and furtive, angry, or frightened whispers flew on every side: *Won't let me in; they've no record of my cousin . . . Allowing no one past the gates without references known to the magistrates . . . Our fruit will rot if we have to take it town to town; those inside the walls will starve . . . Good riddance to them . . . Afraid to piss wrong . . . Vanished, they said, not a hair left behind . . . Cripples arrested . . . Who carries proof they live in the city? We just live here. . . .*

The levy wagons, of course, disappeared quickly through the gates, but all other travelers were required to join a queue and wait to explain their business to a seated clerk. Those travelers who demonstrated noble connections, royal business, or a full purse moved quickly to the front of the queues. Those the clerk approved were given a pass to admit them to the city. The heavily armed swordsmen flanking the clerk wore the king's red livery, and more soldiers stood just beyond the portcullis, armed with pikes or drawn swords.

Radele's blue eyes roamed the crowding beggars, the filthy river, and the squat gate towers and city walls that had been gouged, pitted, and scorched in the years when war touched this close to the heart of Leire. "Vasrin's hand," he said, as he shoved away three ragged, giggling urchins who were pawing at my cloak and doing their clumsy best to rifle our pockets. He wiped his hand on his cloak. "What is this place?"

A scuffle broke out just in front of us. A guardsman

dragged a portly man from his horse, shouting, "Here's one! Only one leg, and look at the size of him!"

"Lost my leg in the war is all! Let me go!" The terrified man writhed on his belly as the pikemen surrounded him and a soldier bound his hands. "My daughter lives in the Street of Cloth Merchants . . . respectable . . . I've served the king . . ." A guardsman's boot smashed into his face, drowning the rest of the man's protests in bubbling incoherence.

"We'll find out how respectable you are," said one of the soldiers dragging him through the gates. The man's horse was led away.

A young couple was turned away when the clerk noted burn scars on the husband's face and that he was missing one ear.

Radele took my elbow firmly, keeping his eyes moving and his hand on his sword hilt, as new guards were summoned and formed up around the clerk. He spoke under his breath. "Let us withdraw, my lady. If we *must* proceed, I'll conjure a way in after dark. The danger—"

"Only if we're turned away," I said. "Using your talents is too risky. And sneaking in would likely only cause us trouble further on."

The pennons on the gate towers shifted in a lazy, humid gust, ripe with the stench of the riverside bogs. After a wait that stretched interminably, a guardsman motioned Radele and me to step forward, and I was soon babbling the story of my husband's death in the war and my desire to find a sponsor for my son among our acquaintances in Montevial. Gerick remained standing by the pony cart at the edge of the crowd.

"And who might you be asking to sponsor the boy?" The clerk flared his nostrils and smoothed his sweat-stained yellow satin waistcoat, as he squinted across the trampled ground at Gerick.

My references to several prominent families by their personal names lifted his eyebrows. "Viscount Magior? Not likely. He's dead these two years in Iskeran. And Sylvanus Lovatto—Baron Lovatto that would be, I suppose—is retired to the north country. Lord Faverre, now . . . Ricard Lord Faverre, you say . . . Tell me, woman, how would the likes of you find yourself on such friendly terms with the commandant of the city guard?"

Radele, standing close to my left shoulder, stiffened, his arm drawing slowly toward the sword on his hip. I stepped on his foot. Epithets for my overplayed hand and curses for the self-important little clerk were the words that came immediately to mind. "Good sir, I'm just a soldier's wi—"

"Sheriff Rowan's man of Dunfarrie, bringing horses for the royal cavalry!" A disturbance rippled the crowd behind us. "Let me through. My master's sent ten steeds for King Evard." Paulo slipped easily from the saddle and dropped to the dirt not ten paces from us, his horses forcing both travelers and soldiers aside.

"Sheriff's man, eh?" said the clerk, inspecting Paulo's slouched hat and worn countryman's jacket. Paulo's bony wrists poked well out of the sleeves. "Where'd you come up with these beasts? Been holding back on our suppliers?"

"Brought 'em from Valleor, your honor. Sheriff sent me to round up animals from those who've no business owning them. I've fifty more on the way." Tennice had written out a false manifest for Paulo before we left Verdillon, and now Paulo shoved the crumpled paper into the clerk's face.

The clerk jerked his head to a sleek young guard with a thin mustache. As the clerk read the manifest the soldier proceeded down the row, running his hands over the flanks and legs of the well-groomed chestnut at the head of the string and then giving a cursory examination to the rest of the beasts. "Decent stock," he said, returning to his post at the clerk's side.

"What's your name and how many in your party?" said the clerk, pulling out a fresh sheet of paper and beginning to write.

"Just me. Name's Paulo . . ."

As Paulo took the pass and mounted his horse, the vintner's wagon rolled forward, squeezing into the tight space before the gates, the drover shouting, "We can't get left out here. A baron's waiting for our barrels. Why are the gates closing early?"

Murmurs swept through the crowd. Other travelers bulled their way to the front, waving their hands and shouting. "I just heard those not inside the gates before sunset wouldn't be allowed in at all," cried a woman. Those in the queue behind me surged forward, yelling, panicked.

Paulo's knees nudged his horse's flank, and he led his string through the gates without looking back. The clerk, one cheek twitching and his gaze flicking nervously over my shoulder, motioned the guardsmen to draw close and hold the shouting travelers back.

"Here," he said, scribbling a pass and shoving it at me. "Take this matter up with the master-at-arms. Secure your son a place with these noble friends of yours within two days or get yourself out of this city. We don't want strangers here nowatimes. Now move on. Next!"

"Tell me, sir," I said, "what's going on—?" But the harried clerk waved me away and motioned the vintner's man forward.

Gerick had already drawn the cart up beside the clerk's table. We didn't take the time to climb up, but led the pony through the shadowed archway after Paulo.

We had arrived one day early for my meeting with Evard. The timing was perfect, for it gave us a full night to rest and a full day to get news, yet would not keep us long in the uneasy city. We were stopped three times on our way to the street where we were to meet Paulo, our pass examined by soldiers whose hands stayed close to their weapons. The men required us to show our full faces, hands, and even our legs. "Don't want no more cripples in the city," they said, snickering at my indignant protest at lifting the hem of my riding skirt.

"Insolent vermin . . . degrading . . ." Radele handed me back into the pony cart with such vigor I thought I might spill out the other side. His disgust and annoyance had grown with every step past the walls. Perhaps he was bothered that Paulo was the one who had gotten us through the gates. I had grown up around "men of action" and their tender pride.

"None of this makes sense," I said as Radele threw

himself onto his horse. Gerick clucked to the pony, and we drove on through the winding streets. In truth I was more puzzled than upset. Such searches had never been common in Leire, nor had I ever heard such concern expressed over the number of crippled bodies. Unfortunately our turbulent history had kept us well supplied with mutilated citizens.

"It's the vanishings," said the buxom, heavy-jowled woman who rented us rooms, shaking her gray braids and wheezing noisily as she hefted her bulk up a narrow stair. "Folks stolen from their beds. First it was only cripples disappearin', as if them as wished all the beggars would go away all these years had their prayers answered." She opened a scratched door into the tight little garret room, leaned close enough that I could smell her bad teeth, and dropped her voice. "But I've heard that some as are not cripples have gone now, too, nobles even. That's put a stick up everyone's backside."

"But if crippled beggars are the ones disappearing, then why treat such people like thieves?"

"I don't talk about it," she said, spitting in her left palm and slapping it with her right thumb, as jonglers do to ward off evil. "I'm just telling you this city is an ill-luck place. You'd best go back where you come from."

I wished I could do exactly that. I felt as if I were being rushed along by the strong currents of a river when I'd only expected to stick my toes in a stream.

While Radele and Gerick took care of the cart and pony and waited for Paulo, I washed my face, combed my hair, put on a fresh tunic, and set out through the dark streets for Evard's palace, intending to use my pass from the clerk at the city gates to get into the palace grounds. If I could find Racine, a friend who had once worked for Karon at the Royal Antiquities Commission, he might be able to give me reliable news. But after being sent from one of the heavily guarded palace gates to the next, waiting interminably for unhelpful clerks to be summoned, while standing in the blaze of torchlight and watch fire and begging favors from leering soldiers—all to no result—I returned to the inn.

"Six years ago I was able to talk my way into the palace with the flimsiest of stories," I said, gulping a mug of ale that Paulo had poured for me as soon as I returned to the garret. "Now you can't step beneath the portcullis without a signed and sealed document from the person you're supposed to meet."

The night was well on, and Gerick, Paulo, and I were seated at a small table in the cramped chamber as I reported on my futile venture. Radele sat on the scuffed plank floor beside the door.

"I told my story to three different officials, but they said the master-at-arms won't see me unless I bring a letter from a family willing to foster Gerick."

"I could likely get into the palace grounds if you wanted." Paulo chewed thoughtfully on a strip of jack, the tough, dried meat he favored over every possible sustenance. "Done it before out at Lord Marchant's castle at Dunfarrie . . . as a lark. Hopped on a wagon loaded with hides. Rode it through a service gate. Looked real grumbly, like I was hating the idea of unloading the stuff. Jumped off, looked about, helped unload, then walked out. Look stupid enough, and no one asks questions."

"Appropriate to look stupid, if you're doing such a stupid thing," said Radele, still in a brittle humor. "I saw five clever fellows dangling from gallows a few streets from here. Evidently they'd done nothing but walk someplace they'd no cause to be. Madam, for your safety, I recommend we abandon this absurd venture and leave this stinkhole immediately."

Gerick, who had remained silent throughout my tale, lifted his head and glared at Radele. "What would an arrogant Dar'Nethi peep-thief know of—?"

"Gerick, mind your tongue!" I disliked rebuking him in front of Radele, but his constant edginess was driving me to distraction. The tension between my son and his bodyguard had become an open sore since the fight with the bandits. No use to let him get caught up in defending Paulo's honor.

Gerick leaped to his feet, knocking over his chair. He kicked it out of his way and threw open the shutters, letting the steamy air and the noise and stench of the streets into the close room.

"What has everyone so terrified, Radele? Have you learned any more about these vanishings?"

His movements ever graceful and efficient, Radele rose and poured himself a mug of ale from a pitcher he'd brought upstairs, coolly ignoring Gerick's flushed complexion and hard mouth. "Everyone's in a lather, prattling about monsters and apparitions being responsible. That's why they're after these deformed sorts." He glanced at each of us in turn, as if asking if his own report could possibly be true. "The innkeeper says a sorcerer was *burned to death* last week."

The color drained from Gerick's cheeks. My stomach tied itself into a knot.

"A mob did the burning, so they said." Radele shuddered slightly as he leaned his back against the door and took a long pull at his ale. "Just imagine what they'd do if they had the slightest inkling of real evil. They'd all go bury themselves in caves."

"There's more things wrong than that." Paulo extricated a greasy paper packet from his pocket and pulled another strip of the leathery jack from it, his unhurried sobriety a soothing counter to the rest of us. "A stable lad was telling me about some baron who had to forfeit his land as his soldiers refused to muster for the spring campaign. And the fellow wasn't the first. Another noble got himself and his family killed by his own men. This fellow says no lord in the kingdom is allowing anyone about him unless he knows their face, and even then he'll have no more than two together. I don't know that we're going to be safe anywhere."

"Mutiny?" I said, rising from my chair. The night, already filled with unease, took a turn for the worse. Something was profoundly wrong in Leire. Honor, duty to one's lord and in turn to his, who was, of course, the king, shedding the blood of your lord's enemies . . . these things were more sacred to a Leiran soldier than our gods or priests, the very sum of his manhood. No Leiran man I had ever known, no matter what his grievance on any matter, would refuse to take up arms at his lord's call any more than he would refuse to breathe. Mutiny. My father would have spit blood at the word. "You're right, Paulo," I said. "We're not safe here. We need to be on our way as soon as we can."

Radele nodded and thumped his empty mug on the table. "We can be off within the hour."

"Well, not quite so soon as that!" I said, shaking my head in exasperation. "We still have to learn what Evard wants. This just makes it more urgent."

Radele frowned. "But madam, you just said—"

"This meeting is not to serve idle curiosity, Radele. Something has turned this kingdom wrong way out and people are blaming sorcerers. There was a time when I would have dismissed such accusations as the usual nonsense, but now . . . What if there's something to it? What if the Lords are involved? We need to learn more if we can. I promise we won't dawdle once we've heard what we need to hear."

Sighing deeply, Radele bowed and pulled open the door. "I think you've sorely misjudged your risk, my lady. But, as I can't persuade you otherwise, I'll keep watch. Please lock this door tonight." His footsteps down the passage and the stair soon faded.

"I'd best be off, too," said Paulo, yawning as he stood and threw his jacket over his shoulder, ready to head for the stables to guard his horses. He paused in the doorway, turning back for a moment, looking at me square on. "Radele's not wrong about the danger hereabouts, my lady. You wouldn't think to go to this meeting with the king alone?"

"No. We'll stay together. And truly, we may be on our way home almost as quickly as Radele wishes. I can't imagine how Evard expects me to get past the gates at Windham. I don't know who holds the Gault titles now or even how I'll find out."

Paulo hesitated, looking thoughtful, running his long fingers over the tarnished door latch.

"By the way," I said, "well done at the gates today. We'd likely be there yet, if it weren't for you. And all the rumors about an early gate-closing . . . they helped as well. You wouldn't have seen who started those, would you?"

Paulo's eyes flicked to Gerick. "I had a bit of help with that part. More than this Dar'Nethi fellow are watching out for you."

He straightened up and pulled open the door. "And you needn't worry about getting into Windham tomorrow. Hasn't been no lord there since the last one was done for."

"Where did you hear that?"

He colored a little. "All those years when you lived at Dunfarrie, and Sheriff took you to the Petitioner's Rite . . . he listened to all the talk about you, and then he'd come back and grouse about how high and mighty you were. I was only a nub back then, hanging about the sheriff where I had no cause to be, but I heard a lot of things. King Evard had the place knocked down and burnt."

The night passed uneasily. The thought of Evard destroying Windham had me alternately seething and weeping. Rain drizzled mournfully as midnight tolled from the palace clock tower. At least Gerick had finally succumbed to sleep. No nightmares, either. Even a drunken commotion outside in the street didn't stir him.

About the time blackness yielded to faint gray, someone tapped on the door. "It's Paulo, ma'am." I cracked open the door and peered into the gloom. A straw poked out of Paulo's tousled hair. "Radele asks that you please come to the stable, ma'am. Quiet-like, he says."

I threw on my cloak and followed him, leaving Gerick curled on the floor. He hadn't so much as changed position.

The innyard was pooled and pocketed with muddy rainwater. Servants stepped gingerly through the mud, carrying slops jars and water jugs, while boys with soaked leggings staggered toward the kitchens hauling heavy coal hods. Wagon wheels splattered through the muddy streets beyond the fence. Though the gray morning already rang with jangling harness, clattering pots,

and orders yelled at the legions of kitchen maids, the
stable was dim and quiet when we shut the door behind
us. Gerick's Jasyr nickered softly as we walked past him
and Paulo fondled his ears. A mouse skittered past my
foot. We found Radele in the farthest corner stall sitting
atop a pile of straw in the near dark.

"What is it, Radele?" I said.

As Radele jumped to his feet, the straw seemed to
shift. The Dar'Nethi swept the straw aside to reveal a
strongly built man in ill-fitting clothes huddled in the
dirt. Only after a startled moment did I notice the ropes
binding his hands and feet. The man strained against his
bonds, twisting around so that he could glare up at me.
A purple bruise covered half his forehead, and the unintelligible words trapped by the rag tied around his mouth
could be nothing polite.

"When I left your bedchamber last night, I met this
fellow skulking about in the passage. Not someone I
wanted nearby, so I ran him off. But then, on my rounds
this morning, wasn't he in the stableyard telling another
fellow that he'd heard some treasonous gossip that was
going to make his fortune if he could just locate a con-
stable to tell? And this time he carried quite an ugly
introduction."

Radele presented me with a long, curved dagger. "His
friend seemed to have an antipathy for constables and
ran away, so I used the opportunity to snag this one. I
wasn't sure what to do with him. We should probably
dispatch the villain, but I thought perhaps a corpse or
another disappearance might draw more attention than
whatever he might babble."

Horrified at the thought of our careless conversation
last evening—sneaking into the palace, my low opinions
of the king, the upcoming meeting, sorcery—I couldn't
think what to do. If the man had heard any of it . . .
"No, of course, we can't kill him," I said, shaking off my
urge to do that very thing. I'd never faced this particular
dilemma before. Danger had always come from my enemies, not balding, inept thieves. "We just want him to
keep quiet."

"Pay him, maybe?" said Paulo, scratching his head.

I pulled my cloak tighter. "We don't have much to offer. And bribes are unreliable. Too easily overbid."

Straining grunts and growls had the veins in the man's beefy neck bulging. His eyes blazed in the dusty light.

"But silencing is easily done." Radele cocked his head thoughtfully.

"We should question—"

The teasing, unmistakable telltale of enchantment filled the air, as Radele laid his hand over the captive man's eyes and murmured a few words. The man's struggles grew feeble and then ceased; his wordless protests fell silent. When Radele removed his hand, the stranger's eyes no longer burned, but wandered over the stall, the straw, and our faces with equal disinterest. Radele motioned us to step back as he untied his prisoner and dragged the fellow to his feet—a big man, dressed in the kersey tunic and shapeless trousers of a common laborer.

"My grandfather taught me this," said Radele, straightening the man's tangled clothes and nudging him toward the stable door. "It's designed especially for those who have dangerous mouths."

Without so much as a word or a glance, the man stumbled away, straw sticking up from his rumpled hair and clothes as if he were a scarecrow come to life. Paulo and I followed as far as the stable door, watching as the man walked into the busy lane and halted uncertainly. A woman bumped into him. He staggered, but stayed upright. And then a wagon narrowly missed knocking him flat. Soon he was being brushed from one place to another like a splinter of driftwood floating on the tide.

"What have you done, Radele?" I said, uneasy. "We should have questioned him, found out what he heard, what he was after . . ."

Radele stood at my shoulder, arms crossed, his face sober. "It would have taken us three days to sort out his lies. This is much better. Your secrets will be quite safe. Unless he can recite a list of names he has no possible reason to know, he'll be able to tell no one anything about what he's heard. And you needn't trou-

ble yourself about him. He'll remember how to eat and
drink, just not much beyond that. My family is very good
at these things."

"Shit," said Paulo, quietly.

In slightly less earthy terms, I echoed his sentiments.

"We must leave this city, madam," said Radele.
"You've seen the risk."

"We'll set out for Verdillon the moment my meeting
with King Evard is done. And, Radele, I thank you again
for protecting us, but what you did here . . . I can't think
the Prince would approve."

"Your safety is imperative. The Prince was most
emphatic."

"But in this world some things are not permissible for
even the best of reasons. Some things are not right in
any world."

Radele dropped his hands to his sides with an exasperated sigh.

Leaving Montevial and its poisonous atmosphere behind us felt like walking out of prison. We abandoned
our disguises. Paulo had sold the pony trap and his extra
horses, and we rode our own mounts through the southern gates of the city in early afternoon. Only after a
wide detour did we circle northward toward Windham.
The shadows were long when we first caught sight of the
towers rising above the leafy sea of its vast parkland. A
host of chittering blackbirds heralded our approach from
the spreading beech and lime trees that lined the road.

Windham's graceful towers symbolized everything joy-
ous in my girlhood. For a girl of seventeen, they had
represented the stimulating company and unending entertainment so at odds with sober Comigor. For a naive
young woman of one and twenty, romantic encounters
with Martin's mysterious and charming protégé. For a
worldly matron of five and twenty, a haven of friendship,
the one place Karon and I could go where there need
be no secrecy, no deceit, and no fear. Windham had
been the most beautiful place I knew, welcoming the
wide vistas of the world through its tall windows, just as
its master welcomed the vast landscape of ideas into his

great heart. How my cousin would have relished our
strange adventures.

A little way into the park, just beyond iron gates that
hung bent and broken from rusted hinges, sat a brick
gatehouse where the housekeeper and head grounds-
keeper had once lived. Though its windows and doors
gaped, its wood trim had splintered and peeled bare of
paint, and vines had overgrown the front stoop and garden wall, the shell of the gatehouse remained intact. We
halted at the weedy semicircle of the carriage park just
in front of it.

"If everything looks safe enough when Radele returns
from his reconnoiter, he and Gerick will remain hidden
here," I told the three of them. "I want Paulo patrolling
outside the walls. The king will have attendants and
bodyguards, but I would expect them to be a small number and remain in the courtyard in front of the main
house when he enters the garden. Anything beyond that,
and I want to know about it."

"There's fresh tracks all over," said Paulo. "A number
of people have been here today."

"I'd expect nothing less," I said. "And very likely ten
spies along the road watched us ride in. But if he brings
in a large party, or if they move to surround the house
and gardens, or do *anything* that looks remotely suspicious, before, during, or after the king's arrival, Paulo,
you're to warn Radele. And, Radele, you *will* get Gerick
away, using whatever means necessary."

"But, madam—"

"You have no other duty."

Radele jerked his head irritably and rode away.

"One of us should be with you," said Gerick, the first
speech beyond single-word responses he'd offered us all
day. "You've said again and again that the king is a
treacherous villain. Tennice has told me—"

"Yes, Evard is a despicable bastard, but he'll not
touch me. I know this seems illogical. He's had a thousand opportunities to do so over all these years, but he
promised Tomas he wouldn't, and, whatever else he may
be, Evard keeps to his word. He loved Tomas like a
brother; I witnessed his grief when he heard Tomas was

dead. Truly I'd not have been afraid to confront him in
his own palace today. But on no other matter do I trust
him. It's *you* must stay out of sight."

Gerick looked very young in that moment, too much
worry creasing his slender face. What kind of mother
was I to bring him into such risk? I brushed his smooth
cheek. "Be alert, dear one. Stay safe, and we'll see our
road more clearly."

Half an hour later, Radele returned from his survey
of the gardens. Having reassured me that no one lurked
anywhere on the grounds, Radele tethered our horses
behind the gatehouse and took up a position in a tree
where he could watch both the gates and the gatehouse.

The sun dropped behind the forested hills. Gerick
watched from the hollow doorway of the gatehouse as
Paulo waved and rode back through the gate the way
we'd come, and I walked up the carriage road through
the tunnel of trees. Shorter footpaths led from the gatehouse to the main house and gardens, but I was still
a bit early, and I wanted to approach the house from
the front.

At the point where the road emerged from the trees
and skirted a wide, open lawn gone to weeds, I got my
first look at the ruin of the main house. Every window
was broken. The south wing, all the guest bedrooms and
the great ballroom, lay in charred rubble. The north
wing, including the drawing room where Karon and I
had wed in the light of five hundred candles, looked as
if a ram had been used to cave in one wall.

Astonishing that Evard would pick his murdered rival's
house for us to meet. Did he think I would feel safe in a
place so familiar? More likely it was a pointed reminder
of his power. Whatever his motive, the ruined house only
served to remind me of everything I despised about
Evard, a shallow, arrogant, ambitious man who had destroyed Martin and his friends because he was not fit to
be one of them.

As the last glow of red dulled to gray in the west, I
circled the skeletal house and strolled into the back gardens. The plantings had gone wild, of course, only the
hardiest left to compete with thistles, brambles, and en-

croaching forest. I could find no remnant of the rose garden, and all the ponds and streams were dry. Surprisingly, the arched bridge remained intact, overlooking a choked oval of knee-high weeds where a reflecting pond should have been. Only a few birds and a lonely frog mourning the loss of his lily pads disturbed the quiet dusk.

A warm breeze riffled my hair as I waited. Not a long wait. My every sense was on the alert, so I heard the muffled hoofbeats long before the solitary rider reached the edge of the gardens. A horse nickered softly. Light steps crunched on the gravel, only to hesitate next to a wild mass of honeysuckle that had overgrown the path. Through the tangled shrubbery glimmered the faint beams of a lantern.

"Straight through. Angle right. The gardeners have been sorely lax. You'll have to mention it to the lord." My voice sounded harsh against the subtleties of the evening. Despite my resolution to be open-minded, I couldn't hide my bitterness at the desolation this man had wrought.

The newcomer pushed through the branches until I could make out a shadowy figure at the far end of the arched bridge. Odd . . . Evard was never as tall as my brother, only average in height, much to his youthful disgust, but this person was not even as tall as me.

"Who's there?" I said, retreating a few steps. "Speak or I'll be away from here before you can blink."

I listened until I thought my ears must crack and whipped my eyes from side to side, searching the gloomy plantings for any sign of stalkers, but I sensed no one else about. The figure moved closer, and I backed away.

"Wait. Don't go!"

A woman! Her voice was low and mellow, yet bore such authority that my feet stopped moving of their own accord. My eyes stopped their suspicious search and riveted themselves to the slight form that followed the lantern beams up the arching span.

"The conditions of this meeting are not changed," she said. "You've agreed to it, and I've endangered myself and others to come here. You cannot leave."

She wore a lightweight cloak of the deepest sapphire, its full hood draped gracefully about her face, keeping it in deep shadow.

I walked to the foot of the bridge. "But the person I agreed to meet—"

"Is unavailable tonight. I speak for him."

"I cannot believe he would permit anyone to speak for him, especially . . ."

"Especially a woman?" She set her lantern on the stone parapet. "Perhaps you don't know him as well as you think you do, even after such long acquaintance. And, of course, you don't know me at all." With slender, pale hands, adorned with a single, slim band of sapphires that gleamed in the lamplight, she lowered her hood. On her brow she wore a gold circlet, graven with a dragon and a lily—the crest of the Queen of Leire.

CHAPTER 7

Mariel Annalis Karestan Lavial, Princess of Valleor, had been a child of eight when her father's kingdom fell. She had witnessed the beheading of her father and brothers, and the rape and execution of her mother, who had vowed to lie with the first Vallorean man she could find and so produce a new heir to rival the Leiran conqueror. Princess Mariel alone was allowed to survive untouched, secured in the virginal captivity of a remote temple school in case the Leirans ever found a use for her. She was the living symbol of Valleor's subjugation. I, as so many other Leirans, had never thought of her as having any other identity, even when she was brought from her childhood seclusion to wed the Leiran king.

"I've wanted to meet you for a long while"—the queen raked cool green eyes over me as I sank into a genuflection I would not have offered her husband—"the Lady Seriana who threw away a kingdom for a sorcerer. The woman to whom I was forever being compared and beside whom I was always found wanting . . . by my husband, as well as everyone else at court."

"Your Majesty, I—"

"I decided early on not to hate you. After all, you'd given me a life. If you'd married him, I would have been dead by seventeen. And even if you'd never existed, he would not have cared for me in the beginning. A Vallorean princess was no more to him than a looted castle or captured horse. But he doesn't speak of you in that way any more."

The queen's light hair was piled on her head in smooth coils, and her features were ivory in the lamplight, an impassive courtier's mask that revealed little of the person beneath. Though her face was too long and angular to be called beautiful, and her stature unimposing, she carried herself with assurance. Her age would be somewhere near five and thirty.

"Why am I here, Your Majesty? How did the king know I was alive?"

She moved a few steps closer. "As you surely know, our people have suffered some . . . disturbances . . . of late that have left them in great fear. No science or philosophy offers any explanation. And so my husband's thoughts turn to other unbelievable tales he has heard. To sorcery. To you. Who else in this land knows anything of magical beings or would be bold enough to speak of such to her king?" Her manner was businesslike, her voice clear and intelligent. "And, despite his many faults, Evard is not a fool. He said he would not believe *you* were dead unless he saw your corpse."

But I refused to allow her easy manner to dilute my caution. "To speak of sorcery is forbidden, my lady. By His Majesty's decree, I have been pardoned of my earlier offenses, but I would not bring the hand of the law around my neck again."

"I'm not here to entrap you, Seriana. I know everything you told my husband: about this other world and the magical passage between us, about the sorcerer prince and his enemies and their war that somehow affects our own lands. If I wished to arrest you for speaking of such things, I'd not need to come to this wilderness and set about playacting. When I tell you the whole of these matters, you'll understand why the king seeks your advice."

"Well, then . . ." She hadn't left me much to say. "You, of course, may speak of whatever you please."

She sat gracefully on the parapet next to her lantern, the light-beams dancing on the crystal beadwork of the riding gown visible beneath her blue cloak. "We heard the first reports more than two years ago," she said, "whisperings among those bold enough to touch on forbidden subjects in the presence of the king: a commander with reports of a maimed soldier who disappeared in the middle of one night . . . a duke's vanished mistress whose legs were crippled by a disease in her bones . . . a military governor investigating accusations of witchcraft. My husband thought little of these incidents until a man named Maceron demanded an audience, claiming he had evidence of an invasion from the world of the sorcerers."

"Maceron!" I almost left the garden right then. The murderer Maceron, the despicable hunter of sorcerers who had exposed Karon's secret to my brother and the king, who had served the purposes of the Zhid when they tried to use the Prince of Avonar to destroy the Bridge, the mundane henchman of the Lord Ziddari. "Madam, Maceron is a vicious, lying scoundrel."

"Yes, you have every reason to despise the man. But you must hear me out." She motioned me to sit beside her. "Maceron brought us a list of more than three hundred disappearances from all corners of the kingdom. Tales of disturbing dreams, fantastical visions of roads or doorways or impossible landscapes, almost every one of them including mention of three odd strangers with mysterious powers. Magical powers. These sorcerers were said to be most bizarre in their aspect: one of them huge with a beast-like hide, one black and emaciated like a creature of charred bones, one a dwarfish man with only one eye, crude in his speech and action. They were blamed for thievery, for tormenting of beasts, and for every manner of mischief and ruination. Strangely enough, almost every person who had disappeared was also deformed in some way, lame or blind or otherwise afflicted."

The queen's hands rested quietly in her lap, pale against the dark blue folds of her cloak as she posed her query. "One would never have believed such a history. Yet identical descriptions of the three villains originated from every region, from people who had never left their villages and from people who had traveled widely and were little amazed at any oddity. And the ruffians had been seen in places hundreds of leagues apart on exactly the same day! Though we hold no admiration for this

Maceron—indeed he is a repulsive villain—his evidence
is compelling. So, tell me, Seriana, are these beings from
the other world? If not, then who are they?"

I shook my head slowly, my thoughts in a jumble.
"This cannot be an invasion from Gondai, Your Majesty.
As I told the king, though the skills and talents of Dar'-
Nethi differ from ours, their appearance does not. They
are not monsters, but human creatures fair or plain as
the case may be. Even the Zhid are but Dar'Nethi who
have been wickedly enchanted. The works of the Lords
of Zhev'Na in our world are far more subtle and terrible
than these nursery frights."

I believed what I said, but her description of the three
odd thieves had shaken me with echoes of another story.
*A bent man, no taller than your waist . . . a one-eyed
jongler . . .* And the storyteller's son had been born with
only one hand. So, had the storyteller heard the tales of
monsters and adopted it to explain his son's disappearance or was there something of truth in the old man's
account? In the past, some of Karon's ancestors, exiled
in this world, had used illusions of monsters to impose
their will upon the people of the Four Realms. Anxiety
needled my spine like a kitten's claws.

The queen held her tongue, and her gaze did not
waver.

No, no, no. Except for the very few like Kellea and
Gerick, the Exiles—those Dar'Nethi who, like Karon's
family, had lived in this world for centuries—were all
dead, hunted to extermination, burned and forgotten by
men like Maceron and Evard. My blood surged hot.

"These events you describe are beyond the capacities
of either Dar'Nethi or Zhid, Your Majesty. Only the
Prince of Avonar can cross between the two worlds at
will, and he is certainly not abducting lame or deformed
Leirans. I'm sorry, I'm unable to explain your mystery."

The queen touched my hand. Her pale fingers were
freezing. "Then you must investigate the case for us. My
husband trusts no one but you in these matters. The
kingdom is in the most terrible danger."

I snatched my hand away. "Excuse my boldness,
madam, but I've heard nothing to justify such a claim.

These incidents are tragedies, yes. Crimes, yes, and mysteries, certainly. But since when has the disappearance of *healthy* citizens concerned King Evard, much less these pitiful creatures you name? If crimes are being committed, then look, not to sorcerers, but to Maceron and his kind, these vermin that your husband has nurtured."

"The danger is unquestionable!" The queen jumped to her feet and crossed the bridge to stand gripping the broken remnant of a sculpted naiad that had once marked the apex of the span. "The very circumstance that has brought me here tonight in my husband's stead is but another confirmation of it."

She folded her arms tightly across her breast and faced me again, her back to the broken statue. "Last evening, I left the King of Leire in his bedchamber with two valets, preparing for a feast to celebrate our daughter's birthday. When he failed to meet me as we had planned, I went back to fetch him. Though the guards swore that the king had not left his room as yet, my knock went unanswered. I returned to the feast and made excuses to our guests. But then my daughter left the feast abruptly . . . and soon sent word for me to join her in the king's apartments.

"Evard sat on his bed, his garments immaculate, no evidence of injury. But he was not, and is not, himself." She stared at me unblinking, her huge eyes demanding I believe her, insisting I answer her charge. "My husband is mute, Seriana. He is deaf, perhaps blind. I cannot tell. He says nothing, responds to nothing. Our physician, the finest in the realm, cannot tell me what ails him. I had the valets and guards questioned—seriously questioned— and I am convinced that the king was himself when the valets left him and that no one entered his apartments. Every door and window was locked from the inside. What can this be but sorcery?"

"My lady—"

"No one knows of his condition save his physician, one servant, two of our most trusted counselors . . . and my daughter, of course. With their help, I've deceived even the Council of Lords. Everyone believes my husband merely incommoded with business. But you can understand how difficult it will be to keep up this masquerade for long. And you can imagine the results if the truth becomes known."

Evard and his queen had produced only a single daughter to inherit the Leiran throne. Though Leiran nobles would never tolerate being ruled by a woman, the promise of a royal betrothal would have given Evard a stranglehold on every nobleman who was unmarried or had an unmarried son, nephew, or cousin. But with the girl yet unpledged, and Evard incapacitated . . .

She pressed harder. "I know of your past and the part my husband played in it. I do not excuse his actions. But I also know Evard would trust you with our lives and those of our subjects. You must leave behind your personal judgments, Lady Seriana, and come to the aid of your king."

I shivered, but not from any evening chill. If things had changed, if the Lords had truly found a way to send monstrous henchmen across the Bridge to destroy a king in his own bedchamber, I couldn't even imagine the danger. Panic. Riots. Murder. Civil war. The chaos caused by the destruction of the most powerful man in this world could be the very fodder to strengthen the Three of Zhev'Na beyond any possibility of defeat. And Karon was on the verge of his attempt on Zhev'Na.

"Tell them," I blurted out. "Tell the people that King Evard has set out on a mission to take care of these disappearances, that he's attacking those who are disturbing their sleep . . . as near the truth as you can make it. You'll have to spirit him away, of course. As long as he's in Montevial you'll never be able to hide his condition long enough for us to learn what's happened. So use the time to his benefit. Tell his people that he's working to save them, and then do something in his name: proclaim a general amnesty, repeal the poaching laws, shorten indentures, revert a portion of their taxes to the landowners, anything to divert attention."

I couldn't believe what I was doing—advising Evard's wife on how to protect his throne. But I would not see what civilization we had dissolve into anarchy. Chaos was exactly what our enemies wanted.

"And what will you do?"

Despite her protestations, to confess to the Queen of Leire that I was guilty of acts for which she could have me executed still caused a twinge in my gut. But evasion would profit nothing. "Prince D'Natheil must be told of these matters. He can investigate, decide what's best to do. And if anyone can heal the king's affliction, it is he."

"He's the sorcerer you told of, the ruler of this other place who has the power to travel between?"

"Yes."

She turned sharply, her blue cloak swirling in the lamplight. "Perhaps he's the one who causes all this! Perhaps he's not as benevolent as you think."

"Your Majesty, you have honored me with your trust"—indeed her secrets were worth her life and her daughter's, as well as Evard's—"and I ask you to extend it a little further. Prince D'Natheil is the most worthy of allies, bearing a deep love for this world and those who dwell here. For a thousand years, his family and his people have borne the burden of our survival as well as their own. Their Bridge is designed to balance the worlds, to restore them, to heal the evils their kind have caused."

"How do you know? Perhaps he deceives you with his magics."

I sighed and prayed I was not acting the fool. "Because he is my husband, lady, and he would do nothing to bring my people harm."

"Ah." She relaxed her shoulders as if I'd finally told her something that was clear. "Tell me more of these people and their war. Clearly there are things you didn't mention to the king."

"Indeed it's a very long story, Your Majesty. Too long for tonight. I need to go." I was anxious to talk to Radele. Surely he had some way to contact someone in Avonar. Karon had to know what was happening.

"Before you go, you need to know of one more complication." The pain on her face and the slight tremor in her voice signaled the first breach in her composure.

"My daughter reported seeing a cloaked man in my husband's chambers when she first entered. We found no one there; it was impossible, as I've told you. I gave her report little credence. Over the past years my daughter has reported a threatening man in her apartments a number of times, but we've considered her stories merely a girl's prattling. Last night I scolded her for continuing such foolery when her father was so ill. After we carried the king to a private chamber, my daughter locked herself into Evard's rooms, vowing to prove me wrong. Today . . . she is nowhere to be found. What if these monsters have attacked us yet again?"

"Ah, my lady, surely she is just angry with you. Playing a cruel prank."

"I pray that's so. But you must understand how precious is that which I entrust to you and your prince. Roxanne is so young . . ."

"I'll do whatever I can, Your Majesty. I promise."

She lifted her chin, no further slip betraying her emotions. "Have you need of funds? Men? Weapons?"

"Not yet. I can't say what might be needed in the future." Her honesty compelled me to add more. "My lady, I'll not insult you by pretending feeling for Evard. The simplest reason declares that to be impossible. But I honor the crown he wears, and I would see it safe until a better man wears it. And I do not avenge myself on children."

"Your frankness serves you well, Seriana." She gave me her cold, pale hand, drew me close, and kissed me on each cheek. As we parted, she dropped a small brooch into my hand, an opal encased in gold filigree, fashioned in the design of an owl—the symbol of Valleor. "If you should have need of me, this will gain you or your messenger instant admittance to my presence. Good night." She picked up her lamp, and hurried down the bridge and the path. The light-beams danced among the shadows.

"Good night, Your Majesty."

CHAPTER 8

The bridge parapet was still warm from the queen's lantern. I sat sideways on the wall, knees drawn up under my gown, eyes growing accustomed to the thick darkness. Though anxious to get back to Gerick and away from this haunted place, I needed to make sure no one lurked nearby, waiting to follow me back to him. Martin had always said that love and honor among royalty was very like their bread, described by the same words, but usually of a very different flavor from that found among the common run of people. Besides, I had a great deal to consider. Somehow I had to convince my husband to aid the man who had burned him to death. Even Karon's generous spirit might not stretch that far.

All seemed secure. No incongruous shape appeared among the shadows of flora gone wild. No untoward sound intruded on the rustlings of the wind and the occasional hoot of an owl. After perhaps a quarter of an hour, I swung my feet to the ground. As I left the bridge and started up the long path to the road and the gatehouse, I heard footsteps on the gravel path. Enchantment stung my skin like a shower of ice crystals.

"Where is he, Seri?" said a low voice behind my shoulder.

I spun on my heel, thrilled and delighted, certain that the vehemence of my wishing in the last hours had drawn him across D'Arnath's Bridge to help me solve Leire's great mystery. But news and greetings died upon my lips when I saw his face and felt the grip on my arm. "Karon, what is it?"

"Where is the boy?" he said. His fingers came near

cracking my bones. "Tell me where the deceiver lurks, in what web he hangs waiting to dispense more of his poison. Oh, it was a fine performance. No thespian in any world could fault him. Now the actor is unmasked . . . but at such cost . . ."

"Earth and sky, Karon, what's happened? Is it Gerick?"

"He is *not* Gerick!" His lips curled in disgust. "Give him the name of his own choosing: Dieste the Fourth Lord, the Destroyer. No name has ever been more apt." The night darkened with his anger. His hand quivered, and his eyes sparked gold and blue like a blacksmith's forge. "Tell me where he is."

I wrenched my arm from his grasp and stepped backward, moving into the path between him and the gatehouse. "What makes you say such things?"

"The boy is not what you think, Seri. Not what I thought. My healing . . . your nurturing . . . our worry and hope and love . . . all wasted. He remains as he was in Zhev'Na. But tonight he stands within range of my sword, and I must and will destroy him before he can compound his evil."

"Karon, tell me what you're talking about." Panic left my voice ragged, my veins hollow. "Gerick has scarcely been out of my sight for four years. There is no deceit in him. What do you think he's done?"

"Murder, Seri. Torture and betrayal done at his word as surely as if the bloody implements were yet in his hand. Only six knew of Jayereth's work. Now she lies dead, her promise, her brilliance, drowned in agony so terrible I cannot think on it. Only six knew of Marcus, Nemyra, and T'Sero and their mission in Zhev'Na, but two days after Jayereth was destroyed, their corpses were returned to Avonar . . . defiled." His voice shook. "And the Circle, Avonar's noblest, most skilled men and women, each one leaving home, husband, wife, children to stand vigil on the borders of the Wastes, awaiting my command, every one of them attacked that same day. No more than fifteen out of two hundred survived. All our preparation . . . four long years and we were ready to begin, and now it's all gone, and we've no time to

start again. Need I tell more? Will you ask me how I
can be sure? Must I show you his bloody works as they
will ever remain burned into my soul?"

All Karon's plans for healing the ravages done to his
world and mine, all his hopes of rescuing the Dar'Nethi
slaves from bondage, everything had been bound up in
Jayereth and the Circle and the three who had once
been Zhid. But why did he blame Gerick?

"There must be some other explanation. A spy. One
of your Counselors suborned . . . Think! Gerick left
Zhev'Na freely, saved our lives. Sword of Annadis defend us, Karon, you've linked with his mind repeatedly.
How could he have deceived you?"

Karon gripped an outstretched alder bough as if it
were the handle to his fury. "I didn't want to believe it
either," he said, his rage cold and controlled now. "Of
course I didn't. I would sooner have believed that I myself had done it, than it be my son. But on the night I
last came to Verdillon, I spoke to the boy alone. He was
the fifth I spoke to that day. Each one of the five I told
a secret, unknown to anyone but myself, each secret a
prize the Lords could not refuse. All false, of course,
but of such a nature that I would know if any betrayal
was done."

I remembered Gerick listening intently in Verdillon's
garden. Arms folded. Expression unreadable . . . as it
was so often. *No, I won't believe it.*

"Four traps remain unsprung, their mythical prizes un-
claimed. The fifth was ingenious, I think." His hollow
laugh was worse than his rage. "I told him that Jayereth
had left transcripts of her work hidden in an abandoned
bathhouse in Lyrrathe Vale. I said that the secret of
nullifying mordemar had not died with her, but would
remain hidden there until I named her successor, telling
him that he needed to know these things in case anything happened to me. Then, I set a watch on the bathhouse. I willed the cache to remain untouched, Seri. I
prayed to be left with unfathomable mystery, rather than
unimaginable betrayal, and on each day that passed, I
gave thanks. But yesterday I named the Alchemist
Mem'Tara to the Preceptorate, saying she would take

up Jayereth's work. And last night, the fifth trap was sprung."

"But Gerick was here in Montevial with me. It's impossible."

"The Lords never dirty their own hands. They use others: Some are tools who do evils of their own will, some like the Zhid have been transformed, and some"— he almost spat as he said it—"they inhabit. They can abandon their own bodies, insinuate themselves into a man and displace his soul, leaving it a cowering, silent witness to the evils they do. They take on his life as their own, reaping the harvest of his senses so as to savor his fears and pleasures, controlling his movements and deeds for their own purposes. You would think the boy merely asleep. But when our son possessed another's body and came to the Ravien Bathhouse, ready to destroy Jayereth's work before it could be used, I was waiting and I recognized him."

I was fascinated and horrified together. This story could have no relation to the boy I helped with school lessons and comforted when he had nightmares—serious, reserved, unsure of his place in a world he was only beginning to understand. Uneven in temper, yes, but so had I been at sixteen. Yet last night he had slept for the first time in days . . . weeks . . . Karon's cold anger battered me like a storm tide, drowning my feeble protests, choking me with his horror and conviction.

"I wanted to kill him then," he said, his jaw rigid. "So we are taught in Avonar: Kill the possessed body and you will kill the possessing soul before it can return to its own body. The host is left dead when the Lords are finished with him anyway. But Lord Dieste had chosen his host well, and I hesitated. It was Gar'Dena, you see, that came to the Ravien Bathhouse. No living soul but Gerick knew the hiding place. But Gar'Dena came and spoke the word that was supposed to open Jayereth's cache, the very word I had told Gerick and no other. Before I could convince myself to slay Gar'Dena's body, the Destroyer abandoned him and left him dead. Our dear friend, the good and generous man who helped save our lives, plunged a dagger into his own heart."

"Gar'Dena . . . no . . ."

Karon's voice was on the verge of breaking, but, instead, he roared and snapped the branch from the alder tree. Launching it into the trees where it crashed to the ground, shredding leaves and twigs on its way, he turned and confronted me again, scarcely containing himself. "This time the Destroyer will not escape me. No matter whose shape he wears, I will close my eyes and see Jayereth's torment and mad Gar'Dena shedding his own blood, and my sword will find its mark. Do you understand, Seri? He was able to stretch his arm across the Breach. Powers of night, I've told him the defenses of Avonar."

I could not accept it. Gerick had rejected his perverse nurturing in Zhev'Na. He had given up immortality because he would not harm us. "Talk to him, Karon. This is impossible. A mistake. Perhaps it was really Gar'Dena after all . . . turned Zhid . . . a vicious trick of the Lords. What of the sixth? You said there were six who knew the secrets. Perhaps that one—"

"The sixth was you."

My heart sank like lead in a pool.

Karon gripped my shoulders and glared at me until my head came near cracking. "I say again, Seri, where is he?"

Of course, Karon would recognize Gerick no matter what form he wore. He had shared Gerick's mind for hours working at his healing. And he was right. There would be no containing one of the Lords outside of death itself. Yet my heart ripped and bled and wept at the vision of Gerick curled up in boyish sleep in this beloved place . . . and Karon plunging his sword . . .

As if that very sword had cloven my skull, for one moment a suffocating fury engulfed my mind. My mouth opened to scream with anger that was not my own. And then it was gone, leaving me drained and empty and helpless.

"So he lies in the gatehouse! Oh, powers of night, we

are at Windham . . ." Karon had stolen my thoughts. His shoulders sagged, as if the fury had left him. He shook his head, closed his eyes, and spoke softly. "Ah, Seri. I am so sorry."

But then he shoved me aside and ran up the path, sword drawn and death in his stride. Our son's death.

"Karon, wait!" This could not be happening, not after so much pain and so much hope.

A sliver of yellow moon hung low in the east. I ran for the gatehouse, leaving the broken path and cutting straight across the vast wilderness of Windham's gardens, stumbling over weeds and rocks in my hurry to reach Gerick before his father could. But I was too tired and too slow, my thoughts shredded like hay under the scythe. In the distance I heard a bellow of rage.

"Karon, no!" I screamed, running onward, ducking tree branches that seemed to get thicker and lower the farther I ran. "Gerick, run!"

A musty cellar gaped before me, its floor a mat of rotted leaves, bare roots crumbling its walls, its wooden doors rotted away. I teetered on the edge, then backed away and forced my way through a bramble thicket that tore at my clothes and my arms.

Odd, tittering laughter burst out somewhere to my right. "Who's there?"

How could anyone laugh? The incongruity brought me to a halt. Was this a dream, my own nightmare, peopled by shades of princes and queens and houses and gardens, stories that made no sense, Gerick a murderous deceiver, Karon, my gentle Healer, in this bloodthirsty rage? A dream, that had to be it.

I pushed through a wall of sprangling lilac bushes. In the center of a circle of alders stood four men. I called them men. No other name that might serve came to mind. One of the four was incredibly thin, his naked, sinewy body colored the pure black of ebony. His hair was silver, his huge eyes burning amber like fireflies in the summer garden. He was half again as tall as the tallest man I had ever seen. The second man was as broad as three blacksmiths together. His skin brown and leathery, his hair red tufts springing from an oddly rounded skull, and he was badly stooped, his hands almost dragging the weedy ground. The third was a bearded man no taller than my waist, perfectly formed except for the skin grown over one eye socket. The three of them were exactly as the queen had described them to me, exactly as the terrified citizens of the Four Realms had described them to Maceron. They were laughing, as I could see by the greenish light of a lamp carried by the leathery man. The fourth person stood with his back to me.

"Who are you?" I said. "What are you doing here? Sword of Annadis! Tell me this is a dream."

The odd trio greeted me with more hilarity. In a burst of green light the three men vanished, leaving only their laughter and their fourth companion behind. He whirled about, squinting as he peered into the darkness. Gerick.

I wanted to touch him, to reassure myself that he was my son whose pain I could ease. I wanted to tell him I still had faith in him and that I knew these accusations were all a mistake. But he stayed back, his wary eyes fixed on my hands, and I realized that in my fear and confusion I had snatched my knife from its sheath.

I dropped the weapon to the ground as if it were newly drawn from the forge. "Gerick! Your father— Gerick, tell me who you are."

"Mother? Are you all right?" He stepped closer. I couldn't see him clearly; the shadows were so very deep, the bushes tangled.

But I already knew I was not in a dream, and I was very much not all right. The pain in my breast was too harsh. A warm flood drenched my tunic, and the circle of trees began to spin. A knife covered in blood . . . Gerick lowering me gently to the ground, his narrow face rising quickly above me, worried, confused . . . his lips moving, but I couldn't hear him for the rushing in my ears. . . .

Then Gerick was gone, and Radele's calm face hovered over me, washed out and vague like the sun's disk seen through a fog. Others joined him, too shadowy to see. "Oh, my good lord, he's killed her!"

I wanted to say I wasn't dead, but the words lodged

somewhere in my chest before leaking away with all the blood. I wanted to say Gerick hadn't done it, but I didn't know who had. If I could only remember what Gerick had said to me . . .

Somewhere in the distance came a howl of grief, but it was much too far away to concern me, and I was much too tired to care what sorrow could be so terrible. So I gave it up and embraced the cold darkness.

CHAPTER 9

Gerick

I knew my mother's hair should be long, plaited into a shining, loose braid that fell halfway down her back. I knew it in the same way I knew that my father—my real father, the man named Karon—was slender and dark-haired, and had a left wrist that ached whenever the weather was cold. I shouldn't have known those things. I'd never seen a portrait of my true father nor heard anyone describe how my mother wore her hair before my father was burned to death.

So how could it be that I would hear my mother laughing to herself while riding in a pony cart, and look over to see her, not in her chosen disguise of widow's cap and purple velvet dress, but with hair braided halfway down her back, wearing a dress of emerald green and a gold locket that I knew had bits of dried rose petals inside it? Or when Prince D'Natheil walked with me in the garden at Verdillon, clasping his hands behind his back and remarking how strange it was to be at Professor Ferrante's house again, why did I sometimes see a smaller, dark-haired man with high cheekbones who never clasped his hands behind his back, but rather held his left wrist in his right because of the way it had broken and healed crooked? Professor Ferrante's journal had only confirmed what I already knew about my true father, though I could not say how I knew it.

This was not my imagination. No portrait and no person's telling could have shown me all I saw and felt and

knew in my . . . visions. I didn't know what else to
call them.

Such experiences were not a normal part of being a
sorcerer. I knew that much. I might have believed the
Dar'Nethi, Radele, was playing mind games with me,
except the visions had started months before he'd come
to Verdillon. And too, I didn't think a Dar'Nethi could
put things into my head without me knowing it, except
perhaps the Prince—my father—who was exceptionally
powerful.

Whatever the cause, I believed the visions were all
bound up with the other things going on with me, my
dreams and nightmares and all the rest of it. Most days
I felt that if I didn't keep myself buttoned up tight I was
going to burst like a rotted cow, strewing every thought,
every memory, every wicked, evil thing I'd ever done all
over the place, exposed for everyone—my mother, my
father, my friends—to see. I told myself I didn't care
what people thought of me, but, of course, I did, and I
believed that if I ever lost control of myself, the Lords
would find me.

That's why I didn't want anyone in my head any more,
why I couldn't let the Prince "help" me get over my
nightmares. I had been one of the Lords, living for a few
hours as the fourth physical expression of their single
malevolent mind, my true identity lost, my soul a pit of
corruption. I had been able to feel nothing in those
hours, no love, no pain, no horror or disgust or joy. I
could have stuck my hands in fire and not breathed a
word. I could have crushed an infant under my foot and
considered the deed no more than smoke in the wind.
All the love and honor in two worlds would have been
nothing more to me than dust on my shoe. Power was
everything. I was filled with such craving for it that even
after four years, to think of it set me trembling.

Only a single thread had bound me to the person I
had been—my mother's voice, telling me the truth of my
lost life and those people who had been a part of it. I
had held on to her lifeline, and eventually I began to
understand how strong it was and how fiercely the Lords
fought to snap it by making me kill her. Paulo had con-

vinced me to believe in my mother, and I had let her pull me out.

In the days and weeks that followed my escape from Zhev'Na, my father had linked with my mind and my body, and with power I never imagined a Dar'Nethi could possess, worked to undo the things the Lords had done to me. But he couldn't touch what remained of my life as a Lord of Zhev'Na. I'd locked those hours away behind a door that even he could not open. If he were ever to see behind it, he would understand what I had been, and if he was the man my mother believed him to be, he'd try to heal that part of me, too. I couldn't allow that. The festering ran too deep. I would surely die or lose my mind, and most probably he would, too. Dieste the Destroyer was a part of me, and I didn't believe he could be excised any more than the remnants of the Prince D'Natheil could be separated from the soul that had been my father's. I had to learn to live with Dieste, to keep that door closed and barred.

There were times when staying in control was easier: when I was studying or working hard or riding with Paulo. There were times when it was more difficult: when I was angry or tired. And there were times when it was almost impossible: when I would touch a sword, or when I tried to work the least bit of sorcery. That's why I'd had to leave Paulo and Radele to protect my mother from the bandits on our journey. The last place I could afford to be was in the middle of a battle with a sword in my hand, pain and blood everywhere. When I saw people suffering, I remembered the taste of pain and bitterness and despair, and how when I filled the dark places of my soul with those things, I could call down lightning or explore the stars or the depths of the ocean. That's when I would hear the cunning whispers of the Lords as they searched for me, and I had to work hard to barricade the door. They were very close.

I couldn't decipher my dreams any more than I could understand my waking visions. The dreams had started just after I left Zhev'Na. When my father had done all the healing he could do—all I could let him do—and I started living again, sleeping and eating and feeling things like a human person, I started dreaming about a barren country with a purple-and-black sky and stars that were green. It wasn't fearful, just a place. But I dreamed of that same place every night, and that made me curious.

Gradually, over the next year, the dream landscape began to change, so that one night I might see a barren moor, and the next there'd be a track across it, and maybe a scrubby tree or a boulder. Then, on another night, a mound of stones would sit beside the track, or the track would be more like a road or wind up a craggy mountainside. After two years or so, I started seeing the dwarf with one eye and his two companions, just sitting on a boulder, maybe, or a wall, or engaged in some commonplace activity like sharpening a knife or carving wood or mending a shoe.

Of course those weren't the dreams that had me waking up the household like some bawling infant frightened of bears or snakes. The nightmares had to do with the Lords: waking up blind and knowing I could only see by putting on the gold mask with the diamond eyes the Lords had given me, or feeling myself trapped alive inside the giant stone statue the Lords had made of me, or discovering my mother injured and bending over to taste her blood, feeling the hunger for power devour me.

Though my entire life had been shaped by D'Arnath's Bridge, I had never seen it. Back when I was a child and Ziddari had carried me across, I had been in a stupor from his enchantments. But after the Prince shared his secrets with me that night at Verdillon, and said for the thousandth time how much he hoped I would come to Avonar before too long, my curiosity got the best of me. No matter what the Prince had in mind, I did not intend ever to live in Avonar. The thought of sitting in D'Arnath's palace and ruling the Dar'Nethi turned my stomach. Therefore, I thought I'd take the opportunity to get a look just that once.

A terrible mistake. The journey had been interesting, just as I told my mother, but I had never felt so out of place and so exposed, as if from the moment we set foot on the Bridge my flesh was torn open and my bare bones showing. And from the night I'd come back, my dreams of the dwarf and his world had become nightmares, too.

The terror would always begin with the dream world falling to pieces like a puzzle knocked off a table. The dwarf might be on one fragment, waving his hands at me in a panic, and the road might be broken up across a few others, and a mountain on another, and in between all the pieces blazed searing white fire. The fire burned up the fragments of the dreamscape like dry leaves, and, all the while, I felt like I was being burned up right along with them. When I woke, I felt hollow and dry, as if the white fire had scorched out everything inside me.

If the dreams had burned out the dark places behind the door, it might have been all right. But, instead, they left me wanting to open that door and escape into the cold and the dark. I don't know whether it was the white fire or the cold dark that made me scream the most. Walking D'Arnath's cursed Bridge had twisted my mind worse than it was already, and I didn't know what I was going to do about it.

Then we traveled to Prydina, and a half-drunk sheepherder described the dwarf and the dream world. I'd told Paulo about them, and how I thought they were real, but I never expected anyone else to know about them. I almost took off right then to go see the place where the sheepherder's son had disappeared, thinking that if I saw it, maybe I could rid myself of the dreams or at least learn what they meant. But I couldn't leave my mother until I knew she'd be safe.

My mother had no idea how fiercely the Lords hated her. The only reason she'd lived for one moment after they discovered her in Zhev'Na was their conviction that I would kill her and thus make my corruption complete. What worried—frightened—them most about my mother was that they didn't understand her at all, how someone with no touch of magical power could oppose them so successfully. They hated her after the affair of the Gate, when they chased her and the Prince to the Bridge. Instead of laughing as D'Arnath's last Heir doomed his world, they saw the Bridge strengthened, the Gates opened, and their nasty plan come to nothing.

But that disappointment was minute compared to what they felt when I followed her into the Prince's portal and left Zhev'Na. They were a finger's breadth from everything they had ever wanted, complete victory, utter control over the worlds. If I had become both the Heir of D'Arnath and a Lord of Zhev'Na, the Lords and I could have destroyed D'Arnath's Bridge with one thought, breaking the balance the Dar'Nethi believed it preserved between Gondai and the mundane world. Then we would have set our enchanted brass ring—the big one called the Great Oculus—to spinning, and used it to feed forever on the chaos we made. No one in any world would have been able to stand against us.

But my mother had stopped it, and the Lords wouldn't rest until she was dead. So I couldn't leave her, because I didn't think anyone else could recognize the Lords when they came for her. After crossing the Bridge with my father, I believed it even more strongly. They *would* come.

I worried about the summons from the Leiran King, of course. It could be the first feint to draw her out, but it seemed too obvious for the Lords. They liked the subtler ploys, for there was amusement as well as outcome involved in their games. No matter how much a hunter desires to bag a Cyvernian tiger, taking it while it sleeps away the winter in its cave has little pleasure. It is only in the tracking across the wilds of Cyvernia, and seeing in the trapped beast's eyes the knowledge of its defeat—only in that completeness of victory does the hunter truly savor his triumph and know that everyone else acknowledges his mastery.

And so I raised no protest when she proposed the trip to Montevial, but I planned to stay close throughout her audience with King Evard. The Dar'Nethi watchdog was with us, too, and I was willing to concede that he might be useful if danger was about, but his eyes were focused on me, not my mother or anyone who might be a threat to her. The Prince had set him to watch me—not watch out for me. That was a subtle distinction—subtle—and so it worried me very much more than the summons from the king. And my mother didn't see it at all.

*   *   *

"I'll be damned if I'll stay here with the watchdog. Someone's got to be with her."

"You oughtn't. She said for you to stay out of sight. I would stay with her—you know I would—if she hadn't told me to watch outside the walls. And it makes sense for me to see what the king's men are up to." Paulo handed me his gray saddle pack, which held supplies for our return to Valleor.

"And what will you do if they made a move to take us? Yell?" That wasn't fair to Paulo. But I was so tired of Radele looking at me as if I were going to shapeshift into a monster, instead of watching for real danger. And except for the previous night when I had collapsed like a dirt wall, I hadn't slept more than an hour or two a night in weeks. The night's sleep had just made me more tired than ever. My head felt like porridge. Something wasn't right in this cursed place, but I just couldn't see what it was.

Paulo and I were standing in the doorway of the gatehouse at Windham. Paulo glanced over his shoulder to where my mother and Radele were talking. He lowered his voice. "If you would only *listen*, you know—like you could if you wanted—I could yell in your *head* and the Dar'Nethi wouldn't even know.

"I can't do that." I threw the bag across the floor of the gatehouse, kicking up enough dust and leaves to look like a whirlwind had come through. "Reading your thoughts is sorcery every bit as much as changing you into an elephant. I've got no power worth talking about, and I don't want any, and, what puling little I have, I daren't use. Not ever."

"Look, why don't you lie down over there in the corner and try to sleep? We won't bother you until we're ready to leave." I looked up to see if Paulo had suddenly lost his mind, but he was waggling his eyebrows in the direction of the Dar'Nethi who was walking toward us leading his horse. "We'll figure out something."

"Figure out what?" Radele unwrapped my horse's reins and those of my mother's horse from the dead tree beside the stoop.

"How to get Master Gerick to stay asleep longer than an hour," said Paulo. "I offered him brandy, but he don't like the taste. Says he'll sleep fine if we'll just leave him alone. Say"—he stepped from the stoop and walked across the carriage park, drawing Radele with him—"I found a place back behind here to leave the horses. Good grass, some water, out of sight. Can't see the gatehouse from the ground, but if you was to climb that elm, you could likely see the gates and the road and the gatehouse, too. I'll show you." Taking the other reins from Radele, he swung up onto Molly's back and started around behind the gatehouse. I never understood how he could get up so easily. As always, Radele looked at Paulo as if he were dirt, but he wasn't too proud to follow him out of sight. My mother waved and started up the road toward the main house.

Taking Paulo's hint, I quickly piled leaves in the darkest corner of the gatehouse, took off my cloak, and threw it over the pile. Then I slipped out of the doorway into the tangle of shrubs and brush and followed my mother into the gardens.

I almost came back and crawled under my cloak when I took my first look at the main house. Another vision. Two images, one on top of the other. One was the silent, dead shell that stood before me, and the other was a great house ablaze with light, the music of flutes and strings and laughter floating through the gardens. I would have sworn I was dancing, though I didn't even know how. My skin flashed cold and hot; my nose claimed that this weedy thicket smelled like roses and perfume and candle smoke. Anger, joy, excitement, and curiosity wholly unrelated to my own state of mind set up such a confusion in my head, I came near banging it on a tree to stop it. After a few moments, the vision dissipated, leaving me in a cold sweat.

From my hiding place in an overgrown arbor, I heard the queen describe the very creatures of my dream world, come to life in Leire: the dwarf again, and the beast-like man, and the one I thought of as the runner, the dark-skinned one, so very tall and thin, who sped up and down the black roads and the mountain paths in my dreams. These were not creatures of the Lords. I felt nothing of Notole's teaching in their magics, nothing of Parven's strategies in their mischief, nothing of Ziddari's wiles in their interaction with me. They were something else entirely. I just didn't know what.

After the queen rode off toward Montevial, my mother sat on the bridge parapet thinking. I did the same in my hiding place, trying to decide whether to tell her of my dreams about the one-eyed dwarf and his friends. My hesitation saved my life.

". . . He remains as he was in Zhev'Na. But tonight he stands within range of my sword, and I must and will destroy him before he can compound his evil."

So the Prince of Avonar wanted to kill me. Everything he'd claimed about trusting me and wanting to help me was a lie. He'd almost had me fooled. For the first time since Zhev'Na, I wished for a sword. Well, even without a weapon, I wouldn't go down easily. I knew some things. As the Dar'Nethi watchdog kept reminding me, I had learned from the masters.

But as my father raged, I saw he was convincing my mother, too, so I started listening more closely to his accusations. "The Lords never dirty their own hands . . . some they inhabit . . . insinuate themselves into a man and displace his soul . . . take on his life as their own . . ."

It was true he'd told me of the secrets hidden at the deserted bathhouse, and it was true what he said about the Lords taking on the bodies of others to do their will. I had done it when I was one of them, and pleasure was far too simple a word for it. But I'd not taken myself into any Dar'Nethi, nor had I used even one jot of magic since I'd left Zhev'Na. It was too risky and too painful, and I hadn't power enough, because the passive ways of Dar'Nethi power-gathering nauseated me.

What was happening?

Fighting the Prince would not provide an answer. I had to get away until I could sort out the truth. My mother couldn't save me from the Prince, and I couldn't save her from anyone if I was dead.

So, using everything I'd learned of stealth in my training in Zhev'Na, I slipped out of the arbor and away from the bridge and the grassy ravine, deeper into the trees. I had to move slowly, watching for sticks and branches and piles of leaves. The weak moonlight didn't penetrate the trees. The previous night's rain had left the dead leaves damp, which helped me move quietly, even though the dew coating the shrubs and vines left my shirtsleeves wet and flapping. I headed away from the gatehouse, thinking that with everything so overgrown I would surely be able to get up a tree, over the wall, and out into the forest. I could probably hide longer than they could look for me.

I skirted a weedy thicket and crept toward a grove of alders. As I neared the circle of trees, I stumbled over something thick and soft in the dark, and landed facedown in the damp undergrowth. Whatever had tripped me didn't smell too fine, so I assumed it was dead, until it hissed and pulled away. I resisted the temptation to leap up and run. Instead I slithered silently forward on my belly. A faint greenish light glimmered through the leaves. I scarcely dared breathe. Then, all at the same time, the branches in front of me parted, and a hand yanked at my hair, lifting my face up so the green light glared directly in my eyes.

"Who is it? Another spying one? A servant of the sword-carrier?" A gravelly voice spoke in my ear.

Hands grabbed each of my arms. I twisted my arms to loosen their grip and drew up my knees to kick their feet out from under them. But I couldn't get loose, and my captors dragged me out of the bushes and slammed me onto my knees, pinning my arms behind me.

Night's mother! Standing right in front of me, as if he had just stepped out of my dream, was the one-eyed dwarf. On one side of me, holding my arm in a grip worthy of a Zhid wrestler, was the wide brown man, and on the other was the wiry black runner, every bit as strong as his leathery friend.

"Who are you?" I whispered, amazement taking all the fight out of me for the moment.

"It is he!" said the dwarfish man quietly, putting his

finger to his lips and grinning through his beard. "Joyful! Oh, tell us that we have not damaged you, great Master!"

The two big ones didn't let go of me, but they eased up enough that I wasn't afraid they'd break my limbs any more.

"I'm all right. Where the devil have you come from? What do you want with me? The dreams . . ."

"It is not yet time for your questioning, great Master. You must come to the Bounded . . . if you are the one we seek. Best follow. And soon! We are here to help you find your way!" He bowed deeply, bursting into giddy laughter. The other two followed suit, the brown man laughing in dry, hacking bleats, and his tall companion in rolling rumbles as deep as the midnight of his coloring.

"Karon, no!" My mother called out from beyond the trees, distracting me from the mystery of the three. "Gerick, run!"

Satisfaction rippled through me at that moment. The Prince hadn't changed her mind; she still believed in me. I would not let her down.

I shook off the brown and black hands and jumped to my feet. The three of them were still chuckling merrily. I didn't believe they meant me any harm. "I need to get away from here," I said. "Someone's trying to hurt me."

"Away?" said the dwarf, scarcely able to swallow his laughter. "We could take you away. A short away. Not all the away. Our way is not your away. You must find your own. But come—"

He was interrupted by the snapping of branches behind me. "Who are you? What are you doing here? Sword of Annadis! Tell me this is a dream." My mother.

The three burst out laughing again and crammed themselves behind a thick-boled oak tree, while I turned to tell her what I planned. She stood in the shadowed tangle of lilacs, hard to see. Moonlight glinted on the knife in her hand. Perhaps I had been mistaken about her, too.

Yet even as I hesitated, she threw down her weapon and extended her arms. "Gerick! Your father— Gerick, tell me who you are."

I opened my mouth to say something, but things

quickly became very confusing. I needed to get to her. The sounds coming from the shadows . . . I knew them well: the soft thud, the rip of muscle and crack of bone, the brief expulsion of air, followed by the quick intake as the pain shot upward. Such sounds always accompanied the hard curve and smooth feel of a knife hilt, and the satisfying release as rubbery flesh and tough cartilage yielded to the honed edge of the blade.

The tangled, twiggy shrubbery snagged my clothes as I fought to get to her.

"Mother? Are you all right?"

But she wasn't. Her garments were soaked with blood. Wide-eyed, she touched her breast where the knife hilt protruded, and her hand came away covered in blood. I caught her before she fell.

I had no healing skills, and only the small amount of power that lay unbidden in the hands of every Dar'Nethi. That would never be enough. Only one way to get her the help she needed. Mustering every dram of power and will I could scrape together, I held my back against the door in my mind and called out to the Prince with sorcery. *Father, come. Hurry . . .*

Such anger . . . withering fury . . . cold death did I find when I touched his thoughts. Only in its absence did I even begin to realize the grace my true father had brought to my healing.

She's here in the alder grove beyond the ruined root cellar . . . wounded . . . That was all I could get out before the storm of his wrath engulfed me. I broke off the contact, panting and sweating as if I'd run half a day in the desert. No use to tell him I hadn't done what he thought, or even that my mother would die unless he came instantly to care for her. He would come. And I had to be gone when he did so.

I peered through the thick limbs, strained my ears to hear a footstep . . . a cough . . . a breath . . . to tell me that the villain who'd done this was within reach of my justice. The three odd creatures from my dreams were still chuckling, hidden behind their oak tree. Several pairs of boots pounded the leafy ground, but the three men were running toward me, not away. Paulo. Radele. The Prince. Where had the assassin gone?

I laid my mother in the damp leaves beside the lilacs. She fought for breath, and her hands grew cold though I chafed them unceasingly. Her eyes clouded. What could I say to her? I needed her to know . . . "Hold on. Trust me." I couldn't think of anything else. She wouldn't want to hear what I was going to do to the person who had hurt her.

And so I left her, trying to ignore the rumbling in my head that felt like an approaching earthquake, and I hurried to where the dwarf and his companions awaited me. "I must go away from here now."

"To what awayness would you go, great Master?"

"Outside the walls of this parkland, to the outer gate. Can you show me the way out?"

"Nicely can we do that. But not more? Not into the treeland or the grassy abiding? Not to the place of many walls?"

I had no idea what they meant. "No. Just show me how to get over the walls and back to the main gate without being seen"—the shouts were getting very close—"and it has to be now."

"Now!" said the dwarf.

"Now!" echoed the brown man and the runner. The two grabbed my arms again and gave a tug. As the thought occurred to me that they were not planning to lead me down any ordinary path, I fell off the edge of the world for the span of two breaths and stepped back onto it right next to the gates of Windham.

The only ill effect of the strange transport was a distinctly queasy feeling. My nausea wasn't helped in the least by the bloody knife in my hand. My mother's knife. Stupid to pull it out of her. I dropped it hastily. My hands were sticky, and I stank of blood. Thank all gods that my father was a Healer.

"Unsettles the belly," said the dwarf, grinning. He patted his own substantial paunch and then did the same to mine.

"That's a truth," I said, "but I've no sword sticking

through my gut, either, and that would be more unsettling yet." I gave the three a proper bow, and thought that perhaps when I had finished the next step of my escape plan, we might try their magic again. "I thank you, Sir—?"

"Vroon?" said the dwarf, hesitantly.

"I thank you, Sir Vroon. Well done."

The dwarf puffed out his chest and grinned hugely. "A name! Do you hear it? The great Master has given me a name! My debt is unstoppable, sir. My honor is to serve you always until the Unbounded is no more, and the Bounded has grown ancient in its days."

There simply wasn't time to decipher his odd speech. My father's rage rent the night. If I just had enough power left to do what I needed. A simple thing . . .

I did. After a long few moments, Jasyr raced through the gates and stopped right in front of me, quivering and tossing his head, just as he did when I galloped away from my dreams. The only problem was that another horse followed right on his tail. And that horse had a rider.

"I knew it, you bloody bastard. I'll kill you for this. How could you do it?"

He was off Molly and on top of me before I could blink, and I was afraid I might have to break both his arms to keep him from doing what he said. His eyes were blazing, and he obviously didn't care in the least what I did to him, unless it was kill him before he'd done the same to me.

"I didn't do it," I gasped, getting him pinned and making sure I didn't leave him a finger's leeway before I'd convinced him. "Any of it. I swear."

"She's dead. You killed her, you black-hearted devil."

"She won't die. He'll save her. If it's possible, he'll do it. I don't have the skill for healing, so I called him to come. Would I have called him if I wanted her to die? I don't. Of course, I don't."

"I don't believe you. Her blood is all over you."

Vroon and his friends grabbed Paulo and yanked him out from under me, and he didn't even notice, any more than he noticed the blood dripping from his nose into the dirt or the fact that his shirt was half torn off him. He never took his eyes from my face.

"Why should you believe me?" I said. "I wouldn't either, if I were you. So believe what you want; it doesn't change the truth."

"I don't want to believe it. I thought I knew you."

"Then listen to what I say. I'll swear on anything you want that I didn't hurt my mother. I could never do that."

"You'll swear, but it don't mean dung on my boots when you don't have a lick of truth in you." He kicked the bloody knife toward me. "Pick it up and kill me, too. It's the only way you'll get away with it."

"Go back and help them. Tell my mother what I've said. I've got to get away or I'll be dead, too. Then we'll never know who really did it, or what's the truth of any of this business. Look who's holding you. They showed up tonight and helped me get away. Do you remember what I told you about my dreams?"

He had finally settled down enough to take notice of the three odd-looking fellows who had his arms pinned behind him and were folding his legs underneath him so he couldn't get off his knees. The sight of the thin black arms, the thick brown ones, and the one-eyed face scowling straight at him, no taller than his own face, surprised him just enough to make him listen. "Bloody Jerrat!"

"I've got to go find out what's going on, Paulo. It's all connected: the dreams, these disappearances in Leire, the shepherd's story about his son disappearing . . . I'll wager these very same events the Prince is set to kill me for are part of it, too. I didn't do those things he says, and I didn't hurt my mother. If you end up believing I did any of it, you can break my neck at your pleasure. Now, go away."

"I won't."

"Suit yourself, then. Stay here and rot." I mounted Jasyr and motioned to the three to let him go.

He strode across the trampled grass to where his Molly waited for him. I squeezed my eyes closed, trying to erase the image of a skinny, freckled boy who twisted painfully with every step. Another vision. A flush of shame heated my skin as jeers of "donkey," "thief's brat," and "cripple" echoed through a dusty street I had never walked. With every mental discipline I knew, I willed the vision away. I had no time for madness.

When I opened my eyes again, I saw Paulo only as he was that night: tall, wiry, surprisingly strong, thrusting himself into the saddle with the two good legs that the Prince—no, that my father, Karon—had given him. He ripped the tail off his shirt, wiped the blood from his face and threw the rag on the ground. "I'm going with you."

"With a murderer? A traitor? Would you ride with a Lord of Zhev'Na?"

"Maybe. Maybe not. You've got some convincing to do." He didn't say which way I'd have to convince him.

CHAPTER 10

Sometime after freeing Paulo and before the two of us rode off together, Vroon and his friends had vanished. Perhaps I hadn't thanked them properly for saving my life twice in one night. I dared not wait around for them, so, as the moon rose, I set a brisk pace through the winding lanes to the highroad, and then headed northward at a canter. We didn't stop until dawn.

As the light crept over the countryside, we searched for a place to rest and water the horses. I picked a spot where the road crossed a wide, sluggish stream, riding a few hundred paces upstream along the marshy bank in hopes of finding cleaner water to fill our empty waterskins. As soon as we dismounted, Paulo settled himself on a hummock of grayish grass that seemed to be the only dry spot within half a league of the stream. From the scowl he had worn since we had left Windham, I saw that asking to share the seat would be of no use.

So once I had filled the waterskins, I stood stupidly in the mud, stroking Jasyr's neck and rummaging in my saddle pack, hoping to find my cloak and something to eat. The morning felt chilly, as my shirt was soaked and muddy from my adventures in the damp Windham gardens. All I found in the pack was one spare shirt—an ugly, useless green silk thing my mother had dug out of Tennice's attic—a change of undergarments and leggings, the silly-looking hat I'd worn as part of my "disguise," a blanket, two cups, one spoon, a small pot, and my flint and steel. No cloak and not so much as a dry biscuit to eat. Then I remembered I'd left the cloak in the gatehouse at Windham wrapped around a pile of leaves. And as for the food—

"You won't find nothing in my kit, neither," said Paulo, as if he had read my mind or heard my stomach rumbling. "All in the gray saddle pack. You threw it into the corner of the gatehouse. Remember?" He wasn't finished being angry with me yet.

"We'll just have to figure out something. Stop in a village and buy what we need, I suppose." I turned out my pockets and found exactly twelve coppers. About enough for half a dozen mugs of ale or three loaves of stale bread. I glanced at Paulo.

"At least you didn't *steal* from the Lady before you stabbed her," he said. "I gave her the silver from selling the horses and the pony trap."

No point in arguing guilt or innocence again. "So you don't have any money, either?"

"Not a copper. Looks like if we want to eat, I'll have to go begging. Most people will give you something if you look sorry enough. Bad as I look, that ought to be easy . . . unless they see you with me, wearing your own mother's blood."

"I'll go hungry before I beg a stranger for a meal."

"Then you've never been hun—holy great demons!" Paulo just about jumped out of his skin when Vroon popped out of a willow thicket just beside him, bowing and chuckling. The other two followed right after him.

"We've come to accompany you on your way," said Vroon, gaping at a pair of moorhens skittering across the sluggish water. He waved his small hand away from himself and his friends. "Pay us no mind."

Tired of Paulo's surliness, I tried asking Vroon a few of the questions that had been bothering me, such as where he'd come from, why he was looking for me, and how he got into my dreams. But no matter how loud I spoke, the three acted as if they couldn't hear me. It was so annoying that I soon turned my back on all four of my companions.

But Paulo wasn't finished with his grumbling. "Too proud to ask for help. That's nothing new. Serve you right to starve."

"We can't be seen until we're farther from Windham. The Prince is not going to give up finding me so easily." But he wasn't likely to come searching until my mother was all right . . . or dead. Even as I voiced the thought, I was disgusted with myself. Vile . . . what kind of creature was I even to think such things?

"That leaves stealing, then, if we're going to eat. You'll make a thief of me. Get me hanged or worse. I didn't steal even when I was a nub in Dunfarrie! Curse this day everlasting!" He threw a rock into the stream so hard it startled a flock of lapwings, who flapped their way noisily upriver, and Jasyr, who almost stepped on my foot.

I dodged the horse, but ended up on my knee in the mud. As if I weren't wet enough . . . filthy enough . . . vile enough . . . "Blast it all, you pigheaded oaf! Just leave, then."

"Better an oaf than a murdering sod."

"I swear I didn't hurt her. I couldn't." Powers of night, couldn't he understand how I felt about my mother? The two of them—my mother and Paulo—were the only reasons I was a human person. And I didn't even know if she was alive.

"Cold-hearted bastard . . . just leaving her like that."

"What good would I have done her, staying there to get my throat slit? If anyone in any world can help her, it's my father. You know that better than anyone. He won't let her die. He can protect her." I had risked using sorcery to call him.

"Who else could have done it? You had the bloody knife in your hand."

"I pulled it out of her after she was down. I don't know why." Stupid to pull the weapon out of a wound like that. "Everything was dark . . . confusing. I was walking up to her. I heard the strike"—*felt* the strike deep in my own gut—"and she fell. I just don't know. I didn't see it."

"Lying coward."

"Thickheaded dolt!"

We traded insults and curses for half an hour. I told him he should stay here and soak his head in the stream while I went looking for the truth. He told me I wasn't going to throw him away like a gnawed bone. That got us back to how hungry we were and how ridiculous it was that we didn't know what to do about it.

Meanwhile, the wide, leathery man and the scrawny black runner examined our horses. They didn't touch the beasts. Just sniffed at their skin, studied their legs and flanks, their hocks and tails and hooves, and stared into their eyes as if trying to read their thoughts. Vroon was more interested in Paulo and me, poking his head in between us and watching our faces as we yelled at each other.

When Paulo and I finally ran out of anything new to say, we mounted up as if we had thought about it at the same moment and started back along the muddy bank toward the road. Vroon and his friends trailed along behind. As I turned northward on the highroad, the three of them vanished.

Paulo shaded his eyes and stared up the road, as if the three might have just sped away exceptionally fast, rather than disappearing in midair. "Maybe they don't like our prospects. Looks like the wide one eats pretty regular. Do you figure they're gone for good this time?"

"I don't think so. They came for more than just getting me out of a scrape."

I just had no idea what that reason might be, and I was too relieved at the moment to figure it out. Foolish to get so angry over nothing. Careless. Dangerous. Why did meaningless things bother me so much? It didn't matter what Paulo thought of me.

Before we'd covered another league, a streak of green light split the air above the road just in front of us. I wasn't too surprised to see our three friends show up again. But now Vroon and the wide leathery man rode horseback, while the runner jogged along beside us on his long, thin legs.

The brown man offered me a wad of cloth. "Yours?"

I reined in Jasyr and took the bundle. Everyone else pulled up, too, and gathered around as I shook out the cloth. It was my cloak. "Yes," I said. "Thank you. How did—?"

"And this to be the other's?" said the runner in his rumbling voice, holding out a bulging gray saddle pack to Paulo.

"How did you get these?" I asked, suspicious. I didn't see how they could have sneaked past the Prince or Radele. "Were the people still there? What was happening? My mother . . . a woman with hair the same color as mine . . . was wounded. Did you see—?"

"Great magics were happening," said Vroon. "We could not see into them."

Great magics . . . healing, I hoped. I ignored the hard look from Paulo and tried to stay focused on the present. I could do nothing for my mother. "So you just walked in and took our things without anyone noticing?"

"We are skilled at acquirings," said Vroon, and the three joined in their now familiar wicked chuckling. "None saw us."

Paulo had already opened the bag and pulled out a handful of flat biscuits. One was halfway to his mouth, when he stopped and offered it to the runner who was staring at the dry lump with his glittering amber eyes even wider than usual. "Are you hungry, too . . . uh . . . sorry, I didn't get your name?"

The runner waved the biscuit away and bowed his head. His skin glowed blue-black like polished onyx. "No name belongs to me as yet. No gift of a name."

Paulo took a bite and chewed for a moment, watching the long-limbed man draw circles in the dirt with his toe. "Everybody ought to have a name. In this land we got names even if we're nobodies."

"If I could have a name, I think it would be Zanore," said the runner, cocking his head thoughtfully. "I feel that name. But it has not been granted to me. Perhaps someday, if I live well."

"Nobody has to *grant* you a name here. If you want to be called it, then just say so." Paulo passed me the food bag. "Don't you think he should be called Zanore if he wants?"

I chose two biscuits and shrugged. "I'll call you Zanore. Whatever you like."

The black runner seemed to grow two hands taller

right there in front of us. He bowed first to me and then to Paulo, scraping the dusty road with his spiky silver hair. "I am honored beyond tellings by your naming, great Master. And I thank you for your goodwill, Horseman Mighty."

Paulo turned pure scarlet. "My name is Paulo. Does *Zanore* mean something special, or is it like mine . . . just a name?"

"Oh, sir, *Zanore* is not 'just a name.' No name is 'just a name.' Names are realness. Hereness. Names are bounded." He grinned hugely, as if he had explained everything.

Once I had swallowed the last crumbs of biscuit and drunk a bit of the tepid, murky stream water from my waterskin, my disposition was much improved. I offered the waterskin to the leathery man. He was so much wider than his bony horse, he looked like an owl astride a twig as he sat gaping cheerfully at his two friends. "I suppose you have a name you're interested in, too."

I would have sworn the red tufts of hair on his brown head wriggled in delight. "Ob."

"Well then . . . Ob . . . I thank you for your help. Have a drink if you want."

"Honor." Though he spoke only one word at a time, his words seemed to have a great deal more bulk than other people's. He declined the water, but he bellowed a laugh and tipped sideways, making the deepest bow he could manage without toppling from his horse.

The three begged us to say what else we might need that they could acquire for us. I didn't want to be greedy, for I had a feeling that their "acquirings" would be at the expense of some terrified villagers. The two horses they rode, though not exceptional, were surely being missed by someone.

"Nothing just now," I said. "Unless you could transport us farther away as you did before. I want to go to the dream place, the place you've shown me with the black-and-purple sky."

The three gave a huge, satisfied sigh.

"Ah, not so far can we carry you," said Vroon, grinning so widely it crinkled the skin over his missing eye.

"You will find your own way there . . . if you are the one. If not, you will fail."

"If I'm the one what?"

"The One Who Makes Us Bounded. Who gives us names. His coming is awaited most eagerly."

"I've no idea what you're talking about. I've seen you three in my dreams—you know that?"

They looked at each other with unreadable expressions. "We came searching for the dreamer. For such a long time we have searched, listening for tales of kings and rulers. Following. Hoping to recognize the dreamer. We felt urgently to come to the fallen fastness, and there we find you! You were not fearful, and so we believe you are the one we have been waiting for. You have . . ."

". . . wholeness," said Ob. His broad brow wrinkled into deep furrows, as if his thoughts were as ponderous as his body.

Silly. I pulled my cloak around me and nudged Jasyr to get moving.

The day grew warmer. We continued northward. I tried a few more questions, but our companions held their tongues and shook their heads. They just weren't going to tell me what I wanted. Part of their game must be making me guess.

"So how far *can* you take us?" I said as the road narrowed and curved into the shadowed ravine between two brown hillsides.

Vroon thought for a moment. "Next topland, anywards. Or mighty treeland sunwards traveling. Or stone-walled fastness coldwards."

I puzzled at the odd descriptions as we rode in and out of the patchy shadows and sunlight of the rolling hill country. *Topland anywards* . . . Hilltops? In any direction? *Mighty treeland* . . . A forest, most likely . . . a big one. *Sunwards traveling.* East? No, west, following the sun. The forest of Tennebar lay west of us. And there were a number of stone-walled *fastnesses* hereabouts—fortresses and castles built to control the approaches to Montevial. And *coldwards* would be north. Comigor was perhaps five leagues north. . . .

Of course! Vroon must have picked up the destinations directly from me, not reading my thoughts exactly, because I'd not voiced them even to myself. But he had offered hilltops because I was worried about pursuit, and we couldn't see more than a half a league in any direction from where we were. He considered Tennebar because that was the route to the Vallorean highlands where the shepherd's son had disappeared. And Comigor, because I could not ride these hills without thinking of the castle where'd I'd grown up always afraid, and where I'd first met my mother without either of us knowing it.

The choice was easy. "The mighty treeland," I said. "Sunwards traveling." The time wasn't yet right for going back to Comigor. But a fast journey to Tennebar would give us a terrific head start on any pursuers, putting us two days closer to Valleor and the shepherd's lay.

"As you say." And with no more fuss than if they were preparing supper, Zanore jogged up between Jasyr and Molly and grabbed my right arm and Paulo's left, while Vroon and Ob rode to the outside, taking my left arm and Paulo's right. Then we fell off the edge of the world again. The last thing I saw was Paulo's puzzled stare at Vroon and me. And the last question on my lips was answered before I could blurt it out. The horses could indeed come with us, for after some indefinable, unsettling instant, I sat on a nervous Jasyr under the green shadowed eaves of Tennebar.

"Bloody hell!" Paulo and Molly were backing in nervous circles, and Paulo had to use all his particular skills to quiet his big-hearted mare. Truthfully, I think Paulo was more disconcerted than Molly.

"Can you take us across this treeland?" I said. " 'Sunwards traveling' yet again?"

"No more," said Vroon, grinning. "Your own way must you make. Ob, Zanore, and I will beside you watch, for acquirings you need or guardings. But the way must be your own." He bobbed his brown beard. "We believe you are the one we hope for."

"So what do you make of them?" said Paulo, after the three winked out again, leaving us to ride alone through the forest in the bright noonday. "They're not from Avonar, are they? I didn't see nobody like them there."

"No. And they're not from Zhev'Na, either." Paulo's face didn't change when I said that, but he fixed his eyes on me as if he might see something different if he looked long enough. I watched the road. "No one in Zhev'Na had any deformities. Think of the Zhid warriors, still Dar'Nethi in form, but all very much alike, even the women. Perfect variations of the same mold. Similar in stature and strength. No weaknesses. They never transformed Dulcé into Zhid. The Zhid considered them too short, too small." I hated thinking about Zhev'Na, much less talking about it.

"Then are these three from yet another world?"

"I don't know . . . though I'm beginning to have an idea."

"What's that?"

"Not yet. You're hard enough to convince of things I'm sure of. Let's get closer and see."

"Closer to where?"

"The place where the shepherd's son disappeared. I think it's a portal to the world I see in my dreams."

At sunset, we stopped somewhere in the middle of the forest and made camp—if rolling off a saddle into last year's leaves and Paulo telling the horses not to go away could be called making camp. It had been two days without sleep for both of us, and little enough for me before that. On that night in Tennebar, we slept from sunset to sunrise, and only at the end of the long night did I fall once again into dreaming. But the dream was as strange as everything else. . . .

When I heard him screaming, I knew I'd best get Jasyr saddled. He'd be wanted within the hour, and me and Molly, too, I guessed, no matter it was the time when nobody but wolves and owls and highwaymen had any business abroad. The moon was half grown and half risen, so I couldn't claim it was too risky. Never could get myself out of it on that account anyway, but the young master wouldn't take the horses if it was full dark. He used to want it so, but I pointed out that Jasyr didn't have

*no magic in him to make him see better in the dark, and
if he was to break his leg, we'd have to put him down.
So on those nights we'd run on our own feet down the
forest tracks until one or the other of us dropped from
it. It was always me dropped first. I'd only had two good
legs for a bit more than five years, since the Prince had
healed me with his magic, and I'd never yet figured out
why running on 'em had any great attraction.*

*"C'mon, Molly. Don't know why you can't saddle
yourself by now, we've done this so much." She blew in
my ear nice and warm.*

*The three of us—Molly and me and Jasyr—would al-
ways be in the stableyard when he came.*

*"Don't you ever sleep?" he said. I don't think he knew
how wicked his screams were, or maybe he just didn't
like to think about it.*

*"Thought it'd be a good night for a ride," I said back
to him.*

"You don't have to." He always said that.

*"You know there's nothing I like better'n riding—even
if it's the middle of the night."*

*Like always, we rode an hour or so as hard as Jasyr
and Molly could go. We came to a lake we knew of, and
I slowed Molly down to a walk. She had a big heart and
good wind, but not as strong legs as Jasyr. We'd cool 'em
down and rest 'em before we rode back. The young master always listened to me about horses.*

*We let the horses drink and feed a bit while we flopped
on the ground in the moonlight. Lots of times we did that
and never said a word, but on this night, the young master
told me again about his dreams. Before I'd thought about
it, I said, "Are you sure . . . ?"*

*He wouldn't even let me get the question out any more.
"It's not the Lords. I'd know it. It's not! It's not!"*

"It's not!" I shouted, and sat bolt upright, causing a
shower of dead leaves to fall all over Paulo, who was
waving a knife in the air blindly while trying to extricate
himself from his blanket.

"What's happening?"

"Nothing," I said, and flopped back against the tree. "The usual."

"Dreams again?"

I nodded, and closed my eyes against the bright sun, and didn't mention to Paulo that it appeared I'd been dreaming *his* dreams for a change, instead of my own. I was going crazy.

We rode west and north as hard as we could get the horses to go. Paulo could coax a horse to do anything he asked, and he coddled and pampered them, staying up every night talking to them, rubbing them down, and feeding them any special tidbits he'd found along the way.

Once the gray bag was empty, Vroon, Zanore, and Ob kept us supplied with food, so we could avoid villages and towns, leaving no evidence as to our course or destination. The three would pop in and out so often that after a while we scarcely blinked at their odd comings and goings. I commanded them to pay for whatever they took with a copper from my dwindling hoard, but they didn't understand the concept at all. Trading made some sense to them, but when they bit the coins, examined them, and spun them up in the air, they couldn't come up with any use for them and told me I must be mistaken. I insisted, and, though I couldn't be sure, I think they complied with my wishes at least in that matter. They still wouldn't answer any more questions.

On the twelfth day of our flight, we rode into the highlands of Valleor, climbing unending slopes of grass littered with white rock and detouring around a thousand cold lakes and a few scattered sheep lays. The sky stayed thick and gray, and it rained every day. Our boots were sodden and our feet cold, but just when I was ready to beg Vroon to find us dry boots, the three vanished and, this time, failed to return. By the chilly sunset when Paulo and I lay behind a scattering of giant, smooth boulders tumbled on a grassy hillside, observing the shepherd's lay, we hadn't seen Vroon and company for three whole days. Paulo's stomach was rumbling like a herd of oxen.

"It won't behave," he whispered, when I motioned him to be quiet. Sound carried amazingly far in rocky places like that. The pounding of a hammer from one of the sheds below sounded as if the anvil were sitting between my feet. The bleats from the flock grazing in the valley, and the gurgling and whispering of fifty trickles of water across the slopes, echoed sharply through the thin air.

We had been watching the lay since early afternoon when I spotted the shepherd—easily identifiable as the storyteller from Prydina. When he had finished mending a holding pen, we followed him home. Both the shepherd and his son carried bows. I didn't want to test how quick their hands would move if they thought we were wolves or thieves, so I decided we would wait until dark and slip around the dale without bothering them. The moon would be up soon after, and though it was still young, it was big, and the night was clear. It would show us the way to our destination. Then we'd see what we could see.

The sturdy-looking younger man milked the goats, carrying the pails into the sod-roofed hovel that squatted in the middle of the valley. Fine smells floated up from the chimney. When a girl called out that supper was ready, my own stomach growled. The valley got even quieter after the burly shepherd laid down his hammer and went into the house. Paulo and I shared out the last cold, hard bits of a meat pie that Vroon had acquired for us three days before. But the meat smelled bad and we weren't willing to risk it, so we threw that part away and ate the stale, greasy crust.

As dusk faded into night, the family reappeared only briefly: the girl to empty a bucket onto a little garden and fill it again at a catchpool, the younger man to relieve himself out by the sheep pen, and the gray-bearded shepherd to smoke a pipe. A short while later they were all inside, and the house was dark.

Paulo slipped back up the hill to retrieve the horses, and we led them quietly around the edges of the lay, keeping downwind of the sheep and the dogs. The gibbous moon was huge and yellow over the southeastern horizon, and we used its light to find the stunted fir tree the shepherd had told me marked the entrance to a steep rocky defile. We scrambled up, leading the horses, glad the earthen banks along either side weren't high enough to cast the treacherous path into deeper shadows. The defile led to the top of a low, narrow ridge that stretched northward.

"Are you sure this is right? This don't look like any road to anywhere."

"This is exactly what he described to me. He was very precise. I think he wanted to prove he wasn't just making the whole thing up. Watch for a patch of junipers that looks like a giant cocklebur. A hundred paces past it, the track and the ridge will angle east. That's where we start looking."

And there, where the ridge abruptly joined the shoulder of a craggy mountainside, we found the rock pile and the wide flat rock where they'd found the one-handed boy's things on the day he vanished.

"I don't see nothing here," said Paulo, whispering for no reason as we examined the rocks and the soft flat ground in the moon shadows.

A few scrubby bushes poked out of the rocks. Only a goat could climb up the steep hillside behind the boulder pile, and in every other direction were endless slopes covered with short, stiff tuck-grass, and endless clumps of sheep's folly, and endless night. No road. No black-and-purple sky. And the stars were their familiar white, not at all green.

"Maybe it's the wrong place or the wrong time." What had I expected? I'd been so sure. . . .

Paulo snorted, pulled a scant handful of oats from a cloth bag and began apologizing to Jasyr and Molly for the long hard riding on a wild-goose chase.

Nothing to do but sleep and rethink everything in the morning. I could talk to the shepherd, perhaps, to make sure of the story, the place, the season. It *had* to be right. I had no other clue.

We rolled out our blankets on the damp ground, and

Paulo was snoring in seconds. He could sleep in a tree limb or a saddle . . . or tied to a stable wall half dead, like that night in Zhev'Na when we'd become friends.

I hated thinking about Zhev'Na. I had lived there only a little more than a year, yet I could still close my eyes and feel the desert sun on my skin and smell the dust and smoke and blood from the Zhid practice fields. Life before Zhev'Na seemed unreal, as if it had happened to someone else—as I suppose it had. Comigor was like a castle in a story. It was easier to recall the flowery scent of Philomena's ugly apartments than to remember her face. It hadn't been at all difficult learning she wasn't my mother. She'd never acted like my mother. She'd never felt it, nor had I.

It was easier to remember Papa's face—Tomas's face—though it kept blending into my real mother's face. The brother and sister had resembled each other closely. I had always liked occasions when Tomas first came home from his travels, because he smelled like horses and leather and the oil he used on his swords. After he'd been home a while, he smelled like Philomena's bedroom.

I owed Tomas a great deal. He had never known that Ziddari, the Exile, Lord of Zhev'Na, had switched his sister Seri's doomed infant with his own child. He had tried to be a good father, but I'd been terrified he would find out I was a sorcerer and have me arrested. Ziddari twisted Tomas's mind for ten years and lured Tomas into a battle that was never his. What would have become of me if he hadn't thought of me when he was dying and asked his sister to tell me how much he cared for me? Maybe none of this would have happened, and I would be the Duke of Comigor right now, fighting for King Evard, betrothed to the king's daughter Roxanne, perhaps. That's what Tomas and Philomena had planned. Or maybe I would have been found out by the Leiran sheriffs and burned to death like my real father. More probably, Ziddari would have discovered the magic that had joined my dead father to Prince D'Natheil and taken me to Zhev'Na anyway. Then my mother wouldn't have been there to stop me from destroying the Bridge. Enslaving the world to the Lords.

I pulled my blanket up over my cloak and around my back between me and the rock. The night was getting cold. I wished very much that I could talk to my mother. Ask her advice. She was good at puzzles and knew so much about so many things. A few times I'd been tempted to tell her more about how it was with me. But she would have felt awful and sorry, when there was nothing to be done. And I hadn't wanted her telling the Prince everything; she didn't like keeping secrets from him. Now I didn't know if she was even alive.

I sat up long into that night. I'd had more sleep these last few days traveling with Paulo than I'd had on any night since Zhev'Na, so sleep just wouldn't come. Instead I went over everything again and again, worrying about my mother, and about the Prince, who wanted me dead, and the Lords, who just wanted me.

By the time the moon had crept across the sky and dropped low on the horizon in front of me, my thoughts weren't making sense any more. I was just staring at the moon that got bigger and brighter as it fell, until it filled the entire span of my vision. As the light swelled and filled me, the world receded. Paulo's snoring sounded soft and distant. The chilly wind no longer made me shiver, and the hard, cold ground seemed only remotely connected to me. Only the moon was in my eyes . . . the moon . . . What had the shepherd said? *Tom come late to the hold, and the moon was in his eyes. . . .*

"Paulo! Wake up!" Without turning my head, I reached out for him, and his arm seemed farther away than the moon. I felt him stir. Careful not to let anything distract my glance, I closed my eyes and turned exactly a half circle to face the rock at my back. I opened my eyes again . . . and there was the path of moonlight, leading straight into the hillside. Only the hillside wasn't there any more. I was looking into another place altogether. Night, yes, but a very different night. The sky was purple and black, and unlike those that burned behind and above me, the stars were green.

"Hurry," I said, my voice emerging at some vast distance behind me, barely audible though I made no effort to whisper. "Untether the horses; leave everything. Take

my hand." And from that same vast distance, I heard
Paulo, answering me. "Good Jerrat, save us! Your eyes
are yellow. What's happened? Are you—?"

"Don't worry about it. I can see the way. Hurry. And
hold on tight. I can't feel your hand."

Moments later, the lightest brush of a feather touched
my fingers, and I set foot on the hard-packed road that
led into the dream world. His words came so faint that
I felt them more than heard them. *Oh, cripes. You're
halfway into solid rock . . . and you want me to come
with you.* Until I pulled him after, and we stood wholly
in the place of my dreams.

"We found it," I said, my voice quite normal again.
Paulo stood quite solid beside me with a crushing grip
on my hand. "Welcome to the Breach."

CHAPTER 11

"This can't be the Breach." Paulo pressed his back against the rock cliff, ensuring he was as far as he could get from the outsloping edge of the precipice. "I don't care nothing for your feelings about it. That was a fearful place. I never told you, but I saw such things . . . And though no man could call this place rightful, it's nothing so wicked as that. This is just different, like Avonar is different. Well, maybe a bit more. . . ."

We stood on a narrow spit of rock that jutted out high over a barren landscape. Streaks of blue-and-green lightning split the sky, and thunder rumbled across the dark plains that stretched in every direction below us. Storms clustered about the horizon, boiling clouds of midnight that continuously changed shape in the bilious light.

"You're right that it's changed—or at least this part of it has changed—since we came out of Zhev'Na," I said. "I can't explain why that's so. By rights we should already be going mad."

"Maybe it's because you're the Prince's son, so you're protecting us like he did. I'm not getting so much as a handspan away from you; you can just count on that." I could feel him willing me away from the edge of the precipice, back toward the dark shape of the doorway in the rock, a black arch outlined with yellow moonlight.

"But I'm not doing anything! When the Prince brought us through the Breach, he was using sorcery every moment, expending every bit of power he could possibly manage." Even when he crossed the Breach by way of D'Arnath's Bridge, the Prince had to concentrate and hold the way open, like someone holding back branches to let you pass through a thick forest. "So this doesn't make sense at all. Maybe Vroon and the others will show up and explain it, now we've arrived."

I was not mistaken. We were nowhere near D'Arnath's Bridge, yet we were standing in the Breach between the worlds. The Breach had been a part of me once, and I recognized it, just as you can look at a childhood portrait and know it is an image of yourself, even recalling the fancies going through your head as it was painted.

The Breach was chaos itself, the warped, broken, distorted bits left over from the birth of the universe, drawn together a thousand years before when three Dar'Nethi sorcerers named Notole, Parven, and Ziddari had reached too far for power. Since that event—the Dar'Nethi called it the Catastrophe—the Breach had divided the mundane world from Gondai. This chaos had no form of its own, but took horrid shapes created by the deepest fears of the traveler who had the misfortune to wander into it. Monsters, flesh-eating rains, rivers of blood, pits full of snakes, spiders the size of a house . . . terror in a thousand guises awaited anyone who walked into the Breach.

Only the ancient Dar'Nethi King D'Arnath and his Heirs had ever been able to control this chaos. According to the Dar'Nethi, D'Arnath's Bridge across the Breach was all that kept the worlds themselves from slipping further into ruin. According to the Lords and the Zhid, the Bridge was a blight on the world that prevented the full use of power and enslaved all true sorcerers to the greedy, spineless royal family of the Dar'Nethi. Whatever the truth, until the day the Prince led Paulo, my mother, and me out of Zhev'Na, no one had ever survived a passage through the Breach without using the Bridge. Even the Lords could not travel there, nor could they feed on the terrors of the Breach to expand their power. That's why I was such a prize for them. I was to be nurtured until I could give them the Breach.

I had almost gone mad on that journey out of

Zhev'Na. In the desert I had seén men staked out in the sun until their skin shrank and grew black and brittle, so that it cracked and tore every time they moved. That's what it felt like with each step away from the Lords. And all the while, the Three were offering me release from the pain and reminding me of the power and immortality I was leaving behind, tempting me to take refuge in the cold, unfeeling darkness we shared.

But my masters had taught me well to ignore pain. As my father led me through a sea of rotting corpses and gales of acid wind, I rid myself of every thought, every sensation, every memory, every instinct. I forced my whole being—mind, soul, heart, senses—numb and empty. That should have been enough. But the pain got worse, and the Lords whispered and teased and tempted until I was half crazed with it.

I wasn't sure what happened then. I tried to drown myself in chaos, thinking that only death or madness would silence the Lords' whispers. For the rest of that crossing, I was very much a part of the Breach, like a bottle of seawater submerged in the ocean. Only when my father carried me into the green world once again did the chaos drain out of me like the water running off as you walk out of the sea. Then I was just empty again.

So that's how I knew where we were as we stood on the dark crag, buffeted by a gale that blew cold from one direction, and then hot from another, and then slowed to a balmy breeze sighing and swirling about our legs like a cat's tail. I knew it in the same way I knew how to walk and how to breathe.

Our perch stuck out of a rugged ridge that stretched as far as we could see to our right and left. In the distance the eerie light revealed clusters of twisted shapes that looked like trees, but my dreams had shown me that they were, in fact, oddly formed towers. A few spidery paths threaded their way through the lowlands from the vague distances to left and right, converging on a low range of hills in the center of the horizon. Beyond the hills . . . yes, there it was again, lit by another flash of green lightning . . . stood the spiral tower from my dreams. Vroon had shown it to me when I dreamed of this place, but I had never determined whether he was trying to get me to go there or warning me to stay away.

Paulo stood at my shoulder. "So what do we do now we're here, whether this is the Breach or somewhere else? How does this tell us what happened to the Lady, or why the Prince is so sure you're still one of the Lords?"

"I don't know. I just think the answer must be here. But we ought to wait for better light before we head down, I think."

"I'll stand watch. Can't go back, and I'm not going anywhere without you're close, so you might as well get some sleep if you need to."

I huddled in the lee of a mottled gray rock, cracked down to its heart with a dead shrub sticking out of it, but I didn't think I could sleep. I just sat there wondering if my real life would show up in my dreams, now that my dreams were outside of me.

"Here." No mistaking Ob's massive presence. I peered out from under my heavy eyelids. The leathery man squatted beside me, smiling. Astonishing how the sound of a word can tell you so much. He wasn't offering to give me anything or calling me to come somewhere other than the place I was. His simple word was spoken in pure wonder. I was *here*. In this place.

"I am most definitely here," I said, standing up and wishing for the cloak and blanket I'd left behind on the moonlit ridge in Valleor. The alternating gusts of hot and cold wind were equally unpleasant through my damp clothes. " 'Where next' is likely more important right now."

"Most eagerly are you expected," said Vroon. "Your subjects await your command. Devastatingly honored are we to lead you to your abode, where you will take up your kingdom and order it as to your least desire. May you reign until the Unbounded is no more, and the Bounded has grown ancient in its days!" It was somewhat difficult to interpret these pronouncements, as Vroon's face was flat against the stone at my feet.

"Take up my what?"

"Your kingdom, sire."

"Vroon, would you please stand up? I can't hear over this wind."

Though it seemed I had dropped off to sleep, I could not have slept long. The land was still locked in night, and I didn't feel as if I'd slept an entire day around. Storms raged across half the sky. Vroon popped to his feet, but kept his eyes cast down. "We have prepared a wall place of magnificence, a fastness as befits our king. If it pleases you not, we will slay the makers who chose wrongly and start again."

If my damp and dirty clothes hadn't itched me so sorely, and if my empty stomach hadn't rumbled so convincingly, I might have thought this was another bizarre dream, where everyone makes sense to each other, but not to you. "Where is your king?"

"*Here*, great Master! *You* are the king, the One Who Makes Us Bounded. You have found your way here as the Source prophesied, and have come to lead us to victory over other bounded worlds. Your glory will be everlasting!" The dwarf snuffled in his beard and fell down to the ground again. By this time Ob and Zanore had flattened themselves on the damp rock, too.

"No, no. There's been a mistake. I'm not a king . . . and not likely to be . . ."

I was the designated successor to a king. Yes, the person who reigned in Avonar was called "the Prince" or "the Heir of D'Arnath." But that was just because the Dar'Nethi thought that no one since the great D'Arnath himself had been worthy of being called king. But even if I had wanted the title, I had no illusions about my claim to D'Arnath's throne. The Dar'Nethi would have something to say about the Fourth Lord of Zhev'Na sitting in D'Arnath's chair.

". . . and I'm certainly not the king of this place. I've only come here to find some answers."

"Whatever answering you desire shall be yours, most majestic one."

Paulo had propped his shoulder against the sheer cliff

face. In between yawns, he cast a hostile eye on the rest of us. "Might start your reign by asking about breakfast, Your Majesty. They seem set on pleasing you."

I wanted to kick him. Zanore popped his silver-haired head up from the stone, his amber eyes gleaming in the dark like hot coals. "Shall we slay this rudeness-speaking, Majesty?"

The three of them seemed to know everything I felt and take it much too seriously. "No! Most certainly not. Don't kill anybody."

"Appreciate that," Paulo grumbled. "Just let me starve slowly. Do you know how long you were asleep? It was at least—"

"Look," I said to the three, "is there someone who can answer some questions? Someone with some authority? Who sent you to find me?"

Vroon lifted his head, the wind threatening to tear off his curly hair and beard. "For all the time of our remembering, we have awaited the king. He dreamed of us, and we felt his presence . . . your presence. But even with a manylight waiting, you had not come, and it was thought you could not remember us because of the time passing. And so we traveled through this moon-door, searched, and found the one who dreamed us, and then we saved you from the Sword Wielder who would have left you unbounded. The Source it was that commanded our sending—the Source knows all about you and about our waiting—and the Guardian chose the three of us from all Singlars to go. Our honor was unmatched, though we know not why—"

A constant rumbling thunder like a stampede of herd beasts interrupted him. Fat drops of hot rain spattered on us from fast-moving, purple-streaked clouds. The wind had shifted so that it was blasting straight up from the plains, and it seemed to be staying cold for a while, so that as soon as we were thoroughly soaked from the hot drops, our teeth were clattering.

"Let's continue this somewhere more sheltered!" I yelled in Vroon's ear. "Can you lead us to this Source?"

"To the Source we cannot take you. Only to the

Guardian. The Guardian can make answerings . . . if he will."

"All right, then. Take us to the Guardian."

Vroon prostrated himself again, apologizing that he could not transport us instantly as was sometimes possible outside the Bounded. I interrupted his abasement. "It's all right. I wouldn't want to travel that way in this land anyway. Please, just show us the way before we freeze. We need shelter and food."

The three jumped to their feet. After a brief consultation which I could not hear, Zanore, his amber eyes like two great fireflies, bowed and took the lead, jogging ahead of us down a steep, narrow path. Though the path zigzagged sharply, every pitch seemed to head directly into the bitter wind. We stepped carefully. The rain made the black rock slick, and a misplaced boot would have left little to scrape off the sharp rocks below. The half-dark was no help, either. Each lightning bolt left me squinting to see beyond an arm's reach.

"When does the sky get light?" I shouted at Ob and Vroon, who hovered around me like hummingbirds at a red flower.

"No sky-brightness shines in the Bounded, not as in the other bounded worlds."

Paulo, raindrops dribbling down his face, nodded knowingly. "I tried to tell you. You slept a good four hours, and the sun never showed up."

Vroon chimed in again. "Mayhap *you* will bring us sky-brightness, Majesty! By you could it be done."

His eager assurance struck me colder than the wind. "I don't do that sort of thing. If you expect sorcery from me, you'd best think again."

Vroon halted abruptly, looking like a fountain gargoyle as the rain cascaded down his crinkled forehead, long beard, and ample belly. I walked on.

The dwarf did manage to soothe my annoyance after a while. About the time I realized that the unnatural quiet was his absence, I sensed rather than heard pelting footsteps on the track behind us. I stopped, holding on to a stunted tree that poked out of the rock so a wind gust wouldn't knock me off the path. Vroon skidded to a stop right beside Paulo, his one eye hidden behind a pile of cloaks and bags.

"I happened across these things," said Vroon. "The moon-door was open, and the One Who Makes Us Bounded wished them here."

By the time I dragged my cloak out of the pile, Paulo held his gray saddlebag in one hand and was cramming a biscuit into his mouth with the other. He offered me the bag. "Breakfast."

We trudged downward. The provisions stowed in our recently empty saddlebag were no more than dry, sweet-ish biscuits, old cheese, and weak ale, but they settled in the stomach as nicely as a Long Night feast.

Even if Vroon could have transported us straight to our destination, I would have insisted on walking. The Lord Parven had been a master of military strategy for a thousand years, and he had taught me everything he could stuff into my head during my time in Zhev'Na. Several of his lessons came to mind that night. Never accept favors from either an ally or an enemy unless it is to save your life. And never enter an ally's stronghold without knowing how to get out of it as easily as you got in.

We walked briskly in the wild purple-and-green storm, able to move faster as we headed out of the craggy foot-hills into the lowlands. The ground was packed hard and mostly barren, though at a distance I could see a few twiggy trees no taller than I. Between the trees, the land showed a softer profile that might indicate low grasses or scrub.

Distances were deceptive. The closest tower had looked to be a good two hours' march, but we'd not been walking half that when we passed by it.

Paulo stopped and looked over his shoulder. "Did you see him?"

"See who?"

"The fellow by that pile of rock back there. He had two arms on one side of him, a regular one, and a little, stubby one. Never saw the like."

"No, I didn't see."

"He bowed as we went by. Look . . . there's another."

A ragged, hunchbacked old woman was standing beside a short squat tower. As we walked past she lifted her hands and fell to her knees, her eyes fixed on me. Just beyond her, a man with bright red hair and no eyes popped into view just beside another tower, as if he'd been inside and had stepped right through the wall onto his front stoop to learn what passed by his door. The towers looked like piles of solid rock, but I began to wonder if they were dwellings of some sort. The eyeless man's head followed us just as though he could see, and as we left him behind he bowed very low.

"It's like they're worshipping you. Like you were their *Lord* . . ." Disgust boiled out of Paulo like sap from a burning pine branch. I kept walking. He could believe what he liked.

The rain lashed our faces until we were numb, and the gale made it difficult to stay upright, but every tower produced someone to pay homage as we passed. All were dressed in shapeless tunics of grayish brown, and almost every one of the people appeared to be malformed—missing limbs or extra ones, bodies too wide or too tall, twisted or misshapen. Yet they were men and women, not monsters.

Seeing these people made me think about the shepherd's son whose tale had led us here. He had been born with only one hand, so his father had said, and had believed he was going to a "place where he belonged." And the Queen of Leire had said that most of those who had disappeared from the Four Realms in the past year had been people mutilated or malformed. But I had never seen such monstrous deformities as some of these.

Soon we came to an even larger cluster of towers, hundreds of them crowded together like a city. As Zanore threaded his way between them, I pulled off my hood and wiped the rain from my eyes so I could see more. The towers were every shape and size, some as tall as the towers of Comigor Keep, some no more than a jumble of stones, some smooth-sided spirals soaring into the low clouds, some squat and ugly stacks of pebbles or piles of sticks and mud. Most were made of a greenish stone streaked with dirty pink, though a few were dark-colored or of indeterminate grays. In the dim light I could see no doors or windows or other openings in their sides. The occupants moved in and out with a soft *thwop*.

The rain finally stopped, and the sky settled to a mottled black and purple, with charcoal-colored clouds floating across the sparkling green stars. The wind turned warm and died down to a sighing moan.

I stopped for a moment to gape at an immense tower, the tallest in the cluster, knobby and bulging at its base, but soaring smoothly upward into a bulb-shaped knot on the top. The colors of the stone seemed unsettled: here more pink, there more green, now reversed or taking on a purple cast. I couldn't tell whether the shifting was a property of the stone or only a result of the uncertain light.

"That is the tower of the long-lived one, the Singlar who taught us how to harvest tappa and use it to—"

Vroon was interrupted by a sharp snapping sound over our heads. Someone in one of the towers gave a horrific shriek. Then, the world fell apart.

Skull-cracking explosions thundered behind, above, and on either side of me. Jagged rents of searing white shattered earth and sky into a hundred fragments. The huge tower sheared down the middle, a blurred cascade of color pouring out of the ruin into the white brilliance of the gaping chasm that opened between its halves. Three . . . four horrified faces plummeted through the air and vanished into the white fire, shrill, agonized screams trailing behind them, as the stone shells cracked and toppled after.

"Majesty! Have care!" screeched Vroon, yanking me aside as I gawked at a snaking white line that ripped the black road threatening to pass right between my legs.

This was my dream all over again. Every streak of white that split the world stabbed a red-hot lance into the region just behind my eyes.

A rift appeared underneath a young man with a twisted shoulder who was running toward us down the road. Screeching, he reached out his arms toward me as he hung for just a moment over the fiery void. But I couldn't move. His cries filled my head long after he had dropped into the rift . . . or perhaps I was screaming, too, as I held on to my head to keep it from shattering right along with the world.

"Wake up. Wake up," I yelled, as I always did when my nightmares became unbearable. But this time, I didn't wake.

Vroon and Ob were cut off from me by another rent, and a powerful hand jerked me away from the brink of a yawning white chasm.

"Demons of the deep, watch yourself." Paulo.

Three more times he pulled me away from toppling towers or flaming cracks. Our dark island grew smaller. Shards of rock bounced around us like granite hailstones. Dust and ash swirled and stung my eyes. I had to end this. Even if a tower didn't crush us or a rift open up under our feet, if this world came apart . . . if I couldn't ease the pain in my head . . . I was going to lose control of myself. The Lords would find me . . . take me back.

In my dreams I could quench the fire, but here . . . I needed darkness. Not the empty, cold dark—the dread, unfeeling power of Lordship that I was trying so hard to keep shut away—but darkness soft and enveloping like dreamless sleep, like hiding your face in your father's cloak, like racing through a cool midnight on Jasyr's back. I knew only one place dark enough, even in a world as dark as the Breach.

Forcing my lungs to keep breathing, I sank to my wobbling knees, closed my eyes, and turned inward. As I knew it would be, the firestorm was inside me as well as outside, the network pattern of blazing white seared into the blank canvas of my mind. But here I could control it.

Blot out the light. Paint over the streaks. Follow their patterns and rub them away. Make the world gray again . . . dark and safe. Seal the cracks. Let the white fire burn as it will behind your dark walls. Pain is nothing to one who has come of age in Zhev'Na. It will go when the burning is done. When the need is ended. For now, just make it dark. . . .

"Stay away from him. Let him breathe." From some indescribable distance, I heard Paulo. "Curse it all, leave him be."

I opened my eyes. I was sprawled on the hard, damp earth, two sharp, pointed rocks digging holes in my back. Paulo stood at my side, his long arms spread out to either side of me, shielding me from a growing crowd of people creeping toward us, hands outstretched. Craning my neck, I saw that Vroon, Ob, and Zanore had their arms spread, too, the four of them making a complete circle about me.

"Cripes, I thought you'd never come out of it," said Paulo, grabbing a scrawny youth with mottled skin who had crept past his barricade and was tugging at my cloak.

"I wish Jasyr and Molly were here," I said, hoarsely, rolling to my side. "I could use a ride." I felt as dry as a September hay field, and I was shivering like aspen leaves.

"They'd be dead of fright," he said. "I was close enough to it." He used one of his long legs to prevent a bald woman from pulling off one of my boots. "It was your dream, then . . . come to life just like the rest of this?"

"Yes."

I pulled my cloak tight and climbed to my feet, surveying the destruction. About a quarter of the towers in this group were crumbled to dust or missing altogether. The road we'd traveled was erased, and, in fact, the whole landscape was in a jumble, like broken pottery hastily crammed back together. Ridges and ravines, pits and potholes and piles of rubble had appeared where there had been none before.

"Let's go," I said.

Paulo marshaled my protectors, and we set off again before the anxious, the curious, or the awestruck could prevent us. "No wonder you'd wake the house when you dreamed."

"It never lasted so long as this," I said, rubbing my

face. Cheeks and nose and lips felt numb. "What happened?"

"You stopped it. As soon as you knelt down, every crack headed straight for you. But before very long, they stopped coming. Closed up. The earthquake, whatever it was, quit like it never happened. *Everything* stopped. The whole cursed world went black as pitch, so's I thought we were all dead. But then the world started up again, or I woke up, or whatever. We just couldn't get you awake for a while. You lay here like you were dead. An hour it's been."

"I can't explain it."

The stars cast a soft greenish glow on the path. Zanore trotted ahead of us, Vroon and Ob to either side. After a time Paulo nudged me. "Have you noticed? Behind us."

I glanced backward. For as far as I could see into the gloom stretched a straggling crowd of the misshapen residents of the Breach. Only now that I looked did I notice the constant rustling noise of shuffling feet and excited whispering. The dim air was warm and dry, and the starlight illuminated a sea of oddity. They all caught their breath when I turned to see them better and sighed as one when I shrugged my shoulders and turned back to follow Zanore again. Unless I was sorely mistaken, they would have followed me had I walked off a cliff.

CHAPTER 12

With gestures and shouts, a horrified Vroon tried to shoo the ragtag mob back to their homes. "Begone, begone! The maintainers will see!" But the strange folk shook their heads and stood their ground, and when we started walking again they trailed after us.

"Punishment terrible do they risk for leaving their fastnesses," said Vroon. "The Guardian did not give them allowing to do so."

I certainly didn't know what to do about them. If they had such rules, it was up to them to obey them or take the consequences. "Tell us about the towers," I said. "These people live in them?"

The firestorm seemed to have left our three companions chastened and ready to answer at least a few of our questions. Each tower housed a single being—a Singlar, Vroon called them. The larger or more elaborate the tower, the longer and more successfully the Singlar had been *real*. Neither Vroon nor his friends could explain how the Singlars had come to be real, or what they were before they were real. If I understood him correctly— and that was never certain with Vroon—the towers were actually part of the land itself, shaped and nurtured by the thoughts and deeds as well as the hard labor of the residents. That is, they grew.

I looked at the towers differently after that. As we walked through the dark, wet, misshapen land, I wondered if I would observe them changing right in front of me. Of course I didn't see any such thing. I supposed it was like a person's growing. You never saw the change happening, not even in yourself. Only the result of it.

No Singlars had names, they told me. A name was the greatest gift one could receive, the culmination of the mysterious process of becoming *bounded*. But Singlars could not give each other names. I gathered that it would have been something like one loaf of baking bread telling another it was done.

The three admitted, reluctantly, that while traveling the world beyond the moon-door in search of the king, they had come across persons who looked like Singlars and acted like Singlars, and so they had brought them to the Bounded even though they had not been specifically commanded to do so. They promised to introduce me to some of these newcomers, once my business with the Guardian was done.

They didn't want to talk about the other things they'd done in my world. Vroon said they would do so only at my "royal command." As I had no intention of encouraging their foolish beliefs in the matter of royalty, I let the matter drop. "We'll talk more of these things another time."

"Quietness," said Ob, nodding sagely and smiling at the other two as he lumbered alongside us.

Vroon smiled and poked Ob's massive, humped shoulder in a brotherly way, and then leaned close to my shoulder. "Ob has always believed our king will be a quiet person, whose words are deep like his own. One person we found, a noisy, ever-talking one who claimed to be a king already, we took straight to the Guardian, lest perchance we be mistaken. But we always believed that the one we sought would be unmatched in wholeness. As you are."

Eventually, our strange procession arrived at another cluster of hundreds of towers and wound our way through them to a wide open space paved with stones. A *commard*, we would call such a place in Leire, suitable for markets or ceremonies or celebrations of thousands of people. Rows of braziers, flame-filled bowls of stone that stood on slender pillars taller than a man, lined three sides of the commard. And on the fourth side, beyond a set of wide steps, stood the largest tower yet, an elongated spiral of pale blue, imposing in its height

and sweep, though nowhere wider than five men standing shoulder to shoulder. The tower was the one I'd seen
in my dreams.

Our three guides gestured excitedly toward the place.
As we ascended the steps, the crowd behind me milled
about, people settling themselves on the flagstone paving
as if to watch a festival pageant.

"This is the place? The Guardian's place?" I said,
standing on the top step and gawking up at the soaring
tower somewhat stupidly. I felt foolish that I couldn't
find a gate to walk through or a door to knock on in
the smooth curved flank of the structure.

"No, Majesty, this is *your* place, formed by many Singlars working as the Source commanded us through the
voice of the Guardian. Of course, yes, the Guardian lives
here, keeping it for you." Vroon stood on tiptoe and
whispered in my ear. "He will expect your calling out
to him."

I whispered back. "How would I go about doing that
properly? I'd like to understand more about the
Guardian. . . ." And the towers and this grotesque land
and my dreams and a number of other things.

Vroon put a finger to his lips, and pondered the question for a moment. "Mmm. Quite . . . uh . . . unim-
pressed is he with your standing as the Bounded King.
He doubts. Willfully, he doubts. Until the king is among
us, only the Guardian speaks the Source. When the
Bounded King rules, the Guardian's ears will be closed,
and his voice will be very small. But, of course, he dearly
wants a name . . . not that giving it will friendly him
completely . . ."

"I think I understand," I said. "Guardian!"

"Who calls?" The words echoed from the stone walls
and steps as if the speaker were shouting from out of
a barrel.

"A traveler," I called out. Then, I bent down to
Vroon and spoke quietly again. "So do you happen to
know a name the Guardian likes?"

"Contemplating *Mynoplas* was he at my last hearing,"
whispered the dwarf, grinning. "A noble name it would
be for the Guardian."

"What seek you here?" echoed the booming voice from the tower.

"Answers. Shelter if the rains come again. Nothing more." The wind had picked up again and smelled ominously damp as it raced out of the muddy lanes and across the wide commard. I ran my fingers over the blue stone. The surface felt warmer than you might expect and was threaded with tiny veins of purple and silver.

"There are no answers here for you, traveler."

"But I understand that you have great knowledge, clear authority, high standing in this place. Surely many come to you for answers."

"Not you."

"Why not?"

"I await the One Who Makes Us Bounded. Go away."

Vroon's estimate of this fellow's state of mind seemed quite accurate. Exasperating.

"How will you know him—your king?"

"You will not trick me into giving you answers."

"Then I will take this noble name I carry in my head and spend it elsewhere. Good day, Guardian."

A very long, straight, and well-proportioned nose poked itself through the curved blue walls, quickly followed by a prominent brow, a pair of wide lips, and a jaw with a sharp, square edge, grizzled with wiry black hair. One cheekbone bulged grotesquely from the otherwise ordinary face of a man of middle years. His eyes protruded from under the dark brows in a rather belligerent fashion.

"Humph! I knew it. You are but a youth. Bounded perhaps . . . yes, clearly so . . . but a mere youth, ignorant of important matters. No surprise that you seek answers. A frivolous person. A child." His gaze skimmed over me from head to toe, then his protruding eyes settled on my own for a moment before looking quickly away. "Well . . . perhaps not a child. No. Perhaps not excessively frivolous. What name is it you carry?"

"The name *Mynoplas* dances on my tongue, but this good friend at my side could use such a sturdy name to good effect, so I might give it to him." I gripped Paulo's shoulder with one hand and gestured toward my Singlar companions with the other. I tried to act as if I saw heads protruding through stone walls every day. "Your messengers bear their new names nobly: Vroon, Zanore, and Ob. Come, friends, let's go."

"Wait! Singlars, has this traveler truly bestowed names?"

Vroon bowed to me first and then to the Guardian. "He is the One Who Makes Us Bounded, Guardian. I feel the wholeness of being Vroon. It is unmatched in glorious truthfulness that I tell you: I am Vroon. I am bounded."

A rippling murmur swept through the air behind us, surged over us like a whispering tide, then faded into a long sigh.

"Who else . . . ?" The Guardian poked a sinewy neck farther out of the tower and caught sight of the mass of beings sitting quiet and expectant on the command, their oddness and deformities almost hidden in the shifting pools of light cast by the flaming braziers. "Confound you, disobedient Singlars! Why have you come here? You trespass the law!"

He is the One . . . the king . . . the One Who Makes Us Bounded. He ate the white fire in the old one's cluster. He will save us from the storms. The flurry of words floated on top of the crowd.

I wanted to leave, but we needed shelter.

"No, he is not the king! He is but a boy. Return each to your fastness and wait as you have been commanded. Any who remain outside will be thrown from the Edge."

I turned and started down the steps.

"Wait, traveler! I shouldn't— You're not— But if you've given names— Well, come in, then, and I'll give you hearing. Then we'll see. Maintainers, herd these unruly Singlars back to where they belong. Whip them if they do not obey."

Two ranks of thuggish fellows, all wearing elaborately knotted rope belts about their tunics, emerged from the shadows and herded the rapidly dispersing crowd away from the command. The Guardian popped back into the tower, leaving no clue as to how to follow him. An icy blast of wind curled around the towers and peppered us with sleet.

Vroon grinned up at me, his single purple eye twinkling. "Well done, Majesty."

"Now, how do I get inside?" Even watching the Guardian's movements closely, I had missed the door.

"Think of yourself in," said Vroon. "More in than out. Enclosed, as to say."

Think of myself in . . . This world was too odd. But I gave it a try. I considered what might lie on the other side of the curved wall. Then I ran my fingers across it—the smooth blue surface felt like stone—and imagined how it would feel to walk through it. I considered the *thwop* sound I'd heard for the past hours. No luck.

"*In,*" said Vroon, quite seriously. "Not *through.* Not *beyond.*"

I imagined the curved walls and turned them inside out so they were curved around me instead of away from me. At the same time I brought to mind all the ideas of "in-ness" I could: being under the blankets in my bed, closing a door behind me, walls, clothes, gloves . . . And then I was in.

No storm raged inside the tower, no wind blew. I saw no dim, gray light or black-and-purple sky or green stars, and certainly I found nothing I might have expected to be inside the narrow, twisting spire of smooth blue stone.

Here I was, gawking again. The chamber in which I stood was large and round, centered by a gracefully spiraling stair that reached toward a simple vaulted dome of pale yellow, almost impossible to see as it was so high. At every one of at least ten levels the tower was ringed by a gallery of sculpted stone. Though this soaring space seemed larger than the outer dimension of the tower could accommodate, I could have accepted that my eyes had been fooled in the uncertain light of the land. But this rotunda was not the whole of the tower's interior.

Beyond a great open doorway to my left was a chamber that could have enclosed the great hall at Comigor with the ballroom thrown in for good measure, both of them strung together lengthwise and stretched into a chamber that was at least ten times longer than it was wide. To my right was a set of double doors of a size equal to the open doorway on my left, with no hint as to what might lie beyond them. Behind the stair, I glimpsed smaller doors, some open, some closed. The place was immense.

But I didn't dally to peek into the other rooms, for the Guardian had hurried into the grand hall on my left. I gaped at the vast chamber as I stepped through the doorway.

The vaulted ceilings reached to at least half the height of the rotunda, and the walls, hung with simple rectangles of plain dark green and red fabric, bowed slightly outward. Near the ceiling, far out of casual reach, iron rings held hundreds of burning candles, casting a glow of burnished bronze about the space. The floor was dark green slate, huge, square plates of it, smoothed and set in simple rows.

The room was sparely furnished. On a raised dais at its farthest end stood a simple high-backed chair of smooth light wood, set in front of a heavy gold drapery. A few padded benches stood along the walls, and a long wooden table sat in one corner. Nothing in the way of variety or the gaudy decoration you might see in a Leiran palace marred the simple structures or disrupted the mellow light. But, considering what I'd seen so far of this strange land, it was very fine. Quite pleasing, in fact.

The Guardian hurried toward the far end of the hall and the dais with an irregular, awkward gait. A plain, close-fitting shirt and breeches and a sleeveless gray robe revealed that he was strongly built, thick-chested and wide in the shoulders. His limbs might have been twisted of coarse steel wire. But his joints appeared to be all knobs and knots like his malformed cheek, as if he had three joints everywhere ordinary men had only one. Perhaps that's what made him so ungainly. Difficult to say how such deformity might affect a man's fighting abilities.

As I surveyed the room from the doorway, Paulo popped into view beside me, his eyes squeezed shut and

his arms thrown over his head. Vroon, Ob, and Zanore
were supporting him. "Am I here yet?"

I couldn't help but smile. "You got here."

"Cripes. This is the damnedest— I told 'em I wasn't
no good at imagining. They said they weren't allowed to
come in uninvited, but I said that if they didn't get me
in, I'd unbound their hides and bounce them so hard
their new names would fall right off again." He lowered
his arms and craned his neck about as I had done.
"Demons, how'd they squeeze all this inside a pile of
rock?"

"Come on. We need to talk to this fellow."

By the time we crossed the length of the hall, the
Guardian had taken his seat on the dais, not the simple,
fine-looking chair, but a backless stool just beside it.
Though his apparel seemed plain for such imposing surroundings, he had set a thin gold circlet on his unruly
black hair, and a heavy gold chain hung about his neck.
From the chain dangled a gold key, embedded with
rubies.

"Who is this person?" said the Guardian, glaring at
Paulo.

"My companion," I said as we approached the dais.
"And a defender of justice. He allows no one to harm
those he cares for." I failed to mention that I was no
longer included in that number, but the Guardian had
no way of knowing that.

"You have no need for protection here. He was not
invited to come into my fastness." The man surveyed
Paulo with flared nostrils and a curling lip.

"I'll judge my own needs, sir. And I understand that
this fastness is not yours, but was built for this king you
are expecting. Is that not the case?"

"I am the Guardian. I hold the King's Fastness until
he comes. You are not he."

"I make no claims. All I seek is to understand this
land and perhaps a place to stay while I hear the story."
And as this person seemed to be the only one with the
answers, I needed to stay here. Besides, I'd seen no one
else along the road who looked capable of providing
much in the way of hospitality.

"About the name you carry . . ."

"I couldn't possibly discuss names until my business is done. *Mynoplas* is so pleasant on the tongue and sits on the mind so solidly. I'll try not to forget it. My companion and I are very tired after our long journey."

"I suppose you wish refreshment." He didn't exactly grind his teeth, but he was very close to it.

"That would be very gracious. We've traveled a long way with little sustenance. And my new friends, your messengers"—the three of them were still bunched up at the door from the rotunda—"I'd like them taken care of in whatever way they'd prefer. They've done good service."

"If you were the king, you could command me, but you are not. *I* decide who shares the king's bounty, and it is not Singlar messengers. They must return to their fastnesses like any other of their kind."

I didn't know exactly what prompted the Guardian's cooperation. Perhaps the anticipation of the mysterious naming ritual, or possibly the secret fear that, despite his assertion and my own, I might truly be the awaited king. But for whatever reason, I was grudgingly accommodated. After commanding a serving man to bring food, he himself led me up the curved staircase to a modest bedchamber.

It might have been a small bedchamber at Comigor: a narrow box-bed piled with blankets, two small square tables and a slightly larger round one, one chair, and two backless stools. On one table stood a washing bowl, and under it a lidded urn that I took for a night jar. Several lamps hung high on the walls, but the room had no hearth. A single slot window opened to the cold and very wet wind, though you couldn't see out of it worth anything. The wood floor underneath it was damp and puddled.

"This appears quite comfortable, Guardian. My thanks. Now where will my companion sleep?"

"This person is not welcome in the King's Fastness. He must remain outside."

"On the contrary, sir . . ."

And we went through it all again. The Guardian argued that two guests were just too difficult to manage, that Paulo was dirty and clearly had no business in a king's house, and was so very . . . crude. I finally prevailed by saying that Paulo would share my room and my plate if the king's Guardian could provide no better, threatening to leave immediately if he didn't agree.

"You ought to keep your eye on his nasty little thoughts," Paulo said when we were finally left alone. He stuffed an extra blanket into the slot window, which left the room somewhat drier and warmer, while I pulled the chair and a stool close to the table. Two serving women in belted brown tunics and wide white ruffled collars had delivered a tureen of hot soup, a heaping basket of fragrant breads, and four flagons of wine. "I don't trust that one no farther than my boot. If I could get into his head like you can, I'd do it in a spit, and see what's filthy growin' in there."

He knew well enough that I'd do no such thing. I sat on the stool and started eating.

"I still can't figure out this place." Paulo had dropped into the chair and wolfed down three bowls of soup, four hunks of bread, and most of a flagon of wine before I could blink. "If this is the Breach, then why didn't we see all this when we got dragged through four years ago? Why don't the Prince know anything of it?"

"Maybe he does," I said, but not really believing it. "He told my mother that the Bridge was getting more difficult to cross. That was one reason he couldn't come to Verdillon more often. He wouldn't have lied to her. So, maybe this is a different part or a new part."

"Do you think you'll get a straight answer out of this fellow?"

I refilled my stoneware cup with the sweet wine. "Probably not. The Source—whatever it is—sounds more promising."

"I'll say this: They got good food."

And so they did. By the time we'd emptied the dishes, I realized the wine was far more potent than I was accustomed to. I was about to roll off the backless stool.

"I should stand first watch," I said, trying to force the

words out past a tongue that seemed three times thicker than usual. "I slept last . . . this morning . . . whenever that was we arrived."

"Looks to me like they got no morning here. And it looks like you got no head for strong spirits, being a nub as you are, so I'd recommend you take the bed and let a man as can keep two eyes open at once do the watching."

I never liked it when Paulo reminded me he was full-grown and I wasn't yet, but I was in no condition to argue. Somehow I made it to the bed, and I didn't know anything else until a clearly exhausted Paulo dragged me out of a dreamless sleep. "Come on. Shake yourself up. I got to take a nap, so's you've got to get up."

"Don't want to," I mumbled. "Best night I've had in forever."

"Look, I've caught the devil in here once already, hanging over your bed, and I showed him out with a good look at my knife. He gave me a, 'Oh, pardon me. Just makin' sure everything's cozy,' and I've heard him outside the door three more times. But now I'm swiped. You got to get up."

The room was dark, and the bed was comfortable, but Paulo's words had me awake and alert instantly. "The Guardian was in here?"

"Like I said. The lamps went out all of themselves, right after you was asleep. Wasn't an hour till he poked himself through the door real quiet. He about chewed his teeth when he found me awake. It's been three . . . four hours."

"Go on to sleep. I'm all right now. I'll watch."

He was already asleep as he curled up on the floor. He didn't stir as I dragged him up onto the bed. He wouldn't care one way or the other, but it made it less tempting for me to get back under the blankets. I wrapped a blanket around my shoulders and sat on the floor. Only once did I hear soft footsteps beyond the door. I asked quietly who was there and got no answer.

A few hours later the lamps mysteriously lit themselves, and a polite serving man summoned us to breakfast.

*   *   *

The Guardian was drinking from a silver cup when we were taken to him. I told Paulo not to mention the midnight visits. We would be as closemouthed as our host was. Leave him guessing and on edge.

"Greetings, traveler," he said to me, spreading his wide lips over yellowed teeth that spoiled his appearance far more than his bulging cheek. "I look forward to completing our business, so that you—and this other person— can be on your way to wherever you're going."

"I'm also looking forward to concluding our business," I said. "But it may take several days."

His smile withered from the inside out. "We'll see about that."

I bowed to him with my palms extended, as was the Dar'Nethi custom in greeting, but he averted his eyes and motioned a servant to seat us.

Our plates were already heaped with a selection of foods, and the cups were brimming with something so deliciously fragrant that it cleared your head to inhale the steam. His expression near ecstasy, Paulo speared a chunk of sausage with his knife, but I laid my hand on his arm and pushed the plate away. "We'll choose our food for ourselves."

Paulo's disappointment was short-lived, for a dozen or more platters with a fine array of breads and meats and fruit sat in the middle of the table alongside several steaming silver pots. We served ourselves from the generous spread, and Paulo filled new cups.

I was dreadfully thirsty and gulped the hot liquid— wine or cider of some kind—much too fast. The pungent stuff shot straight through my head, so that I came near choking. Just when I was trying to be dignified.

Paulo grinned and was more careful. The Guardian didn't seem to notice my discomfiture.

The man made no pretense of conversation. Every time I addressed him he began shouting orders at the servants, men and women of all manner of odd appearance who scurried about without speaking. I soon gave it up.

Before Paulo and I were half done, the Guardian popped out of his chair. "I have duties to attend," he

said. "My morning audience awaits. We will have to
commence our talk afterward. Our king's business cannot wait on a stranger's idle curiosity."

"If the king happened to be watching, I'd wager he'd
be pleased to see his business being taken care of," said
Paulo to me in a whisper that was far too loud, while
savoring the last bites of an anvil-sized slice of ham.
"But then, too, he might think his Guardian was enjoying it bit too much."

The Guardian hissed and worked his mouth until spit
oozed out of it. As he swirled his robe and stomped
away, he bumped into a small table, sending it topsy-
turvy across the room, and he elbowed two unwary servants so that they juggled their stacks of dirty dishes like
performers at a jongler fair. I tried to stay properly
sober. But Paulo wheezed and burst out laughing, and I
soon joined in. We laughed until we almost choked, and
I had no doubt the Guardian could hear us, no matter
where he'd gone.

A foolish lapse, to laugh at a man who felt precarious
in his high position. I hoped we wouldn't regret it.

When we'd eaten so much that we rolled our eyes at
the sight of another sausage, we asked the servants to show
us to the Guardian's audience hall. They bowed silently
and showed us to the long room we'd seen the day before.
It was jammed with people of every possible shape and
size. Through the middle of the crowd stretched a single
long queue—petitioners, it seemed. The Guardian, arrayed
in his gray robe and gold circlet, sat on his stool beside
the chair in front of the gold hanging.

I almost felt sorry for having annoyed the Guardian
so sorely, as he spent the entire morning snapping at
everyone who appeared before him. The petitioners
were asking the Guardian to intercede with the Source
for help in re-creating towers destroyed in the firestorm,
in resolving disputes regarding property or insults, or in
redressing their grievances about services unperformed
or agreements broken. The session could have been the
duke's assizes at Comigor but for the oddly shaped petitioners and the bizarre circumstances of their business.

A one-legged man spoke of a well of stone chips,

drained dry by a neighboring fastness. A woman with three snakelike fingers on each hand complained that a newly arrived Singlar was harvesting more of something called tappa from her diggings than was his right. She wanted him to be starved for some span of time until the difference was made up.

People gasped and shrank backward when four men hauled in a monstrous hairy creature, tied with sturdy ropes and rags to muzzle it. The catlike beast's matted hair and clawed hands were caked with blood, and it fought wildly to get free. I couldn't understand why they had brought the animal indoors instead of caging it while they did their business.

"This creature has raged through the Gray Fastnesses for a manylight, Guardian," said one of the four when the Guardian gave the group permission to begin. "It destroys weak fastnesses and rips up tappa, but does not eat or use it. Now matters have worsened. One Singlar was dead a twolight since, and another in the light just past. We found this beast . . . eating . . . the dead one. Our asking is to be allowed to slay the murdering creature before it eats us all."

The beast growled and strained against its bonds.

"The Source has said Singlars must not kill creatures with minds," said the Guardian, nodding. "But clearly a beast that eats a Singlar is mindless. Your petition is granted."

Two Singlars held the writhing animal, while two of them forced back its grotesque head and bared its throat. But its struggles dislodged the binding across its mouth.

"I ate no Singlar!" cried the beast, snarling. "My denmates will avenge this lie. And no Singlar in the Gray Fastnesses will live a tenlight more. They—"

But the creature, whether monstrous man or intelligent beast, did not finish his threat. One of his captors plunged a sharpened stick into his throat. As they dragged the carcass out of the hall, the blood that streaked the slate floor appeared quite red and ordinary.

"This place is the damnedest . . ." said Paulo.

"It's part of the Breach," I said. "All manner of strange creatures could exist here."

The next petitioners were two Singlars together: one a dark-haired girl of perhaps my age, whose face on one side was fairly pretty, though the other side was horribly disfigured, and the other a man about Paulo's age. The fellow looked very odd for this place in that he had no visible deformity. But when he began to speak, he could scarcely get out a whole word for his stuttering. He asked permission for the girl and himself to share a single fastness, a matter that didn't seem too mysterious to me, but clearly shocked the Guardian and the crowd of other petitioners.

"We . . . we've feelings to . . . to be t . . . t . . . together," said the young man. "But our headman says no Singlar has done so . . . ever . . . and w . . . w . . . we must make asking."

"Feelings? Together?" The Guardian gaped like a particularly stupid fish and then exploded. "Inconceivable! Are we to throw out all our customs for Singlars' *feelings?* How dare you propose such a thing? Maintainers! Take this villain and flog him ten. The female is to be taken to the Edge to see where she is headed if this insolence persists. Leave her there to make her own way back to her fastness. If these two speak even a single word to each other ever again, they are to be put over the Edge."

Gasps rose from some observers. Others nodded their heads. The girl dropped her hands to her sides and wept silently as the youth was dragged away. But as he wrestled with the two thuggish maintainers who grabbed his arms, he cried out after her. "Denya!"

The crowd fell into stunned silence.

"Flog him fifty!" roared the Guardian, shooting out of his chair like a bird startled from its roost. "And bind him outside his fastness for a twelvelight. He must be an example. To throw him over the Edge would take his crime from our eyes. So is the judgment of the King's Guardian." He left the dais, sweeping through the gold fabric hanging behind it.

Two more of the maintainers, easily identified by the knotted rope belts about their tunics, led the sobbing girl away. The crowd broke up and straggled out of the room, murmuring in shock. *A name! He's named her! A portent . . . evil begets evil . . . inconceivable . . . should be thrown from the Edge . . . will unbound us all . . .*

"Demons!" said Paulo as we walked toward the curtain. "Don't leave me here. If a fancy for a lady gets you ten lashes and calling her by name fifty . . ."

We stood unobtrusively in a corner, watching the crowd of Singlars file out of the audience hall and through the rotunda. I glanced at Paulo, wondering if his thoughts had wandered the same path as mine. Though most Leiran commoners were wed by eighteen, Paulo's comments about the village girls near Verdillon had always concluded with an avowal that none of them could compare to some particular girl he had met in Avonar before he went to Zhev'Na. I guessed that a Dar'Nethi family wasn't likely to welcome Paulo's attention any more than the Guardian and his folk welcomed their two rebels.

When the hall was almost empty, I bade Paulo wait in the audience hall and grabbed the sleeve of one of the house servants who was hurrying past, licking his fingers and brushing crumbs and hair from his white ruffled collar. "Please take me to the Guardian. He agreed to meet with me when his audience session was over."

Without a word, the servant bowed and led me, not through the gold curtain, but around through the passageway to a proper door—perhaps so I could see the two maintainers who stood beside the door holding quite normally efficient-looking swords and spears. The servant knocked, stepped inside at a growling summons, and, moments later, held the door open for me to enter.

The small room, furnished with a wide table, several chairs, and a shelf with cups and porcelain jars on it, was tucked away in an alcove behind the gold curtain. A retiring room, a Leiran noble would have called such a retreat adjacent to his audience hall. The Guardian sat behind the large table, hammering his fingers on the polished wood top, fuming. The morning's events had clearly unsettled him.

When the servant closed the door behind me, the Guardian jerked his head toward one of the chairs, and then popped up and strode around the room, fingering the ruby-studded key about his neck. On every circuit his rapid pace billowed the heavy gold curtain that separated him from the audience hall. "Singlars . . . sharing a fastness . . . male and female . . . Disgusting! And names! I must report this to the Source . . . seek counsel to stop such perfidy. Fifty lashes were not enough. Should have been a hundred. Two hundred."

"Your customs here are very different from those of other lands," I said, folding my hands in my lap. The chair and its lumpy cushions were uncomfortable, but I tried not to shift or fidget.

"Question our customs, and I'll show you and your insolent companion the same punishment as that wicked Singlar! We are satisfied with our ways, and you'll not come here and muddle them. It doesn't matter who you are or what you can do, or what any empty-headed Singlar thinks you are. *I* make the rules for the Bounded!" His distress seemed to have lowered his guard on his tongue.

"Remember, Guardian, all I want is answers." Well, I also wanted to meet this Source, whoever or whatever it was, but this didn't seem the time to mention the fact.

Abruptly, he stopped his pacing, returned to his chair, and began our interview as if nothing had happened. I had come to this meeting alone, not wanting his antipathy for Paulo to make an accommodation impossible. Paulo should be just beyond the curtain, close enough to come if I called, though I wasn't sure how well he could hear.

"What answers do you seek, traveler? I have many responsibilities. The dwarf and his companions have clearly disrupted your life with their mistaken opinions. They will be disciplined for it, but not too severely, due to your kind interest in their welfare." He smiled, but he could have cracked nuts in his jaw. "I would send you on your way as soon as possible with our apologies and good wishes."

I played it just as he did. Answers were the important thing. "I appreciate your time and patience, Guardian. So, tell me, what is this land? Where do you and the

other people come from, and why do you seek your king
in my dreams? That should do to start."

He sat back in his chair, his spine straight, his shoulders rigid. "This land is, of course, the Bounded. We
have lived here always, except for the few persons that
our overeager seekers have brought us from other
bounded worlds. The Source has said that our king
would come from another bounded world and would discover us in his dreams, but that he might be lost upon
his way. Therefore I was commanded to choose seekers
to go to certain places and be visible to the dreamer, so
perhaps to lure him here, and then I was to send the
seekers through the moon-door to find him. And so I
have done. I know nothing of their dealings with you.
Many many persons dream of the Bounded, I am sure.
Beyond that, we are as we are. It is satisfactory."

"And the Unbounded . . . what is that?" If there was
a Bounded, its opposite must also exist.

He shifted a bit, and a shadow touched his eyes and
his face. "It is beyond the Edge. It is nothing. Terrible.
Nothing."

He was afraid. His fear, deep and profound, shaped
his thoughts and deeds. To know more of that fear could
be a useful thing. "Was the Bounded at one time the
Unbounded?"

He pursed his thick lips and clasped his hands together
tightly on his fine table, considering his answer as if my
question were not rampant nonsense. "Some say it. I
don't hold with it. I say we are as we are. I certainly
have no memory of such a time."

"Why is your king to lead you to victory over all
bounded worlds?"

At this, the Guardian drew himself up even tighter
and glared at me. "The dwarf told you this?"

"I heard it said."

"He should not have said it. The dwarf and those like
him are too eager. You are *not* the king. You are *not*
to know our business."

"But now I do, so you may as well explain."

He considered for so long a while that I was sure he
would refuse. But after a time he rose and circled the

room again, brushing invisible specks of dust from the plain tables and chairs set about the room. "You have seen a firestorm?"

"Yes."

"I suppose they are quite common outside the Bounded." The slightest hint of a question in this statement.

"No. Not common."

"But you know of them. The Singlars claim you caused one to stop, so you must understand their nature."

"That was only a coincidence. In fact, I was going to ask you about them. What are they? How often do they occur?"

"Humph. They come from the same place as you, so your question is clearly foolish and deceitful. The storms tell us that those outside the Bounded—maybe you and your uncivil companion—do not care about our survival. The Source prophesies that our king will not allow this destruction to continue, and that he will shape the destiny of all bounded worlds. We do not know how that is to occur. Because of the firestorms, some believe it will be a great violence, and thus our king will be victorious in this conflict."

"And what do you think?"

He stopped behind his table, directly in front of me, and drew up to his full height. "I think only as the Source commands me. But I have not yet seen our king. So I encourage our people to nurture their fastnesses and wait."

"Does the Source know the nature of the storms?"

"The Source knows all."

"Can you take me to the Source?"

"Certainly not!" He ground his thick, knobbed fingers into the edge of the table. "Only the Guardian and the king may visit the Source. I think you've asked quite enough questions, traveler. I think you should take your leave of the Bounded." He pointed to the door.

The Guardian's fear washed over me like a heavy sea lapping at the sides of a boat. Frightened men were always more dangerous than they might appear, so I didn't think it wise to push him further. I hadn't forgotten the two beefy maintainers outside the door.

I stood up to go and bowed respectfully. "I am not your king, Guardian. I have no desire to be a king of anything. I just want to understand about my dreams, and about your world, and how they are related. Nothing more. And so I present you with this proposition. Allow me to stay here for a while. Tell the Source of me and see if it is willing to hear my questions. If not, I promise to go peacefully, leaving you my sincere thanks. And in either case—answers or none—I will grant you the name you desire."

"You make no claim?" Incredulity dripped from his tongue.

"No claim. I don't want to rule anyone. Ever. I'm not suited to it. And I have no wish to make my home in the Bounded."

He dropped into his chair and drummed his fingers while he looked at me. When he made his decision, he leaned forward. "And if I tell you the Source refuses to answer . . ."

". . . I will present you the name Mynoplas, and then I'll go. Do we have a bargain?"

"For now you may stay. Until I consult the Source."

He dearly wanted a name, for he was still very much afraid of me.

CHAPTER 13

It is a strange fact of war and politics that fortunate circumstances can condemn the best of strategies to ruin. Another of Lord Parven's maxims. I wasn't sure that I had actually stopped the firestorm on my first day in the Bounded, only that I had kept myself intact, but it happened that no more of them struck in the days following. And because this astonishing and welcome eventuality was associated with my arrival, the people of the Bounded came to believe I was their king.

Whenever I explored their city, they bowed or cheered as I passed. When I attended the Guardian's daily audiences, the petitioners knelt before me and begged my indulgence or my hearing. They would not attend to the Guardian, even when I insisted they do so. I started sitting in the retiring room behind the gold curtain to listen discreetly, but it only took them two days to find me and come after me again.

And, of course, all this made my bargain with the Guardian go sour very quickly. At first he only grumbled and snarled at me as we sat at meals. Eventually I decided it was politic to stay away from his audience sessions, which annoyed me, as I was learning a great deal about life in the Bounded from listening to its troubles. But even that did not pacify him, and whenever I asked if he had yet spoken to the Source, he turned red and tightened his lips. "The Source has said nothing of you. No answers to your queries have been spoken." Then he clamped his mouth shut. But he didn't send me away.

I was no less irritated than he, because seven days had passed, and I'd learned nothing of real importance. I was worried about my mother and worried about what other untoward events my father might be blaming me for. But nothing could be done about either concern, and I didn't know of anyplace else to look for the truth. So we stayed and tried to learn what we could.

Though the Guardian disapproved of our wandering, Paulo and I spent our days poking about the Blue Tower, also called the King's Fastness, and the Tower City, trying to discover how the place worked. Everyone in the Bounded seemed to be holding his breath, waiting: waiting for the mythical king, waiting for the next firestorm, waiting for someone to come and give all of them names. Life was dreadfully dull.

The Blue Tower itself revealed little. The lamps lit and darkened themselves in a rhythm quite familiar to those who'd lived in sunlit worlds. You could control them with your fingers, too, in the way of ordinary lamplight. A few other fastnesses in the Bounded had slot windows and lamps like these, and the Singlars watched the lights in those towers to measure their days, passing the information from tower to tower. Besides his maintainers, the Guardian had an army of servants at his beck, a hundred quiet, oddly shaped men and women who wore ruffled collars over the same brown tunics as the other Singlars wore. Neither servants nor Guardian seemed to understand why the lamps behaved in the way they did. It was only one of a thousand things they didn't know.

Beyond the tasks of serving or protecting the Guardian, the servants in the Blue Tower could tell me nothing of other people's occupations. The Guardian's food was grown or raised, fabric was woven and thread was spun, but no one could say who did those things or where. Meat and flour, oil, fruit, fabric, pottery, and all types of goods arrived in the storerooms of the Blue Tower, seemingly without the interference of servants or laborers, and were used as the Guardian desired.

The Singlars had no such luxuries. Their diet consisted entirely of the tappa root, a white vegetable that looked something like a turnip and tasted worse. They boiled it, baked it, or fried it in oil squeezed from its stem. They dried and ground it for flour and baked it into a flat, slightly sweetish bread. They made their clothing from the woven fibers of the tappa and the other stunted shrubs that grew in the dim light, and they made a thin bitter ale by fermenting the tough skin of the tappa root along with its shredded gray leaves. We saw little evidence of commerce or trade, only rudimentary bartering.

Most of our information we gleaned from observation, for the Singlars were too much in awe of me to speak, and I didn't know how to make them. Frustrated, I asked some of the Singlars where I could find Vroon and his friends. Everyone knew the three Singlars who had been granted names, and they pointed us toward three towers not far from the Blue Tower. One was tall, straight, and gleamed silver in the starlight. One was shaped like a stepped pyramid of ruddy sandstone, and one, Vroon's, curved upward from a wide base to a crown-like peak.

Vroon, Ob, and Zanore were delighted to accompany us in our explorations, despite the Guardian's having specifically forbidden them to have contact with me. They said that since I was certainly the king, all would be made right eventually. Every morning after the lamps came up, the three waited for Paulo and me in a lane near the Blue Tower and guided us about the confusing countryside.

"Tell me, Zanore," I said, "does anyone know the shape of the Bounded or make maps or charts? Perhaps if we could see a map, we could get some idea of where to go." The morning was dismal and rainy—morning in name only, as it was still and always night in the Bounded. The constant dark and the wild, fickle weather made it difficult to estimate the size and shape of the land or even to decide if we had been in some particular place before.

After a quick consultation with the other two, Zanore nodded and led us through the muddy lanes to a beehive-shaped fastness. He entered and, after a few moments, poked his head out. "This Singlar will be honored to have you come into his fastness."

Inside was a single round room, cluttered with stacks

of flat stones and wood scraps, some of the stacks taller than my knees. A sputtering wall torch made from damp branches provided smoky yellow light, but revealed no evidence of mapmaking. The Singlar pressed his over-large head to the stone floor.

"Thank you for allowing us to come in," I said, tilting my head in an attempt to see his face. I'd found no easy way to address people whose heads were on the floor. "I'll do my best to see you reap no punishment for it. I would like to know about the Bounded . . . its shape and size. I understand you have made some kind of a chart. . . ."

He didn't move or answer, except to quiver a bit.

"Are you sure he doesn't mind us being here?" I whispered to Zanore, who had come inside with me. Paulo and the others waited outside, alert for any maintainers taking an interest.

Zanore pointed his bony black finger around the room and shrugged his shoulders.

At my left hand stood a stack of flat stones, one of the fifty or more such stacks that crowded the little room. The one on the top had lines scribed into it, and when I picked it up to examine it, I saw that the one underneath had a similar pattern, but not quite identical. And the ones below, the same. A quick survey evidenced that every scrap of wood and stone in the stacks had a sketch on it.

"This room . . . this fastness . . . the whole thing is your map," I said, as the clutter suddenly took on new meaning. "Each stack placed in relation to the others. Some stacks tall, some short. Each layer of a stack a new version of that particular area or feature."

The big-headed Singlar peeped up and grinned.

"Please, would you show me? It's marvelous."

Scarcely enough room to walk remained between the tall stacks in the middle, and the sketches on these pieces were quite detailed. Some wider gaps existed between the stacks at the outer margins, and those stacks were very small.

"Out here must be the Edge. Is that right? But I can't tell which direction is which."

"The mark on the wall represents the entry of the King's Fastness," came a whisper from the floor. "That is Primary."

The mark was an arrow smudged on the stone wall with a charred stick. I nodded at the man who had now lifted his head slightly. "Come, please, show me the rest," I said.

I learned a great deal that morning. Where a mapmaker in Leire might labor for three years on a new version of his map, the mapmaker of the Bounded had to create a new one every day, or perhaps it would be more accurate to say he was never able to finish one map. The place called the Edge was truly the edge of their known world, and it moved outward with every change of the light—every day. The firestorms kept him even busier, for while the Edge always moved outward, changing only the dimensions of his works, the firestorms wiped out clusters of towers, and shifted or erased landmarks, whether roads, ridges, or even mountains. He collected his information from Singlars who moved around in search of tappa or wood or to build new towers and from those who traveled in from the Edge.

"Would you . . . could you . . . possibly tell me of the places you've traveled in the Bounded, mighty one?" he asked, once he'd taken me on a tour of his current work. "Zanore"—his soft voice caressed my guide's name with wonder—"has a natural ability to find his way, but he lacks greatly at describing what he has seen. But he says . . . all say . . . that *you* see much. If you would honor me . . ."

It seemed only fair to tell him what I could. He grew comfortable with me very quickly then, peppering me with questions about where we'd been and what we'd seen, sketching my descriptions with charred sticks on more bits and pieces that he could transfer to his map, exulting whenever he could lay a new chip on the floor to start a new stack in between two others. The Bounded was much larger than I'd imagined, home to thousands of beings in hundreds of tower clusters, scattered across the landscape. Two hours we spent examining his torchlit stacks.

"I'd like to repay you for your time," I said, as I stood by the silvery trace that marked his door. Easy to guess what payment the mapmaker would want. Though the Guardian had specifically forbidden me to grant any more names, the mapmaker had already violated the law by allowing me into his fastness, and I certainly hadn't anything more useful to give him. "A man named Corionus was the most famous mapmaker in my home country. My grandfather collected his maps. Would you accept the name *Corionus* in thanks for your help?"

I held his arm so he couldn't put his head on the floor again. I already felt like I was cheating him.

"What next, great Master?" said Vroon, after Zanore and I rejoined the others and told them about the map. "Shall I show you the tappa planting at the Gray Towers?"

"No," I said. "Take us to the Edge. I'd like to see it for myself."

Before the horrified dwarf could answer, a huge, leathery hand fell on my shoulder, almost pressing me to the ground. "No." Ob didn't need to say it twice. As with all of his rare words, he communicated a great deal more than the simple meaning of the word.

"So what makes it so dangerous to walk there, even just to take a look?"

Before answering my question, Vroon furiously herded us away from the nearby towers into open country. "Before companioning with me, Ob wandered close to the Edge," he said, more relaxed as we walked down the road toward the Tower City. "For a manylight he watched the land writhe and groan as it grows and pushes the Edge. Not overfearing is Ob, and he came to no harm. But the risk is true—to fall or be crushed or be burned by spewing vapors—as long as the Bounded is incomplete. Too risky for the king."

"We'll be careful, then. I want to see it." I did not intend to be in the Bounded whenever it was finished with its growing.

Paulo, the three Singlars, and I set out early the next day, heading away from the Tower City in the direction Corionus had named Primary, approximately opposite

the moon-door—the passage to Valleor. The stacks of
stone and wood said it didn't actually matter a whit
which way we went, as the Edge was about the same
distance from the City in every direction. But it made
sense to see something new along the way.

Unfortunately, for half the day a steady, cold rain kept
us from seeing anything more than twenty paces from
the track, only the flat ghostly outlines telling us when
we passed a cluster of towers. After six or eight soggy
hours of walking, Zanore stopped at the top of a small
rise and peered steadily into the gloom ahead before
directing us to the left, in the first obvious deviation
from our straight-line course. Zanore's amber eyes must
have seen more ahead than human ones could. Neither
Paulo nor I could see anything that wasn't gray or wet
or immediately under our feet, and thus no reason to
turn aside.

"Danger to pass through here," said Zanore, when I
asked him why we were going out of our way. "Strange
tales have I heard of this place. Best stay away."

"What kind of tales?"

The three conferred among themselves and couldn't
come up with anything but the words *hurtful* and
troubled.

"If you've no better explanation than that, we'll go
straight," I said. "I want to get to the Edge today, and
I don't think we'll want to spend the night there. I won't
let anything happen to us." Except for the firestorms,
I'd seen nothing of the Bounded or its inhabitants that
we couldn't deal with. I felt safer here than at Verdillon.

The three were afraid to argue, so with many sighs
and muttering and shaking of heads, they led us on the
downward path and into a wide, rocky gully, where we
found ourselves ankle-deep in mud. We soon glimpsed
a cluster of perhaps fifty or sixty dreary fastnesses, low,
crude things of rocks and mud, none better than the
others.

The Singlars who stepped out of the rock piles were
mostly naked, all of them thinner than Zanore. If they'd
not smiled cheerfully and bowed at our passing, I might
have thought them standing corpses from some long-

finished battle. One of the Singlars stepped forward with
his hands raised over his head and spread wide apart—
in greeting it appeared—offering the same welcome
shown me by all the Singlars, without the speechless
groveling that usually accompanied it.

"Greetings, weary traveler. Such happiness you bring
to our valley." The spokesman was a tall, emaciated man
with dark skin and a twisted back that left one shoulder
higher than the other. He wore nothing but a tattered
loin wrapping, yet his shaggy black hair was clean and
tied back with a piece of vine, and his air of dignity
would not have been out of place in any fine house. His
protruding bones vibrated with the rumbling of his voice.
"Too rare is our delight in seeing new faces. Will you
stop for a while?"

"No, no, no, no," whispered Vroon, pawing at my
arm. "We travel in haste. No stoppings."

A smile radiated like sunlight from the man's huge,
pale eyes. "To hear a word from the world beyond our
fastness would be a joy unmatched. So empty is our
experience of travelers; I must think that you are someone of importance, someone who has much to share with
us. If we could persuade you to share a dry seat, a mor-
sel, and a sip, you might, in that brief time, provide us
a feasting of words to last until the Bounded grows
ancient."

There was no danger here. I could snap this man like
a twig.

"Of course, we'll stay," I said, dismissing Vroon's urgent gesturing without a second thought. I'd not heard
a Singlar so well-spoken, nor so cheerful and mannerly
in his greeting. Besides, I was ravenously hungry, and
even the prospect of a Singlar's unvarying menu of tappa
root had my stomach growling.

The man clapped his hands in delight. "My fastness
awaits. If your companions wish to come, we will be
crowded, but happy. Others will bring sustenance for
them."

I glanced at Vroon and he shook his head. "Out here
we'll stay waiting, if you insist on going inside, my—"

"I insist." I interrupted him before he could come

out with some honorific that might make my host less
at ease.

Paulo came inside with me, but Ob, Vroon, and Zanore stubbornly remained standing in the rain.

The Singlar's dim and smoky shelter was the most
barren I had seen, its rock-and-mud walls unrelieved by
any decoration, its furnishings no more than two smooth
rocks beside a tiny fire pit scraped in the center of the
dirt floor. A small heap of dark, spongy squares sat to
one side, their purpose revealed when the tall man set
one in the fire pit and carefully blew a small ember to
life underneath it. In northern Valleor, where wood was
scarce, the villagers used such material cut from the
ground to make their fires. The fire seemed hardly
enough to warm the Singlar, much less dry out two such
soggy guests.

"Tell us of the wide world, traveler," said the man,
easing his bent frame onto the ground across the fire
from us. "We hunger to know of it."

"You surely know more than I," I said. "I'm new to
your land and few speak as freely as you to teach me
of it."

He squinted pleasantly. "Hmmm . . . you've not the
look of a new-birthed Singlar who wanders from the
Edge. You have been real longer than any I've known,
longer than any who hold fastness here. I see it in your
bearing. I hear it in your words. You come from the
center of the wide world to which we send the new-
birthed on their way, never to see them return. Mayhap
even farther than that."

"Perhaps you could tell me of your life here and what
you know of the wide world, then I can tell you whatever new I can."

The man laughed and flushed a little. "I've given these
Singlars so many guesses, told so many stories of what
I imagine or surmise, I can hardly say what is fact and
what is only my foolishness. You must catch me up
where I err."

While he emptied a small lump of tappa root from a
woven bag, sliced it thin with a stone knife, and fried it
in a chipped clay pot over his little fire, he told me of

storms that lashed their valley, and earthquakes and lightnings from the Edge. His villagers welcomed the occasional wanderer who struggled in from the Edge naked and bewildered, and they tried to calm those who arrived frightened and ferocious. Often they had to fight off raving man-beasts who roamed the wilds and were known to kill Singlars and eat them. The Guardian had forbidden the rift dwellers to leave their valley, but they were determined to make the best of it until the king came to the Bounded to change everything.

His stories, though interesting and dramatic, fit with what I knew already. It was only when I asked him about his knowledge and theories of the "wide world" that I heard anything extraordinary.

"Have you not wondered about the Bounded?" he asked, leaning toward me, his eyes alight. "I sit before my fastness and watch the passing of the storms and feel the earth shaking under my feet; I see the new-birthed Singlars open their eyes to the world, and my head will not stop wondering."

"And what have you concluded?"

The man almost whispered his answer, as if these wonders of his reason were too much to express. "Our land is *alive*. We feel the beating of her heart, and we experience the pain of her growth. She is bent in her aspect as are we, and it pains her as do our own misshapen parts. Our life here is hard. But I tell my people that the Bounded is only just learning of Singlars, and that we are hidden here in our valley where she cannot see us as yet. When she learns of our hardships, she will share her abundance and shepherd us through the storms."

As he talked of his strange theories, I ate his fried tappa as if I'd not eaten in a week. I would have eaten five times as much if it had been available. Paulo left his share to me, saying it was clear I was far hungrier than he, and our host shook his head when I indicated he should take his own portion.

"What of the firestorms?" I said, picking the last crumbs from my hand and wiping my fingers on my breeches. "Do you have an idea about those?"

"I tell the Singlars that there must be a guardian beyond our lands who flogs the Bounded as our Guardian flogs Singlars, even if they do not understand their offense. We must help our land endure her punishment, just as we must ourselves endure."

His gentle philosophy was sorely at odds with my view of the Guardian. I almost hated to tell the man that the only news of his "wide world" that I had to report was the judgments and activities of an iron-fisted despot. But the man listened so intently to my own discourse that I guessed he could have repeated my words more exactly than I could have re-created them. I mentioned nothing of the Singlars' beliefs about me.

"And the Guardian believes our king will come from outside the Bounded?" he asked, his face hungry for my tale.

"It seems so. He sends searchers into lands beyond the Bounded—other worlds—to seek him out."

The man wrinkled his brow, his first sign of disagreement. "No, no, that's wrong! The king must be *of* the Bounded. He will speak for her, and mold her, and ease her suffering. How could he be from outside?"

"I agree with you," I said. "It makes no sense."

After we spent a few moments quietly pondering these mysteries, I took my leave, thanking him for his hospitality.

Outside the smoky hovel, the rain had eased into a warm drizzle. Pink sheet lightning flickered constantly overhead, illuminating the dismal settlement. Two Singlars, one a rheumy-eyed young woman wearing a sack-like covering, and the other a naked man with one foot like a tree stump, stood to one side waiting patiently for my host. Each of them carried a woven bag, just like the one from which my host had taken his tappa root.

"Abide a moment and I will serve you," my host said to them. Then to me, "I must leave off my prattling and give these two their portion of tappa. They hunger much. Joyfully, I may share your words to fill out their stores."

"Do you keep a common store of tappa then?" I asked. "I've not seen that custom among other Singlars."

"It serves us best. Tappa grows only in one small part

of our valley." Not hard to understand, considering the steep, rocky walls, and the river of mud that comprised the valley floor. "To prevent disputes and to share equitably, we decided long ago to appoint one person to share out our stores. This waking, these two have come for their portion. Next waking, two more."

He moved the stones from a small shelf in the steep embankment to reveal a root cellar, dug high enough up the wall that it wouldn't flood when a capricious storm set the valley awash. With his stone knife, the man cut a sizable lump of dusty white from the huge knotted root in the little alcove. Then he allowed the woman to cut the lump in half, and the man to choose which piece was his. The two stuffed their portions, each roughly the size of a loaf of bread, into their bags, smiled and nodded at Paulo and me, and hurried away.

"Your people must trust you very much," I said. "And it must be a great deal of trouble to feed everyone on every day."

"Only two come each waking," he said, flushing with embarrassment as he carefully replaced the rocks about the precious root cellar. "So it is no trouble. Farewell, kind traveler. I am honored by your speaking. Have care in your journey."

Paulo and I started toward Vroon and the others, who stood waiting for us a hundred paces down the track. As the five of us trudged through the mud toward the end of the valley and the Edge, the gaunt Singlar began to sing. His song told of the suffering land and his people's long waiting, the haunting tune echoing through the mists long after we lost sight of him.

I thought a great deal about the cheerful Singlar as we slogged down the road out of his muddy valley. It was easy to dismiss his fanciful imaginings. Yet, as we began feeling the slight tremors beneath our feet as we approached the Edge, I couldn't completely rid myself of the image of a beating heart.

We hadn't traveled far before Paulo pulled out a piece of flatbread to munch on, and my mind wandered onto the Singlar's problem of feeding his people. If there were fifty towers in the cluster—fifty Singlars—and only two per day could claim a share of the tappa root, then the loaf-sized lump would have to last a person twenty-five days. No wonder then at their gaunt appearance. And then I thought back to the meal I had eaten . . . the thin slices of fried tappa, so much more appetizing than the boiled mush that could last for many days. The man had emptied his own woven bag for me—his month's ration.

"Vroon!"

"Yes, my king?"

"What stores do we have?"

"Flatbread for us all to last a twolight, the hard sausage the Horseman Mighty favors though it is not what he is used to, five of the Guardian's round fruits that you have named apple-things."

"Each of you take one piece of flatbread for yourselves, none for me, then take the rest of our supplies back to the man we just visited."

"But, great Master—"

"Tell him it is our custom. I want him to have it."

"But the Guardian—"

"Blast the Guardian. He need never know if we don't tell him. He can't mean for those people to starve." I would have to speak to the Guardian about the place. Even if the man kept all of our rations for himself, it wouldn't hold him a month.

Vroon bowed, wearing his most long-suffering expression.

We proceeded through the increasingly rough country, along the path Zanore devised, slowly so Vroon could make his delivery and catch up with us.

"He seemed a right fellow," said Paulo.

"A natural leader," I said. "Probably the best mind we've run across in this place."

After we had tramped through the gloom for another hour or so, Vroon rejoined us. "The Singlar delighted in your gift, great Master, praising you unstopping."

"What did he do with it? Did he take it?"

"Five pieces of the flatbread he shared out among all his people, each taking a portion. Himself, too. The rest he put in the common store—"

With an ear-splitting roar, a plume of steam shot skyward not fifty paces in front of us. We dodged sharply left to avoid a shower of glowing rock shards. Soon afterward the wind came up, a frigid gale, blowing right in our faces, even when we had to reverse our course again to skirt a bubbling pit of stinking yellow mud. I had no more time to think about the people of the rift.

"How long until we reach the Edge?" I shouted to Ob over the roar of the wind. We'd just made a third hour-long detour, this time in order to circumvent a bottomless crevasse. The earth groaned all around us.

"Long," said Ob in the nuance of speech that I'd learned meant, "a very much longer period of time than you possibly could imagine."

Even that would have been all right, if I hadn't begun feeling so wretched. At first it was merely dizziness. But then waves of hot and cold that had no relation to the character of the wind left me variously sweating and shivering. My stomach tried turning inside out. I blamed the evil-smelling gasses from the sinkholes and steam vents, but no one else seemed at all affected.

Eventually, knees wobbling and head spinning, I had to stop and lean against a massive boulder that seemed a bit more stable than the heaving earth, forcing myself to hold on to the generous Singlar's meal. I didn't think my malady had anything to do with my humiliation at so callously gobbling up a starving man's last provision. Before long, I could think of nothing but a warm dry bed and a lifetime of sleep. It had been hours since the others had eaten their flatbread, and I didn't want to see them among the starving either. "Let's go back," I said. "I still intend to visit the Edge, but I guess I'll just have to wait."

For the rest of the journey back to the Tower City, sickness and exhaustion muddled my head. I kept hearing the faint echoes of the starving Singlar's song of joy drifting through the stormy ever-night, soaking through my soggy clothes and into my skin and bones right along with the dismal rain.

Wait I did, and it drove me to distraction. I'd not come to the Bounded for lessons in geography or eco-

nomics, no matter how odd or interesting. I had certainly
not come to see that the Singlars were fed or to drag
them out of their mud holes. I didn't like it that the
place felt so familiar or that the people took it for
granted that I was their king.

The Guardian continued to ignore me. He even
stopped coming to the table for meals. Maybe the damnable villain thought I'd go away if he paid me no attention. We had been in the Breach three weeks by my
reckoning when I decided I could wait no longer.

"He'll never take us to the Source willingly," I said
one day when Paulo and I were wandering aimlessly
through the deserted streets of the Tower City. "And
no one else seems to have any idea what it is or where
to find it. We'll just have to learn when he goes, and
then follow him."

"He goes somewhere every third evening before the
lights go down," said Paulo. "That's the times he don't
come to the room to check on us, and he's always fired
up nasty the next morning."

"I don't think the Source will let him send me away.
Otherwise we'd be on the road or dead by now."

"What is this Source? Is it some*body*?"

"That's what we're going to find out. So, he came
sneaking around last night and the one before. That
means he'll go this evening. There's an alcove on the
third landing . . ."

The winding stair of mottled red stone, polished and
smoothed like marble, was the heart of the Blue Tower.
Though the rooms one found beyond its landings had no
relation to the outside shape of the tower, the staircase
followed the exact curve of the spiral. The audience hall
and the retiring room, the dining and reception rooms,
were on the ground level. Paulo and I slept in guest
apartments on the second level, and the Guardian had
his private apartments on the third level. The storerooms were below ground, so we understood. The maintainers guarded them ferociously and would not allow
us to go down the narrow stairs. All the other rooms on
the ten levels of the tower, including a luxurious bedchamber on the fourth level and a rabbit warren of wind-

ing passages and large and small chambers that had no clear function, were reserved for the king.

Paulo and I slipped out of our room right after supper. The upper levels of the Blue Tower were quiet, as always. And we didn't fear running into anyone. The servants seemed to disappear as soon as we were fed.

We crowded into an alcove near the third-level landing, counting on the fact that the Guardian would use the stair if he was going anywhere, and we'd be able to follow him. No more than an hour after we'd begun our watch from the cramped space behind a slender column that supported the spiral stair, we heard steps approaching from the direction of the Guardian's quarters.

Surprisingly, the knob-jointed man started *up* the stair, not down. We crept after him, staying just close enough to keep his gray robe in view. He climbed all the way to the uppermost landing.

The yellowish wall at the head of the stair glowed softly of its own light, plain and undecorated save for a carved circle about the size of my full armspan. The Guardian seemed to be running his fingers slowly around the circle. Crouching low on the stair one turn of the spiral below the Guardian, we couldn't see what else he might be doing or hear him saying any words. But after only a moment, the center of the circle dissolved into a curtain of deep shadows. And a moment after that, the Guardian stepped through and vanished, leaving us staring stupidly after him.

We hurried up the steps and examined the wall . . . now solid stone again, colored the pale golden yellow of ripe wheat. The devices carved on the stone circle at top, bottom, left, and right seemed quite ordinary: wheat sheaves, grapevines, flowers, and so forth. In the center of the circle was a small raised area about the size of my fist, having an oddly shaped hole in the center of it. Nothing told me how to invoke the enchantment.

But as I ran my fingers idly around the carved border, much as the Guardian had done, the center of the circle melted away again. "Well," I said. "That was easy enough. Keep watch—"

"Wait," Paulo whispered, laying a hand on my arm.

Without bothering to discuss it, Paulo pushed past me
and stepped into the opening.

No alarm rang out. No one shouted or cursed. But I
was furious. *Fool! Why did you do that? You should
have let me examine the opening . . . to look for enchantments. Dangers.* I was sorely tempted to charge after him
straightaway. But, of course, that would risk compound-
ing the blunder if he was going to fail, or wasting his
courage and luck if he was going to succeed. So I didn't
follow him, but I listened until my ears hurt, and probed
the emptiness and the silence with every sense. The Lord
Parven would claim Paulo had done exactly the right
thing. As my skills were potentially more useful, it was
only right that the "expendable partner" lead the way
into unknown dangers.

About the time I was ready to damn the risks and lay
my hand on the carved circle yet again, Paulo stepped
back through the wall as if he were walking out of the
stable door. Even if we'd have been standing in pitch
dark, I could have felt his grin. "It's the damnedest! You
won't believe it. It's safe enough, but watch the first step.
It's a rouser."

First things first. I grabbed his head and pulled his ear
close to my mouth. "Don't you *ever* do that again."
Paulo was *not* expendable.

Then I ran my fingers around the circle and walked
through the dark hole. The effect was quite the same as
when Vroon and company transported us from place to
place, as if the solid earth had dropped away beneath
my feet, taking my stomach with it. No shapes were visible. Only a nauseating smear of gray, swirling and
streaking by. And I heard nothing but a fast, dull throb
in the ears that might have been the beating of my
own heart.

Before I could force my stomach back where it belonged, my feet jolted onto solid ground, and the world
came to a standstill. My eyes blinked open to a sight so
alien to everything we'd experienced in the Bounded
that I almost burst out laughing.

Paulo leaned over my shoulder, whispering. "The
damnedest, right?"

We stood in a doorway that opened onto a graceful, curved gallery, its floor made of diamond-shaped tiles of red clay, its roof supported by a row of slender columns that were joined by a waist-high railing of carved stone. Beyond and below the gallery lay a garden, acres of trees and shrubs of a thousand varieties; vines with stems as thick as my arm looped about the columns and railing; flowers of colors beyond my ability to count them. Bounding the garden on every side were sheer cliffs of varying height. Our perch was embedded halfway up one of them. To our right, maybe a quarter of the way around the roughly circular expanse, beyond the spot where the gallery ended in solid rock, water splashed down in a silver ribbon from the heights into a pool far below us, all of it sparkling in brilliant daylight. Not sunlight—the smell and taste and feel of the air told me we were not outdoors—but from some other fiery yellow source lost in the glare above us.

I stepped to the railing and hung over it, marveling. No storms. No black-and-purple sky. A pleasantly warm breeze, wafting a fine spray all the way from the waterfall, rustled the huge trees and stirred the scents of flowers and herbs. A cardinal, as deep a scarlet as King Evard's banners, flicked by at my eye level, mocked by a crested jay perched in the highest branches of an oak.

Pressing a finger to his lips—wise in the echoing vastness—Paulo gestured toward the pool and the falls. He led me quickly down a flight of narrow stone steps, and onto a well-worn path through the garden. We hurried past masses of pink and violet flowers, between rose bushes taller than my head and covered with red, pink, and white blooms, past fragrant patches crowded with herbs, and rocky mounds, their niches and crevices home to a hundred varieties of low-growing, thick-leaved greenery dotted with tiny, starlike flowers of yellow and red. The path led us around the pool past the base of the falls, a pool which must have drained directly into the earth below, for its only visible outlets were a dozen threadlike runnels that spread out through the garden.

Just past the pool, we entered a stand of massive maple, birch, and hemlock trees, the undergrowth thick

with hobblebush and shiny-leaved laurel. On the far side
of this clump of forest, the path ended at a rounded hole
in the pale yellow stone of the cliff wall.

Motioning for silence, Paulo flattened his back to the
rocks and peered around the corner into the cave. After
a moment, he signaled me to follow him. I crept around
the corner and into the heart of a jewel.

The modestly proportioned cave, perhaps twice my
height and similar in width, was lined with amethyst. The
light of two small torches set into sconces near the cave
mouth bounced and glittered from the crystal walls and
ceiling. As we slipped deeper into the cave, past more
torches, the rush of the nearby falls was muffled. Soon
we heard only a trickling of water and two voices, both
ahead of us.

". . . need not fear. No murder will be done in the
Gray Towers. Set watchers about them to prevent any
attack."

The speaker, whose soft voice sounded neither male
nor female, was nowhere to be seen. Only the Guardian
was visible in the glittering purple light, standing beside
a niche in the back wall of the cave, his head bowed.
Inside the niche was a stone basin worn in the rock. I
could not see the source of the water, but it overflowed
the basin, dribbling down the rock wall onto the cave
floor.

"I rejoice at your saying, O mighty Source of Wisdom.
Next must I seek answer to a new heresy sprung up
among the Singlars. Two of them, one male, one female,
have petitioned to be together in one fastness. I have
punished them for their crime. I beg knowledge of how
I am to halt such villainy before others take it upon
themselves to ask the same." His voice cracked and
quivered with emotion.

"Do not grieve, Guardian. It matters not how the Singlars arrange themselves. Until the king takes his place,
the Singlars will not be other than they are," said the
speaker. "The king will bring an end to the old ways
and order the Bounded as he sees fit."

"I knew I was right."

"Tell me, Guardian, has the king not yet found his way to us?"

"No, mighty Source of Wisdom. Our seekers have failed. I worry that he may have been killed by the beasts of the Edge or by a foolish Singlar. We must constantly defend ourselves and you, Source of Wisdom. I try to be vigilant, to send away those that have no business here and punish those who do evil. You have said I may punish those who threaten your safety, have you not?"

"Heed my words. Welcome all newcomers; greet them and keep them close until you understand their origins and purposes. Protect the root of the Bounded, yes, but have care with your judgments. You are forbidden to dismiss or banish or slay any being who might, in any imagining, be our king. You will rue the day your hand harms our king."

"Truly I follow your teaching. But if I should discover interlopers, disgusting, foolish, insolent strangers who are clearly not our king . . . impostors . . . scoundrels . . . ?"

"Do with them as seems right to secure the Bounded. My only concern is to draw the king to us and keep him safe."

"As you say, O mighty Source, so shall I do your will."

"Though our king is young, Guardian, just out of boyhood, he will save his people from the storms of fire so that never again will they fear the breaking of the world—"

"I will watch for him, great Source."

"—and his hand can shape the destiny of all bounded worlds, for his strength is unbending. You must teach the Singlars to watch for him, too: The color of fire shines in his hair, and his hands and heart bear scars of bitterness that time can soothe but not erase."

"Our king has not come, O Source of Power. But when the glorious time is upon us, I will bring him here." The man's voice had sunk almost to a whisper.

"You have done good service, Guardian. Wear your burdens with honor, for your time as steward draws to a close. Seek the king once more in the bounded worlds. Though he no longer dreams of us, the moon-doors remain open for your seekers to pass. Thus I am sure that our king lives and is not changed. I hunger for the fulfillment of my prophecies."

The Guardian's fingers danced on the rim of the stone basin. His tongue danced over his wide lips. "Good Source of Wisdom, I struggle to maintain all as you have said, but the battle is wearing, and I fear I am too weak to fulfill your commands. If I could but taste of the spring . . . one sip . . ."

"O, Guardian, the spring is not for you. Its power would destroy you. Rejoice in your faithful service, and yearn not for that which can never be yours. You must not fail."

Paulo tugged at my arm as the Guardian hurriedly dipped his hands in the water and poured it over his head, so that the splattering droplets glimmered like a shower of gems in the jeweled light. "Of course, Source of Power. As you say. It's not my place—not mine . . ." His jaws ground as he spoke, and his hands that had touched the water so lovingly curled into shaking fists.

Time to go. The cave provided no place to hide. We slipped out of the cave and dived into the laurel thicket just as we heard the Guardian's footsteps clattering on the stone floor of the cave.

The Guardian hurried out of the opening, muttering. ". . . but it will never be his either. Young. Yes, far too young. He could never control the Singlars. It would be chaos all over again. They just don't know . . . don't remember. I'll not be unreal again. Never."

The hurrying footsteps crunched the gravel path past us. Paulo urged me to follow as soon as the knob-jointed man was out of sight. Lagging behind risked the doorway being closed or locked before we got through it.

Nevertheless I held back. "I need to question the Source myself. This might be my only chance."

"I was afraid you'd say that. That voice . . . this place . . . there's something not right here. Thought maybe you'd feel it, too, and want to consider it a bit before you tried anything."

Our instincts were usually quite similar, but I'd felt nothing of the kind. The voice of the Source had resonated deep in my bones, warm and comfortable and right. Strange as it all was, everything about the garden and the cave, indeed everything about the Bounded, seemed very natural, as if I were turning the pages of a favorite book long unread. Perhaps I couldn't remember what occurred on the next page, but it all unfolded just as expected as I read the familiar words. I didn't question that such a place as this garden could thrive in a sunless world. And it seemed right and reasonable that the Edge of the world moved outward, and that the Singlars' towers grew and changed. Though I didn't know its cause, I'd known what had to be done to stop the firestorm. From the moment I had stood on the windy precipice and surmised that this place somehow existed in the Breach between the worlds, I had gaped and wondered at its marvels. But I didn't think the Bounded held anything that would really surprise me, which, of course, surprised me very much.

"I'm going back inside," I said.

Paulo sighed. "I'll watch then. Best be quick."

I nodded and stepped out of the laurel thicket, only to have something large and fast and heavy slam into my head. As the darkness closed in, I caught a hazy glimpse of a knobby cheekbone and grinning yellow teeth.

CHAPTER 14

One tentative finger on the throbbing knot that was my temple sufficed to remind me of the thick wooden stick I'd seen coming at my face when I stepped out of the laurel thicket. The manacles had come later, as well as the fiery laceration about my neck that felt like someone had started to slice my head off, but changed his mind halfway. My eyes didn't seem to be working. I hoped that was a result of the sticky glop that coated them— probably blood from my head. Though I was wickedly thirsty, anxiety enabled me to muster enough spit to wipe it off and reassure myself that I could still see.

I was neither in the amethyst cave nor in the garden of the Source. A dungeon would be more apt a name. Comigor Keep had housed two levels of dungeons, long abandoned in the days when I would explore them, crawling through rotted straw and pools of murky sludge to play at knights and sieges. This dungeon looked and smelled disturbingly well used.

My cell was small, its stone walls relieved only by an iron door with a barred window set into it. Somewhere beyond the door was a blazing torch that sent dancing shadows through the bars. The floor was straw-covered stone, not clean, but dry, at least. My wrists and ankles were chained to the rear wall of the cell, loose enough that I could sit, lie down, or stand as I pleased.

The chains clinked heavily as I staggered to my feet. Standing up allowed me to peer through the barred window, but I quickly decided sitting was preferable. My head spun like a whirlpool. Besides, I didn't like what I saw when I stood: more cells like mine across the way, two dark-stained flogging posts standing sentinel in between, and a wooden rack with a variety of whips, straps, hooks, and other metal implements hanging on it. I sank back to the straw, just as happy not to know whatever else lay beyond my field of vision. I'd used such things in Zhev'Na and needed no reminders. The place stank of untimely death.

"Hello," I called out, as authoritatively as I could manage from my swollen face. "Is anyone there? I want an explanation!"

"Not bloody likely." The faint voice came from somewhere beyond my cell door.

A knot in my gut loosened a bit, and I rested the back of my head on the wall. "Are you all right?"

"Been better. Should of kept my mouth shut early on, I guess. Knew it."

Venturing to my feet again, I stretched my chains to their limit and squinted through the barred window. He sat at the foot of the second flogging post facing away from me. His hands were secured behind the post to a chain that dangled from a beam over his head, twisting his arms up awkwardly behind his back, and bending him forward so that his head almost touched his knees.

"How'd we get here?"

"The old man's quick . . . give him that." Paulo's speech was tight, halting, breathless. He must be hurting. "Had you snoring and a noose around your neck before I could get untangled from the bush. Told me the cord would take your head off if I didn't carry you back through the portal real careful. Sorry. Didn't believe him at first."

"I'm all right. So we're back in the Blue Tower?"

"I took you as far as the stair. Maintainers come . . . hauled you off. Don't remember much after that. Woke up here and wished I hadn't. He's wicked afraid of you."

"He believes I'm the king."

"You heard . . . in the cave. Not much mistake about it."

"It doesn't make sense."

"Best make sense of it. In a hurry, maybe. They're not even asking me any— Oh, demonshit . . ." He began retching violently.

"Hold on. I'll get us out of here."

After a little while, I couldn't hear him any more. Not even a moan.

"Hey, are you all right? Paulo!" No amount of shouting or rattling my chains roused him. I almost broke my wrists jerking on the cursed manacles.

The Guardian despised Paulo. I remembered his question to the Source about insolent strangers. I had to get Paulo away before the bastard killed him. But I had nothing to work with. My cell was absolutely bare. Not a spoon, not a pebble, not anything to use. No weak links in my chains. My wrists were already raw.

That left only one way to do anything in a hurry, no matter how much I hated it. I focused my attention on the shackles that bound me to the wall, hearing the words the Lord Notole would have used to teach me: *Mold your thoughts around the iron. See it. Feel it. Hear it. Take in its essence of brittle strength, of holding, of restraint and connection. Now reach for power . . . draw it together . . . shape it to your desire . . . thrust it between the links and wrench them apart. . . .*

Nothing happened.

Pitiful beggar . . . Try again. I worked harder, shoving aside my worries about Paulo and maintainers and Singlars, concentrating only on the work, drawing together everything I knew of such enchantments, reaching for whatever power I could find while keeping my back against the door in my mind, and my thoughts as far as possible from the Lords of Zhev'Na. No better result.

Demonfire, how could I have nothing? Maybe sorcery didn't work in the Bounded or it was dampened by some binding enchantment around the cell or the dungeon. Surely I'd know whether or not something like mordemar was hampering me; it would have eaten away half my mind as it had done to the Dar'Nethi slaves in Zhev'Na.

A faint moan came from beyond the cell door.

"Paulo! Come on, answer me! Wake up!" If sheer will and effort could have broken chains or pulled down a stone wall, I would have been free at once.

Silence.

Try again. Dropping to my knees and closing my eyes, I delved deep inside my mind, clawing for any scrap of power. Something had to be there. I was Dar'Nethi. I tore through my stores of knowledge and experience, pushed past the evidence of my senses, tossed aside sounds and images and memories, seeking the power born in me because I was my father's son, the power nurtured and grown in me because I was the Lords' favored pupil.

Deep . . . very deep . . . something huge and unidentifiable began to expand within me, crushing my lungs until I could not breathe. Swelling my chest until I felt as wide as Ob. Stretching my skin to the verge of ripping. Filling my veins until I must surely spray blood from my fingertips. My eyes felt pushed out of their sockets, and my head seemed to split in two until I could see myself cringing in terror against the wall of my cell while still feeling the enormous pressure within.

Horrified, certain that this was exactly what I had feared, some intrusive power of the Lords, I fought to push the monstrous thing back where I'd found it. Control. I needed control.

It required every thread of will and strength I could muster to bury the monster again. But, after much too long a time, bury it I did.

"Gods and demons, Paulo, I can't . . ." I was on all fours, my head drooping, sweat dripping from my face and neck. My breath came in wheezing gasps; I could scarcely even whisper. "Wake up, Paulo. Please, wake up."

Somewhere amid the slowing beats of my heart sounded a dull thud, accompanied by a soft groan. Hanging onto the wall, knees wobbling, I got to my feet again, strained forward, and peered out of my cell.

Paulo couldn't possibly answer me. Two of the Guardian's thugs had unlocked him from the suspended chain and thrown him on the floor between the flogging posts. Bloody stripes crisscrossed his back and shoulders. He had curled into a ball, and even as I watched, the taller of the two guards aimed his heavy boot at Paulo's head.

"Stop," I shouted. "I command you. Leave him alone."

The tall fellow paused, his jaw slack and doltish. A second maintainer, who had legs like tree stumps and clawed hands the size of a sheep's haunch, nudged him. "Go tell the Guardian the impostor's awake."

As the taller maintainer trotted out of sight, the claw-handed fellow grinned at me and kicked Paulo in the gut. Paulo's body jerked backward, and he retched blood.

"Leave off!" I said. "You're killing him."

He did it again.

A mistake to let him see I cared about his victim. I had to get control here. "How dare you disobey me? Don't you believe I'm your king?"

"Guardian says you're not." He wiped his piglike snout with the back of his hand. "He'd never put our king down here. Kings are fine folk."

I babbled about greed and fear and motives, but the dolt ignored me and shuffled out of view. After the distinct sound of water sloshing in a stone cistern, he came back into sight, carrying a pail, which he emptied over Paulo.

Paulo jerked, choking and coughing, wrapping his arms about his gut. With his huge paws, the guard caught Paulo's wrists and dragged him onto his back. Paulo's face was battered, his eyes swollen shut, blood running freely from his nose and mouth. He breathed in tight, irregular gasps.

"Now this is a sorry sight." The Guardian strolled into my range of vision. He bent down to get a closer look, shaking his head. "The impudent lad is feeling a bit pinched, it seems. Well, we'll relieve him of his burdens soon enough. And you"—he approached my cell and peered through the bars—"you who dared violate the Source—"

"Have you told your people of the garden?" I said. "Do they know what marvels lie so close to this deadness you've left them? Do they know of the light? Or are you the only one who sees the jeweled cave, a wonder such as I've not seen in three worlds?"

"You know nothing of our life or our laws. You are an impostor, and your mouth is filled with lies."

"I see. So you *do* keep it all to yourself. You protect your pleasures well, just like you keep the good food and fine linens. And there are so many pleasures . . . Tell me, Maintainer, does this Guardian come down here to watch the floggings? Does he smile and lick his lips when you torture Singlars in the name of safety? Does he go to watch when Singlars are thrown over the Edge?"

"Silence, impostor!" He did those things. I could see it in his face. And behind him the two maintainers were nodding their heads as if such pastimes made perfect sense.

"You can't bear to give up your sovereignty, for you enjoy the nasty bits so very much. The king might not agree with what you've made of this place, or he might not let you watch any more. Have you told your people what the Source says concerning the Bounded King?"

All I wanted to do was to keep them from killing Paulo, but my mouth wouldn't stop. "Did you tell them that he was just out of boyhood, that his hair was shot with fire, or that his hands bore scars of bitterness that would never fade?" I held up my palms, burned on the day I became a Lord of Zhev'Na. "Look on these, Guardian, and tell me I'm not your king!"

He snarled and averted his face. "I see no king. Only an insolent boy. It doesn't matter, anyway. I'll neither kill you nor send you away. Those things the Source has forbidden me. But I was not told to feed you, and if you're locked up here for trespassing our laws then that's your affair, not mine."

"So you'll never allow them their rightful king?"

"We don't need a king. *I* care for the Bounded. The Singlars listen to me, and they are better off for it."

He snatched a whip from the maintainer's clawed hand, and the air whistled and cracked, as he laid another bloody stripe across Paulo's arm and shoulder. "If you are a king, then show us your strength, traveler. The Source has told me that our king will shape the destiny of all bounded worlds. If he cannot fight a weak Guardian like me, then that seems very unlikely."

He tossed the whip back to the tall maintainer and pointed to Paulo. "Have your way with this one; just make sure he's dead at the end of it. Leave our 'king' where he is. Then, seal this dungeon so that no one will ever come here again."

"What of the other prisoners, Guardian?" asked one of the brutes.

"They can be his subjects."

His laughter echoed long after he was gone, until it was drowned out by the sounds of Paulo's beating. I tried to make them stop, to command them, to bribe them. I babbled about the garden and the jeweled cave, about the other worlds and the Breach, which they called the Unbounded, and of what I believed about the miracle of their existence. They would pause and listen carefully, then shake their heads and go back to their fun.

Once, Paulo stirred as if he might get up, and I threw a screaming fit to distract the maintainers' attention, but my friend made it no farther than his knees before the short one spotted his movement and kicked him sprawling again.

"Sorry." That was the only word he spoke in that awful time. Gods . . . *sorry.* As if he were responsible. . . .

Before very long, Paulo was too far gone to give them sport, and they began to discuss how they would finish him. They laughed and stretched him out on his back, tracing a shallow, bloody circle on his heaving chest with their knife blades. They would cut a little deeper each time, they said, until they could take the heart out of him.

"Paulo!" I begged. "Get up, Paulo. Fight them!" He tried, but could not. His face was unrecognizable, his hands pulp, his breathing ragged.

I willed him to wake up. To find strength. *Paulo, don't die.*

Their gross, callow ugliness set me tearing at my bonds again. I saw in them the same things I'd seen— and felt—in Zhev'Na: the enjoyment of pain, of fear, of horror and death. I'd seen it in both worlds and in myself, and I loathed it with a fury that burst from me like a firestorm. This was Zhev'Na all over again, but I was powerless. . . .

"No!" A mad fury exploded through me. This was Paulo, who had made me care about him when I cared about no one in the universe. He and my mother had saved my soul. My mother might lie dead from whatever wickedness had followed us to Windham—I could do nothing for her right now—but if I could summon one scrap of strength or power to prevent it, Paulo would not suffer the same fate.

And then the monstrous thing lurking in my depths broke free. Again my chest swelled and my blood surged, and again my head split until I could see myself collapsed in a limp heap at the extent of my chains. *Paulo! Get up and fight. You will not die here. I won't let you.*

Ready to summon power, I took a deep breath . . . and almost fainted from the pain of it. *Ribs broken . . . three, four at least. Don't do that again.* Suddenly my hands were screaming at me . . . worse than the ribs and the lacerated back, worse than my aching gut and my throbbing face, so swollen I could barely see the knife hanging in the air above me . . . ready to cut out my heart.

One, two, roll. Hook your leg around the tall one's ankles. Yes, that's it. Pull him down. As Radele is always reminding you, you had the finest masters in Zhev'Na. These are stupid, arrogant beasts who know nothing of true combat. Get his neck between your thighs and hold it if you want to live. Do it. Your heart is still inside you and still beating. Everything else will heal. Pain is nothing to one who has come of age in Zhev'Na. You were never handsome anyway . . . freckles all over . . . ears too wide. The girl in Avonar is blind. She's the only one who never saw how awkward you are.

Now take the short one when he comes in for the kill . . . twist! Control the knife and turn it back on him . . . for the Lady and the Prince and the young master . . . your friend. Concentrate. Squeeze harder. The tall one thinks to get away, thinks to play dead so you'll let up, for he knows your ribs are trying to come through your skin . . . through your lungs, so you can't get a decent breath. Harder. The Zhid taught you how to kill.

Force the knife back on the one who would take your heart. Your heart belongs to those who looked past the squalor of your childhood and called you friend, who showed you your true worth, and who honor you with their love across three worlds.

I felt the maintainer's neck crack between my legs, and with the last of my strength I forced the other one's knife into his own belly and jerked upward until I felt the satisfying rip.

One more squeeze with the legs to make sure . . . one more twist of the knife to make sure . . . I shoved the corpse off my chest and struggled to get air into my lungs.

For a long while I lay on the stone floor of the dungeon, fighting to stay alive. *Breathe, don't think. Rest. What I wouldn't give for my father's healing touch! Don't sleep. It's death if you sleep . . . maybe death if you don't. Sit up. That will ease the breathing . . . ah, demonfire, how can it hurt so much?*

Carefully, I eased myself up until I was leaning on the flogging post. I couldn't use my hands. They'd crushed them early on with wooden clubs until I fainted from it, until I begged them to cut them off as it wouldn't be half so bad. But then they stomped on them instead, saying as how the impostor was plotting to destroy the Source, and they would see him stopped. Breathing was a little easier, as long as I kept it shallow.

Ought to stop all this blood. It's going to leave me dry as an ale barrel at midsummer. But I couldn't see where all of it was coming from. Everything was blurry.

Stay awake. Sleep just won't do it. Not yet. Got to stay awake and get enough strength back to unlock the cell door.

But I couldn't figure out why I had to unlock my cell. I was already out. I'd come out to fight . . . to save Paulo . . .

My sluggish mind riffled through thoughts and images as if they were pages in a crumbling book. Holy gods, what had I done?

The pain was real, the agony of each breath, the

screaming fire in my hands, the dangerous dull throb in my gut. But this pain could not be mine.

I squeezed my eyes shut, afraid to see. But the darkness was too tempting. If I kept my eyes closed, I would sink into sleep just to escape the pain, and then I—whoever I was—would die. So I opened them again and saw what I was terrified to see. My legs were long, perhaps two handspans longer than they should be. And my arms were long, like a scarecrow's I—he—had always said. But he'd never seen the strong back and shoulders that held them together. And the shirt that hung in tatters on my bleeding chest was not the blue silk the Guardian had provided me, but the rough brown kersey my friend had worn since the dwarf had acquired it for him.

If I could have shrunk from myself in horror, I would have done so. In my zeal to save Paulo's life, I had violated every oath I had sworn since leaving Zhev'Na. I had taken possession of my friend's body and had no idea what I had done with his soul.

CHAPTER 15

Stay awake. Breathe. Only the necessities of staying alive held horror and revulsion at bay.

How was I to get him back? When I was in Zhev'Na and had done this thing—taking another's body for my own use, for my pleasure—I hadn't cared what became of the soul I had displaced. The bodies died when I left them. I didn't know why or how, only that they did, and it didn't matter for they were Zhid or Drudges or slaves who existed to serve my need—my power. But this . . . I had to find Paulo, put him back, and put myself back where I belonged.

Holding one arm tight around my ribs, I eased to my feet. One step. Two. Slowly, using the flogging post, a bloodstained headsman's block, and the implement racks to hold myself up, I staggered across to the wall where the maintainers had hung the keys to the young master's cell—my cell—on a peg. Cold, shivering, I had never hurt so much in all my life. After every step I had to stop and rest, trying not to heave out my insides.

Forgive me, Paulo. I've got to keep you alive . . . get you back right . . . and I don't know how. So I've got to use you while I can, make your body work even though it may make it worse for you.

It took an agonizing time for me to get the key, insert it in the cell door, and make it turn. Only two of his fingers were of any use at all, and they shook ferociously, refusing to cooperate until I was ready to scream.

"Cripes! You've got to do what I tell you!" I yelled, and almost turned around to see where Paulo was. But it was me, using his voice . . . even his words . . . as I'd used his very thoughts while I was wrestling with the maintainers. As I fumbled with the key, I considered what had run through my head in that time. Not just my own thoughts, not by any measure. Paulo had been there, too, with ideas and feelings I had no way to know. That I had no *right* to know.

I'm sorry. So sorry. Don't be dead.

An hour it seemed until the cell door swung open, and I saw my own body lying insensible on the floor. So many bizarre things had happened to me in my life, but unshackling my own wrists and ankles, and dragging myself out of my prison cell, were truly among the strangest. At least I was breathing.

Once I had my body out of the cell, I sank to the floor beside it, waiting for the waves of pain and dizziness to recede so I could think what to do next. If Paulo was still somewhere inside this body, then maybe all I had to do was get out. I had to hurry. The Guardian could come at any time, eager to see if his will had been done. But first . . .

Gods and demons, my head was in a muddle, and everything hurt. The light began slipping away from me, as if the torches were falling down a deep well. I reached down the well, trying to catch them. My life depended on it . . . Paulo's life . . . but I lost my grasp on the light, and lost my footing, and tumbled into the depths after it. . . .

"Cripes, are you going to sleep all day? I thought I was the one busted up, but you've got a head like a rotten melon. We've got to get out of here."

"Can't you be quiet? My head hurts." Why was I talking to myself, when all I wanted to do was stay asleep?

"Let somebody crack a rib or three for you. Or put a boot in your gut. Make you forget your head."

I was still leaning against the flogging post, holding myself together with my bloody, smashed hands. I looked more than half dead. But how was I able to see it? And why was the filthy stone floor pressing so brutally against my face at the same time?

I sat up quickly, ignoring the aches that were so trivial next to those I'd experienced earlier.

Paulo was leaning against the flogging post. Some-where in the mess of his face was a particular crooked grin I'd not seen since we'd left Windham. "Got to stop traipsing after you. Man could get himself killed."

"It's you," I said, gaping like a fool. "And I'm— Oh, blast it all, I must've been dreaming. I don't want to go to sleep ever again." My head felt like a mountain had fallen on it. But at least it was my own head, and my own arms and legs attached to it.

"Wasn't no dream." His smile had vanished, but the anger that should have displaced it didn't follow.

Not a dream . . . He should be furious with me . . . revolted. He should feel violated, but he just sat there looking at me, waiting for an explanation. I wanted to be sick. "I'm sorry. I don't know how I— I didn't mean to do it. I swear."

"Didn't *mean* to? And here I thought you'd done magic just to keep my hide in one piece. Ragged, but one piece all the same." A laugh burst out of him, though it sounded more like a hoarse whoop.

"Well, of course, I meant to help. But not that way . . . taking you. Never that. I didn't know I could. Not any more. Only when I was a Lord. When I had power and did it on purpose, the person always died after. I don't know how this happened. I just wanted to help." It sounded so childish, such a pitiful excuse for an act so reprehensible.

"You saved my life. I was a dead man. I *wanted* to be dead."

"It's an evil thing. I could have killed you." I still wasn't sure why I hadn't.

"I won't argue that it wasn't a touch fearful. It's not something I'd want to do over again . . . or even to talk about. Not yet. And one more thing"—he jerked his head at the dead maintainers—"I don't *ever* want you that riled at me."

"No time to figure it out right now. We've got to get you someplace I can take care of you."

I didn't know how long I'd been insensible, and Paulo wouldn't be able to move fast. How well I knew that. I got to my feet and across the floor, ignoring the way the walls seemed to dip and swirl as I squatted beside him.

"I'm as ready as I'm gonna be for a while." He was shivering so badly he almost couldn't get the words out. His breath came in short, tight gasps.

"Don't try to talk."

"Don't forget the others."

"Others?"

Paulo waved toward the cells lining the block. "Other prisoners."

Earth and sky . . . "All right. Hold on. I'll be right back."

I grabbed a torch and the keys I'd dropped, and then I ran the length of the room, unlocking every cell door and throwing it open. Most cells were empty. In one I glimpsed a dead man. He had been dead a long time, but I think he'd been foul even before that. He had scales.

In another cell I found the disfigured girl from our first day, sitting in the middle of the floor watching the door. I waved my hand impatiently. "Come on, you're free." She didn't move.

I stepped into the cell and offered her my hand, but she refused to take it. "I must stay here for punishing. We took Joca down from his fastness. They'd tied him to its wall." She gripped her knees, and tears rolled down her cheeks. "He was so broken. Bleeding terrible. The Guardian's servants grabbed me, but good Singlars carried Joca to safety. I wish no more hurting for him. Ah, Joca . . ."

She looked half starved, but no one could call her weak. Not by half. It took me an eternity to persuade her that allowing the Guardian to punish her would not save her friend, that Joca would surely come for her and risk more punishment himself.

"You're doing the right thing," I said, when I finally got her moving. "Take care of each other. Just be careful. Don't let anyone see you."

"I would never want Joca's hurting. All I want is goodness for him . . . and being with him."

"Things will change," I said. "I'll see to it before I go. You and your friend can be together as you should be."

She knelt and took my hand, bowing her head over it. "You are all kindness, mighty king."

I shoved her toward the stairs and closed my eyes for a moment so everything would stop spinning. I was in too much of a hurry to explain that I had no intention of being her king.

The last cell in the row appeared to be empty. But just as I turned to go, a slight movement caught the corner of my eye. A rat, most likely, assuming they had vermin here. But the infernal place was as dark as pitch, and I'd left my torch behind when I'd taken the Singlar girl to the stairs, so I stepped through the doorway and squinted to get a better look. "Come out," I said, just in case it wasn't a rat. "You're free."

A chip of stone smacked into my bruised head. Ten more followed it, stinging all the wrong places.

"Stop that!" I yelled. "Are you crazy? I've come to set you free."

I fumbled around in the dark, fending off a flurry of ineffective blows, and dragged the prisoner out into the torchlight. No sooner had I shoved the fellow up against the wall, than I dropped my hands and stepped back, confounded.

The bedraggled, furious person before me was a girl very near my own age. Though her fair hair was matted, and her face streaked with dirt, she was no Singlar. She had no obvious deformity, and her torn and filthy garment had once been white satin. Even more astonishing, she looked vaguely familiar.

She darted out from between me and the wall, and grabbed an ax from the implement rack, keeping her eyes on me the whole time. "Don't touch me, you villainous scum. My father will cut off your hands. He'll put out your eyes for looking at me. Don't think he won't." Though her voice quavered a bit, she brandished the ax with some authority.

"Your father?"

"My father. The King of Leire."

"Roxanne?" The rock-throwing prisoner was none other than my long-ago playmate, the Crown Princess of

Leire. Though shorter than me by a handspan, she'd grown up considerably since I'd seen her last.

I had been eight or nine years old the last time King Evard had come to Comigor to visit. He had sent the two of us off riding with six grooms and six ladies-in-waiting. It had been a miserable afternoon. Roxanne spent the entire time tormenting her servants, arguing with her chaperones, and calling me names. I spent the hours mute and paralyzed with terror that she'd spot me working some sorcery and have her father burn me to death. A most uncomfortable acquaintance. Tomas and Philomena had planned that I would marry Roxanne, but on our return from our ride, the princess announced to her father that I was the stupidest boy in the world, and she'd sooner marry her horse.

"You needn't be afraid," I said, holding up my hands, palms open. "We'll take care of you. My friend and I were prisoners here, too."

She snorted as if she were sitting in her salon in Montevial. "You don't look like you're capable of caring for your boots, much less me. And as for him"—she glared at Paulo, who was looking like a particularly grotesque gargoyle on a castle battlement—"I've seen livelier fellows at their own hanging. If you want to 'help,' then you will show me where I can take a bath, find me a decent garment to put on, and send a message to my father to come for me. He'll kill every nasty villain in this hellish place." She did not lower the ax.

Paulo started choking, and I forgot all about the princess and hurried back to him, worried to death until I realized he was laughing and about killing himself with it. "Oh, damn . . . oh damn . . ." He held his ribs, gasping for breath.

"Don't turn your back on me, boy," the princess yelled at me, brandishing the ax. "I said—"

"You listen to *me*, Your Highness," I said, crossing the space between us in two steps. We had no time for this.

Ready to dodge, I raised my hand as if to strike her. She swung the ax. Ax swings are not easily recovered . . .

especially by someone inexperienced. In one swift move-ment, I ducked the blow, grabbed her arm and the ax handle, and yanked the ax from her hand, throwing it across the dungeon well out of reach. Though she wrig-gled and hissed, I gripped her arms tight while I gave her the rules.

"I don't know if you have any idea where you are or how different is this place from anywhere you've ever been, but if you ever want to see Montevial again, you'd best take heed. I don't give two coppers for you, your father, Leire, or anything else you're likely to care about, so if you cross me, I'll leave you behind. There are people here who would as soon eat you as look at you. By the remotest twitch of chance you've fallen in with someone who not only might be able to get you home, but also knows that when you were nine, you stuffed three cherry tarts into your jumper, and ended up with them leaking all down your leg. You were so angry at your own stupidity that you ripped your jumper and told everyone you'd been chased through the woods by bandits and fought them off with your riding crop. It was lucky a whole village wasn't hanged for it. So I know you, and you'll not pull your tricks on me."

I don't know whether it was the disarming, the threats, the sight of the two dead maintainers facedown in a pool of blood, or simple mystification at my familiarity with her past, but she stared at me speechless, an unaccus-tomed state for this particular princess as I remembered. I let her go and steadied her on her feet, gesturing toward Paulo. "My friend here needs care. You will help me carry him out of here, and you will help me tend him. Then maybe I won't toss you back in that cell for our jailers to play with. Do you understand?"

I motioned her to take Paulo's ankles. Without a word, she did so, and we jostled him up three long flights of steps and through a maze of passages until we came to the rotunda and the spiral stair. The lamps were turned down, and I warned Roxanne to remain silent. I didn't need to tell Paulo. He'd passed out the instant we moved him. The climb up the curved stair was awkward, but we reached my apartments without meeting anyone.

Once Paulo was on the bed and I had turned up the lamps, I set to work trying to clean him up a bit, pleased that we had made it so far without detection. My satisfaction was short-lived.

A sharp metal point pricked the skin over the heart vein in my neck. "You will take me back to Montevial immediately or to the nearest Leiran military post. Maybe I won't have you hanged if you do it."

It took me exactly two heartbeats to have her on the carpet with her hands twisted behind her and Paulo's spare knife pointed at her eye. "If you ever do that again, I'll cut out your eyes. It makes a very interesting popping sound when it's done right." Clearly you couldn't mince words with a Leiran princess.

The knife that she'd snatched out of a bowl of fruit went back in its sheath and into my boot. Then I hauled up the princess and shoved her into a cushioned chair, untangled a sheet from the jumble of bedclothes, and dropped the sheet in her lap. "I need this torn into strips."

She spat at me and threw the sheet on the floor.

I picked up the sheet and dropped it back in her lap. "Rip it up, or I'll tie you up with it and hang you from the ceiling. We don't have much time until the alarm goes out, and I've got to take care of him before anything, even before saving your royal skin. He *will not die.*"

She must finally have believed me, for she started tearing the sheet, grumbling to herself and shooting murderous glances at me as she did so.

I tied long strips tight about Paulo's ribs, then cleaned and bandaged his hands. His worst injuries were those I couldn't see; his heart was racing, his skin cold, his breathing fast and shallow, his belly purple and hard. I propped his feet up higher than his head and covered him, but I knew nothing else to do for him.

"Who are you? How do you know those things you said to me? No one knew of the tarts, not even my nurse."

"Be quiet. I need to listen." As always, soft noises filled the Blue Tower: unidentified creaks and shuffling

that I always imagined were the sounds of its growing,
wind sighing up the stair and under the doors, rain spat-
tering in our slot window, distant doors closing. At any
moment the alarm would be raised, and the place would
come alive. I just wasn't sure what I was going to do
when it happened.

I tied off a bandage on Paulo's left leg; with bandages
around his chest, his head, his leg, and his hands, he
looked like a stuffed doll. Just as Roxanne threw me
another wad of narrow strips, a small lamp, sitting on
our eating table, brightened on its own. I had left that
one lamp turned down as I worked, so I would know
when the normal change of the light occurred.

I untangled one of the new strips and soaked it in a
cup of wine. No time to dawdle.

The princess's mouth fell open when I pulled Paulo's
knife out of my boot and pressed the hilt into her hand.

"If anyone tries to touch him—or you—kill them. If
he wakes, give him this cloth to suck on. Nothing else.
His name is Paulo." I threw the wine-soaked cloth on
the table and shoved the bowl of fruit toward her. "You
can have whatever you want of this. It's not poison or
anything. I'll be back as soon as I can."

"How do you know I won't kill him myself and run
away?"

Though I didn't touch her, I made sure she was looking at my face before answering. "I once cut the skin
off a man and tied him to a stake in the desert for a
week. He crossed me far less than if you even think of
hurting Paulo. And you have no idea where to run."

"Where are you going?"

"To kill a man if he doesn't do what I want."

She didn't even blink. "Don't you need this, then?"
She waved the knife at me.

I shook my head. "A knife is too simple for him."

"Is he the one responsible for all this?" She pointed
to Paulo and to me, her gaze traveling up and down,
taking in a full view of the blood and muck spread all
over me.

"This is only one part of what he's done."

She lifted her chin. "I don't believe you cut a man's skin off."

"You had best believe it." I didn't do such things any more, but then, it didn't seem to matter what I really intended. Dieste the Destroyer, the Fourth Lord of Zhev'Na, was still with me.

I slipped into the passage and closed the door softly behind me.

I needed to get this business over with quickly, so I could find Paulo some help. It would have been far better if I could have hidden him somewhere other than our bedchamber, but I didn't know anyplace else with water and blankets and a bed. His hold on life was precarious. That left me few options. No time for anything subtle.

The plan that came to me needed only a few preparations. Fortunately, the time was right, and the help I needed most would be waiting for me just outside the Blue Tower. I crept through the passage and down the stair to the ground floor without seeing anyone. Just as I reached the rotunda, doors slammed down below, and men started yelling. Footsteps pounded on the stairs up from the dungeon.

I crammed myself into a niche underneath the stair. Two maintainers burst through the door from the lower levels, passed within a rat's tail of my nose, and raced up the spiral stair. I popped out again and watched their feet. To my relief they bypassed the second floor, heading for the Guardian's apartments on the floor above, no doubt. I thought myself out into the commard, and hurried around the corner into a narrow lane. Vroon, Ob, and Zanore were waiting for me, as they did every morning.

Once I told them what I needed them to do, I hurried back into the Blue Tower and waited at the bottom of the stair, just long enough for another one of the Guardian's thugs, a red-haired fellow with wiry tufts sprouting from his nose, ears, and lips, to trot up from the dungeon. He caught a glimpse of me and shouted the alarm. "The Impostor!"

I bolted for the staircase, mapping out the warren of the tower rooms in my head. The hairy maintainer lumbered up the steps behind me.

Vroon had promised to be quick. Half an hour should be all I needed.

More shouts rang out from both the third level and below. I sprinted up the stair to the fourth-level landing and into the deserted rooms, making sure the red-haired maintainer and the three others who had joined him saw where I went. I led them up and down and in and out, shoving furniture in their paths, throwing pots to lead them into blind corners, then dodging past them and into another passage. Before very long, ten maintainers were after me—the entire posting in the Blue Tower. I tripped the red-haired fellow, and he slammed his head into a marble column. Nine pursuers.

After a pass through every nook and niche on the fourth level, I raced up to the fifth, and then the next, leading them away from Paulo and Roxanne. Trying to use up time.

Afraid I'd be trapped there, I didn't stay long at the uppermost level. Rather, as soon as I had led most of the party around a blind corner, I doubled back to the stair, dropped over the rail and past three twists of the stair, grabbing the rail and vaulting over it again onto the marble treads, just below the two maintainers posted to block my descent. Rather than running away as they would expect, I engaged them and toppled them both down the long stair. Seven in pursuit. The maintainers weren't chosen for intelligence.

Level by level, I led them down again. Another speedy tour through the Guardian's rooms, taunting the villain himself along the way. I shoved another pursuer into a wall and heard the satisfying crack and scream when I slammed my boot into his kneecap. Six left, plus the Guardian. Four would be better, but I was slowing down. Another drop and vault, skipping the second level, and skittering into the ground-level dining room. *Careful now . . .*

I deliberately slowed—not a comfortable situation, as it gave me leisure to note that the fiery cut on my throat was bleeding again and my skull on the verge of exploding. But then, things were not going to be comfortable for a while yet . . . if ever. My instincts were still good; I felt the pursuers closing in.

Wiping my hand across my throat, I smeared blood everywhere I didn't have it already. As the chase caught up to me—six maintainers led by the scarlet-faced Guardian—I staggered backward through the short passage. There, in the doorway of the retiring room, the small room adjacent to the audience hall, I collapsed into a heap.

Things settled out rather quickly. Two maintainers grabbed my hair and arms and dragged me to my feet. The Guardian squeezed past us and sank into his chair, a grotesque grin baring his ugly teeth. I ignored the vigor with which the maintainers twisted my arms and shoved me into the retiring room. My only worry had been that they'd kill me right away.

As the two pressed me toward the Guardian's desk, the rest of the chase party tried to crowd through the door behind us. But the retiring room was small, and the Guardian sent two men to guard the main entry of the tower, left two outside the door we'd just come in to prevent my escaping that way, and kept just the two close at hand to prevent my exiting by way of the gold curtain and the audience hall.

"We have unfinished business, Guardian," I said, wrenching my right arm from one of my captors and using my shirttail to blot the blood dribbling down my face.

A brutish Singlar did his best to break my arm while recovering his grip on it. I resisted . . . moderately.

Smugly, the Guardian motioned the two maintainers to leave off. "He can't get away."

They released their hold, but stayed close, growling under their breath.

Eyes glittering, the Guardian leaned forward on his elbows, his knobby fingers twined in a knot under his square chin. "We have *no* business, impostor. We will continue exactly where we left off, but with better supervision and better result."

The gold curtain that closed off the audience hall swayed slightly.

I raised my voice. "You mean where you left me to die in your dungeon?"

"Your dying is your own business," said the Guardian. "I will just give you ample opportunity."

"Yet when I made claim to be your king, you did not deny it."

The Guardian motioned one of the maintainers to close the door to the outer passage. "It is no matter who you are. *I* rule the Bounded, and that will not change. Not ever."

"Yet I showed you my scarred hands, and you noted the color of my hair and my age, and you agreed that all is exactly as prophesied by the Source."

The Guardian's pale skin stretched tight over his bones. His smile lost its mirth. "That makes no difference."

"And so, when the firestorms come again, the Singlars will do as they have always done. Mourn their neighbors. Rebuild. You will allow them no king who might help them change their fate. You will allow them no names."

He jumped from his chair and moved around the desk to stand between me and the gold curtain. He towered over me. "This conversation is at an end. Maintainers, take this impostor back to the dungeon and seal it closed forev—"

"Hold, Guardian!" I yelled it loud enough to make the two brutes stop. Time to play my last card. "If I'm an impostor, then you must slay me immediately. I've escaped from your prison once and may do so again. What if I found the Source and listened to what it had to say? You claim I tried to destroy it before. What if I tried again? Surely it is your duty to execute anyone who might damage the Source. Maintainers, give the Guardian a weapon so that he can perform his duty."

The Guardian, skin flaming, spluttered incoherently as one of the Singlars, accustomed to instant obedience, pressed a sword hilt into his hand.

"You have the power to pass mortal judgment on anyone save your rightful king," I said. "Surely that could not be causing your hesitation?"

I dropped to my knees before the astounded man, spreading my arms wide as did the Dar'Nethi slaves in Zhev'Na. "Before these witnesses, I lay claim to the throne of the Bounded. I say that I am the one spoken of by the Source. I have granted names. I quelled the firestorm. If I am an impostor, a danger to the Source, it is your duty as Guardian to slay me. But, of course, if I am your king, then you are forbidden to take my life. Make answer, Guardian. Choose my fate, for there are witnesses to your deeds."

And so, I laid down my wager. I believed the Guardian to be a cruel despot. But I also believed him driven by his ignorance, too fearful to blatantly disobey the Source.

The Guardian's big hands massaged the sword grip, and his face twisted slowly into a feral snarl. "Hold his arms. Spread them wide so I can take him cleanly."

The brutish pair had me before I could move, each taking a firm hold of one of my arms and stretching it so far to the side, I could not shift a finger's breadth. With an experienced two-handed grip, the Guardian raised the sword, a wide, efficient-looking edged blade.

So my gamble had failed. I whispered a quick apology to Paulo.

But as the air shivered with the passing blade, my neck remained intact. Amid spouts of gore, the red-haired head of the guard on my left thumped to the floor and the massive body slumped. Then the dripping sword slashed again, severing the neck of the surprised maintainer on my right. The Guardian was astonishingly quick, and I was astonishingly unlucky that the grossly heavy left maintainer fell on top of me, pinning me to the floor.

The bloody sword tip teased at my lips. "I cannot slay you, my king, but I've silenced the witnesses to your claim. And when the two outside the door come at my call, they'll find you tongueless. You'll not put me in such an awkward position again."

I smiled then, as will any gambler as he sweeps the coins into his purse. "I would advise you to pull back the gold curtain before you act so rashly, Guardian."

The color fled from his face. He stepped away and flicked aside the curtain that separated us from the audience hall. The sword clattered to the floor.

I craned my neck to see.

Vroon had managed what I asked of him. Filling the vast hall was a sea of faces: misshapen, grotesque, ugly, some beautiful, too, atop malformed bodies. All silent. All listening. Every one of them my witness.

"You cannot kill them all," I said.

"Behold the One Who Makes Us Bounded!" cried Vroon, standing proudly in the first row. The cheers did not die out for more than an hour.

And so it was I gained myself a kingdom, and the most unlikely subjects any ruler had ever governed. Unfortunately, I had not found any answers as yet, only a fistful of new questions.

CHAPTER 16

I didn't kill the Guardian, nor did I allow any of my more bloodthirsty subjects to do so. I might need him to help me unravel the mystery of the Source and get it to answer my questions. So I had six Singlars take the bitter man to his apartments and confine him there, and I commanded Ob not to leave his side.

While they took him away, I stood on the dais of the audience hall, thanked the residents of the Tower City for saving my life, and asked Corionus the mapmaker to record the identity and description of each one present on the vast walls of the audience hall. "On the third light from this one," I said, "each of you will receive the name of your choosing. Until that time comes you must tell everyone you meet what treachery has been done in the name of greed, and that no more of that will be tolerated in this kingdom. From this hour, all judgments of the Guardian are overturned. I will rehear all grievances beginning on the first light after the naming day."

They cheered and wept and babbled among themselves.

"Listen to me! One more matter of importance . . . is there one among you who is a healer?"

The cheers and chattering faded away. No one moved to speak.

"Surely someone eases your pains or cares for wounds or sickness. . . ."

Some of the Singlars shifted uneasily.

"It is forbidden for us to take such service of another," called out a youth. "That one would be flogged for changing the course laid out by the Source."

"The Guardian said it was an evil thing," said a bent old woman.

"No longer," I said, already questioning my decision to keep the villain alive. "Healing sickness and hurts will reap no punishment. I promise. By the Source, I swear it. My companion—the tall traveler—has great need of healing. If anyone is skilled in such matters, I would be very grateful for help."

A murmuring rose in the middle of the crowd, and a woman stepped, or was pushed, forward. She wore a veil wrapped about her head, covering all of her face except her eyes, which she cast down.

"Know you of healing, madam?" I said, trying not to let my urgency frighten her.

She dipped her head shyly, but voices rose from every side of the audience chamber.

"Her hands know much for easing those of us who are unstraight."

"She gave me potent waters to clear my breathing when I could not."

"When the graver's fastness crushed his legs, she worked him whole again."

"With caring she walks."

"You are much praised," I said to her, "and very brave to do such kindness when it was forbidden. Would you look at my friend? Help him, if you can?"

She bowed.

Dismissing the Singlars, I hurried the woman up the stairs and threw open the door to my bedchamber. No sooner had I stepped across the threshold than I felt an uncomfortable prick in my back. A duck, a spin, and a hammering blow with my stiff arm, and the knife clattered across the floor.

Roxanne sagged against the wall, cradling her right arm, but looking more relieved than hurt. "Blessed holy Annadis." The princess's voice was shaking.

I lifted the Singlar woman up from the floor where she crouched with her arms thrown over her head. "I'm sorry. This lady princess was just a little too—"

I broke off. One of the Guardian's claw-handed maintainers lay sprawled on the floor. I nudged the body with my boot and rolled him over onto his ugly face. No question he was dead. Most likely the bloody, well-placed hole in his back had done it.

"What *is* that?" The princess pointed a trembling finger at the ox-hided corpse.

"He was a man, a vicious, bloodthirsty servant of the former ruler of this place, but a man, nonetheless."

"I thought . . . I thought it was just nightmares or my imagination when I saw them in the dungeon. I was sure it was the bad light or bad food. I didn't know they were real."

Before I could answer, she screamed. "Behind you!"

She shoved me to the side, dropped to the floor, and scrambled across the tiles toward the knife.

I whirled around, crouched and ready, but instead of hurling myself at the newcomer, I sprang toward the princess and caught her arm before she could launch the knife. Her target was Zanore.

"I told you that you're a long way from Montevial," I said, catching her wrist and removing the knife from her hand. "A lot of things will appear strange, and a lot of people won't look like those you're accustomed to. That's the way it is here. It was good you killed that one, for he meant no good for you and Paulo. But don't kill anyone else just because they look odd. This is my friend, Zanore."

I tried not to show how relieved I was that Zanore had not come to the room any earlier. I needed to be more careful with my orders.

Roxanne wrenched her arm away, picked herself up off the floor, and flounced into a chair, her face a deep scarlet.

"Do you understand, Your Highness?"

She sniffed and averted her face. Straightened her back. Crossed her arms. Tucked her shaking hands out of sight quickly.

I had no time to play courtier. "What is it, Zanore?"

Zanore did not seem flustered by the commotion. "I've come to serve you as you require, my king. The good Vroon said you might have need of me."

"Thank you. If you could just wait a bit . . ." I left
him at the door and hurried over to the bed, where the
veiled woman had begun running her fingers over Paulo.
One by one, she peeled away my crude bandages to
examine his cuts and bruises, feeling every bone and
muscle from his head downward. When she pressed her
fingers on his bruised belly, he cried out sharply, though
he didn't wake. Quickly she brushed her palms across
the discolored skin, and he quieted again. When she unwrapped his hands, she shook her head before rewrap-
ping them carefully.

"Can you help him?"

"The cutting and pounding marks will ease of themselves," she said. "The bones of his middle I can work
to make whole and strong. The milk of the knotted tree
with forked leaves will I bring to close the bleeding inside that makes him hurtful, emptying him so that he
may eat and drink again and be well. But the hands have
taken disease in their wounding, and I have nothing to
appease it. If the disease does not go away, I cannot
work the bones, and he will be forever unhanded."

It was very hard to make out her words. She spoke
softly, and seemed to lose half the sounds through her
veil, but I understood enough.

"Disease in his hands . . . Festering, you mean, sepsis,
mortification that makes them hot and putrid and filled
with poisonous fluids?"

She nodded.

"Have you no medicines here, no herbs: woundwort,
wild indigo, pond lily?" My mother's Dar'Nethi friend
Kellea had taught me something of plant medicines.

"I know nothing of these."

Of course she wouldn't know them. So few things
grew in the sunless Bounded, except . . .

"Perhaps I can find something to help. Do what you
can while I'm gone. Send Zanore here for anything
you need."

As I started for the door, the princess jumped from
her chair and dodged in between me and the exit.
"You're not leaving again. Not with creatures like
these about."

"I'll come back." I motioned her to move aside.

"Your friend might wake up. He woke while you were gone before. He asked for you. "Young master.' I suppose that's you."

"What else did he say?"

"I told him you'd gone to kill a man, and he said you'd likely come back a king."

I gave her a second chance to get out of my way.

She stood her ground between me and the door. "Are you going to kill someone else?"

"I hope not."

"Aren't you awfully young to be killing people and such?"

"You seem to have done a most efficient job at killing this morning, and I am exactly one year, ten months, and five days younger than you." I took her by the shoulders and moved her aside, leaving her with her mouth agape.

In half an hour I returned with a fistful of herbs, leaves, and roots. It had taken no trick at all to find my way back to the garden. Running my hands around the stone circle opened the passage as before. I had been pleased to find many plants I recognized. Some others I just seemed to know would be helpful, though they did not resemble any Kellea had taught me.

The veiled woman was amazed at the variety of things I brought her and my explanation of their uses. Once we had boiled, cooled, pressed, or squeezed enough of them to do some good, and dressed Paulo's hands with the medicines, she rolled him to his side and began kneading his back and stomach muscles. "While you were away, I gave him tree milk," she said. "Now I must work him so it may nourish and heal him. Soon he will bring up all the blood that's pooled inside."

Though still out of his head, Paulo groaned at her every touch.

"She's killing him." The princess had moved to my table and was making short work of the apple-like fruits sitting in a wooden bowl. "You seem to think of nothing else but him, yet you're letting her torture him. And

there's a dead creature . . . excuse me, a dead *man* in
the room with us, and probably more of them on the
way, and you stand there like a post."

Paulo moaned again. A trickle of blood rolled out of
his mouth. Zanore was kneeling by the bed, and the
woman motioned to him to hold a basin close to Paulo's
face.

I grabbed the woman's wrists before she touched
Paulo again. "Have you done this before?"

"Oh yes, great king. Many Singlars are given punishment, and such injury as this is not rare. The tree milk
draws the blood together in his belly so he can be rid
of it. Perhaps it would be better if you would leave us for
a while. Come back before unlight and see the change. I
care for him as if he was yourself."

"She wants you to go so she can steal from you," said
the princess, who'd come to peer over my shoulder.
"You should set someone to watch her. Anyone who
won't show her face is up to no good."

I released the woman's wrists and watched her work.
Her hands moved carefully and gently, not at all unsure.
Paulo groaned and brought up more blood along with a
pinkish milky liquid. The woman bathed his face tenderly.

"Maybe you're right," I said to the healing woman.
"We'll leave you alone for a while. Zanore will stay
close and fetch you anything you wish."

"I will apply the yellow root oil to his hands as you
have instructed me," she whispered, lowering her eyelids. "I bless you for your trust, Majesty."

"Why don't you speak up?" said the princess. "You're
hiding something . . . fooling this boy, so that his friend
will die, and I'll never get out of here."

In a move so quick I couldn't prevent it, Roxanne
snatched away the woman's veil.

With a moan of quiet distress, the woman crossed her
arms and held them up before her face, but not before
we saw that which made the princess run to the washing
basin and vomit. I fought one of the hardest battles I'd
ever engaged in not to do the same.

The Singlar woman had no face, nothing but bone and
cartilage below her eyes. What little skin she had was

almost transparent, a thin layer over strips of muscle that allowed her jaw to work. No lips, no cheeks, no nose . . . she was paralyzingly horrid.

The woman stepped backward toward the door. No wonder, that. She might as well have been stripped and flogged. What could repair such an act?

"Tell me, have you a name that you desire? I need something to call you. You are one of my Witnesses, and I promised you a name."

She shook her head, keeping her arms curled over her face and her tear-filled eyes cast down. But she stopped moving away.

Swallowing my gorge, I pulled her arms down. Carefully, I took the trailing ends of her veil and wound them around her head as she'd had them. "Near my home, very far from here, grows a rare plant called *nithea*. It is very plain, no flower, only thorns. But if you dig deep, you discover that its root is bright red, long and silky— quite beautiful. When you open the root and spread it over a wound, it takes the pain away and makes the wound heal with no scar. If you would permit me, I would give you the name *Nithea*."

She sank to her knees, her head bowed.

I raised her up quickly. "Take care of my friend, Nithea. Send Zanore for me if he wakes."

Then I took the pale princess by the arm and propelled her into the passageway. "If you ever again lay your hand on one of my people without my permission, I will cut it off. Do you understand me?"

She tried not to answer, but I held her tight until she nodded her head.

"Paulo was right. I am the king of this desolation, and I plan to get you out of it and back where you belong as soon as possible. But until then, you are my guest, and you will behave like it whether anyone is paying attention to you or not. You will treat every servant, every beggar, and every person, no matter what their appearance, with the respect you expect for yourself. This is *not* Leire."

She remained silent, her pale face rigid, her lower lip trembling.

                              *   *   *

We found Vroon, and I dispatched him to install Roxanne in guest apartments as befit her rank, leaving instructions that she was to be clothed and fed and allowed
to go anywhere she liked, but that she was never to be
left unguarded. The rest of the day I spent securing my
position in the Blue Tower.

I had Vroon interview all the tower servants, weeding
out any who demonstrated too much loyalty to the
Guardian. The maintainers I dismissed entirely, forbidding the Singlars to exact revenge on them for their
crimes in the name of the Guardian, but threatening to
revoke that protection at the least provocation. In their
place I installed twenty Singlars that Vroon designated
as trustworthy, men and women who had stood witness
in the audience hall. I granted these Witnesses their
names along with their duties and believed, somehow,
that no sovereign would ever enjoy troops so loyal as
these. By "unlight," the hour when the lamps went
down, I'd done all I could do.

I returned to my apartment to check on Paulo and
found him sleeping peacefully under Nithea's eye. I bade
the woman good night, but before I could find a new
bed of my own, a servant brought an urgent message
from Vroon, asking me to come to the Guardian's
rooms. I hurried up the stair to the third level, through
an open foyer, and down a passage toward several Singlars, who stepped aside and bowed when I arrived. My
leathery friend Ob stood just inside the doorway. With
a thud that shuddered the walls, he dropped to his knees,
crossing his thick arms across his chest. His voice
boomed in massive distress. "Failed."

"Failed . . . Has the Guardian escaped?" My mind
was already racing to the Source. Would the Guardian
damage it? Set it against me with lies?

But Ob shook his red-tufted head. "Dead." With Ob's
word, the world itself mourned. His wide shoulders
were trembling.

I squeezed past the bulky Singlar into the Guardian's
large, sparsely furnished bedchamber. Evidently the
Guardian had decided he would rather be dead than give

me a decent answer. He lay on his bed, wearing his gold circlet. His blue robes were smooth and orderly, his hands folded primly across his chest, holding the ruby-studded key. The only discordant note in his presentation was the black swollen tongue lolling out of his mouth.

The untimely death of one's adversary was not the best way to begin a reign. I had wanted to expose the Guardian's misdeeds to all the Singlars before deciding what to do with him. But hiding his death would be very difficult. I picked up a small gold flask that lay on the floor beside the bed and sniffed it. The faint odor was sickly sweet. Moving closer to the dead man, I bent over and sniffed his mouth. Not at all nice. "Handle this carefully," I said, giving the flask to Vroon who had followed me into the room.

He took it gingerly, scrambled around the floor until he found the glass stopper that had rolled under the bed, and closed the flask. Ob knelt by the door, head bowed, quivering in shame.

"Vroon, how do you dispose of dead bodies here?"

"We dig them into the ground, Majesty. Under a tappa field, so they are still part of the Bounded."

Though I left the gold circlet on the Guardian's head, I removed the ruby key from his cold hands and dropped it in my pocket. Then I turned to the leathery man.

"Ob, stand up." I spoke as a commander, briskly and without sympathy.

The leathery man lumbered to his feet, standing as straight as possible with his deformed back, and kept his eyes pinned to the floor. The Singlars in the passage drew close to the door. Vroon stepped forward, anxious. "My lord, please—"

I held up my hand to silence Vroon. Softness could ruin a strong man. I needed Ob strong. "Ob, I charge you to dig the Guardian into the ground as is your custom. Bury this poison flask with him. Choose two Singlars to help you. Make no honor or special ceremony out of what you do, but do not hide it. And to all who ask, you will answer clearly and willingly that the Guardian took his own life out of selfish pride and shame at

his failure to heed the Source in the matter of the king.
Some may be angry at his death and make accusations
against me. But you will not fight them or hurt them in
any way, except to save your life or that of your assis-
tants. Do you understand your orders?"

Ob straightened his shoulders and bowed deeply.
"Majesty."

As he came up, I motioned for him to look at me,
forcing his watery red-and-yellow eyes to meet my own.
"Next time, watch closer."

As the wide brown man set to his duties, I stumbled
my way to the royal apartments on the fourth level, fell
into a bed the size of a banqueting table, and slept for
an entire cycle of the light.

CHAPTER 17

By the time I crawled out of the royal bed on my first morning as the Bounded King, Vroon had taken most efficient charge of my household. A young male servant with only one ear and a wooden stick for a leg was waiting for me with a tub of steaming water and fresh clothes suitable for royalty. I accepted the fine-woven red shirt and black breeches, black hose, and calf-high boots—all of them, amazingly enough, made exactly to my measure—but diplomatically postponed wearing the gold-encrusted doublet and elaborately jeweled belt. Feeling properly human after the bath, I sent the servant to inform Princess Roxanne that I would wait upon her in an hour, then grabbed two hunks of hot bread, dripping with butter and honey, from a tray beside my bed, and set off to see Paulo. With my breakfast had come word from Nithea that he was awake.

When I arrived, Nithea had him propped up on pillows and was feeding him tiny spoonfuls of a thick whitish substance that smelled like rotten fish.

"Demons, have you come to rescue me?" he said weakly.

"Only to see that you're not making Nithea too miserable with your complaining."

"She's got me so flat, I couldn't lift a horse's tail, then shoves more of this mess down me so I'll puke out what insides I've got left. I thought it was a new torture from the Guardian."

"You look better," I said. And so he did. Some of the swelling had gone down in his face, his color was healthier wherever he wasn't purple, green, or black, and his eyes had a spark of life in them.

Paulo screwed up his forehead and looked me up and down. "You look cleaner than last time I saw you, and your outfit's pretty fine, but I think this lady should work on your busted face for a while and leave me be. You look like a mountain fell on you. What do you think, Nithea?"

"The king said *you* were to be made well before anything else. I do his will."

Paulo squinted up at me. "The king . . . I was right, then."

I shrugged.

Nithea took the pillows out from behind him and rolled him onto his side. I sat on a stool beside his bed and told him what I'd done.

"So why haven't you gone to the Source yet?" he said, wincing as the woman spread a salve over the lash marks on his back.

"I just woke up. I had to come here first."

He kept looking at me.

"All right, I don't know. It's what I wanted . . . what I came here for . . . the whole reason we got caught . . ."

"You're scared. That's what."

"I'm not scared. I'm just waiting for you to get on your feet again. You heard something 'not right' in that cave, and I didn't. So, maybe you need to be with me when I go back."

He pressed his face into his pillow, muffling a miserable groan. Around all the cuts and bruises he had gone a sickly yellow. "Maybe tomorrow," he said. "This lady and her tree milk have done for me again."

"Maybe tomorrow," I said.

Nithea shook her head, holding up four fingers, then five, but her eyes smiled reassuringly above her veil. So it would take more than a day, but he would be all right.

"I'll come back later when you're feeling better."

Nodding to Nithea, I left the room and headed down the stair in search of Roxanne.

Was Paulo right? Was fear what made me feel like a battle was going on in my chest every moment we stayed here? My connection to the Bounded was very deep. The land, the people, the problems . . . Every day, the place revealed itself a little more. I could look at the Singlars and know what names they would choose. I understood what had to be done to release them from their peculiar confinement to their towers, and I was already trying to figure out how they might share the wonders of the gardens. But I didn't *want* to know these things or feel them. I didn't belong here. I had to go back and clean up the mess I'd left behind in Leire, and then find some place to hide where no one could ever find me.

I wasn't looking forward to my interview with Princess Roxanne, but unlike the Bounded, she was full of surprises. She wasn't waiting for me in her apartments, but was bustling about the audience hall, peering into every nook and cranny, pulling back curtains, examining columns and doorways and every handsbreadth of the walls. Two Singlar women, dwarfish like Vroon, trotted after her on their stubby legs, while a male servant observed her from the wide doors to the rotunda.

The princess had gotten cleaned up as she wanted. Her hair hung heavy and damp halfway down her back. Evidently no one had found any gowns to fit her, so she wore a simple wool robe, much too large, that she had tied at her waist with a gold cord. Not very elegant, but the color, a rich blue, made her light hair look like gold thread.

When she saw me enter the room, she immediately altered course and hurried across the floor, planting herself in my way as if I had intended to walk past her. Her face, now that it was clean, looked like a fine sculpture, perfectly smooth, and rounded just enough to look soft. But you could have struck sparks from her eyes. They were gray, like steel. "So I'm a prisoner again. A fine rescuer you are."

Why had I decided to visit her? Yes, I'd been harsh with her. And this was a strange, ugly place, bound to be frightening for someone with no experience of sorcery. But her father had burned sorcerers alive, slaughtered them and anyone who knew them: my father,

Tennice's brother, their friends, the infant they had thought was me. I had no reason to think the princess would do any different in his position. I ought to put her off the Edge.

"You are free to come and go as you like."

"What a polite thing to say. But *most* houses provide doors and windows that make it a bit easier. Do you see any such things hereabouts?" She pulled back a green curtain, only to drop it again once she had shown me the blank wall behind it. With her lips pressed together, she strode from one drapery to another, nearly tearing them from the wall to illustrate her point. "And my chambers have none either. But then perhaps you still have plans to cut off my skin if I complain."

She was certainly afraid—the Lords had taught me to smell and taste fear—but she did a good job of hiding it. I followed along behind her, hands clasped behind my back. It was true I had told Vroon to give her rooms without window slots. I had thought peeking through them might frighten her worse than she was already.

"Didn't these women tell you how to leave the tower?" I nodded to the dwarfish women just out of politeness. They turned scarlet, placed their hands on their ruffled white collars, knelt, and bowed their heads to the floor. Roxanne glared at me. I nudged the women to get up, wishing myself ten leagues away. I'd give her a quarter of an hour and that was all.

"They only told me this 'think of yourself out' idiocy. Does it give you pleasure for your servants to be insolent or were you testing my obedience? I didn't kill them for it, nor give them even a gentle slap for their rudeness."

"But it's the truth. They just don't understand that you're not used to such things. This is . . ."

". . . not Leire. Yes, I remember." She spun on her heel, almost causing me to collide with her. "So tell me, O great king, where in the blighted universe are we?"

"Its inhabitants call this world the Bounded."

"This *world*—" She sat down abruptly on a plain wooden bench next to the wall. To her credit she lost none of her color. "You really mean that, don't you?"

"Yes."

"I heard a story once of another world . . ."

". . . and a bridge of enchantment that joined it with our own."

"I remember some of it. Such a wild tale . . . sorcery . . . other worlds . . . villainous creatures with no souls. I thought the woman must surely be mad."

"That woman was my mother." My mother had been astonished that King Evard had kept his daughter in the room as she told him about Gondai and the Bridge and the battle that had killed her brother.

"Your mother . . . truly? I couldn't believe my father would even listen to her. I thought it was only because she was related to his sword champion, the Duke of . . ." Her voice trailed away, and her gray eyes grew wide, staring at me again. "*That's* who you are! Duke Tomas's son!"

I bowed. "The stupidest boy in the world—at your service."

Her brow wrinkled. "But the woman who told the story was not Duke Tomas's wife."

"There was a mix-up early on. He wasn't really my father, but my uncle. His sister, Seriana, was—is—my mother."

She shook her head. Her hair was curling as it dried and a few of the curls fell down on her face. She didn't seem to notice. "Gerick. That was your name. And you were so unfriendly! You wouldn't say anything and wouldn't play anything I wanted. I told you about the cherry tarts to impress you. And later you were stolen by bandits. Everyone believed you were dead."

"It's complicated. I didn't die."

"So this is the world your mother told of?" She looked around the audience hall with new interest.

"No . . . or rather, I'm not exactly sure. It's a long story. Would you like me to show you how to leave the Blue Tower? That's probably enough strangeness for one day." Then I could leave her to her own devices.

"Yes. Certainly. It might prove to me that I'm not your prisoner." She popped up from the bench. "This is so odd. We played together. It seems a thousand years ago right now. This place . . . these people . . . You

know . . . I don't care if it's complicated to explain where
we are. I want to hear it. I'm not stupid. And I'm not
some ninny who faints at the least fright. But, yes, show
me how to get out of here first."

Roxanne didn't stop talking the whole way down the
length of the audience hall. Without giving me much
time to tell her anything, she peppered me with questions, not always the ones I expected.

"Who is your friend that you care so much for him?"

"His name is Paulo. He was born in the village of
Dunfarrie. My mother befriended him there, and four
years ago he helped her rescue me from the people who
abducted—"

"A common boy, then."

"Those words have no meaning with respect to Paulo."

"All right, all right. I can see not. Are you really as
fierce as you say?"

I kept my eyes on the doorway at the end of the hall,
wishing we were in the rotunda already so I could push
her through the wall and be done with her. "My childhood was very unusual. I've done everything I say."

She thought about that for a moment, her sidelong
gaze feeling like fire on my skin. "There are a number
of people who would say you are young to be a king,
but I think it would be more accurate to say you are
very old to be a year, ten months, and five days younger
than me."

The main entrance to the Blue Tower, where Paulo
and I had first come through to visit the Guardian, was
centered on a sheer curved wall, identifiable as a tower
entrance only by the narrow silver band at its edges. I
traced my finger over the outline to show her. "A
dwelling in this world is called a fastness. They look
like towers to us. But dimensions—height and width
and depth—are measured differently here, so the interior spaces don't reflect the exterior shape. And though
the interior doorways between rooms look familiar to
us, those which pass through the walls do not. The
women were exactly right. You have to think of yourself out. . . ."

I explained the passage to her as Vroon had explained

it to me, and I described the thoughts I had used successfully. That was not easy, as I didn't even have to consider them any more. Then I gave her a demonstration.
When I popped back in, she was already yelling at me.

"Sorcery! I should have known it! How is it *you* are
capable of such wickedness?" The princess was flushed,
whether with anger or fright I couldn't tell. "And how
could you think that *I*—"

"It's not sorcery, though I'm sure to you it appears
the same. But you and every person in this land can do
it. And no one burns you for it."

This time, she did turn pale. I thought she was going
to run. But she just stared at me until my skin grew hot.
"Well then," she said at last. "Explain it to me."

It took me a few moments to decide how much to say.
I'd done a lot of thinking about the Bounded. Anyone
in the Four Realms would call Nithea's healing practices
sorcery, and the same for Zanore's route-finding, Ob's
weighty words, and the whole business of towers that
grew. Yet I'd felt no telltale prickles of enchantment
when the healing woman had massaged my shoulder—
twisted when the dead maintainer had fallen on me—
and I could suddenly raise my hand above my head without passing out from the pain. And I summoned no
power to think myself out of the Blue Tower. The
"prickles" were a sign of the resistance of the natural
world to the use of a sorcerer's power. So I had concluded that the Guardian had pronounced no magical
winding to open the stone circle passage to the garden
because no magic was needed. The fundamental nature
of the Bounded was magic.

The princess's fingers tapped impatiently on her
folded arms.

"Well, first you have to understand the distinction between natural law and sorcery. Natural law is the set of
rules a world works by—which can be different depending on the world. Sorcery is the use of a particular
kind of power to stretch or extend or nullify those rules.
Going in and out of these towers has no more to do
with magical power than does riding in a wheeled cart
or sailing on a lake in Leire. . . ."

I tried to explain how things that would be inexplicable in our world and require a sorcerer's power to accomplish could be a natural part of another one. I felt as if I was making a muddle of it. Roxanne stared at the floor, listening, her frown deepening by the moment.

When I finally gave up and stopped talking, she glanced up. "All right, then. I suppose that makes some kind of perverse sense. Go on."

I was astonished. I wondered briefly what she might say if I told her I'd melted rocks with lightning from the tip of my finger or had swum in the deeps of the ocean in the form of a fish. I stayed with nature. "So, the way to pass between these spaces we call *in* and the spaces we call *out* is to convince yourself which way you're going. Your mind's just not used to being in a world with a different set of rules, and it doesn't believe it when you tell it what to do. If you don't want to try it, I could—"

"No. I'm feeling a bit overstuffed with all this strangeness, and I'm tired of this dismal place and these lamps that are forever being turned up and down by creeping servants I never see. I need to walk in the sunlight. Maybe go riding."

"Uh . . . perhaps there are a few more things you should know before we go out. . . ."

Roxanne was very determined, and mastered entrances and exits in short order. She seemed to accept my word that it wasn't evil. I supposed she had no one else to trust. However odd, I was at least someone she knew.

Once we were outside, she marveled at the green stars and massive lightnings of the Bounded, and called the towers "extraordinary" and "exotic." This is not to say she was pleasant company. Mostly she complained about her awful robe, and the wind, and the too-large sandals they had given her for shoes, and the black dirt, and all the inadequacies of service in the Blue Tower. But even though I sensed how she was repulsed by many of the deformities in evidence, she never once showed it to those who crowded around us as we walked.

After a short walk, we headed back toward the Blue Tower. As we crossed the commard, a bent old woman with a jaw that bulged out like a bullfrog's throat dropped to her knees in front of me and kissed the toe of my boots. She wasn't the first Singlar to have done so that day.

Roxanne glared as I sent the old woman on her way. "They *worship* you! You must tell me how you've come here. I don't care how long or complicated the story. How is it you're their king? And why were you a prisoner?"

"I need to go—"

"It's *your* vile henchmen who brought me here, 'King' Gerick, putting a bag over my head and taking me before a horrible man who wore a crown and acted as though he were a king, though he had no kingly manner about him—"

"And I would guess you told him who you were and what he could expect from your father if he so much as looked at you."

Her eyes could have ripped the skin off a rabbit, but her tongue never slowed. "—and in his most disgustingly impudent manner, this vile man threw me into that dungeon, where those other beastly creatures would come and taunt me and look at me, and I refused to believe in them. I spent a great deal of time screaming, until I decided that I must be in the hands of Kerotean priests, and that everything was an illusion induced by their wicked potions and elixirs. I believed they were taking vengeance against my father by driving me mad, and I decided I wouldn't let them do it. So it's only right that you tell me what's going on in this place. Why are you a king?"

"It's all bound up with a prophecy or an oracle or something like that . . ."

I didn't explain about the Breach or the Lords or why I had come here. I just told her about the Guardian and his corruption, and how I'd come to the Bounded for my own reasons, but gotten caught up in their expectations. As I talked, we started walking again, across the commard and back into the city. It rained a little as we walked, but the air stayed warm and still. Roxanne didn't seem to mind. She kept her arms folded and her eyes fixed on the roadway as she listened. But she didn't miss a word, and she kept interrupting me with more questions.

"Is everyone here a cripple or were they made so by this Guardian?"

"They are as they are," I said. "You could say this is a world of outcasts, leftovers, ones people in our world would find unacceptable. They weren't—"

"And those three monsters came and stole people like these from Leire"—she waved her hand to the growing crowd following us through the dark streets—"frightening everyone to death. Brought them here to live like this, as if this were something better."

"Vroon and two friends were sent to our world to look for this king. They just thought . . . Well, they were trying to help, I think. The Bounded is a very new world. They have little experience to—"

"And then they make a boy their king!"

Having a conversation with Roxanne was like walking through a field of dartweed. You ended up getting pricked just about everywhere a needle could stick you.

"I've no intention of being their king forever. I just need some information from this Source. The Guardian was in the way."

"So you're not going to stay here and sort out the mess you've made."

"As soon as Paulo is well, I'll find out what I've come here to learn. Then I've got to go back, get some things straightened out. Make sure some people are . . . all right . . ."

". . . and take me back."

"That, too. But meanwhile, yes, there are some things need doing here, and as I upset the order, I might as well do them. Then they can name someone else to be king if they even need one."

"So why was *I* brought here? Do you know what they did to my father? They don't have any prophecies about driving rightful kings mad or abducting princesses, do they? Whatever my failings, I don't exactly match what your odd friends were looking for."

We had come to the command in front of the Blue Tower again, but here was another mystery laid out right in front of me. "I know what happened to King Evard, and I asked Vroon about it. He swore they had never touched the king. He admitted everything else—taking the other people and taking you."

I waved toward a set of towers we hadn't explored yet, and we set out that way. "What did you see on the night your father was attacked?"

Roxanne didn't balk at extending our excursion. She seemed to be all right about anything as long as she was talking. "It was the night of my birthday feast. We were going to have such a magnificent party—they were bringing Kerotean fire-eaters—but Mama had it announced that Papa was occupied with a messenger, and she needed to attend him. Half the guests stood up to leave. No one wanted to waste their time if Papa and Mama weren't there to see them ogling and coveting me. I was furious with Papa, so before the towels and water bowls were cleared away, I went looking for him. I couldn't find him anywhere he might be 'receiving messengers,' so I went to his bedchamber. The guards didn't want to let me in, but I . . . insisted."

That scene wasn't difficult to imagine.

"Papa was sitting on his bed, looking as if someone had hit him on the head, and a man was touching him . . . *arranging* him." Roxanne shuddered. "The man was tall, dreadful—well I didn't actually see his face . . . and perhaps he wasn't all *that* tall. His size was unremarkable, in fact. He wore a servant's cloak with a hood draped down low. But I'll never forget his voice—soft, gentlemanly, whispering horrid things, calling Papa 'the father of chaos.' "

"Was he the same man you'd seen before? Your mother said you'd seen a threatening man in your apartments."

Roxanne turned approximately the color of fireblossom. "No. He— Well, I made those reports when I was

much younger, and they perhaps weren't . . . accurate.
This was quite different. I screamed for Mama and the
guards, but by the time they came, the man was gone.
No one saw him leave the room."

"When Vroon took you . . . was the man there, as
well?"

"No. I locked myself in Papa's room, telling everyone
I was going to stay there until they believed me. Foolish,
I know, but I couldn't think what else to do. I was so
angry and so afraid. Yes, afraid. I'm not a fool; Leiran
nobles are not the most forebearing of subjects. If word
got out about Papa's condition, he would have been
dead by midnight, and I'd have been married to which-
ever of the closest contenders lived until dawn. Poor
Mama . . ."

She inhaled deeply. "Anyway, I fell asleep on Papa's
bed and got waked up by a huge flash of green fire . . .
The dwarf babbled nonsense, and when I told him who I
was and threatened to have him flayed, the three horrid
creatures dragged me off here like old baggage." As we
rounded a corner and entered the commard once again,
she was glaring at me.

Taking a deep breath in hopes I could get out the
explanation before the next barrage, I tried to explain
what Vroon had told me. "The three Singlars followed
me to Montevial, pursuing this stupid notion that I'm
their king, just because I have these vivid dreams. When
they discovered that a real king lived in Montevial, they
came looking in the palace and found you. And when
you . . . uh . . . went on . . . about being a king's daughter
and how you were destined to rule, Vroon says they got
scared that *you* might actually be the one they were
looking for. They didn't dare let you go, so they brought
you here straightaway."

Vroon had actually said that by the time she finished
yelling at them, they were all but certain she *couldn't* be
the Bounded King, but were afraid of what she might
do to them if they let her go. That detail seemed best
left for later.

"This isn't exactly the kingdom I have in mind. So

I suppose that when they talked about 'the one'—that was you?"

"I didn't— They shouldn't have taken you." I wasn't going to apologize for something I'd had nothing to do with. Certainly not to her.

"I'm the Crown Princess of Leire. I survived it."

We had come to the steps of the Blue Tower again. After "thinking ourselves in" and summoning the waiting Singlar women to join us, I bowed. "I've told the servants to give you whatever you need."

To my astonishment, she curtseyed in return. "Tell me, do you dine alone in your royal dining room, Your Majesty, or may a former playmate join you?"

I almost choked. I'd sooner dine in the middle of a nettle patch. "I eat with Paulo," I said. "He's not used to being laid up and needs me to talk to him. There's not much room—"

She raised her eyebrows, turned her back, and walked away, her soggy, overlarge robe sweeping behind her like coronation-day regalia. I felt like a glob of mud on the floor.

After three days, Nithea declared Paulo ready to eat real food. On the fifth day, I took him walking a few steps through the halls. A week and his ribs no longer pained him so badly, though Nithea kept them bound up tight. His hands remained heavily bandaged. Nithea had begun to "work the bones" now the festering was gone. Paulo didn't want me with them when she did this, saying only that he'd be grateful if I could find some herb that deadened feeling . . . maybe from the neck down . . . while she worked her magic.

"What she does isn't magic," I told him. "It's just the way of things here." I explained it all again as I had to Roxanne.

"And the princess . . ."

"She's civil. Zanore takes her walking every morning, and Vroon says she's trying to teach the servants how to sew and how to serve food properly and make her bed. She's not hit anyone or taken an ax to them."

"That's a surprise. She seems such a . . ."

". . . wretched brat?"

"Yeah, that."

"She is. Whenever I see her, she takes me to task about the food, the clothes, the temperature, no windows, her bodyguards, no sunlight . . . everything. I think it's just she doesn't know how not to complain. I stay as far away from her as I can."

"She is fine-looking, though, even when I saw her. Strange to think you might have been married to her by now." Paulo seemed to enjoy the thought.

I just found it alarming. "So, I guess some good came out of my being stolen away."

He raised his eyebrows and shook his head. "Someday you'll get all this sorcery and doom and king business out of your head and figure out there's other things for a man to think about."

On the day Paulo felt strong enough to climb the stairs to the portal, we set out for my long-delayed visit to the Source. Only an hour or so remained until time for the lights to go down. I had sat all day in the audience hall, hearing the petitions of a far-flung group of Singlars who wanted to dig a trench to draw water to their tappa fields from another tower cluster's supply.

"Are you sure you feel up to this?"

Paulo pushed my hand away. "If you don't get to it, you're going to forget what you come here for. I don't want you getting to like this king business too much. I'd give a deal to see the sun sometime soon."

We made the stomach-jolting passage to the garden that was still blooming as if this particular spot were forever spring. The yellow daylight was hot as we clambered down the steps. Paulo stopped just inside the cave mouth, close enough to listen.

"I'm depending on you," I said. I hadn't thought this venture would make me feel so unsettled, wound up tight with my stomach gnawing on itself.

"I'll be here."

Torches still burned in the sconces on the walls, making the cave sparkle, just as on our first visit. I walked the short distance to the spring. The basin itself was nothing remarkable, a slight depression in shallow shelf of rock that protruded from the mossy niche. The blue-green water seeped out of the surrounding rock to fill the basin and looked to be far deeper than the shallow bowl could possibly permit. I couldn't resist the urge to dip my hand into it.

"So you've come at last." No sooner had I touched the water than the clear voice surrounded me, reverberating in my very bones as if the icy water had penetrated my skin and carried the sound directly into me.

"You know who I am?" I said, peering under and around and behind the basin, examining the niche and the surrounding crystals as closely as possible. Finding nothing. I could see no hiding place in the alcove at the end of the cave, no sign of where the speaker might be found.

"You are the One Who Makes Us Bounded, our long-awaited king. You have lived in two worlds and found your place in neither, but in this world will you find the healing you seek." I still couldn't tell if the speaker was a man or a woman, but the smooth texture of the voice made me think of it as a "she."

"I'm not looking for healing, only answers."

"Only a small part of your questioning can I satisfy. All answers can be found within yourself."

"Who and what are you?"

"I am the Source—the first root of this world, not yet buried deep by the weight of years."

"Why are you so sure that I'm this king? How did you get into my dreams? How did you learn of me?"

She laughed softly. "So many questions . . . Here is one answer to satisfy all. As a stone falls to the land of which it is a part, as the rain finds its way to the sea which is its essence, so have you found your way to the Bounded. The stone dreams of the earth. The raindrop dreams of the ocean. And the earth needs no one to tell it of the stone's existence."

Vagaries and poetic speech—just as I had always read about oracles and prophecies. No absolutes. No matter what happened, a believer could always claim the sayings were truth, and a skeptic call them nonsense. I rested my back on the cave wall and thought about questions. Paulo's presence hovered behind me, so the next would be for his satisfaction as well as my own need.

"Are you . . . is any of this the work of the Lords of Zhev'Na?"

"The Bounded is beyond the reach of the Lords as long as you are beyond the reach of the Lords."

I couldn't decide whether or not that was reassuring. "Then who was the Guardian? The only reason I'm going along with this king business is to undo the things he's done."

"The Guardian it was who first spoke to me. His intent seemed earnest, his hand firm and enduring to guide the Singlars as they emerged from chaos." For the first time the voice reflected surprise . . . puzzlement. "Has he failed you, lord king?"

"He bound the Singlars to their towers with threats and punishments, beating and killing them, forbidding them company and pleasure, even denying them comfort and healing for their wounds and diseases. The Guardian said it was *your* commands he undertook. Why do you control the Singlars so cruelly, starving and punishing them?"

"No, no, my being is not cruelty. I entrusted the Guardian with the search for the king, but his reports never showed these things that trouble you. I shall have to consider the Guardian and hear your tales of the Singlars." Legitimate concern. Legitimate sadness. "Sadly, intents are often flawed . . . misdirected. Sometimes we fail to pay attention to things we ought. *You* know this."

I ignored the personal jab. The amethyst walls glittered in the torchlight, and I traced my fingers over the sharp facets of a crystal the size of my hand. "How long has the Bounded been in existence?"

"I have no concept of *how long*, but my nature is to be buried by the passage of time. A time will come when you and I no longer hear each other's voice, but it is not yet."

"What are the firestorms?"

"They are beyond my knowledge. They come from

outside, and you must stop them or the Bounded will be returned to what it was."

Returned to chaos. "How can I stop them if I don't even know what they are?"

"You are with us and cannot be other than you are."

"That's no answer."

"It is the most fundamental truth. It tells me that you can learn the nature of the storms. Though you belong here, you, like the storms, come from outside the Bounded. And the storms are aimed at you."

I was getting nowhere. How had the Guardian ever managed to get information specific enough to act on? Perhaps I had to frame my questions differently. I still had the most important thing to ask, yet I didn't expect an answer any clearer than those I'd already dismissed.

"Do you know who stabbed my mother?"

"Yes."

"And you know who betrayed the Prince's—my father's—plans?" It didn't seem necessary to explain what plans or who my mother and father were. This voice expressed the same understanding of me that I felt for this strange land.

"Yes."

Cold, tight, I moved toward the basin again, as if proximity might make me hear the answer better. I would tolerate no mistake. "Who, then?"

"I will not answer that."

My fingers gripped the rim of the water bowl as if I could rip it from the solid stone. "Tell me!"

"It is not time for you to know."

"This is madness!" I threw up my hands, wishing for something to break or throw, yelling at the ceiling and the walls and the floor of the damnable place. "You . . . whoever you are . . . whatever trickery you work . . . you've used a thousand words, but you've told me nothing at all! It's so easy to play the prophet, to tell me how wise and knowledgeable you are, but you speak in circles and refuse me the answers I need most."

"To tell you these things would be a distraction from all you must accomplish here. Your people need your care, more even than I—"

"These are *not* my people!"

"Be patient. Learn of your true self. Return in a hundredlight from this, and I will reveal what you ask of me. Until then, think carefully on all I have said."

"A hundredlight! A hundred days? Impossible! I don't even know . . . do *you* know if my mother is alive?"

"That I do not know. Ask me no more this day, O king. Secure your place in this, your new world. Help your—"

"How can I waste a hundred days? I have to go."

"And where would you go that is closer to the truth than in your heart—here, in the Bounded? Power awaits you here, and peace. Only death awaits you elsewhere."

Disgusted with myself for trying to force some meaning into gibberish, I turned to leave.

"Before you go, young king, will you not taste of the water that gives life to your land? To all others it is alien—poison—but for you it holds comfort, strength, and nourishment. It is *of* you, and thus it will sustain you in whatever trials you face."

I dabbled my fingers in the cold blue-green, scooping the water and letting it dribble through my fingers. "I don't think so. I don't trust your all-knowing benevolence."

"As you wish. I will await your return. Come to the Source for counsel as you desire, but wait a hundredlight for your deeper questioning."

"A waste of time," I said to Paulo, as we emerged from the cave. "I should have known no 'prophetic voice' would tell me anything useful. And three months to try again."

I strode down the path through the grove, only realizing, when Paulo grunted, how he was straining to keep up. Stopping at the pool, I gazed up at the falls for a bit, allowing him to catch his breath before we went on. The light had faded while we were in the cave. Sparrows and finches chattered as if the change were true sunset, and the call of a thrush pierced the cooling air with the clarity of a flute. In the shadier corners of the garden, lamps hung on iron posts gave off a warm glow that brightened even as the yellow-orange glare above us dimmed.

"So, what do you think?" I said, when Paulo's expression looked a little less anxious. "Did you feel the same things as before?"

"You're not going to like what I say."

"Go ahead."

"I think you need to get away from here. You oughtn't stay—not even one more day."

"This Source business is idiocy. I'll agree. But"—how could I explain what I felt here in the Bounded, despite the day's frustration?—"she was right about one thing. Where would I go?"

"It wasn't so much the voice, but the place . . . the whole thing. There's something wrong—something hidden. It's what she's *not* telling you that makes me skittish. I think we ought to leave. Go home. Hide out in Dunfarrie or Montevial if we can't go home. Get to Avonar somehow, if that's where you need to be to find out what's going on with you."

Even as the worn rim of the stone basin had yielded to the dribbling water, his arguments and my own resistance were eroded by simple logic. "I can't face my mother, living or dead, until I know who hurt her. There are no answers in Leire or Valleor. All I can do there is hide. And if I go to Avonar without an explanation in hand, my father will kill me or the Lords will take me back, and I won't even know who to blame."

He couldn't answer that. He'd been ready to kill me, too.

I draped Paulo's arm across my shoulders, and we walked slowly around the path and up the stairs to the gallery. "I'll be all right here for a while. But I'll have Vroon take you back . . . and the princess . . ."

"Now that wouldn't be smart," he said between steps. "If anyone was looking for you, and they found out the lady was come back from where you were . . . Well, she's not likely to keep it quiet, now is she? She'd lead 'em right to you."

"I suppose so."

"And I told you I'm stayin' close."

"Even if I decide to stay here?"

"Nothin' better to be at."

Without any further discussion, we stepped into the dark opening that would take us back to the Blue Tower. I wasn't yet ready to ask if he still thought I'd stabbed my mother.

CHAPTER 18

We stayed. The princess was livid when she heard it was to be another three months until she could go home, and she told me I was still the stupidest boy in the world who would take the word of a bowl of water for anything. She didn't speak to me for three days, and then decided maybe it was more of a punishment to make sure I heard her complaining all the time.

I couldn't argue with Roxanne's premise. I certainly needed to learn more about the Source. But a number of things had to come first.

Paulo's condition improved every day, and soon we were able to send Nithea home. I made sure she had a supply of all the medicinal plants I found in the garden and that she knew as much as I about what to do with them. Her eager questions made me wish I had listened closer to Kellea.

As the Singlars seemed inclined to listen to me, I spent the days trying to untangle the mess the Guardian had created, dealing with their disputes and petitions. I remembered how my mother had treated the tenants at Comigor with honesty and respect, and how she had spent most of her time listening rather than talking. Those principles seemed to carry me pretty well.

"You must do something! You're forcing me to stay in this desolation, so it's your responsibility!"

I had never expected to find the Crown Princess of Leire in the queue of petitioners that jammed the audience hall as happened one morning a week or so after my visit to the Source. The Singlars watched in awe and

fascination as she rattled the walls with her yelling. She
stamped her foot and pointed her finger as if it were a
crossbow aimed at my chest.

"I've no idea how you might amuse yourself," I said.
"And I don't care. I've more important things to worry
about." What did she think I was?

"You've no horses, no dogs, no music, no dancing, no
bow hunting, no books, games, lessons, or conversation . . .
nothing. If I lose my mind from boredom, you'll have a
larger problem than this fellow's collapsing wall." She
jerked her head at the Singlar just behind her. "One of
his neighbors has been launching boulders at him, an
amusement I might take up if you don't give me something to do."

"Go away." At least twenty petitioners stood in the
queue, and each one was going to use up two hours or
more explaining who he was or where she was from,
the history of every day since becoming "real," and the
particular circumstances of today's need or grievance.
Some of these people would still be here three days from
this one, and twenty new ones would join the queue in
between. "It's hard enough to sort out these people's
actual problems."

"Well then, I'll help you. I'm no stranger to assizes.
At least I won't rot from disuse."

"No." Leiran laws and customs were not my idea of
reasonable. "Go away. Ob, please see the lady out. . . ."

"Lady." But Roxanne shook off the leathery man's
hand and swept out of the room, her back rigid as a
pillory.

On the next morning, as I labored through the first
case of the day, trying to understand something about
tappa skins from a Singlar who could not get out three
words without an interminable pause in between, Vroon
hurried across the room to my side. I was relieved to
see only three more petitioners waiting, though the ever-
present crush of babbling spectators milled about the
hall. Vroon bowed to the waiting Singlar with a quick
jerk. "Majesty, may I intrude on your speaking with this
good Singlar?"

"Of course, Vroon. What is it?"

As always he swelled with pride when I spoke his
name in public hearing, but his brow was drawn down
in such a scowl, it almost hid his good eye. "It is the
ever-talking woman, Majesty. She is making speeches
with the Singlars, and I fear she is trying to make plots
with them or to prevent their seeking help from you
who can make them bounded."

I jumped out of my chair and hurried down the long
room, ready to throttle the woman if she was trying to
undermine my authority. She was seated at a small desk,
talking earnestly with a knobby-faced young woman and
scratching notes on a sheet of paper. When I walked up
and looked over her shoulder, she twisted her head and
looked up, blinking innocently.

"Ah, Your Majesty," she said. "This young woman
wishes to take service in the Blue Tower. She's come
from a great distance to beg a ration of tappa, but isn't
sure she can find her way back to her fastness—a meager
tower from the sound of it, and isolated, but I'll not
burden you with the details of her poverty or her terrifying journey. She was delighted at the idea of remaining
here and exchanging her work for her sustenance. I have
noted her place of residence and her description on my
sheet—which, of course, I was planning to leave with
you when today's petitions are resolved—and told her
that after a twentylight of good service, the king would
consider granting her a name. Does that seem in order?"

My mouth was open to order Roxanne to stop interfering, but the young Singlar woman bowed her head
and clasped her hands together. "No name is needed,"
she said very softly. "Only to eat. To help. To be
bounded is a hopeful blessing of great joy, but hunger
is deeper. Told was I, that the king valued good service."

"Of course you can stay. And a twentylight . . . that's
reasonable. But you, Lady—"

"And earlier, a gentleman Singlar gave me a very long
description of a device he has fashioned from sticks and
vines. It sounds very like a sledge, which could, of
course, be useful if you think to make anything of this
somewhat . . . primitive . . . settlement you call Tower
City. He was one of your Witnesses, who now feels the

wholeness of being Avero. I have recorded his name and
the precise location of his tower, so that you may go
there and see his invention on your next progress
through the city—assuming, of course, that, as the wisest
of monarchs do, you intend to take up the practice of
periodic journeys throughout your kingdom—and so, instead of standing in this queue, Avero has returned to
his fastness and is excitedly building four more sledges
to have them ready when you come to inspect them."

"All right, but—"

"Have I done ill, Your Majesty? Shall I send for the
good Avero to stand in your queue? His story of how
he has grown his fastness from a mound of mud into a
tower half as tall as this one is truly astounding . . .
and interminable. And then there is the three-handed
woman. . . ." Roxanne had not smiled even once.

"All right," I said, still considering whether or not I
should lock her in her room. I didn't trust her. Didn't
fancy her running amok with her ideas. "But I want to
hear about every one, and if there's the least—"

"I will dispose of only the most obvious requests. In
all others, especially disputes of the kind which form the
foundation of law, I will discover the facts of the case
and note them on a paper which the petitioners will
bring to you. Two of the men waiting for you over there
have already talked to me, and carry my summaries in
their hands . . . or feet, in the case of the one with no
hands. And granting names is clearly your prerogative.
If only Leiran nobles were born without names. . . ."

My daily audience ran smoothly from that day forward. Vroon disapproved of the princess, ever suspicious
that she was subverting my authority. He watched her
so closely, I didn't have to worry about the matter at all.

Though it was hardly necessary, I formally and publicly
repealed the Guardian's rules that restricted the Singlars
to the towers. I had no idea how to get the people to work
with each other or make something out of their cities. I
had to hope they would figure that out for themselves
without killing each other. The Singlars seemed to learn
everything very quickly, even the rotten things.

*   *   *

On the tenth change of the light after my visit to the Source, the morning was less grim than usual. *Morning* was a term only Paulo, Roxanne, and I attached to the first hours after the lamps came up. Before this particular one I'd never seen such a large portion of the sky clear enough to show so many millions of the green stars, enough of them that you could navigate the Bounded without lamps or torches. The wind was moderate and mostly warm. Occasional cool, moist pockets hung in the lee of the taller towers. The storms and lightnings stayed over the Edge, far beyond the horizon.

Paulo and I decided to take an early walk through the city. Roxanne saw us leaving and attached herself to the excursion, saying she wanted to see the new marketplace. Vroon and Zanore had told the Singlars what they'd seen in our world, and gradually the lanes of the Tower City were being transformed into a hive of flickering torchlight and unceasing activity. I wanted to see how things were progressing, too, but I also had a few things I wanted to talk about with Paulo. When you walked with Roxanne, you talked about what *she* wanted.

On this occasion, however, Paulo didn't give her a chance to start. He was excited about some large four-legged beasts Zanore had told him were roaming the lands beyond the Gray Fastness. The Singlar had said the beasts were very like the horses he had obtained for us back in Valleor. "I was thinking I might have to look into that," Paulo said.

As we walked, he held his hands out in front of him, flexing his fingers as Nithea had commanded him. They looked dreadful, discolored and scarred where they stuck out of the bandages that remained about his palms, but he could move them fairly well and was gradually regaining his strength and dexterity.

"I miss Jasyr, myself," I said. "Do you think he and Molly are waiting for us back—Stars of night!" I stopped and pressed a hand to my forehead. If four of my Witnesses hadn't been posted in front, behind, and to the sides of us as bodyguards, I might have thought someone had stuck a rapier right between my ears.

"What is it?" By the time Roxanne asked the question, the sensation was gone.

"Nothing," I said, blinking my watering eyes and kneading my scalp a little, thinking I must have had too much wine the previous night.

Pink and orange lightning flashed from beyond the Edge. We walked on. Roxanne said something about riding. The piercing pain shot through my skull again . . . this time accompanied by screams and shouts from every side.

" 'Ware!"

"Firestorm!"

With a skull-shattering blast, a forked tongue of brilliant white streaked across the green-starred dome above us. Wails of terror rose from the city.

"Face out!" Paulo shouted to my bodyguards, shoving them with his bandaged hands.

The four Witnesses drew close around me, one facing each compass point. Paulo had come up with the idea, thinking they could watch for the rifts heading toward me and get me out of the path. He had forced them to practice it over and over, even when they insisted no storms would dare come again, because the king was come to the Bounded.

"What in the name of Annadis—?" Roxanne's yell was cut off when Paulo shoved her back flat against mine. The princess had never experienced a firestorm. The one we'd survived on our first day in the Bounded had not reached so far as the Blue Tower.

"Alas, the death fire . . . save us . . ." A wailing Singlar, trailing a length of tappa cloth behind him, raced down the lane just ahead of a jagged rent in the earth.

Paulo reached for his hand, but his fingers slipped out of Paulo's grasp, and the Singlar fell screaming into the fire. Feeling weak and useless, I struggled to keep breathing, clutching the sides of my head to keep it from cracking in two. Hands dragged me sideways. A burst of white flame blackened my shirt, scorched my cheek, and incinerated one of my bodyguards.

"We'll watch out," yelled Paulo in my ear. "Do as you need!"

This storm was far worse than the first one. I could scarcely hear him for the thunder and the pain in my head. Another rift split the sky. Fighting not to cry out, I sank to my knees. Gathering what strength I had left, I closed my eyes and plunged myself into darkness.

The canvas of my mind was scarred with searing ribbons of fire, one and then another, coming so fast I almost couldn't keep up. As I had done before, I attempted to seal each rift as it appeared, to absorb the heat, the pain, and the terror that rode the lightning like an enemy warrior on a white charger.

Control the fire. Build your fastness strong. Confine the flames behind these walls, leaving the world dark . . . silent . . . safe . . .

I built the walls thick, muffling the shouts of warning, the clamor of fear and destruction. I no longer felt the hands pulling me to safety, only the soul-searing flames.

Hold, I told myself. *You must hold. One slip, one weakness, will breach this armor you forge, these walls you build, this fastness that is safety. Keep it dark outside. In here, let the fire burn. . . .*

An odd sound called me out of the silent dark. The low-pitched trill might have been the buzz of a hummingbird's wings until it skittered up the scale into a cheerful melody you might hear at a jongler fair. The piper dragged my limp senses along with him until his music was abruptly halted by a harsh whisper. "Quiet till he wakes. Your noise disturbs the king."

"If he sleeps, then my playin' don't disturb him. If he wakes, then he can decide for hisself if it bothers. My whistle must play the last of the storm away. It's been too long silent."

"We'll stuff the stick down your gullet!"

"It's all right," I said, opening my eyes to a string of dusty, whitish lumps dangling just above my nose. Tappa roots. Three pale and anxious faces, bearing a striking resemblance to the lumpy roots, hovered close in the smoke haze that hung below the low ceiling.

"Majesty!"

The dangling foodstuffs had to be nudged out of the

way, along with my relieved bodyguards, before I could
prop myself up on my elbows. The place looked bleaker
than the worst tenant shacks at Comigor. Dirt floor, low
ceiling. My prickly bed felt like twigs with a thin blanket
thrown over them. Beyond a tiny fire flickering in a
freshly dug fire pit, a scrawny, light-haired youth was
curled up against the wall of dried mud, playing a reed
shepherd's pipe.

"How is it with you, sire?" Nithea knelt on the floor
beside me, her cool hands on my forehead and cheek.

"I'm all right," I said, taking her hands and moving
them aside so I could sit up all the way. "What am I
doing here? The storm . . . How bad was it?" Paulo
stood just behind Nithea.

He stepped around her and squatted down beside me.
"Seven towers destroyed in the city," he said, speaking
low. "Twenty-some damaged. Three Singlars lost, including Gant." Gant was my fourth bodyguard, the one I'd
seen catch fire. "It was just as before. All the lightning
headed straight for you. After a bit everything went
dark, and then it was over. You wouldn't wake up,
though, so we brought you to the closest shelter."

"The princess?"

Paulo jerked his head to a shadowy spot beyond the
makeshift fire pit.

Roxanne sat on the dirt by the wall, huddled under a
long cloak, staring at her knees. She must have felt us
looking at her, for she glanced up and met my gaze. Her
face was smudged with soot, and her eyes were bleak.
Pressing her hand to her mouth, she slowly rose to her
feet. After a moment, she inhaled deeply, lowered her
hand, and straightened her spine. "I'm going back to the
Blue Tower now," she said. "I'll be in my bed."

She stepped to the silvery trace on the wall and
vanished.

Paulo gazed after her. "Her mouth was open to
scream the whole time, but she couldn't make a noise.
Pulled you to safety once, though. And grabbed Kalo
before he could fall into a rift. He did the same for her.
When it was over, she followed us in here. Sat here all
day staring like that."

All day . . . "How long have I been out?"

"It's almost time for the lights to go down. Are you sure you're all right now?"

"I'm fine," I repeated. Especially for having been insensible most of a day. "Is this your fastness?" I asked the piper.

" 'Tis."

"If I could have a drink of something . . ."

My three bodyguards almost fell over themselves rummaging about the place as I got to my feet. The piper directed them to a crude clay bowl, and I was soon drinking a cup of weak tappa ale.

"You're Tom from Lach Vristal," I said. The arm he'd used to point out the water bowl had no hand on it.

"Aye. I am that." He grinned broadly. "And you're the new king."

"I followed you here from your father's lay."

The hand holding the reed pipe fell into his lap. "Did you now? How fare they at the lay—Pap and Hugh and Dora? I've a sorrow not to see them."

"They seem well enough. But your father grieves. He thinks you were stolen away by thieves."

"He didn't understand how I had to come here."

"I suppose you'd like to go back now."

The youth had probably not been out of this hovel in weeks. The place smelled like it.

"Why would I want to go back?" said Tom.

"For your family. For the hills. For the sheep. I don't know. What have you here? Wouldn't you go back just to see the sun or eat a slab of bacon?"

Vroon had told me that most of the newcomers had a difficult time learning how to grow their fastnesses, or even how to get in or out of them, much less where and how to harvest the tappa roots. He and his companions felt bad about it, but didn't know how to remedy the problem. The idea of teaching the poor souls had never occurred to them. At least Tom had learned about tappa.

The fellow smiled, then. "Listen." Returning the pipe to his lips and propping it up with his handless wrist, he danced his five fingers over the holes.

I was not a judge of music. Though my mother valued it, and I was told she played the flute reasonably well, four years of listening to her had not made up for twelve years' lack. But Tom's playing was something else again. The song rambled slowly and mournfully for a while, up and down the scales as if looking for just the right note. There it was, and the next, not the one you might expect, but a different note that took you around an unsuspected corner, and before I knew it, I was somewhere else altogether. . . .

They're so green . . . the fair hills of my land. The lake so clear, imaging the bowl of the sky. Or is it the sky what is the deeps of the lake? The sun is blessed hot. Its firm hand feels so fine beating down on my shoulders, and the heather smell floats on the soft air, boiled up from the ground by the sun, Dora says. The sheep are safe, but I've got to get back. Pap'll beat me for leaving the sheepcrook behind. He's a firmer hand than even the sun. But I'm free with my pipes, and running. Up and across the hills just like the music . . . faster and faster, then down, down into the cool valley. Pap says the sheep smell tells of the year's good fortune. . . .

"You see?"
The music had stopped, taking the vision with it. I had never felt so light, so . . . joyful. Now, my bodyguard's bulk close to my elbow seemed to be the only thing that kept me from toppling over.
"Are you sure you're all right?" Paulo. Whispering.
I shook the fragments of the image from my head. "I'm fine." I almost shivered as I wriggled the fingers of my left hand, reassuring myself that fingers and hand were all there. From the puzzled looks, I gathered that no one else had seen what I'd seen.
Tom smiled at me crookedly. "How could I leave? I never made such music in the hills, and it brings the hills to my heart so's I don't sorrow for 'em too fierce. And these good folk here"—he waved his stump at Vroon and Zanore and the other Singlars—"they don't make

jest of a man if 'e's a broken one like me. They're all broken, too. I belong here."

Someone had dropped a cloak about my shoulders. I hooked the clasp at my throat. "Your music is very nice. Stay as long as you like in the Bounded. Come and tell me if you decide you want to go home." I hurried out.

From the outside, Tom's tower was a squat, ugly place, like a mud wasp's nest attached to a grimy windowsill. I told Vroon I wanted Tom taken care of, taught how to live properly in the Bounded, and the same for all the others that he and Ob and Zanore had brought here. If they wanted to return to their homes, Vroon should take them back through the moon-door.

Then, we headed back for the Blue Tower. I needed to sleep.

As I had expected, they were waiting for me outside the Blue Tower . . . the Singlars . . . filling the commard so that I had to pass through them to get inside. They murmured reverently and bent their knees as I passed. I didn't want this. I didn't want any of it.

CHAPTER 19

The condition of the Singlars nagged at me. I didn't understand how the storerooms at the Blue Tower had come to be filled with ham, duck sausage, oranges, and silk, while the Singlars had nothing but tappa, mud, and rock. The answer must exist in the garden. I didn't trust the Source to tell me anything useful, so I decided to do some investigating, putting the question to the Source only if I couldn't discover the answer on my own.

"I need to understand about the light," I said one day, as Paulo and I poked around the base of the cliffs near the waterfall and the amethyst cave. "What makes a light so bright that plants can grow inside this place?" And it was only here. No Singlar I'd spoken to, even among those who had traveled widest, knew of anything like this garden elsewhere in the Bounded.

The pale yellow boulders were jumbled and broken around the waterfall and the grotto, the face of the rock less sheer than the rest of the garden perimeter. Innumerable dirt paths squeezed past the rocks, promising to take you higher, only to taper into nothing or end abruptly at a cliff. I climbed back down from the current dead end.

"This whole world is fair odd. I could believe most anything." Paulo vanished behind a boulder twice my height, then emerged above it, craning his neck upward and shaking his head. "We might try this way. Looks rugged, though."

I squeezed between the boulder and the cliff, and scrambled up the rocks to stand beside him. It wasn't exactly a path. More like a flight of granite steps, sized

for legs three times the length of mine, with a number
of stomach-curdling gaps filled by loose avalanche debris. We started up. Our path held close enough to the
falls to keep the rocks treacherously damp.

A quarter of the way to the top of the falls, Paulo sat
heavily on a wide boulder. His exaggerated groan
bounced off the rocks as he sprawled on his back and
flung his arms wide. "Demonfire, but I'm done already.
I'll just wait here for you to scrape me up on your
way down."

No surprise. The way kept getting steeper. Paulo's
stamina was much improved in the last week, but his
hands were still bandaged and weak. I'd already had to
haul myself over a few of the slabs.

"If I'm passing by too fast on the way down, you
might need to stick out your hand and catch me," I said,
peering up into the glare.

By the time I reached the top of the falls, I was climbing rather than walking or scrambling. The effort required all my limbs and all my concentration. And the
heat had become murderous. Only the spray from the falls
and the eddying air currents set in motion by the massive
movement of water kept me from melting into a heap.

Eventually, the steep cleft in the rock led me over the
edge of the cliff. I rested for a while on a gentle slope
of barren rock that formed both the cliff top and the
riverbank, funneling the water over the edge. Before me
lay the gut-heaving drop to the colorful blot of the garden. I couldn't see the roof or sky or whatever it was
existed above this odd landscape. Great billows of steam
hung over the river as it thundered over the edge of the
cliff, causing a hazy glare that obscured the view. The
rock underneath me was hot to the touch.

Not much farther. What I was searching for was
nearby. My bones told me. My senses and instincts insisted. After the brief rest, I blotted my damp face one
more time on my shirt and climbed up and away from
the cliff's side to see what lay beyond the rocky slope.
When I reached the summit, my heart almost stopped.

The ridge sloped sharply downward and flattened into
a shimmering plain, the shore of an ocean of fire . . . a

sea of sunlight . . . a rippling expanse of gold that stretched as far as I could see into the uncertain reaches of this strange place. From this gleaming ocean, pillars of shifting light rose into the heights, some gold, some blue-white, some red-orange, ever growing and dissipating like the watery storms and spouts sailors witnessed on mundane oceans. The hazy brilliance threatened to blind me; the heat came near blistering my skin. To stay here long would leave me no strength to go down again.

This marvel, like the moon-door and the garden and the heaving Edge, was no enchantment, but the natural substance of the Bounded. Looking on it left the same warm, satisfied feeling in my belly as a good meal and good wine.

I was not tempted to touch the substance of the sea itself. To stand even so near as I was to the scalding water . . . fire . . . whatever it was . . . was debilitating enough. Yet neither could I retreat. For the great crescent of shoreline that swept alongside the river, where it flowed out of the sea and across the plain to cool and plummet over the edge of the cliff, was not sand, but shingle, great swathes of fist-sized golden rocks abandoned by the sea and the river.

The rocks were the key to life in the Bounded. The sea and the rocks would brighten and fade with the rhythm of the suns that warmed more familiar worlds. I could not explain it any more than I could explain the fickle weather of the Bounded or the green stars or the expanding Edge. I just understood it. If you waited until the rocks began to fade of an evening, you could gather and carry them in your hand or a bag or a cart. If you set them in a pit of sand in a tower, they would glow and nourish a small garden with healthy light.

Light, food, a world . . . I could make that happen.

Sharing the sunrocks and the plants that grew in the garden became my highest priority. If I could accomplish what I intended, every Singlar would be able to use the sunrocks to grow a little garden in the heart of his or her fastness, every one of them slightly different. Names continued to be something special that the Singlars had to get directly from me. I used names to recognize those who changed things for the better and obeyed my laws. But although we made a great ceremony of it—that part was Roxanne's idea—*everyone* received the rocks and the plants.

The first supply of sunrocks went to the Rift Cluster. I carried them there myself, excited to tell the bent philosopher of the new things I had seen. So much had happened since I'd sat in his fastness. Weeks had passed. As we traveled through the rain and gloom, I chafed at how Avero's crude wheeled sledge slowed our progress. When we reached the rift, I left the others behind and hurried down into the dreary cluster. A gaunt young woman with a stunted arm stepped forward in the muddy narrows to greet us. My excitement withered.

"Your leader," I said, as the cold rain beat down on my head, "the tall Singlar with the bent shoulder . . . who sings . . ."

"To our loss and sorrow, our leader is unbounded, good traveler," said the woman. "Six wakings before this."

"Was it a beast . . . or did he drown . . . ?" But I knew better.

"He weakened greatly in the cold just past," said the woman, her eyes bright in the torchlight. "But happy was he always, teaching us to endure. He told us that he, a humble Singlar, had supped with the Bounded King, who was traveling his realm in disguise! Is that not a wonder? We hold his thoughts dear, and they warm us more than flame."

A wonder? I could not answer the woman. Could not look at her. All the bright pleasure of my discovery . . . my plan . . . dulled and fell into ash. Why had I not thought to send these people help in the past weeks? *Selfish, stupid fool.* Paulo had warned me. *Too caught up in playing king.* In playing god.

The woman stood waiting for me to make sense of the world.

"Grieved . . . sorrowed . . . greatly sorrowed am I to

hear this," I said. "I had hoped to give him—Well, we've brought things to help you. My companions will show you."

The woman summoned the rest of the rift dwellers who waited shyly beside their towers in the cold rain. Vroon opened the stone caskets and distributed the sun-rocks, teaching the Singlars how to use them to warm their towers and nurture the tappa roots and other plants Zanore pulled out of our wheeled sledge. I stood in the rain contemplating pride and thoughtlessness and how little difference sorrow or shame makes once a deed is done.

When the lesson was finished, I asked the Singlars to stay one moment before returning to their fastnesses. "Though I neither sought nor wanted the office, and though I've neither experience nor wisdom to commend me, it seems I am your king. To your leader"—I nodded to the woman—"I give the name *Vanaya*, which means *wise follower*, for I see that she follows in the footsteps of a great leader, her own kind spirit learning from his wisdom and grace. To the one who is gone, I grant the name *Daerli*, which means *farseer* in the language of my people. This name will be held in the highest respect in the Bounded forevermore, and his life will serve an ex-ample and reminder for us all."

A reminder for me.

Any surmise that my presence in the Bounded had stopped the firestorms was quickly dispelled. Whatever the cause of the previous cessation, it was done with, for at about the same time I discovered the sunrocks, the storms took up with a virulence and regularity the Sin-glars had never before experienced. Every two or three days the world fell apart with a bolt of white brilliance, and I retreated into the fastness of myself so I could put it back together again. Paulo said the storms stopped quickly once I got to work, though I seemed to experi-ence their entirety. By the time the fires burned them-selves out and I slipped into insensibility, I had long lost all sense of time.

Once I came to expect them, I caught most of the

storms early on, so the Bounded suffered little injury or damage. When a particularly violent storm struck one night while I was sleeping, though, it was devastating—fifty towers lost in the Tower City alone, and many more in the smaller clusters throughout the land. Being waked so suddenly made it almost impossible for me to get control. Paulo admitted that I was screaming worse than when I had nightmares at Verdillon by the time I'd stopped the storm. Almost an entire cycle of the light passed before I woke up again.

From that day forward, I posted a guard outside my door whose sole function was to wake me in case of a firestorm. The Singlars considered it the highest honor I could do them, so I kept the position active even after I'd come to sense the storms' birth in my sleep, like any trained warrior who learns to feel his enemy steal through his dreams. Or maybe I never really slept any more.

Though the storms terrified her beyond any sorcery or dungeon, Roxanne suggested that I should let some of the storms have their way and maybe they would stop. Paulo urged me to leave the Bounded until they subsided again. I refused both suggestions. Now that the Singlars had sunrocks and gardens, sledges and kilns, I could not allow the destruction, not to mention the loss of life. And, as storms had occurred even before I came to the Bounded, we had no reason to believe they would stop if I left. Besides, I wanted my answers from the Source, and I wanted to leave the Singlars able to take care of themselves so I wouldn't feel so responsible.

Four or five weeks after the storms had taken up again, a violent firestorm struck on the eve of a long-planned journey to a remote tower cluster. I was insensible for half a day after it. Paulo suggested postponing the trip so I could rest, but I wouldn't hear of it. We were delivering sunrocks.

We left the Tower City just after the lights came up and were soon walking through sparsely settled countryside. The weather was wild, dense clouds of purple and black surging and boiling across the sky. The wind was blowing a gale, and sleet threatened to remove our skin or at least any prominent features we left exposed.

During our first rest stop, I huddled into the lee of a rock while Paulo, Vroon, and the others ate. Even after the rest period had come and gone, I couldn't seem to muster the will to move on. My limbs felt like lead.

"They're eating you up, aren't they?" Paulo lowered himself to the frozen mud beside me. I hadn't even heard him coming.

"What do you mean?"

He offered me a piece of sweet tappa bread. I shook my head and burrowed deeper in my cloak as a gust of wind swirled around the rocks.

"*That's* what I mean. You haven't eaten three mouthfuls of anything since the storm yesterday, and I'll wager I could take you down in three moves as I've not been able to do since you were a nub. The princess could take you down with her tongue."

"I'm just tired. I'll recover."

"Not while the storms keep up."

"I'll figure out something. It's only another few weeks till we can leave this cursed place."

"You won't last that long. And if some of these oddments that still believe the Guardian was their friend find out you can't think straight for half a day after a storm, they might come up with some way to do us in."

We'd had some trouble with some of the old maintainers trying to force Singlars back into their fastnesses, beating them and telling them I was destroying the Source. Most Singlars were still easily intimidated.

"I can't leave now."

"Then go back to the Source. Try what it said would help you."

"Drink from the spring? Not likely. I don't want to take anything from the Source. You said yourself that you didn't trust it."

"I don't. But I don't want you dead neither. I want to go back where they make jack and real biscuits, and where I can plant my backside on a piece of horseflesh. If you're going to be dead, then you might as well be dead from trying to stay alive."

I didn't answer him then. I just got to my feet and said, "I'll be all right. Let's get moving."

Three days later another storm struck, worse than the last. Another sevenlight, three more storms, and I couldn't go up the stairs in the Blue Tower without stopping every third step to rest. I'd lost so much weight, my breeches wouldn't stay up. I felt as scrawny as Zanore, but Zanore could have tied me in a knot with one hand. My mouth tasted like ash, as if everything inside me had burned up. Paulo kept looking at me, and I knew what he was thinking.

I went to the Source while everyone was asleep. I didn't take Paulo with me, didn't tell him or anyone where I was going. I didn't want anyone seeing how hard it was for me to get up the stairs.

The lamps were down in the tower, so it was night in the garden. But it wasn't completely dark. Lamps just like the ones in the tower hung on iron posts, scattered throughout the plants and trees, casting a soft yellow glow on the path. The air felt chilly, but that was no surprise. I couldn't seem to get warm any more.

"Greetings, my king." The voice washed over and through me when I walked into the cave and dipped my hand in the water. "Too long it's been since you've come here."

I didn't waste time. "What did you mean when you said the water from the spring could sustain me through my trials?"

"Just that, my king. The water is of you, and thus will strengthen and nourish you."

I dabbled my hand in the icy blue-green water. It had no smell, no aura of enchantment. I touched my tongue to a drop and discovered no suspicious taste, no unexpected sensation except for overpowering thirst. No instinct warned me of poison. Having eaten or drunk nothing for many days without threat of imminent nausea, and having scarcely made it down the garden steps without falling on my face, I decided it was worth a try. I scooped up a handful.

"Drink deep, my king. Live."

And so I did.

"Oh, stars of night . . ." It was hard not to drain the basin dry. Pure, clean, clear, the water stung each of my

senses awake. After I had drunk all I could hold, I
sagged against the cave wall and slipped down to the
floor, feeling the ash that clogged my veins and lungs
washed away. I did not sleep, but by the time the lamps
faded and the sunrocks began to glow, I could think
clearly again. I must have been perilously close to the
end. The Source did not speak again that night.

From then on I went to the Source after every storm.
Each time I dipped my hand in the water, the voice
would greet me. "Welcome, my king. I rejoice in your
life. How may I serve you this day?"

"Will you answer my question?"

"Not yet. The time of your understanding is not come.
But I would talk with you about many other things."

"Then I'll just drink the water and be on my way."

"Ah, you are hard! I must find something to tease you
into talking with me. I've waited so long for your
company."

"Tell me what I want to know."

"You should expand the realm of those things you
want to know. Your wisdom is lacking in many areas."

It became a game of sorts between us.

"Tell me, O voice of the water bowl, have you a
name?" I said one day, as I sat watching the torchlight
sparkle on the surface of the spring while the water did
its work in me.

"I am the first root of the Bounded. It is perhaps not
an elegant name. Not easy on the tongue."

"It seems strange to call you *Source*. It's not a proper
name. I could call you *Root*, I suppose."

"As you wish—and I could call you *boy*, instead of
king, for at the root of your being is a youth of sixteen,
though you bear the burdens of a king."

Gradually we did move on to matters of more substance in our conversations. I began to talk of problems
brought to me by the Singlars, of difficulties caused by
the changes I'd made, and of freedoms I'd given them.
I asked about the roving bands of monstrous creatures
that I knew were sentient beings who threatened outly-
ing fastnesses, and what to do about the Singlars who

were afraid to leave their towers to join in the awakening life of the city. I began to think of the Source as a friend who spoke to me as an elder sister might. She never told me what to do, but led me through my thinking, asking questions and encouraging me to draw on everything I'd learned: from books, from watching my father and mother—both my true parents and those who had raised me—even from my time with the Lords, though neither the Source nor I ever mentioned them by name. I refused to sully the beauty of that cave with the ugliness of my past.

"The answer is already there," she said to me when I fumed in frustration at some problem. "You have only to uncover it."

And most of the time it was.

I remembered what the Source had said that first time, about how a stone dreams of the earth of which it is a part and how the rain finds its way to the sea that is its essence, and I came to believe that I was indeed linked to the Bounded in some profound way. The firestorms that damaged us both, the water that healed me, the Source that knew my mind, my instincts and familiarity with the strange land and its people . . . even the geometries of the Blue Tower that satisfied desires I hadn't even known I had . . . my nausea at the unsettled Edge . . . everything I had experienced here witnessed to such a mystery.

And so as the days of waiting passed, the Bounded grew, and I felt useful, and I began to think that once I'd settled my business in the mundane world—my mother and the rest of it—I just might come back and finish what I had begun here.

Roxanne became an invaluable assistant in matters of governing, coming up with good ideas about trade laws and judgments and projects. She must have studied every document about philosophy, law, or politics that had ever been written in the Four Realms, and she delighted in quoting them at me, especially when she could trounce one of my ideas. I had never imagined anyone could take pleasure in argument.

She didn't travel the Bounded with Paulo and me. Though she never admitted it, I think it was fear of the firestorms that kept her close to the Blue Tower. The first one had kept her in her bed for almost a week.

When she wasn't helping me in the audience hall or the council chamber, as I had named a large study down the passage from my bedchamber, she was rummaging about the Blue Tower, foraging for furnishings, fabrics she might use for clothing more suited to her tastes, anything to enliven a "house run by male children" as she put it. She had taken over the running of the household, training servants and ordering whatever foods and furnishings she liked from the luxuries found in the storerooms of the Blue Tower, but nowhere else in the city. I was happy to have her deal with those things, as I had more than enough to do, and cared not a whit what we ate or sat on.

That no one could say where the goods in the storerooms came from or how to obtain more when the supplies started getting thin piqued my curiosity, but infuriated Roxanne. She could not abide secrets or mysteries, and took any suggestion that an event was unexplainable in terms of science, economics, or politics as a personal affront. Living in the Bounded, which by its very existence was a mystery beyond her experience, came near driving her to distraction. Even after she'd long given up on science and nature, no day passed on which she failed to look for any small mystery that she could declare solved.

And so she was determined to discover how the Blue Tower was supplied and set out to investigate every part of the place, even the garden. With some misgiving I allowed her to go to the garden, though I forbade her to enter the cave of the Source.

She agreed to my restriction, though not without complaint.

"Come on. You must see what I've found." She was waiting outside my bedchamber, her gold hair in a flurry of curls, her green gown perfect as always.

"Not today." If it hadn't been the hundredth morning

of my waiting, I might have been more interested in her "discovery."

She stuck to me like a grass burr as I headed down the passage to the stair. "I've been trying to tell you about it for a fortnight, but you're always traveling or too busy. Promise me you'll take just a moment to look."

"Later. Have you forgotten? This is the day I get my answers, and I'll not wait a moment longer than necessary. I'd have thought you'd be shoving me up these stairs yourself."

When I reached the stair, she dodged in front of me and backed slowly up the stairway, not allowing me to get past her. "Yes, of course, I want to go back, but I'll never get another chance to solve a mystery like this. Sorcery is against the law in Leire, and my life there is going to be hideously boring. Do you know how annoying it is, always being ignored because you don't have the right private parts, knowing you're going to be married off to someone's idiot son whom you will never love and knowing that the pox-ridden dolt will rule the kingdom that is yours by right?"

"You'll drive the fellow bats and order the Four Realms to your every whim." It could do worse.

"That's not the same."

I tried again to push past her, but she flitted from side to side, blocking the way. I was ready to be angry with her, but in her exasperating, teasing way she dangled a glittering object of red and gold in front of my face, snatching it away and hiding it behind her back before I could see it. "You've never told me these important questions of yours. Perchance I've found one of your answers for you. Did you ever think of that? Though because of your insufferable reluctance to speak more than three words at a time and never what you're truly thinking, you'll never admit it, you know very well I'm not a fool. So when I say I've found something of interest to you—even on *this* day—you really ought to listen, don't you think?"

I halted on the stair. "All right, what do you have?"

She held up the glittering object again. Her trinket

was the ruby-studded key that had hung about the neck
of the Guardian.

"Oh. I'd forgotten that." My first inquiries into its use
had been fruitless, and I'd never given it another
thought. "Where did it get off to?"

"You threw it on the desk in the Guardian's retiring
room, and I didn't think it should be left about to be
stolen. You have a lot more faith in the honesty of these
Singlars than I do. But I've learned what it's for, and I
want you to see. We'll be leaving this world soon, and
this is the only truly important thing I've discovered!"

She'd been a great help to me all these weeks, more
than I'd had any right to expect. And I had to admit
that she'd tweaked my curiosity with the key. I'd already
waited a hundred days. An hour more or less could
make no difference. "So what does it unlock?" I said.

"I went looking for keyholes everywhere, and there
just aren't all that many. But I found one here in the
Blue Tower and one in your garden, and this key fits
them both. Come on."

We reached the head of the stair, and she pointed to
the notch in the raised center of the yellow stone circle.
The ruby-studded key slipped smoothly into the slot.

"Now look at the haft," said Roxanne, "the way the
jewel points to the flowers. I wondered what would happen if I turned the key. Try it."

I twisted the haft of the key and felt a steady resistance . . . until I'd turned it a quarter of the way
around. The teardrop-shaped ruby pointed at a laden
grapevine at the bottom of the circle. I turned it again,
and then again, feeling the pegged end of the key snick
into place at each quarter, leaving the jewel pointed first
at the carved wheat sheaves and next at a cluster of
leafless trees. But nothing else happened.

Roxanne pulled the key from the hole, but she didn't
seem disappointed. "Go ahead and open the way as
usual. You'll see."

I ran my fingers around the circle, and when the wall
dissolved and the passage appeared, we stepped through
it and, shortly after, onto the gallery.

It was winter. Snow lay in thick mounds on the shrubs

and terraces, and the barren trees cracked in the cold. Thick gray clouds obscured the clifftops. Across the expanse of the winter garden, the frozen waterfall hung suspended between the false heavens and the mysterious earth. The air was so quiet, I could hear my own breath freezing.

"Isn't it a marvel?" said the princess. "Each of the four positions of the lock changes the season. I've not determined if it's the same place, only transformed, or another place altogether. But come, you have to see the rest of it. The winter garden has the most intriguing secret."

Powdery snow spilled over the tops of my boots as Roxanne led me down the steps and along the winding path that was little more than a smooth depression scooped in the thick mantle of snow. She hurried past the towering icefall, through the grove, and into the cave of the Source. "I know you told me not to risk entering the cave, but after you got so friendly with the Source, I thought it couldn't matter. I was careful never to touch the water or anything, but I found the second keyhole inside. If you're angry with me, that's too bad, but this is really marvelous."

I wasn't angry with her, only impatient. Being so close to the Source reminded me of how close I was to the answers I cared about. "Just hurry," I said.

The crystals in the cave were not amethyst, but jet and silver. Roxanne crouched down beside the basin and pointed to a notched carving in the rock at its base. "Here's the second keyhole. Watch what happens. . . ."

She inserted the key in the slot. "You just have to wait a few moments. You'll be able to provide the Singlars with everything they need after you've gone . . . solve so many problems . . ."

But I wasn't listening to the princess any longer. I cared nothing for comforts or furnishings, linens or exotic foods. I cared nothing for Roxanne or the Singlars. The answer was so close; I could feel it in the winter garden, brooding, rumbling in the depths of the stone. The hair on my neck rose, and my stomach constricted, and my ears roared with my own blood, drowning out every other consideration, and if anyone had asked me why I was suddenly so afraid, I couldn't have told them.

I plunged my hand into the icy water. It was thick, as if on the verge of freezing, and I lost all feeling in my fingers in the instant I touched it.

"A hundredlight has passed, my king. How quickly have the hours flown." The soft voice of the first root of the Bounded crackled in the frosty air like breaking glass.

"So it *is* you." What had I expected?

"Of course. There is only one root, one Source, but the key allows you to explore many of its aspects."

"So the garden still lives beneath all this? We've not changed it, killed it somehow by using the key?"

"Winter is but another expression of life. No less worthy than its more embracing fellows. My winter aspect is perhaps a bit more dangerous than the others. Would that you had chosen it on a different day."

"Why more dangerous?"

"It is the quietest, the deepest buried, the most private. We do not always like what we see when we explore our most hidden places or what we hear when the world falls silent."

"I don't want philosophy today. I want my answers."

Roxanne stood with her arms crossed, tapping her foot. "Sometimes it takes a little while."

"Have you not found your place here in the Bounded?" The voice of the Source stayed pleasant and even. "If you would but wait a little longer . . . finish the work you've begun. Your people need you. Your life is here. Stay in the Bounded and be at peace."

"The firestorms are hardly peaceful. They almost killed me."

"But you've made an accommodation. You protect your people and renew yourself. You are not the same person you were when you walked into your dream. It is no matter what the origin of the storms."

"No more delays," I said. "I accepted your word and made the best of my waiting, but I must finish the journey that brought me here."

"As you wish, my king. Ask as you will."

"I want to know the identity of the person who stabbed my mother and betrayed my father's secrets."

"Have you not guessed it, my lord?" Her voice was quiet, gentle, and relentless in its truth. "Look into your own most hidden places. Open your eyes. Can you not see?"

"No." But there were no surprises for me in the Bounded, and even as I said the word, the bitter chill of the winter garden settled over my spirit.

"There, you see?" interrupted Roxanne, who had paid no mind to the Source. "You can ask for anything you want—a bolt of red silk or an ivory hairbrush or a cask of sparkling wine—and you'll find it in the Blue Tower storerooms when you go back. Isn't it odd the way the ring catches the light as it spins?"

And even as the back wall of the cave dissolved into blackness and revealed the spinning brass ring, I remembered despair.

The ring was taller than I, and as it whirled about its axis, numbing my cheeks with the frigid air, it snatched the light of the torches and the sparkling reflections of ice and silver and jet, and it wove them into an orb of gray light. An oculus . . . just as I had seen them and used them in the fortress of Zhev'Na . . . just like the one spinning in the Lords' temple on the day I traded my eyes and my soul for power and immortality.

Roxanne stood at my shoulder. I needed to warn her. But I couldn't take my eyes from the oculus, and the hunger grew in me like the storm clouds that raced to devour the skies of the Bounded. It was danger unimaginable for me to stay so near an implement of power . . . an implement of temptation. But I could not . . . would not . . . run from the truth, and I would not believe it until the words were spoken.

"Tell me the name of the betrayer and assassin," I said. Even then I knew the two were one and the same.

"But, my—"

"Tell me!" I roared the command, trying to drown out the thunder of my desire, and the wailing of my fear, and the hollow empty silence within me.

"Oh, my gracious king . . . it was you."

CHAPTER 20

Karon

It was in the fourth month of the war in the Wastes that I received news of a half-dead lunatic found wandering at the fringes of the desert. He was not Dar'Nethi, the panting messenger reported as he drained a waterskin and flattened himself in the shadows of his horse to find a moment's relief from the voracious sun. Nor was he Zhid.

Anyone found wandering alone in the Wastes was assuredly a lunatic, but if he was not Dar'Nethi, then he was not one of our own warriors who had survived a raid only to get himself lost in the desert. That meant he was from Zhev'Na, and therefore suspect, but possibly a valuable source of information.

Ven'Dar, the Preceptor who held the sector where the prisoner had been taken, sent word that the man was severely dehydrated, so it might be as much as two days until he should be moved. But Ven'Dar believed—strongly believed—I would wish to question the prisoner myself. I couldn't imagine why, but I would accept Ven'Dar's judgment. If I could be said to trust anyone in the world besides the Dulcé Bareil, it would be the Word Winder Ven'Dar.

I told the messenger to take his rest, and that he, Bareil, and I would leave for Ven'Dar's encampment at dawn the next day, once I had set in motion the day's battle plan.

The war was going nowhere, unless the matter of hastening our own destruction could be viewed as a positive accomplishment. On more than a few cold desert dawns, as I washed the metallic taste of too much sand and too little sleep from my mouth with a swallow of lukewarm ale, that particular accomplishment seemed eminently desirable.

But then, of course, would come the midnights when I would make my rounds of the day's wounded, the destroyed youths restrained with leather straps and strong enchantments lest they chew their own hands away, the young women who stared silently into unending emptiness or tore at their skin, screaming to rid themselves of unseen terrors, the men writhing in pain from savaged bodies or raving from the relentless barrage of sun and desert. All of them would stretch their arms toward me, beseeching me for help when they should have been embracing husbands or mothers or children, or using their hands to build a life of beauty. On those nights I would swear again that no price was too high to rid the universe of the Lords of Zhev'Na. Perhaps it was because I had already paid the price that I could swear so easily and with such dreadful consequences.

The red half-disk that sat on the horizon had already broiled away the night chill when I called my commanders together the next morning. I told them I would open up the portal needed for the day's attack on a Zhid war camp, but would then leave the portal in the care of the Preceptor Ustele while I went to consult with Ven'Dar. I designated N'Tien, my most able strategist, to monitor the progress of the day's plan and shift our forces as he thought best. Old Ustele was powerful in the wielding of enchantment, but he had no talent for war, particularly for one who was so enamored of it.

Within the hour the battle was joined: the portal that allowed my warriors to bypass unending leagues of trackless desert was open, and I had saluted the valiant men and women who poured through it bearing swords, lances, bows, and sorcery to engage our soulless enemies. The encampment fell quiet once they were gone. The previous battle's wounded had all been sent back to Avonar, and the dead buried or burned according to each one's family custom.

As I expected, Men'Thor showed up at my tent, swathed in his usual mantle of righteous concern, just as I was ready to leave. "My lord, do I understand you are to be absent from the day's battle?"

"If you're here asking me about it, then I suppose you do." I pulled on my gauntlets.

"May I inquire what draws you away? The Geographers have supported our assumption that the Dinaje Cliffs are an essential base for our next stage. The Zhid are entrenched with at least four levels of battle wards. Our own troops are in good spirits and resolute. Today's foray is critical to our plans." A properly concise analysis from the Effector.

Men'Thor was regarded highly for his talent in juggling arcane data and using it to form a plan of action. He could find a way to accomplish anything you set him to—especially if he agreed with it.

"*Every* day is critical to our plans, Men'Thor. When one has no alternatives, one has to make the best of whatever remains. And you may certainly inquire anything you like. I just won't always answer."

Something about Men'Thor always set my back up. He was such an honorable man. "So very worthy," people said. "Destined for greatness." I couldn't see this great destiny, but I also could see nothing to justify sending him away as I might prefer.

"Of course I had no intent to pry, Your Grace. You are the finest battle leader the Dar'Nethi have ever had. When you remind our warriors of the horrors you have seen, of the noble purpose that demands our sacrifice, they respond to your command with twice the fervor they give to any other commander. But if your private business intrudes . . ."

"This is *not* private business, Men'Thor." I yanked one leather strap of a canvas pack too hard and it snapped. I threw the broken piece to the ground, cinched the other one, and hefted the worn satchel. "Ven'Dar has a prisoner he wants me to see. A Drudge escaped from Zhev'Na, I believe. If Ven'Dar says it is important, it usually is, and so I'll go. N'Tien will set our positions. Your father can hold the portal, and the warriors will follow you. You can send for me if I'm needed. Is that enough?"

"I am only concerned—"

"For the welfare of Avonar and our people. I appreciate your attention to duty. Good day."

"Good journey, my lord. I am on my way to the front." At least Men'Thor was no hypocrite, staying back with his maps and plans while sending others to fight the battles he espoused so fervently. He relished being in the vanguard of this mad venture.

"Take me to Ven'Dar," I said to the messenger, who stood waiting with Bareil and our horses as Men'Thor hurried away. "The Preceptor had better be right about the importance of this prisoner, or I'll send Men'Thor to oversee his operations."

The journey would be long and hot, for we had to use conventional transport, rather than one of the Dar'Nethi portals that could link one place to directly to another across a few steps or many leagues. All true power was saved to create and maintain the portals to the battle-grounds, for the battle itself, and for whatever healing could be done after it. I, the Preceptors, and the commanders had to shift the load between us, husbanding our resources carefully to muster enough power even for those most fundamental uses.

Ven'Dar and his small detachment were situated about a half-day's ride from the main encampment. His troop's primary function was to send small, quick-moving teams to harass vulnerable pockets of the Zhid. He considered his secondary mission, liberating the work camps of the Drudges, to be of far more importance. Drudges were not Dar'Nethi, but descendants of people from the mundane world who had been held in generations of servitude in Ce Uroth, the wasteland empire of the Lords.

Ven'Dar also kept up a special watch for Dar'Nethi slaves, sending in rescue parties at the least rumor of them. But we had yet to find any slave who had been allowed to live when we got close. If forced to abandon a position in a hurry, the Zhid impaled their slaves on stakes or set them afire. Death was not pleasant for any

Zhid who encountered my sword after I'd come across
such a sight.

"The Preceptor is in the blue tent at the center, my
lord," said the messenger, as we approached the perimeter of Ven'Dar's encampment. It was nearing midday,
and my primary interest was not the mysterious prisoner,
but getting out of the sun and finding a drink of water
that was not scalding like the dregs in my waterskin.
Hardening oneself to life in the desert required more
than a few months. Four years had passed since my imprisonment in Zhev'Na, and I wasn't used to it any
more.

When I walked into the stuffy dimness of Ven'Dar's
tent, the Preceptor and two sweat-sheened lieutenants
were leaning over a small wooden table, poring over
maps. A young aide was sorting food packets and waterskins in a wooden chest.

"Ah, Your Grace, welcome," said Ven'Dar, pulling
off a pair of spectacles.

"Sire!" The warriors straightened up, each laying his
two fists over his heart before spreading his arms and
opening his palms in greeting.

Ven'Dar came around the table and bent his knee,
extending his open palms to me. *"Ce'na davonet, Giré
D'Arnath!"* He smiled as I touched his palms and gestured him up. "I'm glad you've come. And Bareil, welcome." The Dulcé had followed me into the tent.

Some men and women bend their knees to their sovereign out of duty, others out of fear, or awe, or custom.
Ven'Dar was the only person I knew who expressed joy
in his obeisance: joy in my position, in my life, in my
friendship, joy in his own position and his own life. And
no matter what the circumstances of our meeting, I could
never greet his smile save with a smile in return. Ven'Dar
was a living example of the Way of the Dar'Nethi, accepting, rejoicing, savoring every moment of his life, and
fitting it into the larger pattern of the universe.

"This had better be important," I said, taking a damp
cloth offered by one of his aides and wiping my face and

neck. "We hit five thousand of Gensei Senat's troops at the Dinaje Cliffs this morning. I should be there."

Ven'Dar ushered his warriors and servants out, pointing Bareil to a water barrel and tin mugs sitting beside the curtain that screened his sleeping quarters. The Preceptor was only of medium height, slight of build, fairhaired, his unfashionable beard just starting to show signs of silver. Some might have called him unimposing, but only until they heard him speak or looked closely into his eyes. Ven'Dar could fill a room with his quiet exuberance, and the lines about his gray-blue eyes had been etched deep by sixty years of laughter. But it was the power of his words that could touch the essence of the universe, drawing a man's tears or honing a woman's fury, evoking a holocaust or an infant's laughter. Even those who discounted the Way admitted that Ven'Dar was a formidable enchanter . . . and a formidable warrior when he chose to be.

"I think you'll find this of far more moment than even so dramatic a turn in this pernicious war." Ven'Dar hated the war, and though he carried out his duties faithfully, it was with far less relish than I. The war and its consequences were the only thing that could dim his smile—and so they did, at his next words. "This young wanderer we found—in his ravings, he speaks of your son."

"He is with them then. Back in Zhev'Na where he belongs."

My rage had cooled in the four months since the events at Windham, as lava will cool after it spews and boils its way from the volcano. I could speak of Gerick, even say his name or speculate on his plans and his whereabouts, without tasting blood. But as lava becomes a part of the mountain, my anger had become a part of me: hard, cold, smothering the life of everything it touched.

"Is your prisoner a Drudge?" I said. "Has he actually seen the Destroyer?"

"I don't know. The poor fellow had been out there beyond Calle Rein near the Castyx Rocks for a day or

two without food or water. My Healers have taken care
of him and sent him deep to sleep it off. They should
be able to wake him by tonight. He'll be quite all right; I
perhaps . . . exaggerated . . . his condition in my message.
Slightly. But when he was first brought in, despite his
weakness, he was extraordinarily agitated. He was begging to be taken . . . to your wife, my lord."

"To my wife? I thought you said—"

"He was near frantic. I think he was afraid he was
going to die before he could speak to her. His exact
words were, 'I got to speak to the Lady Seri about the
young master.' "

"Take me to him."

"I had him brought to my quarters, but he's not yet—"

"Now!" Only one person I knew would say those
words.

They had laid him on Ven'Dar's own pallet. The sun
had burned his skin to a deep red bronze. Thanks to the
Healers, his face and arms were merely blotched and
peeling. I dismissed Ven'Dar's Dulcé Guide, Bastel, who
was dripping water into Paulo's mouth, and took over
the duty myself.

"Go on about your business," I said. "I'll watch him."

"Then I'm right," said Ven'Dar, standing between the
parted curtains as I sat cross-legged beside the pallet.
"He is the boy of the stories, the boy who went with
you to the Gate and survived Zhev'Na."

"I owe him my life twice over and a great deal
more besides."

"He vanished with your son."

"We found signs of a struggle outside the gates at
Windham . . . and Paulo's blood. We thought the Destroyer had killed him."

Ven'Dar was a wise man. He made no attempt to give
comfort when it wasn't possible, nor did he intrude with
words when I desired none. He didn't question me during that long, hot afternoon as I sat with Paulo, for the
Preceptor already shared my most painful and intimate
truths. I was not likely to hide anything of importance
from him for long. And when the Healer came at sunset

to check on Paulo and bring him out of the deep sleep to which she had sent him, Ven'Dar knew I would not leave, even though it had become almost unbearable for me to watch a Healer work. So he stood behind me, laid his hands on my shoulders, and cast a whispered winding of words about my pain.

One can never recall the words of power spoken by a Word Winder making his cast. Sometimes you'll hear a phrase in casual conversation, or catch an inflection in someone else's speech that will infuse you with a breath-catching emotion far beyond what is warranted by the current circumstance, and people say it is because the sound has recalled to you a Word Winder's enchantment. All I knew was that for a blessed moment I was eased. Then the Healer was done, and I was offering Paulo a cup of water.

"My lord!" The dismay that glanced across his face when he saw me caused a stone to settle in my gut.

"My friend," I said, forcing a smile and a calm I did not feel. "Of all the stragglers we've picked up in the Wastes, I never expected to find my most faithful companion. Are you feeling better?"

I would have sworn he turned pale under the sunburn. "I thought I was done for," he said. "It's come a habit I got to break."

"I'm glad we found you."

"There was a sandstorm. Guess I took a wrong turn somewhere."

He sat up, took the cup, and drained it, never removing his intent gaze from my face. I wondered what he was looking for, but he spoke before I could ask. "She's dead, then?"

"What do you mean?"

"The Lady. I kept hopin' you'd been able to— But I guess not."

"Seri is alive."

He almost leaped out of the bed. "Cripes! You had me there for a bit. I thought . . . you just looked . . . damn! Where is . . . I mean . . . she's not here, I guess. Not in the Wastes. The ones who found me said you had battles going on."

"She's safe in Avonar."

He breathed deeply and slowly. "It's fine to hear that."

"She was very ill."

His eyes flicked away from my face. "I'd give a deal to see her."

"I'll take you to her, if you want. It might do her good to see you. Once a day we send our wounded back to Avonar through a portal. But we can't keep it open for too long at a time lest the Zhid find our camps. I've matters to attend tonight, but we'll go tomorrow if you're feeling up to it."

The wind billowed the tent walls, rattling the lamps and tools hung from hooks on the cross poles.

Paulo settled back onto the thin pillow the Healer had slipped under his head. "I think I'll sleep then, if it's all right. I got to tell you about what happened and all, but I'm swiped right now. I was afraid to sleep out there in the desert, thinking as how I'd never get up again. Got a lot to make up."

"I'm sure that's true. The Preceptor Ven'Dar and his aides will be close if you need anything, but I'll tell them to let you sleep."

"I'll be all right. I don't want to keep nobody from their business."

"You can tell me all about your adventures tomorrow before we go to Seri. I have to understand how you got here, where you've been . . . You know that."

"I understand. My lord, am I your prisoner?"

"No. You're not a prisoner. Sleep well, lad."

I took my leave and stepped through the curtain. Ven'Dar was waiting, and I motioned him to walk out into the night with me. "Leave him unguarded," I said.

"But, my lord, if he's been with your son . . ."

"I'll be watching."

The night wind blew cold in the Wastes and quickly erased the memory of the furnace that was daylight. For a while I shared my warriors' campfires, allowing them to relive the day's battle for me until they'd rid themselves of enough of it that they could sleep, but always I stood where I could keep an eye on Ven'Dar's dark tent. As the hour grew late and the campfires smoldered, flaring into false life with a gust of wind, then dying again in swirls of sparks, the warriors rolled into their blankets to dream away the horror.

Ordinarily, once I had seen to those who had to face the Zhid another day, I would go to the wounded, but on this night I sat in the dark on a hillock of warm sand and gravel, alone until Bareil brought me warm cheese, bread, and ale. "Do you wish for company, my lord, or should I leave you?"

"You are always welcome, Dulcé. A tree does not consider its trunk 'company.' "

Bareil, the wise companion who had been instrumental in restoring my memory and saving my sanity after Dassine's death, sat cross-legged on the sand beside me. "How fares young Paulo?"

"The Healers tell me he's only blistered and dry. He tells me nothing at all."

"Surely you do not doubt him? He would give his life for you."

"Watch Ven'Dar's tent, and we'll see."

I considered invoking the link between my madrissé and me, to discover if somewhere in his vast knowledge he could formulate any good reason why Paulo would be wandering around in the desert beyond the Castyx Rocks, bearing a message for Seri—any reason that would not speak treason. But, on second thought, I needed no more unproven theories.

Less than a quarter hour passed until the dark form rolled out from under the rear of the blue tent, crept to a clump of dead trees, then slipped through the darkness toward the lights and activity of the pavilion where the wounded lay. Bareil and I followed quietly, staying well back. The boy's timing was perfect. He lay still on the sand, waiting for half an hour or more as the Healers went about their business. But Ven'Dar had no sooner finished the words that left a wavering oval distortion in the air before the pavilion, than the slender figure darted out of the shadows and straight through the portal. A few shouts rang out from those watching, but I assured everyone that there was no cause for alarm, and they soon went back to their grim business of transporting their fellows through the portal, patching the lesser wounds of those who were to stay, and caring for the dead.

I told Bareil to take my horse back to my headquarters, then I spent a few moments with each of the wounded before reopening the portal to Avonar and stepping through it myself.

The portal opened into a large building that had been converted into a hospice for those the Healers could not return to health or those who needed a longer time to recover. I didn't go there often enough; it was too difficult when there was nothing I could do for those who lay in the endless rows of simple white pallets. But on that night, I spent a while with my brave warriors. I knew where I would find Paulo eventually, but it would take him some time to learn where she was and get himself there.

In the quiet hour before dawn I commandeered a horse and rode out of the north gates of Avonar, up the winding road that led to the Lydian Vale and a quiet, graceful white house called *Nentao*, "the Haven." I had refused numerous offers of protection from those uneasy at seeing their sovereign ride out unaccompanied in the night. I hoped what I told them was true, that I had no need of guards. I didn't want to believe that Paulo had turned traitor, too.

When I left my horse in the front courtyard and walked through the rose arbor into the garden, the sky was already a vibrant pink. A hand touched my sleeve from out of a leafy bower. I would have been sorely disappointed if nothing of the sort had occurred, and I stepped into the sheltering shrubbery without hesitation.

"A surprise to see you here, my lord."

"Good morning, Radele."

"She has a visitor this morning. The stable boy . . . but then you must know that. It's why you're here."

"Has he said anything?"

"He's only just found her."

"I presume there has been . . . ."

". . . no change, my lord."

"Yes. Thank you, Radele."

I left him and walked up to the little terrace centered by a dribbling fountain. Seri was sitting in a chair by the fountain as she did every morning, her lovely face bathed in the dawn light. A dusty, blistered Paulo knelt at her feet, panting as if he'd run all the way from Avonar.

"My lady, can you hear me? Please, my lady, what's wrong? I've brought you a message."

"She won't answer you," I said, stepping out of the shade.

He looked up, startled. Seri didn't turn her head.

"She's said no word since her injury. I think she hears us, but she makes no acknowledgment. She walks when we guide her. She eats whatever is put before her. She'll hold a book and look at it, but she does not turn the page. She neither laughs nor smiles nor weeps, but I don't know if she *cannot* speak or if she *will* not. No one has been able to tell me that."

"Oh, my lord. I'm so . . . I never thought . . ."

I brushed my hand over her beautiful hair, silky dark brown with the touch of fire in it. A few strands of gray. Her quiet expression with the little frown between her eyes did not change as she peered into the rising sun.

"And even you . . ."

"I have nothing to give her."

Paulo looked back at my wife, and to my surprise, took her limp hand and kissed it. "Ah, my lady, I'm so sorry," he whispered. Tears rolled down his sunburned cheeks.

"Come," I said. "Let's walk a bit."

He did not move or take his eyes from her.

"I insist." I took his arm and pulled him up, noting that he'd grown again. He was almost as tall as I. "I wanted you to see my son's handiwork for yourself, lest somehow he has managed to retain some remnant of your misdirected loyalty. He's killed her, Paulo, as surely as if she had breathed her last."

He was quiet for a long time, but I didn't push him. There were other Dar'Nethi who would, but I believed nothing could be as devastatingly persuasive as the sight

of Seri in her walking death. I knew what it had done
to me.

"Now, tell me where you've been, and what is this
message you've brought my wife."

He didn't look at me, just walked alongside me, his
hands clasped behind his back. His sand-colored brows
were drawn together in a thoughtful frown.

"Everything's wicked confused; I suppose my head's
still muddled from the desert. I remember I followed the
young master from the gardens at Windham. I was ready
to kill him for what he done to the Lady. I caught him
and took him down, but I don't know for sure what
happened then. We traveled someplace . . . a new place.
It's like a dream that lasted forever, but right now it
won't come into my mind any more than a dream what
slipped away when you woke up. Next thing I remember,
I woke up in the desert thinking I had to find the Lady."

"Where did he take you? Was it Zhev'Na?"

"It wasn't there. I'd have known Zhev'Na. We were
in Valleor for a time, someplace in the north I'd never
been before, but I'm no good at maps to tell you where.
And then we were in this other place. Not an evil place,
I don't think."

"And what message would he have you give Seri?"

"I can't say the message."

I left it for the moment. "Where is he now? Where did
you leave him? Was he already joined with the Three?"

"He's not one of the Lords no more. Even with my
head so thick, I'll swear as it's true, my lord. And he's
not in Zhev'Na. But I can't tell you where he is. He's hiding,
my lord, hiding where nobody can find him. He's afraid
of you."

"As well he should be."

"He knows you won't believe him. He understands
that and holds no blame to you for it. I think that's why
he sent me to the Lady."

"You're a good friend, Paulo. Seri and I, and everyone in both worlds, are forever in your debt. But it will
all be undone, all the suffering and death, all the sacrifice
of thousands of people will be wasted if Gerick rejoins

the Lords. You understood the consequences before, and they've not changed except for the worse."

We had come to the edge of the garden terrace, a white railing beyond which the land dropped away into the soft green swathes of the Lydian Vale, the Vale of Eidolon closest to Avonar. Its sun-drenched woodlands nestled between the spires of the Mountains of Light, and in autumn its leaves splashed fire-yellow and scarlet against Avonar's deep blue skies. In my four years in Avonar, I had often walked this vale and dreamed of bringing Seri here. I had imagined her face reflecting its beauty, enriching it beyond measure with her delight. But now her eyes reflected nothing, and I saw no beauty anywhere. I gripped the white iron railing until my knuckles looked a part of it.

"Do you understand what Gerick's betrayal has cost us? You knew the three who were once Zhid, the ones I healed at the Gate. They were ready to destroy the heart of power in Zhev'Na, while the finest sorcerers in Avonar encircled the fortress and created a barrier of enchantment the Lords could not breach. My counselor Jayereth had found the means necessary to free the Dar'Nethi slaves. We could have won without bloodshed, Paulo. We could have worked a healing on this blighted land. But all was undone by my son, and we are left with nothing but weapons and blood. But even they are not enough. Gerick's betrayal has strengthened the Lords, revealed our vulnerabilities, and if he joins with them again, we will be lost. Both worlds. Forever. I cannot allow it. You must tell me where he is."

Paulo, the youth I thought I knew, looked me in the eye as he had never done, one man to another. Neither fear nor awe nor willful deceit showed itself in him. "My lord Prince, I owe you and the Lady all as is possible to owe. I would lay down my life for you, or ride to the ends of the earth to fetch for you, or give you my legs back if you was to need them, or my arms or my head. If it means you must hang me or put me in irons or send me back to the life I was born to, then so be it, but I cannot tell you what you ask. I've sworn my oath . . .

and I feel it as deep as a man can know what's right.
He is not with the Lords. He's hiding where no one can
find him. I can tell you no more than that."

"You know that any Dar'Nethi could read you and
find out everything you know." Not exactly true. Few
had the ability any longer, but Paulo couldn't know that.

He did not waver. "The Prince I honor wouldn't allow
that. Not if I said to him that I gave him no leave to
do it."

"Maybe the Prince you honor doesn't exist any
more."

"Then this war is lost anyway, no matter what I tell
or don't tell."

And that, of course, had been the whisper in my own
mind for four villainous months, but I would not hear it
from an illiterate boy. I released the fury pent up in my
hands and sent him sprawling across the terrace. "Radele!"

The young Dar'Nethi came running.

"Put this traitor under restraints. He is not to leave
this house until I decide what to do with him. I want
him to serve my wife, to see her every day as a reminder
of what his friend has done to her."

"Of course, I'll do as you say, my lord, but that seems
too good for a betrayer." Radele . . . always ready to
prove his zeal.

"You will not harm Paulo, not in any way. No one is
to speak to him or make any attempt to question him.
I alone will hear what he has to say when I decide he
will say it. Do you understand me?"

"Of course, my lord. As you wish."

"Consider this simple puzzle, young fool," I said, turning my back on the bleeding youth lest I lose control of
my fist again. "What kind of person corrupts his loyal
friend's mind and memory? Or sends him into the middle of a war half enchanted, while he himself cowers in
the shadows? Perhaps it is the same one who rips a
young mother apart at the beginning of her life or forces
a strong and decent man to slit his own belly. If your
tongue is forbidden to speak the truth of where you've
been, then perhaps your mind is forbidden to remember
the truth of what he is."

I did not watch Radele work his enchantments and lead Paulo away. I stood behind Seri and stroked her hair. She sat on the edge of her chair, gazing into the sunrise as if she expected to see someone she knew walk out of it.

But I could not stay long in her company without going mad. So, after only a few moments, I left the garden, threw myself on my horse, and returned to the Wastes. By early afternoon I had slain fifty of Gensei Senat's Zhid warriors. My beleaguered troops rallied around me, cheering and waving their swords, shouting that the Heir of D'Arnath had come to bring death to Zhev'Na. And I, the bringer of death, drowned my fury in the blood of my enemies.

CHAPTER 21

Ven'Dar

Prince D'Natheil's first meeting with the Leiran youth filled me with tremendous hopes. The Prince had such great love for the boy, and as he sat at the bedside through the long afternoon, I could sense his desire to unleash it. But the boy held back. Whether he had truly turned traitor, or whether he had seen the changes in the Prince and decided he couldn't trust him, I didn't know, but I grieved for them both. If the youth maintained his silence, the consequences could be severe, not so much for him as for D'Natheil.

On the next morning, Bareil told me how the Prince had let the youth escape, and I understood his plan. I contrived to be at his headquarters when the Heir returned from Nentao, hoping to hear that the boy had indeed been moved by the distressing sight of the Lady, but I received only a brief account of the Prince's failure. With a troubled heart I saw him plunge into his war once again, and return late that night covered in blood, his warriors praising the glories of his killing. If this continued, a time would come very soon when I wouldn't be able to reach him any more.

And so on that evening, unknown to the Prince or even my madrissé, I slipped through a portal to Avonar. Soon after midnight I let myself into the peaceful darkness of Nentao by a side door. I had no fear of reprisal. After all, it was my own house.

*   *   *

I hadn't known the Lady Seriana before the distraught Prince summoned me in his darkest hour, begging me to save her life. The Healers called to repair her injury had felt her slipping away. She would not grasp the tethers they proffered, as if life was become too painful to embrace any longer.

"Ah, gods, Ven'Dar," he had said, weeping at her bedside. "I've killed her and myself together. And she'll be gone before I can repair what I've done." Guilt can twist truth so terribly.

I had drawn together what I knew of her from four years of the Prince's friendship, and what I knew of this man she had loved beyond death, and I had worked a winding for her.

One never knows what will be the exact result of a winding. You create with a sense of your desired outcome, in the Lady's case the necessity for holding on to a life so beloved and so valued, and you weave it into the words and the knowledge and the power that has been given you, until you are so filled with the enchantment you think it must leak out of your skin. Only then can you spin it out, as the fisherman casts out his line, and hope that the sum of your efforts lands somewhere close to your intended mark.

She lived, and for a brief hour we thought she might awaken to herself. But as the days passed our hopes faded, and when her eyes opened at last, no life dwelt in them. It was as if her injury had healed, but her soul would not. It was then the Prince asked if he could bring her to Nentao. "She wasn't ready to come to the palace," he said, bitterly. "She always said it was D'Natheil's place, not mine. Clearly, she was more right than she knew. I can't leave her there. And I'll have to be away so much . . ."

The Leiran youth was locked in my root cellar, snoring heartily, his hands and feet secured to a drainage pipe that was embedded in the ceiling. The small window and the door were warded and his limbs restricted by various simple, easily detectable enchantments.

I sat down on a crate of turnips and stared at him

until he woke. Almost an hour passed. But I'd always found touching a sleeping stranger a dreadfully rude way to wake him up. And sometimes dangerous.

"Trussed you up like a goose, have they?" I said, when the boy's eyes popped open, and he bolted to a sitting position amidst an avalanche of vegetables, letting out an exclamation of a common barnyard variety when he got tangled in the ropes and whacked his head on the pipe.

"Aye." He slumped against the carrot bin.

"My name is Ven'Dar. I am one of the Preceptors of Gondai. I understand you are familiar with us—both our better parts, and those we'd prefer not to let everyone make jest of?"

"Mmm." He acknowledged the truth with a sour twist to his lips.

"I thought so. Now if I were to untie your hands and feet, and make any number of promises of my honor and goodwill, and any number of threats regarding any attempt on your part to get away, would you consider talking with me for a while?"

He shrugged, his expression uncommunicative. Clearly he had reservations.

I did the untying, but skipped the promises and threats.

"To start, I'll tell you that I'm an advisor of Prince D'Natheil, and also his close friend. I can't set you free. I wouldn't want you to be mistaken about that."

"I figured. Did he send you to steal what's in my mind?"

"Do you think he plans to do that?"

"Before today I wouldn't have thought it. You'll have to ask him."

"You've been missing for four months. Believed dead. Mourned. And now you reappear in the vicinity of Zhev'Na, and you don't deny your loyalty to one we believe to be our deadliest enemy. You weren't expecting to be questioned about it?"

"I wasn't expecting the Lady to be like she is. I wasn't expecting the Prince to . . . to be like he is."

"You find the Prince changed?"

"Demonfire . . . changed! I don't— Well, just say that if you'd have told me he'd gone and got himself switched around again, I'd be more believing it, than that he's the Prince I knew. But then, every once in a while, there's a word or a look in his eye . . . and I know it's really him. That's worse."

A perceptive young man. And a heart that was exactly as I'd been told.

"You swore to the Prince that his son was not allied with the Lords of Zhev'Na. Have you any proof of that?"

"No. None but my word and his—the young master's, I mean."

"Is that why you were so anxious to speak to the Lady Seriana?"

The boy narrowed his eyes. "So you *are* here to read my head?"

"No. Not only did the Prince nòt send me here, I have a feeling that he'll be very angry with me when he learns of it. That's why it is so important that we come to some understanding. I know that you've loved and honored the Prince, as do I, and I need to know if such is still the case or if the young Lord has turned you against him."

"I told the Prince yesterday as I'd give him my life or my legs or whatever he asked. I wasn't lying. I shouldn't have to say it again."

If this boy was lying, then he was by far the most convincing prevaricator I'd ever encountered. Perhaps lying was a particular skill of those who lived in the mundane world, one that we Dar'Nethi never had perfected.

"That's what I thought. So answer my question. Why is it so important that you speak to the Lady?"

"Because she's the only one as I can give the message. The young master believes the Prince won't listen—as has been shown true—so he needs the Lady to convince the Prince to do what needs done. If she was dead, I'd be able to tell the Prince direct, but since she's alive I can't, and I'll be shiv'd if I know what in blazes I'm to do now!"

I sat for a moment trying to sort out what I'd just

heard and had no luck at all. So I pulled a cloth pouch from the pocket of my robes. "Would you like something to eat?"

"I'm not hungry."

Another clue that all was not as usual with the boy. The Prince had told me a great deal about Paulo. I took a handful of dried duskberries from the pouch and munched on them while I watched the boy watching me. I felt a question forcing its way out of him.

"So"—he scraped at a wayward carrot with his fingernail, concentrating on its pale skin—"does Radele know you're here talking to me?"

"No, he does not. You can trust me, Paulo. I promise." Of course, I had to hope he wasn't fool enough to believe just any Dar'Nethi's promise. Only mine. "I need you to trust me."

"I don't know you."

"True. What if I were to share a terrible secret with you?"

"Why would you do that? Don't you believe the young master is evil like everyone else does? And if he's evil, then I'm probably evil, too."

"I choose to believe in you, young Paulo, because if the young Lord is corrupt and you are corrupt, then there's no saving the Prince. He might be able to save Avonar or he might not, but he—the man you know and honor as I do—will be irretrievably lost. I've left to the Prince the task of saving the worlds, but in the stupidly prideful way of Dar'Nethi Preceptors, I've taken on myself the task of saving *him*."

"What do you mean?"

"You know of his two lives, and I would guess you understand that your friend, the man you admire so deeply, is a person named Karon, a Dar'Nethi Healer snatched from death sixteen years ago." Astonishing to think of what my audacious colleague Dassine had done, binding a dead man's soul to a pyramid-shaped crystal the size of my hand, holding that soul prisoner for ten years, and then pouring it into the body of a dying prince.

"I know that."

"And you know that, in some way, he is also the Prince D'Natheil, a magnificent warrior, but one who glories in violence, a man driven and controlled by his anger . . ."

It is always a delight to see the dawn of understanding on a human visage. One of life's greatest pleasures.

"You're saying that he's coming to be D'Natheil and not the other! He even said it—that the Prince I knew mightn't exist any more."

"He sees it happening, but he doesn't know how to stop it. He's fought it since he took up residence in Avonar, believing it was only a matter of his will to make sure D'Natheil stayed in his place. But will hasn't been enough, for his own nature has conspired against him. Anger is the catalyst, you see, for anger was the core of D'Natheil's life."

Had Dassine miscalculated? Had the murdered Prince D'Natheil's soul not completed its journey beyond the Verges before Dassine displaced it with his prisoner? We would likely never know. But the evidence was clear: More of D'Natheil remained than Dassine could ever have intended.

"When our Prince saw the results of the Zhid raids on a village, or remembered the horrors of Zhev'Na and the innocents who suffered from them, D'Natheil's anger began to eat away at him. Slowly. So slowly he wasn't sure of what was happening and told no one, not even his wife. But it was only after his counselor Jayereth's murder, when he suspected his son had betrayed his trust, that he came to believe he was going to lose the battle. Before I could discover a way to help him, his trap was sprung, and our worst fears realized."

Paulo nodded. "That's when he come to kill the young master. I never saw him angry like that. Not in Zhev'Na when he was a slave. Not at the Gate when the Zhid made him fight."

"Yes. And on that darkest of nights, when his beloved wife was at the point of death . . . Paulo, he could not heal her. He could not even begin."

"Blazes."

"He's been able to work no healing since that day.

The foundation of his life has been destroyed. He sees his soul as lost, and his wife lost, and his son, and he can do nothing at all about any of it."

The Prince carried Dassine's crystal with him everywhere now—his suspended death awaiting his touch. I feared for his life as well as his reason and his soul.

"Why are you telling me this? I'm a nobody horse trainer. You need a sorcerer to help him."

"Because yesterday when he sat at your bedside, I saw the spark of his last hope. He desperately wants to believe you. He wants you to convince him that his son is not what he thinks. He knows that if he slays his own son, he will lose himself forever, but unless you give him a choice, he will have to do it."

"But I've got no proof, only what I know to be true. And if I tell him what I know—even if I could—it would just show him where to find the young master so as to kill him. The Prince even said that's what he intends."

"So it appears we're at an impasse. You need to speak to the Lady, in hopes she can sway the Prince to listen to his son. But the Lady cannot hear you, or if she hears, she can do nothing about it. The young Lord himself cannot appear before the Prince to state his arguments, because he would end up without his head. And please, explain to me once more, why is it you cannot plead his case before the Prince?"

The boy kicked at a crate of shallots. "Because the young master put an enchantment on me that I could only give the message to the Prince if the Lady was dead! We never figured on her being like this."

"I was hoping that's what you meant."

The boy's face twisted into such a perfect image of confusion that I burst into entirely inappropriate laughter, a habit I've never overcome since my far-distant youth.

"Tell me, good Paulo," I said, when I had sobered enough to say it. "What do you know of this Radele?"

I had warned the Prince not to put his family at Men'Thor's mercy, not in such a delicate matter as young Gerick. But full of self-condemnation at his indiscretion and mistrusting his own affection for the boy, he

had chosen a bodyguard who would be impervious to
such emotion, the son of Men'Thor and grandson of Ustele, the only Preceptorate member to suggest publicly
that D'Natheil should be overthrown and another Heir
named to lead Avonar to war with the Zhid. The Prince
believed that Ustele's and Men'Thor's opposition was
rooted in legitimate care for Avonar. I had no such
conviction.

Paulo spoke grudgingly. "Radele is a good fighter.
Helped run off the bandits from the merchant caravan
we traveled with. And he's a gentleman, I suppose. Edu-
cated. Manners and all that . . ."

"But he disdains those who are not Dar'Nethi."

"Every moment of every day he was looking down
our necks, all the way down into our boots, thinking we
were dirt. But what he hated most was the young master.
The young master knew real quick that Radele wasn't
there to protect him. The Lady maybe, but not him.
Radele was there to watch—" The boy abruptly clamped
his mouth shut and glanced up at me. "Why do you
care? You're Dar'Nethi, too."

"Did you ever see Radele do anything but watch?"

"I don't know what you mean." I felt him withdrawing. "I don't know what you want."

"As you said, Radele is an extremely skilled warrior.
He is also a Dar'Nethi of more than moderate talents, as
are his father and grandfather. Let me tell you a story
from the long past, before old Ustele was named Preceptor. A woman called S'Patra, a Speaker of immense talent,
was a candidate for Preceptor, as was Ustele. D'Natheil's
grandfather was torn between the two. Both were re-
nowned for skill and loyalty. Both had fought the Zhid
for years on the walls of Avonar. But S'Patra and Ustele
had very different ideas on whether to concentrate our
efforts on strengthening the Bridge or pursuing the war.
Eventually, the Heir named S'Patra to the Preceptorate."

Paulo was listening intently.

"In her term as Preceptor, S'Patra discovered how the
Heir might cross the Bridge, even though it was designed
to allow no passage. But indeed, in the ensuing months,

the war went very badly. The Zhid captured much of the
healthy land that remained outside the Vales, making it
a part of the Wastes. But only a few months into her
tenure, S'Patra fell victim to a wasting disease of the
mind, a strange malady that left her in silence. Ustele,
as you might imagine, was named to take her place.
After the Prince called on me to help with the Lady, I
searched through our archives and discovered this inci-
dent. A rare illness. Only a few similar cases occurred
through the years. Another victim held a position of influence as a judge, a position Men'Thor took over when
the man was stricken, thereby coming to great promi-
nence in our community.

"So, you see, these stories make me wonder. I see no
cause for the Lady Seriana's condition. She is no frail
creature to be confounded by adversity, but a strong
woman, who has borne immense trials with fortitude.
Ustele and his family have no use for the Prince as we
know him, and perhaps they also know that if anything
would transform the Prince in the way they desire, it
would be harm to his wife at the hand of his son."

It was when I mentioned the silencing that the boy
remembered something. When I fell quiet, he sat thoughtfully, chewing on a knuckle. I let him be for a while, but
the night was passing, and eventually, I spoke up. "Tell
me what you remember, young Paulo. We are allies."

He let out a slow breath. "There was something . . .
a man Radele said was listening at our door in Montevial, and we were afraid he'd heard things to compromise
the Lady and the young master . . ."

Paulo told me the disturbing tale of Radele and his
enchantment—surely the same silencing spell used on
the Lady—and how the only way for the spell to be
released was for the man to recite something in his head.
"A list, you say, to undo the enchantment, but no hint
of what list it might be?"

The boy shook his head. "None. Only that it was
things the man had no means to know."

A list could be anything—kings, flowers, stars—
connected to Gondai, it seemed, if a man of the mun-

dane world had no way to know it. Even so, I could not even begin to guess what it might be. I needed more information. "Paulo, I ask for your consent to read you. Something may be buried in your memories of Radele or of that particular event that can tell me what I need to know to unlock the Lady's enchantment. I'll swear on anything you wish that I'll not probe beyond Radele. I'll not pry into your secrets."

"I give you no leave to do that!" His voice was steel, all his mistrust and wariness brought back instantly. "I won't allow it."

Swallowing my disappointment, I prayed that a night's consideration would change the boy's mind. I couldn't blame him. He was in an unfortunate position.

"Then I'll ask that you watch and listen carefully as you serve your Lady, especially when Radele is about."

"I will," he said. "I'd give most anything to help her."

"I believe you."

I had to leave the boy as I'd found him. Apologizing, I secured his wrists and ankles to the pipes again. Then I took myself through the dark and silent house to my rooms, thinking to steal a few hours' sleep before returning to my post in the desert. If I was clever, no one need know I'd ever been away. But, of course, that was before I cast a word at the lamp that sat on the perennial stack of books by my bed. The white flame burst into life and revealed Radele lounging in my favorite chair. The sword and knife I had deposited on the bed upon my arrival were firmly in his hands.

"An interesting young man, is he not, Preceptor? Filled with secrets we would give our fortunes to know, yet he has no power, no talent, and cannot make sense of two words together if they happen to be written on a page. How far are the Dar'Nethi fallen when such a lump of ignorance is our Heir's last spark of hope?"

"Or when a Dar'Nethi stoops to spy upon his Prince or his Preceptors?" What a fool I'd been not to take the simplest precautions. He must have heard everything.

"Spies are the tools of the enemy, Master Ven'Dar. The Prince has commanded me to watch and guard, and

I do his will. You, on the other hand, have trespassed his express command that no one is to speak to the boy or attempt to learn what he has to tell."

I wrestled with a balky latch and threw open the window, regretting my decision to choose a bedchamber on the second floor of the house. I was not decrepit, but my bones would not tolerate a two-story leap to the flagstone courtyard.

"We will not argue the definitions of spies or traitors, or even of enemies, Radele. I've come to my home to sleep for a while, so I respectfully request that you withdraw."

"That is not possible, Master." The young man stood and tossed my weapons on the floor, well out of my reach. Then he walked around me slowly, getting closer with each circuit, forcing me to turn if I wished to keep watch on him. Which I did. He shook his head as he eyed me. "We are at a dangerous pass. Your attempt to keep our Prince weak, encouraging his unhealthy attachment for people who are not our own, has become intolerable. It's time for you—"

"To be silenced?"

His expression did not change. "D'Arnath created the Bridge to maintain the balance of the universe, not to enslave our world to the other. I never appreciated it so fully until the Prince sent me there. We *diminish* ourselves by associating with the mundanes, Preceptor. You should see how they live—the noise and filth and ignorance, the violence they perform against each other. They do nothing but strengthen the Lords. Those who are so enraptured by them must be convinced to let go."

"It must be marvelous to have so clear a vision."

Radele quit his circling, opened the door, and motioned me into the passage. "Master, your meddling must cease. For now, I will escort you to safer quarters."

"And if I insist on sleeping in my own bed?"

"That will not be possible."

We Dar'Nethi were not accustomed to political dispute. Since the Catastrophe, our goals had been so singular and so formidable that we'd had little difference of opinion that could be translated into conspiracies or intrigues or struggles for power. The Preceptor Dassine changed all that, of course, with his belief that a dying young Healer named Karon, a descendent of our long-exiled brothers and sisters, held somewhere in his essence the secret of defeating the Lords and repairing the damage they'd done. Dassine had been stubborn, rash, not trusting his fellow Preceptors to believe a man born so far from our war and returned to life and power under such bizarre circumstances could untangle our predicaments. Yet time and circumstance now conspired against long debate, and our influential people were choosing up sides. I, who had spent my life in the study of those beliefs and practices that made the Dar'Nethi unique among the races of living beings, believed Dassine was right. I could not allow Ustele and his purists to destroy the prince Dassine had given us.

And so, as Radele raised his hand to work his silencing on me, I raised mine to cast a winding over him. My enchantment was formed of *doubt, uncertainty, wavering . . .* drawing the essence of the words to shape the spell. I overwhelmed him with *questions* and *ambiguity*, stuffed his belly with unnamed *anxiety*, bound his hand with *indecision*—a devastating fate for a young man so sure of himself.

Radele's hand trembled and fell, and he watched uncertainly as I moved past him toward the door. Unfortunately, I didn't get very far. A tall, straight-backed man in red filled the doorway.

"Ah, Preceptor Ven'Dar, none of this . . ." I felt the abrupt starved dizziness of a Word Winder whose cast has been snapped before completion, something like having one's stomach and eyes excised at the same moment. It is a most distressing sensation, especially when one suspects something even more unpleasant is to follow.

Men'Thor was an imposing man. His padded doublet was elaborately embroidered and immaculately clean, his boots brushed. His gray hair and beard were trimmed and neat. His whole demeanor cried a reproach to my sand- and sweat-crusted skin and my rumpled shirt and breeches, though he, too, had come here from the battlefield.

I reeled in my cast, taking a breath and squeezing my eyes shut for a moment to convince my mind that my body was still attached. Of course, as I recovered, I considered whether to cast again. Men'Thor, whose expression never changed, whose voice was always calm and equitable, and whose mind could not be influenced once it was settled on an idea, was a very powerful sorcerer. I was likely stronger. But I was not interested in dueling with any Dar'Nethi, as long as the man prevented his son's vicious foolery. Though Men'Thor and I disagreed on many matters, including strategy and ethics, we shared a common enemy—the Zhid and the Lords. So I held back.

The only unpleasantness I had to endure for the moment was Men'Thor herding me back toward Radele, appropriating my chair that his son had so recently vacated, and lecturing us both like schoolboys. "Master Ven'Dar would be well within his rights to have you exiled, boy! How shall a father represent his fool of a son to repair such injury? How shall a Dar'Nethi justify raising his hand to his Preceptor or a Preceptor to one of his own brother Dar'Nethi, while, at the very moment, the Vale of Seraph burns at the hand of the Lords of Zhev'Na?"

"Seraph!" I said. Seraph, the southernmost Vale of Eidolon, was a land of sparkling streams, green hillsides, and white cliffs hung with red-flowered vines. Its perennial springtime produced the sweetest airs in Gondai. The white stone towns and villages housed hardy folk who prided themselves on their abundant fields of grapes so near the edge of the Wastes.

But the significance of Men'Thor's news stretched well beyond the tragedy of a bountiful land touched by war. Since the earliest years of our war with the Lords, when they ravaged Grithna, Erdris, and Pylathia, the Zhid had been barred from the Vales. We had thought the remaining Vales secure as long as Avonar stood.

"Our enemies have penetrated the southern wards

and struck the towns of Tanis and Ephah, withdrawing before the Prince could respond," said Men'Thor, shaking his head. "But the Lords' true power is revealed. Tomorrow the Prince will walk the ruins of Ephah, knowing that the fate of the world hangs by the thinnest of threads. If the Zhid can take the Vales, untouched for a thousand years, Avonar can be surrounded. And that will be the end, as surely as if the Lords' plot to destroy the Bridge had succeeded or the demon son been anointed Heir."

"How was it possible?" I said. "The Watch . . ."

"Someone has compromised the Vale Watch. Though only the Prince and the Preceptors knew the secret of the watch, such an event was hardly unexpected now the Destroyer has shown himself."

"The Prince will be forced to listen to you now, Father," said Radele. "Take down the Destroyer first, then Zhev'Na itself."

"You assume it's the Prince's son who has caused this?" I said.

"The Prince believes it," said Men'Thor. "He says it's possible the Destroyer has read everything of Avonar's defense from him. As soon as he is able, he will come here to extract the Destroyer's plan from our prisoner. Then we'll rid the world of the demon son."

"I don't grasp your logic, Men'Thor. We've had no luck flushing the Lords from Zhev'Na in all these years. If the boy has joined them in their stronghold, their position will be all but impregnable."

"If such is the case, the Prince says he will lead the host of Avonar against Zhev'Na." Doom and awe gave shape to Men'Thor's words, leaching the color from the lamplight.

"At last!" cried Radele. "His eyes are opened!" He strode briskly to the window and gripped the sill as if his own eyes might witness the new battle already engaged.

My spirit recoiled at Radele's glee. *The host of Avonar against Zhev'Na* . . . Our last resort. Every man, woman, and child to march on the desert fortress wielding sticks and swords and magic in a monstrous, mad crusade that would result in the annihilation of either the Lords or the Dar'Nethi. Ustele and his family had been championing such an impossible assault for generations. They had long proclaimed that it was only our hesitation—our doubt in our own power and our reluctance to commit ourselves—that had caused the war to last so long. But to buy our safety with slaughter . . . even in victory we would lose.

"This is madness, Men'Thor," I said. "The Prince will never agree to such a plan. I know his true heart, and if I have to stand vigil and cast for a thousand nights, I will convince him to renounce this absurdity."

"Let me tell you what is madness, Preceptor," said Men'Thor. "A Prince who cannot tell you his name from one day to the next. A Prince whose loyalties are compromised to the verge of corruption, whose 'true heart' is fixed on a mundane woman and a boy who gave his eyes and his soul to become the Fourth Lord of Zhev'Na. An Heir of D'Arnath who can no longer offer the most rudimentary service of his healing gift."

His voice flowed with the grave sincerity he used with equal skill to notify a mother of her warrior daughter's death or to mediate a disagreement with his tailor. It was Men'Thor the Effector's unflappable rationality that had convinced many Dar'Nethi that he was better equipped to lead us than our passionate Prince.

"For a thousand years, Ven'Dar, we have allowed the Lords to taunt us and feed on our weakness, to keep us prisoned behind our walls and hiding in our little valleys as if this were the life Dar'Nethi were born to. Now they are a handsbreadth from putting their nurtured spawn in D'Arnath's chair, and you would not have our Prince fight them? You suggest that some mysterious conjunction of the planets has betrayed our safety, rather than the depraved child who swore undying loyalty to our enemies. And you dare call *our* course absurd!" Though neither volume nor timbre had changed, Men'Thor burst to his feet with the intensity of his speaking. "You are a good man, Ven'Dar, and Avonar will need your talent when her host ventures forth. But you serve us ill—to the point of treason—when you nurture the Prince's madness."

While I blustered like a fool, thinking that yet another round of argument might make some difference, Men'Thor sighed deeply and laid his arm on Radele's shoulders. "I must go. My men hold the walls of Avonar tonight. I just thought I should share this news with you myself."

"Thank you, Father. What do you suggest I do with the Preceptor? He was trying to pry information from the prisoner."

Men'Thor gazed at me mournfully. "We will never convince Preceptor Ven'Dar of our position. The best we can do is prevent cowards of his ilk from influencing the Prince. Our duty is to keep D'Arnath's Heir focused on his proper business—the survival of Avonar, of the Vales, of Gondai, of the Bridge—until holy Vasrin sees fit to give us a sovereign worthy of D'Arnath's throne."

Radele smiled broadly and embraced Men'Thor. "As you say, Father. The tide is turning."

Radele stood in the doorway, watching his father descend the stairs. Then he turned back to face me. "My father is a wise man, Preceptor. Shall I demonstrate how we shall keep our mad Prince focused on his duty?" He was smiling.

Tired, distracted, envisioning our enemies tearing at our heart, I didn't answer him. And so I failed to note the movement of his hand. . . .

I was changed. Like a storm cloud suddenly bereft of rain and wind or a forest instantly deprived of trees, my life no longer had a purpose, and thus no meaning to be expressed in words. A hand took my arm and propelled me toward the doorway. My feet moved as they were directed.

"I'll have to put you with the stable boy, Preceptor. I don't like keeping the two of you together, but someone will need to feed and clean you. I'll have to dismiss your servants. We can't have them snooping about. And when the Prince interrogates the boy, I'll just make sure he has no memory of his cellmate."

The hand led me down two flights of stairs and through the cellar, unbolted a door, and shoved me into the dark. I tumbled onto a dirt floor as the door closed behind me. Even as I grasped to hold them close, my thoughts detached themselves from the world of order and logic and drifted away.

"Who's there?" came a drowsy voice from the darkness. "I know someone's there. May as well answer me . . ."

So tired. I curled up on the cool dirt and weariness closed my eyes.

CHAPTER 22

Dull light beams pushed their way through the dusty air from a tiny grate close to the ceiling.

"Oh, cripes!" An outburst of words quite close to my ear. "They've done for you like they done for the Lady, haven't they? Demonfire! A right fine mess we're in now."

A freckled face . . . a worried face, striped by the dusty light-beams . . . appeared in the air somewhere above me.

Jostling. Sitting upright now.

"Radele brought our breakfast and told me to see that you eat. Very kind he is."

Bread in my hand.

"Well, come on then. Put it in your mouth."

Dry . . . chewy . . . *Teeth and tongue, wits like dung* . . .

"Wasn't supposed to work out this way. 'Be fast,' he says. 'It's got to be fast or we'll all be dead.' So now he's out there likely dying, while I'm rotting in a bin of turnips. They're all going to die if his plan don't work. What in this cursed world am I to do?"

No cursing! No rotting! Carrots in the bin . . . turnips . . . heads and turnips . . .

A mechanical click . . . a buckle? a clock? a latch? *Disturbs the dancing dust motes . . .*

"Come on, horse boy. Time for you to do your duties as the Prince has commanded you. By rights you should be banished to the Wastes as a traitor, though my father says you're only a pawn of the Destroyer. He claims that mundanes are incapable of any meaningful act such as treachery. I'll have to consider that. I think you should be dead."

Clambering . . . crowding . . . bumping. A door slammed. Click. Silence. Colors, impressions, bits and pieces of memories, fragments of music, of song, of stories or poems, showers of words. *Words are my life.* . . . Drifting, pushing, and crowding one another this way and that, like gnats hovering above a pond. Swirling aimlessly like snowflakes in a circling wind . . . like dust motes in the light . . .

Directionless time . . . fading light . . . blindness creeping . . . *Fearful blindness . . . terrible . . . not that, not that, not that* . . .

Click. Snap. Searing brightness. Air shifting. Stumbling boots. An avalanche of turnips . . . Sounds, movements, smells . . . nudging me . . . wandering . . .

"Move closer to the pipes, boy. I'll leave you loose enough you can tend the Preceptor, but we'll not have you getting away."

Intrusion. Crowded. Arms . . . legs . . . boots . . . Click. Snap. *Darkness. Not blindness. Night.* Quiet breathing. *Lungs and tongues, inhale . . . exhale . . . smothering dark* . . .

"Master Ven'Dar, can you hear me? Here, squeeze my hand if you can understand me."

A nice hand. A working hand. Scars. *Don't raise your hand to me, young man!* So much clutter in my head, ready to fly away . . . A sister's ready hand, boxing my ears . . .

"Ah, curse all sorcery and them as practice it!"

The hand withdrew. Cold bread now. Bread in my mouth. Sour ale. Sleep tugging at my eyelids . . .

Light and darkness. Crowding, bumping, silence in the light.

Crowding, bumping, companionship in the dark. Hands in the dark. The cycle . . . whirling past.

"You know, Master"—the spoon popped between my lips yet again—"sometimes the way things happen just turns a man's head inside out. The first clue I get, and in the same breath I hear it's no use to us. I've been trying and trying to find out what was the list Radele used for the enchantment. Today I heard Radele talking to his Grandpa Ustele, the Preceptor, and at last I hear them talking about a list, and I'm thinking it might be the list as is needed to help the Lady and maybe I could somehow get away and find someone to come help her. But doesn't the old man say that *you're* probably the only one in Avonar as could say the 'list of all the Dar'Nethi talents'? And your head is about as useful as one of these turnips."

Drowning!

Figs and pools, pigs and fools . . .

"Ah, plague on it! Now you're a mess. How am I supposed to feed you when I'm tethered to this pipe like a donkey? No way I could run off, anyway. Not with this magic they've put on me that make my feet like lead. Only reason I can talk is that they're just not scared of anything in my head. Not like with you and the Lady."

Dampness . . . on and under me . . . earthen floor . . . soup mud . . . farmyard mud . . . stink . . . of onions and pigs . . .

"I looked about to see if you might have a bit of writing in the house that might be such a thing as this list, but I'm so ignorant, I couldn't even tell if it was the right one or not, nor yet what to do with it if I found it." Cloth blotting. "I'm just not much good to nobody as doesn't have a mane and a tail, am I?"

The list of talents . . . the hundred . . . of all the hundred you received only one . . . in measure large or small . . . your gift . . . to be with you forever . . . to guide your Way . . . *Ven'Dar yn Cyran, proved a Word Winder this day! Fool of a boy, can't you feel it? Look what you've done . . . best learn a cast to repair the steps or father will flay you! So difficult to be good at it. You can't stay at home . . . not with power like yours . . . undisciplined whelp . . . Master Exeget will house you, as well as mentor you . . . prevent your killing anyone . . .* Exeget, cold as an ice cliff . . . *Be worthy of your people . . . be worthy of your gift . . . Truth is the founda-*

*tion of a Word Winder's power . . . Try again . . . and
again . . . You are the living essence of the Way. . . .* Mice
scrabbling through the baskets of turnips and onions and
carrots. Onions rotting. *Men rotting in the desert . . .
dead in the Wastes . . . turnips and carrots . . .*

Light and darkness. Crowding, bumping, silence in
the light.

Crowding, bumping, companionship in the dark. "Can
you hear me, Master? The Lady's fading. Every day I
have to see her. For a man to breathe on her would
kill her."

Light and darkness. Click, snap. Breathing in the dark.

A crash. Again. Fist hammering. "Shit, shit, shit! I
can't believe they'd do it! And here I'm stuck in this
cursed hole, no better off than I was in Zhev'Na. And
you no more help than a two-legged mule."

Pinching my shoulder. Rattling my teeth. "Listen to
me, Master Ven'Dar. We've got to help the Lady. Radele is going to kill her before the Prince comes back
here. He believes that when the Prince looks in my head,
he'll find out where the young master is. But old Ustele
told him that having the Lady around might stop the
Prince from killing their son—just knowing what she
would say about it if she could talk. The Prince has been
in an awful battle, he says, one that's gone on for days,
but he'll be coming here tomorrow. So we've no more
time."

*Words tumbling . . . raindrops . . . hailstones . . .
avalanche . . . buried . . . hurt . . .*

"Do you remember how I told you to think on the
talents of the Dar'Nethi? The list? It's the key to the
silencing. I've tried talking to the Lady to get her to
think on it. But I don't know if she can hear me or if
she knows all of the list, and it has to be every one of
the talents, so Radele says. You've got to name every
one of them in your head, Master."

Warm, bony hands . . . enfolding . . .

"I know some of them: Healer, like the Prince, Word
Winder, that's you. Master Gar'Dena, may his name be

writ, was a Gem Worker. There's Builders and
Horsemasters that the Prince told me of . . . but I don't
know the rest. You've got to name the whole list to
be free."

Gem Worker . . . left for dead like turnips left to rot.
*Hurts! Hurts! Forests rotting . . . souls . . . cabbages . . .
black and moldering . . . soon to be dust, like the
Wastes . . .*

Raindrops of words pelting the sea. *Tiring.* I curled
up on the cool dirt. *Sleeping . . . creeping . . .*

"No, Master! You don't understand. The time! It's
been too long already. Demonfire, I *know* you can
hear me."

Slap! Stinging blow.

"Come on, sit up again. *Think*, Master. Radele's killing the Lady. He's put another enchantment on her
that's going to make her die if we don't stop it. Is there
a Singer in the list? A Tree . . . something?" Words
hard-edged in the darkness. "You want to save the
Prince, you got to save yourself first. I heard Radele
sniggering at the Lady, telling her how he's going to see
she don't save the young master this time. Oh,
demonfire, Master Ven'Dar, you've got to listen, and
you've got to think of the list. Right now."

Hands squeezing cheeks and jaw . . . trembling
now . . . suddenly cold as a glacier . . . cold fire . . .

*Singer, Healer, Speaker, Word Winder . . . Hold your-
self together, Ven'Dar. Ven'Dar the Vainglorious. Dam
up the ocean and replace it with a water jar. Catch the
raindrop words in something where they'll make a
difference.*

*. . . Metalwright . . . Sea Dweller . . . who battles the
tide . . .* Timeless waves . . . drifting . . .

*No! You can do this. You know the list. Exeget taunted
you until you learned them all. Do you need to stand on
your head to do it? Say the list. Every name.*

Stronger now. *Builder, Tree . . . Delver, of course,
Balancer, like the great D'Arnath himself and C'Netra,
yammering, beloved C'Netra . . .*

The list grew . . . The voice in my head . . . so loud . . .
so hard . . . *What next? Say them!*

Gem Worker . . . Silver Shaper . . . and next? So hard to remember . . . leave it go . . .

No, hold on. How do you remember the names? How were you taught? Probing . . . digging . . . holding back the tide of madness. *In the order of their discovery: the Hundred Talents. After Silver Shaper comes Horsemaster . . . You draw them from the depths of your being, not just facts memorized in childhood, but from the essentials of your soul, lived . . . believed . . . cherished . . .*

The list grew.

Is that all? There are more, aren't there? Think . . . remember . . .

Ninety and nine have I spoken, from Glass Maker to Storyteller, from Gardener to Navigator, each one a touchstone of our history, a fundamental of our life, like the heart of a mother and the hand of a father that shape the core of the family.

What is the last? Why do some say the list is complete at ninety and nine?

Because the hundredth is the myth . . . the Soul Weaver . . .

My eyes blinked open. I was kneeling on the dirt floor of my root cellar, cold as a new-caught fish and stinking like a dead one. No sooner had I voiced the hundredth name than the ocean of confusion had retreated, exposing shape and order like rocks emerged from a receding tide: past, present, future, memory, dream, knowledge, deduction . . . and dominating all of it, the driving urgency to go to the Lady. She would be in my parlor, sitting by the fire, lost in a sea of light and shadows as I had been. And close beside me in the dark, very close, someone else was breathing.

"I think I'm all right now," I said, nudging straggling, greasy hair out of my eyes.

How was this possible? I might have thought another Dar'Nethi had spoken in my thoughts, giving me the names and prodding me to attention when I faltered. Yet such a speaking was very different, an intrusion across the barriers of self, instantly recognizable and traceable to the intruder. No one but my sister and I knew of "Ven'Dar the Vainglorious," the young Word

Winder whose first cast had landed so wide of its mark that his elder sister, the humble Balancer, had been forced to make peace with an entire village of infuriated Gardeners standing hip-deep in an ocean of well-intentioned mud. No one but I knew how I used the title so often as a prod to humility. And I'd never told even C'Netra how Exeget had made me stand on my head until I could speak the list. No. Though it was impossible, the words had been mine. But, of course, this lad had urged me to it.

"Thank you," I said to my companion in the dark cellar, while I rubbed my swirling head and shook the last confusion away. He had fallen so silent while I wrestled with chaos that his dark, still shape might have been nothing but another bag of onions. "You were right. The list was the key. I don't know how I was able to do it, but you were right."

"Please, go to her," he said quietly, demonstrating not the least surprise at my sudden speech. "Hurry."

"We'll both go," I said.

"Can't. They've bound me here and not just with rope. Touching the door latch makes my hand feel as if it's being torn off. And you'd think my boots had anvils in them instead of feet."

Stupid that I'd forgotten. I would have sworn he was free, running around me, hounding me like a sheep dog, while he pelted me with words. A foolish image.

"You've run into so many disadvantages in your association with us Dar'Nethi that you've forgotten the advantages," I said, as I produced a soft white light from my hand, crawled over his long legs, and grappled with a tangle of pipes and rope I could scarcely reach. With a knife of flame I split the ropes that bound his ankles and wrists, perhaps a little too vigorously, for he yelped. The backs of my own hands felt singed. As he massaged blood back into his fingers, I countered the simple enchantments that kept him from securing his own freedom. "Now we can go."

"Maybe I should stay here for a while. Distract Radele if he should come to check on us."

"If what you've told me is correct, young Paulo, we

need to get the Lady and ourselves out of this house at
the first instant. I can handle Radele, as long as you
watch my back and yell at me if he should raise his hand
again. You've no idea how embarrassing this has been—
to be caught like a novice. And you've no idea how
lucky we are that I could come up with the list." Enunci-
ating the precise words in a mind scarcely capable of
thought. Vasrin's hand, surely.

"Go ahead, then, I'll follow."

Coaxing the smooth veneer of a binding spell from
the door latch, I allowed my light to die and pulled open
the door a crack. A stray beam of lamplight from the
cellar stair invaded our dusty den. The faintest of magical feelers sent into the adjacent cellars and up the stairs
confirmed that no one lurked anywhere nearby. Evidently our captors were secure in our incapacity. I
stepped through the low door into my cluttered store-
room, stretching my cramped legs and stiff back.

Creaky old man. I glanced back to see if my young
friend had emerged. Paulo had just stepped out, and
when I turned, he threw his hand up before his face, as
if to shield his eyes from the brightness, but not before
I'd gotten a glimpse of them. Odd . . . something . . .

"She's in your front sitting room," he said. "They
leave her sit up till a serving woman is sent in to her
about an hour before midnight."

"Are you well, son?"

"I'm fine. Lead on. And, Master, Radele said Men'Thor
was on his way tonight, so as to be here when the Prince
arrived. To be sure of him."

"I understand. We'll be quick and quiet."

With what stealth a not-young man just out of a
week's trance could muster, I led Paulo through the
maze of pots and paintings, crates of books, and extra
furnishings I'd shoved into my cellars when I ran out of
space in the main rooms of my house. We crept up the
stairs. Perhaps I needed to hire a Builder to make my
stairs less steep, I thought, as we topped the last step
and tiptoed into the back passage that serviced the kitchens and the large doors that led to the front of the
house. What nonsense comes to mind, even in the midst

of great events. Did D'Arnath worry about the steepness of his cellar stairs as he built his Bridge?

The hallways were deserted, but quiet voices emanated from the library. My reading room, what Paulo called the front sitting room, was tucked in between the front doors and the library. I could afford no enchantments lest Radele be monitoring the house, so I cracked the reading-room door ever so slightly and hoped my man Ceddoch had quieted the old hinges as I'd asked him to do some time ago when life was less complicated.

The door opened without sound. The Lady Seriana was alone, exactly as I had envisioned her, even to the deep blue color of her gown and her position on the low stool in front of my favorite fireplace. She stared into the fire, unmoving, unblinking, lost wherever the tides of random thought and memory had taken her. Far from my reading room, I guessed; it had been four months for her. I could afford no anger at those responsible. We had time for nothing but to get her away.

The boy darted past me and knelt by the Lady, his back to me, his whisper barely audible. "Come, my lady. We've come to take you to safety. Don't be afraid."

He took her hands and stood up, pulling her gently to her feet. She, of course, said nothing and made no resistance. She was as pale as starlight, as fragile as a soap bubble that floats from your hand on washing day. A loud voice might dissolve her, or a hasty touch; I guessed that her remaining life could be measured in hours, not days.

Fixing my attention on the passage, I whispered over my shoulder. "When I say the word, take her straight through the kitchen to the stable and get her on a horse. From the rear door of the stable, a track leads down into the Vale. When you meet the main path that traverses the Vale—you'll know it—go left, upward, and ride hard until you come to an arched rock. Half a league beyond it, a path will branch to the left and lead you to a stone tower. You'll be immensely reluctant to go there, but it's only a winding to keep people away. Push through it, keeping your eyes on the path every moment. No harm will come to you, and once inside the tower you'll no longer feel the aversion. If I don't arrive close on your heels, get the Lady to Avonar and tell the Preceptor Ce'Aret all you've told me."

I glanced up and down the passage, listening so intently I could hear my own heart beating. Satisfied that no one lay in wait, I nodded.

With an arm around her waist, the youth led the Lady down the dim passageway. As soon as they had disappeared into the back of the house I hurried the opposite way to an alcove near the front entry, where I kept my old mentor Exeget's weapons. I grabbed two swords, two knives, a bow, and a small quiver, prayed holy Vasrin we wouldn't need them, and slipped out of the alcove into the foyer, heading toward the back of the house where I'd sent Paulo and the Lady.

Fortune plays many games, testing us, I think, or perhaps as part of some grand jest. Why else should Radele step out of the library just then, and the front door swing open to reveal Men'Thor, clad in cloak and battlefield boots and already removing his gloves?

"Ven'Dar!" Father and son spoke in perfect unison.

Happily, I was less shocked than either of them, and more familiar with the plan of the house and the wards I had created to deter intrusions. I sped across the foyer, whispering the word that extinguished every lamp, candle, and torch in the house. I laughed when I heard the bump and curse that could be nothing but the meeting of Radele and my gallery wall. Lest sun or moon guide any ne'er-do-well through my chambers once the lights were doused, the winding shifted the perceived locations of doorways and corners. On my way through the kitchen I grabbed an armful of cloaks, abandoned over the years by my kitchen staff, and a small leather bag I always kept hanging by the door, a habit retained from my youth in a village in constant danger of Zhid raiders. A wise man was always provisioned for a hasty retreat.

Trailed by shouts and curses, I burst from the kitchens into the warm, starry night of the kitchen yard. Through the windows behind me, a pale light flicked into life. Radele and Men'Thor were no fools. My enchantments would give us only moments.

"Best hurry!" I yelled as I burst into the stable.

The Lady was already astride a chestnut gelding, and Paulo was swinging up behind her. The back door of the stable stood open, and my own Jocelyn stood ready for me. I threw the cloaks across Jocelyn's saddle and tossed the spare sword to Paulo, but to my surprise he dropped it as if it were newly pulled from the smith's fire.

"I've no place to carry it," he said. "And I'm no good with 'em." He spurred the chestnut, and they shot from the stable like a meteor across the night sky.

I didn't follow immediately, but buckled on the second sword belt and hung the bow and quiver over my back. Forcing myself to ignore the commotion, the shouts and slamming doors, the lamps winking to life one by one as the men searched for us, I took a deep breath and worked a winding of somewhat more weight than the house ward: *wood, paper, straw, consume, huge, shield, home, safety, necessity, heat, sudden, confusion, terror, escape . . .*

Focus on the words, Ven'Dar. I sought the truth of the words, the meanings buried beneath centuries of use. I drew them together and infused them with my gift, my knowledge, and my intent. *Patience. Let it grow. Lives could depend on how long you hold before the cast.*

My hands rested on Jocelyn's flank as the enchantment swelled within me. I resisted the urge to set the spell free before it broke through the boundaries of my body, holding my focus until the main door of the stable was thrown open. One person was out of the house. The others would soon realize where we'd gone and follow him. At last, out of time, I made my cast. *Fire!*

No chance of this winding going astray. Nentao was my own house, after all. As if the ground beneath had opened to the fiery heart of the earth, yellow-orange flames burst through windows and walls, engulfing my home.

I urged Jocelyn through the back door and galloped down the track in the light of the flames. I didn't look back to see Nentao burning, nor did I listen to the shouts and screams. I might have been tempted to moderate my work, and we needed every advantage we could get.

Paulo had told me that most of my own servants had
been dismissed; my wards would warn the rest and lead
them safely away. Radele's men would be confused and
desperate to find their way out, but they also would escape. I had left them a thread.

Men'Thor's bodyguard, who had opened the stable
door, raced down the path after us. But, poor soul, he
didn't know the track well enough and was too cautious.
If he'd come at full speed he might have overtaken me
before I could cast again, and taken care of me as young
men can do to those more than double their age. But
he hesitated and got himself tangled in what, on the next
morning, he was going to swear was a massive spiderweb
with a dinner-plate-sized spider lurking in it. In fact, it
was a particularly thick patch of vine-draped trees and
a small, very shy raccoon.

The fellow didn't know that the time for caution was
past. As I galloped through the Lydian Vale, the world
galloped right alongside me, history's ragged banners
flying as we raced into the dark midnight.

CHAPTER 23

Just before moonset I turned Jocelyn loose to refresh herself on the sweet grass of the Lydian Vale. The white stone of P'Clor's Tower gleamed like pearl in the moonlight. As I wearily climbed the wooden stair to the single plain room at the top, a lazy, humid breeze soughed through the empty window slots.

P'Clor's Tower was my refuge, my solitude, the place where I would strip down to essentials: bread, water, sun, wind, forest, and words. A Word Winder has no more fundamental necessity than such a retreat, where he can hear the truth of words unmuddled by society and business, come to understand their nuances, and prepare a place for them to dwell within himself.

The Lady Seri stood beside one of the narrow windows, as if she were watching the drift of clouds that rushed past the setting moon. She appeared to be alone in the circular chamber, but the vigilant Paulo materialized from a shadowed window ledge behind me as I topped the last stair.

"It's only Ven'Dar the Vainglorious," I said, tossing him one of the spare cloaks and laying another about the Lady's shoulders. "I think we've a little space to breathe for now."

"Can you do it?"

"Help the Lady Seriana? If her mind was locked with the same key as mine, and if she's not drifted too far away to hear me, I think I can."

"You've got to hurry. I can't—" Taut, anxious, the youth remained by the top of the stair.

"Can't what?"

"I can't stay with you. Don't ask me to explain. Just hurry."

The urgency in the youth was indisputable, even if I'd had a thought of delay. I removed my weapons and laid them on the floor beside the table where I kept my supply of candles and paper and ink.

Even if young Paulo hadn't urged me to it, I would have made the attempt. Lady Seriana's life was less substantial than the waning moonlight, and I had no faith she would survive the coming of day any more than the angled beams pouring through my tower window would.

I guided her to my chair, a straight-backed wooden thing I'd crafted on one of my sojourns in P'Clor's Tower. Then I sat myself on a flour barrel I'd pulled close, laid my hands on her temples, and intruded on her mind.

My Lady, forgive my entry unbidden. My knowledge of your character and history tells me that you would grant me this privilege were you able. I have dwelt in the place you wander, and I know how impossible is the task of mastering a coherent thought, but for your freedom and your life, I beg you try. With all you are and all you have been, grasp the words I give you and hold them close. Then I opened myself to her.

Great Vasrin, Shaper and Creator! I came so near drowning in a fog of incoherent images, I almost had to withdraw. She was very far away.

Well, nothing for it but to begin and to hope. *Singer, Healer, Speaker, Word Winder . . .* One after the other, I gave her the names and all I possessed of their essence, just as I had carved them from my own chaos a short few hours before. Each one I forced into the stream of her thoughts, holding it firm until I felt the flow snatch it from my grasp and whirl it away.

Never had I been involved in so intense a speaking. Twice I came near losing my place in the list. After no more than a quarter of the names, my sending faltered. My head pounded unmercifully; my arms weighed like lead; and my shoulders screamed at me to let them fall. She was so very deep, and I had been through so much myself. Unutterably foolish of me not to rest for a while before trying this. I would have to stop and try again.

Focus, Ven'Dar. Send the tale deep. Etch it in letters of fire, like a beacon she cannot fail to see. Twenty-seventh in the list is what? Say it.

Twenty-seventh is Scribe. . . .

Just as earlier that night, there arose in me such a strength of will, a veritable lodestone that drew together every fragment of steel I possessed, so that I could not wilt or wander or falter.

. . . Seventy-fifth is Sea Dweller, who breathes water, and tends the gardens and herds of the deeps. . . .

It was as if I had four hands, two of them invisible, but strong and tireless, supporting the two that trembled lest they lose contact with the sad and lovely face before me. But whose hands were they? The Lady and Paulo were mundane. The only hands they possessed were the pale, slender ones that lay passively in the Lady's lap, and the strong and capable pair belonging to the youth who sat silent and still in the shadows.

Almost at an end . . . what is the next? Stand on your head. . . .

Ninety-ninth in the list is Finder, who sees beyond the visible and can sort one essence from another in the great blending of the world that is life. And the hundredth in the list is Soul Weaver, the myth.

As the last words echoed from my inner voice, monumental weariness overwhelmed me as if my very bones had been drawn out of my flesh and discarded out of reach. My aching arms fell to my sides, and the moon-streaked darkness spun slowly about my head. Paulo jumped off the table and caught my shoulders from behind before I fell off my barrel, while from the distant forest, an owl's clear hoots broke the expectant silence—the silence of failure, I believed. The Lady had not moved.

But then she gasped with one great breath, and the great brown eyes that for four months had reflected only profound emptiness blinked and focused on my own. Her lips curved into a smile, and as her gaze slid over my face to the one standing behind me, her expression blossomed with deep affection.

But as I sighed and slipped into happy oblivion, the

smile faded. Grief and horror claimed the territory of
her eyes. "Oh, my dear one, what have you done?"

I'd thought to enjoy the sleep of satisfaction, of deeds
accomplished and battles won, but the Lady's stricken
countenance wrapped me in a blanket of unease, and
only fearful visions were my night's companions.

The soft, scratching sound would stop for a moment,
then take up again, somewhere close to my head, sometimes farther away. Sometimes it was interrupted by a
rhythmic picking, then a flutter, and a tickle of moving
air across my face. Ah, sparrows, the permanent tenants
of P'Clor's Tower, so tame they'd nest in your hair if
you were still long enough.

My aching bones begged me not to move. Only a blanket separated me from the floor, and someone had
thrown a cloak over me in the chill predawn hours after
I'd collapsed. Now the day was warm, and the angle of
the sun shallow. I already felt like a piece of raw meat
that had been dragged through the streets by a starving
dog, and if I stayed under the warm cloak I was going
to smell like it, too, worse than I did already. I threw
off the cloak and creaked to my feet.

The Lady was sleeping on my thin pallet, her red-brown
hair loose and scattered, her cheeks blooming with life. A
cloak had been laid over her. Likewise deep in slumber,
Paulo had curled on the bare floor at the head of the stair
like a faithful hound guarding the entry. Somehow I had
expected the boy to be gone when I awoke.

Grabbing an empty bucket from a hook on the wall,
I eased around the sleeping youth and tiptoed downstairs to where a rain barrel stood in the glade, a dipper
hung over the side. The water was cool and sweet. Then,
ignoring all modest caution, I stripped and poured three
buckets full over me. Somehow the water felt colder on
my back than in my mouth, but to waste enchantment
to heat it always seemed inappropriate at P'Clor's
Tower. So, I smothered my yelp and snatched up my
filthy shirt to rub myself dry.

Refreshed now the ordeal was over, I donned the
damp shirt and breeches, vowing to burn them at the

first opportunity, along with the underdrawers Vasrin
herself could not have forced me to put on again. Then
I refilled the pail and carried it upstairs for my companions, planning to lay out the meager bounty of my refu-
gee's provision bag for breakfast.

Lying on the worktable next to the leather bag was a
folded paper, a sheet from my own small supply,
marked, FOR THE LADY. Odd. I didn't think I'd taken a
yen for composition in my sleep, and I assumed the Lady
wouldn't have found it profitable to write a missive to
herself. And from everything I understood, Paulo was
illiterate.

"What puzzles you so this morning, Master . . .
Ven'Dar, I think?"

I didn't quite jump out of my skin at the quiet interruption. "Ah, my lady, what a pleasure it is—a most
profound pleasure—to meet you at last." I bowed, extending my palms. "I am indeed the one you name."

I gave her my hand, and she rose from the pallet,
returning the politeness. "My thanks are inadequate,
Master."

Her smile was genuine and kind, but her mind was
not on our pleasantries, only on the youth who lay unmoving by the stair. She crouched down beside him, laying her hand on his back as if to assure herself he was
breathing. Only after a long while did she rise and move
to the window slot to survey our green haven. She folded
her arms across her breast, one thumb pressed pensively
to her lips. Her eyes flicked repeatedly to the boy.

I hated to intrude on her thoughts, but our time was
not unbounded. "Please, come and share breakfast, my
lady: dried fish, some old, but well preserved bread, and
fruit. You need nourishment. As for my small mystery,
it is yours to unravel." I handed her the letter. "The
contents are not the puzzle—I've not taken it upon myself to peruse your correspondence uninvited—but only
the author. The message was written last night here in
the tower, for I recognize the paper, and the ink is fresh.
But we've had no visitors, and that means, eliminating
you and me, the scribe must be young Paulo. I believed
the boy unschooled."

She fingered the folded paper, but made no move to read it. "Paulo cannot read or write," she said softly. "You'll have to tell me what it means that he could do this."

"I'm not sure . . . If I may ask, what transpired last night after I so unamiably collapsed?"

"I was tired, too; it was like a dream. He laid you on the blanket, covered you with your cloak, and then led me to the pallet. The next thing I knew I woke to the sunlight." She threw the letter onto the writing table. "It's impossible. Impossible. I won't believe it." Her vehemence seemed little related to the matter of Paulo being able to write.

"Perhaps reading the message will answer your questions."

I busied myself by squandering a small enchantment to heat a cup of water and measuring out chamomile and meadowsweet from the small supply in the leather bag. I offered her the tea along with a chunk of ancient dried fruit that I hoped would not break her teeth. But she had picked up the paper again and was turning it over and over in her hands. What was she afraid of? Finally, after taking one more glance at the sleeping boy, she unfolded the letter.

Though it was only a single close-written page, she studied it for half an hour or more before silently offering it to me. I set aside my cup and took it.

My dearest Mother,

I hope beyond all hopes that this morning finds you completely recovered from your grievous injury. I beg you not to destroy this in disgust at my hypocrisy, or in revulsion at the truth you guessed last night. Rather I ask you to indulge one last time in the love and trust you have so generously—so unquestioningly—given me in the past.

Paulo will tell you of all that has befallen us, and with it of the revelation that has only lately come to me. On my life I swear to you I did not consciously seek your death, nor did I knowingly betray the defense of Avonar. I cannot expect anyone to believe

*this, save perhaps you, who have always been willing
to think the best of me. Paulo, despite his generous
service, has doubts. I doubt myself, yet both deeds
were so alien to my desires that I cannot admit their
possibility. Of course I must, for the future of the
worlds is once again at risk because of me, and the
remedy is once again in your hands, and, through
your intercession, in the hands of my father.*

*The world that Paulo will describe to you is not
Gondai, nor is it the familiar home where we were
born. The Bounded is a third world, a world still
forming, still growing, peopled with a strange and
wonderful variety of beings, who, while bearing little
of beauty or grace, are no more evil in their souls
than any race of humans. This world was newly born
from the chaos of the Breach at about the time we
traveled through it on our escape from Zhev'Na. In
some way I do not yet understand, my actions on
that journey and the state of my mind at that time
have created a profound bond between me and the
Bounded, so that I know and feel and experience its
life as if it were a part of my own body.*

*Unfortunately, the magic of the Bounded has
shown me the truth of something I have suspected
and feared these four years. The Lords maintain their
hold on me as well. I believe the Lords themselves
discovered this when I crossed the Bridge four
months ago and now threaten ruin to all the worlds
I touch. If the situation remains as it is now, the
Lords will surely gain everything we denied them
four years ago. Just as the Prince so rightly fears,
they will control me, and they will control the
Breach. It seems they can already use me at their will
to wreak havoc; you and my father's counselors and
subjects have suffered grievously from it. This is not
to excuse myself from those deeds, for ultimately, as
with all the evils I have done, I am responsible.*

*The remedy seems very simple. My death will re-
move this danger, and if that were the only concern,
I would kneel willingly before the Prince and let him
finish what he so badly wants to do. But because*

of my strange connection to the Bounded, I believe thousands of innocents would die with me. I am a conduit of the Lords, and when the Dar'Nethi focus their power against the Lords, it is funneled through me onto that land in a storm of fire. As the land is injured, so I am weakened, and so I believe that when I am destroyed, so would it be, and all who dwell there.

Two things must be done.

First, the attacks on Zhev'Na from Avonar must stop until I am dead. The Lords do not suffer from them, but reflect them on me, using them to return the Bounded to chaos and thereby strengthen themselves.

Second, my father must enter my mind and sever my connection to the Bounded before he slays me. I cannot ask him, because I don't know how to find my father in Prince D'Natheil, and the Prince will not listen to me before he strikes. You must convince him to do this, if not on the strength of your desire, then in mercy for people he has no reason to hate and no reason to destroy.

Now I wait. I haven't power enough to stay any longer, and Paulo is at risk every moment I do so. He will be able to reveal my location when he is convinced that all will come about as I have said. But if the time goes too long, more than five days from this, only one course will remain open to me. I will have to send the Singlars into the world where we were born, hoping they can find some haven there once I am destroyed. I have a friend of some influence who says she will do what she can for their safety.

Know that your faith and love have saved me from despair countless times over. When all is done, I would like to think you might visit the Bounded and see its wonders. Have Paulo introduce you to Vroon and his friends, whom I met in my dreams, and Nithea, who spends her life giving what she can never possess, and Tom, the shepherd's son, who led me there, and will play music for you such as you've never heard.

Trust me.
Your loving son,
Gerick

"He was here, then. While we were asleep? Astonishing that he could pass my wards . . ."

The Lady knelt by the boy, shaking her head, and my words dwindled away. How foolish is all certainty that can so easily lead us away from the obvious. She kept her tear-filled eyes on him and stroked his hair, and only then did I begin to understand. I recalled how her expression had changed as she looked on Paulo the night before, and the words that had formed on her lips. "Oh, my dear one . . ." She had not addressed the boy Paulo, but her son, recognizing him within the body of his friend. Her son had possessed Paulo, displaced a living soul for his own purposes.

I dropped the letter on the floor, overwhelmed by revulsion, the reaction bred into me by fifty years of hearing tales of the Lords of Zhev'Na and their hideous games.

"Is there any chance Paulo can survive this?" whispered the Lady.

"I've known no one to survive such a violation. Paulo will be dead when the . . . being . . . leaves him. Unless I kill him first in order to kill the one controlling him." I was horrified, nauseated. Yet . . .

I retrieved the folded paper and studied it again. A trap, surely. A devilish son begging his father to enter his mind . . . to open himself . . . to leave himself, the Prince of Avonar, vulnerable.

Yet, the words were so at odds with such villainy. The words . . . Interpretation of words was my life. Never had I read words so fraught with loneliness and pain, a desolate honesty that belied the writer's tender years. I could not reconcile what I assumed . . . what I believed . . . what I had been taught . . . with what I read.

Could the boy I knew as Paulo truly be the heinous manifestation of a depraved Lord of Zhev'Na? I thought back to our first encounter in my tent in the desert, and then in the root cellar that became our prison cell. He had clearly been himself in our first interview. When could the displacement have taken place? The youth's care for me in the days of my madness had been kind and earnest, and the only alteration in his manner came after . . . no, just before I broke Radele's enchantment, when his hands grew icy, and his voice fell silent, and I . . . I was changed . . .

"Great Vasrin!" I bent over the sleeping youth and shook him with a vigor that would have roused a dead man—as indeed the Lady believed I was trying to do.

"Master Ven'Dar, have mercy. Leave him in peace!"

I ignored her. "Paulo! Wake up! I know it's you."

"Cripes, can't a body have a decent sleep without somebody has to bully 'em up and—?" The lanky, disheveled boy sat up, rubbing his face and yawning. When he caught sight of the Lady, her mouth open in shock, he stopped in mid-complaint. "Oh, my lady, it's a fine thing . . . a fine thing to see you."

"Then you're not—" She picked him apart with her eyes, and then glared at me as if I'd pulled some student's prank on her. "He's all right. And himself. We must have been wrong." She snatched the letter from my hand and read it again, while I tried to contain my excitement. If this were true . . .

"Paulo, we were afraid for you," I said, squatting so I could look him in the eye. "You weren't exactly yourself last night."

The boy leaned up against the curved stone wall, scratched his head, and sighed. "He wouldn't hurt me. He knew it was a risk, and he hated the thought of it, being so evil a thing as it is, and not even sure how it is he does it. He let me decide. I agreed it was the only way."

"So you know what happened," I said. "What he did to you."

"Of course, I know. We planned it. Well, we didn't plan he would have to take over like he did. Only that he would hide . . . inside me . . . and be here to help if he was needed."

"So he left his own body and took up residence in yours. And when he saw I could not free myself, he left

your body and came into mine." The sustaining hands.
The strength and reason I could not muster on my own.
Directing, not controlling my thoughts and actions, though
sharing an awareness of my memories and capabilities.
And when the deed was done, he had relinquished his
control, returning my mind and soul intact. Not corrupted. Not dead. Free.

"We never expected the Lady to be so bad off. And
then you was the only one as could help. He had to get
you free." His steady gaze met mine and nothing . . .
nothing lived in him but simple truth.

"What are you talking about?" demanded the Lady.
"I thought Gerick had taken Paulo as he did Gar'Dena.
Why isn't Paulo dead?"

I had to work to keep from laughing aloud, struggle to
remember the dire situation of the world. This discovery
would not even be a footnote in history if we didn't
think carefully about its consequences. But my excitement could not be contained.

"Madam, young Paulo lives and breathes and delights
us with his company even after sharing his person, because your son is no more one of the Lords than are
you. It is the myth, the legend, the hundredth talent in
the list. Twice I tallied the names last night, not knowing
that the one who enabled me to speak the list was its
capstone . . . its enigma. Who could relinquish his own
life so completely, taking unto himself the full body,
mind, and spirit of another being—lending strength or
courage, skill or knowledge—and then be able to yield
the other soul undamaged? Who could do such a thing
and himself remain whole?

"Your son, my lady, is Dar'Nethi and he is sixteen
years of age, and, as happens with most of us, his talent
has come upon him with ungainly, overwhelming, and
mystifying suddenness. And in a charming convolution
of the Way, it seems he has turned out to be a Soul
Weaver, the rarest of the Dar'Nethi talents, bearing a
gift that carries the most magnificent possibilities and
the most complex ramifications, and he doesn't even
know it."

CHAPTER 24

Karon

I spent five days bathed in blood. My anger had burst all its bounds when I walked the blackened ruins of Ephah, past the poles on which children had been spitted like suckling pigs and the pits where old men and women had been set afire. When word came that Zhid marauders had been sighted near the Vale of Seraph, I would hear no caution, but led twelve hundred warriors in pursuit. They drew us into the Wastes, where three thousand smirking Zhid lay in ambush. But they would have needed twice that number to evade my wrath, and when they were all dead or run away, I wept because none were left to kill.

On the blistering evening of our bloody victory, we rode back into the encampment just as the last light faded, dropping a mantle of darkness over the dead and wounded we had packed into carts or draped over horses. After an ordinary foray, warriors would light fires and heat water for bathing their wounds and those of their fellows, for washing off the filth of battle, for preparing food. Sounds of camaraderie and consolation would give a wholesome texture to the night: men and women rattling pots and restoring weapons, singing songs or telling tales. But as this night crept around us, the camp remained dark. Warriors dropped onto the hard, bare ground and did not move. But I didn't think they slept.

I slid from my horse and shoved the reins at a smudge-eyed boy who gawked at my scorched, blood-soaked gauntlets. "Have him ready for me at first light."

"Aye, my lord." The boy dropped his gaze.

Two aides rode up behind me, their pale, sand-crusted faces like some primitive artwork in the deepening dusk—inhuman. I gave orders for the watch, sent news and a commendation to Men'Thor, who had led his battle-weary company all the way to Avonar to fortify the garrison, and dismissed them. A few hours' sleep and then I would return to the business of Paulo and my son. I could not allow Gerick to live one more day, to betray us one more time.

"My lord!" Bareil held open the tent flap. The Dulcé's garments were sweat-stained and bloody. While I'd led the troops into the desert after the Zhid raiders he had remained in Seraph Vale, helping with the survivors and seeing that all the information they could give us about the attack was recorded for me to review. "I was just about to ride out in search of you. I've sent for Master Ven'Dar, as you commanded me, but neither his aides nor Bastel have seen him for several days. They believed him to be with you. And you've an urgent message from Nentao. The quartermaster says it came five days ago."

Nentao . . . Seri. My annoyance with Ven'Dar's lack of communication would have to wait. I yanked off my stiff gauntlets and threw them on the ground, snatched the paper from his hand, and broke the seal. Every crack and ridge in my hand was caked with dried blood. "Five days! What incompetent bastard let it lie here five days?"

> *Your Grace,*
> *It is with great distress that I must inform you of the events that have transpired since your last visit to Nentao. Preceptor Ven'Dar arrived shortly after your departure. He attempted to interview the prisoner, despite my insistence that he show me some token of your approval. Only when I forcibly prevented his violation of your orders did he relent and leave the premises. I assumed he had returned to his duties.*

But on the next morning, I came upon two of my father's guards I had set to ward your lady's bed-chamber. They were grievously wounded, sire, one dead already. But the second man claimed that Pre-ceptor Ven'Dar himself had done this terrible deed, boasting that this man and his fellow were but the first two "Dar'Nethi Watchers" to be slain that night. I assumed this accusation to be some confusion of the man's last agony. Yet when I heard of the death of the Vale Watch that preceded the attack on Ser-aph, it gave me pause.

Regretfully, I must report that your wife's condi-tion has taken a serious decline since that day. She grows weaker by the hour, and the Healers have de-spaired. I urge you to come quickly, my lord.

Your obedient servant,
Radele yn Men'Thor yn Ustele

Five days! I rode out without changing my blood-soaked garments, without cleaning the death from my hands. I recklessly conjured an early portal to Avonar, and by the time the night was spent, I was galloping up the winding road to Nentao, dread sitting in my belly like lead. When I smelled the telltale of charred timber on the dawn wind, I could not contain my fear. Bel-lowing like a speared boar, I spurred my horse unmerci-fully until I reached the smoldering ruin.

"Where is she?" I leapt from the saddle and charged through the billowing smoke toward the blackened stone-work, nearly throttling the first person who chanced within my reach. "Tell me she's dead and you'll wish you were likewise."

The man in the red shirt didn't answer, only choked and gasped and fought, dragging me to the ground with his struggle.

"She isn't here," said the calm voice behind me, "and killing my servants won't get her back . . . my lord." Men'Thor peered down his straight nose and bowed slightly. What a portrait I presented: groveling in the dirt with a common soldier, the filth of battle dried on my clothes. "Radele says Ven'Dar has abducted both your wife and the Destroyer's minion. And it appears as if the Preceptor is responsible for two murders a few days ago. The situation is unfathomable. The man must have gone mad."

"Seri and Paulo abducted? By Ven'Dar?" I shoved the gasping soldier away and scrambled to my feet, fighting for composure, for clarity. "Why the devil would he do such a thing? Where did he take them?"

"Having just arrived myself, my lord, I've no answers for you. No sooner did I walk into the house than the man set the place alight over our heads. One of my men saw the three of them ride deeper into the Vale, but we've searched and found no sign of them. Ven'Dar's surely made a portal to transport them elsewhere. They could be anywhere by now."

Calm yourself, fool. Breathe. Think. I could not help Seri if I could not think. Heat pulsed from the rubble. I ducked under a smoldering beam and wandered through the broken walls, waving a hand at the destruction. "You're saying Ven'Dar did *this*, too?"

Men'Thor folded his arms as we moved through the ruin, scuffing the ash with the toe of his knee-high boot. "The Preceptor cast as he escaped. We're fortunate no one else lies dead. Happily Radele had dismissed the servants. The whole thing reeks of madness . . . of the Lords."

Blackened piers and beams stood at rakish angles, a macabre pattern against the morning. Wind sighed across the hilltop, swirling smoke and ash in our eyes and fanning the embers. This was lunacy. I could certainly comprehend that Ven'Dar had decided he could no longer support me. But beyond the simple matter of desertion, nothing of this story held together. Two guards murdered by a man who so treasured the Way? By Ven'Dar, who understood and grieved for what I had become? Persuasion was Ven'Dar's favored weapon, not a knife, not fire and destruction. He wielded power backed by virtue and wisdom, not hostages or blackmail.

And a mystery of less mortal consequence, yet still profound: Nentao had once belonged to Exeget, Ven'Dar's mentor. This house and garden had held everything that remained of a brilliant, honorable, difficult man that only Ven'Dar had truly loved. What circumstance could cause him to destroy a place he so treasured? If it was the Preceptor . . .

I whirled on Men'Thor and gripped his arm. "Are you certain it was Ven'Dar? Did you read him?"

"These events transpired but moments after my arrival, lord." A man of infinite patience was Men'Thor. "If you remember, I have been fighting Zhid the past five days. Besides . . . I would never take it on myself to read a Preceptor." Men'Thor's voice did not falter, though my fingers ground his flesh against his bones.

"You took it on yourself to come here unasked."

"On the contrary, sire. You did not respond to my son's urgent message and so, very properly, he summoned me. Radele indicated that your wife was ill beyond the continuing sad state of her mind, a disease of enchantment the Healers did not recognize. My son was concerned for her life."

"Not enough, it seems."

Men'Thor's jaw tightened, bulging his cheeks; the sinews of his arm stiffened like taut rope under my fingers. Yet even now his voice remained even. "Speak as you will to me, sire, but I'll not have my son's abilities or loyalties questioned, even by you. Neither man, nor Zhid, nor cowardly tool of the Lords of Zhev'Na has ever prevailed against my son in combat. He has defended your kingdom since he could hold a weapon, as have my father and I. Tell me the same of *your* son, Your Grace."

His words laid down a gauntlet that I could not pick up. I released his arm.

"Yes, Men'Thor. Radele is very accomplished. And a man of honor, as is his father." That's why I had chosen the noble bastard to watch Gerick and to guard Seri. "Where is the man who witnessed Ven'Dar's escape?"

Men'Thor called out to one of his guardsmen that the Prince wished to see H'Kale as soon as possible. It was Radele, his mouth set in an uncharacteristically grim line, who held a youngish man firmly by the sleeve and dragged him stumbling through the ruins a few moments later. "Here's the fool who let them get away," snapped Radele.

The fellow fell to his knees, stammering. "My lord, I've never seen the like. The spider . . . I've a horror of them . . . caught me up . . . By Vasrin Creator, I saw it as the size of a dog, and so real . . . I felt the pincers . . . felt the web sticky . . ."

"Just tell me where they went—the Preceptor and the others."

"Into the Vale, my lord. I'll swear it. Down the track where I was caught, back behind the stable, and then up farther into the hills. They didn't circle back as . . . some others say. On my mother's bones, I'll swear it. First the youth and the Lady, and then the Preceptor close behind just after he set the fire."

Radele sneered at the blubbering young guardsman, gripping his hair and jerking his head back, allowing us to see the slimy evidence of terror dribbling from his nose and mouth and smeared across his cheeks. "You're either blind or traitor, H'Kale. There's nothing in the Vale within a day's ride. We sent—"

"Did you search the tower, Radele?"

"My lord?"

"Ven'Dar's tower in the Vale. Did you examine it?"

"We searched every house and rock and glade within ten leagues of this house. We saw no tower."

"Bring my horse," I bellowed, kicking the young guardsman to his feet and sending him stumbling through the blackened ruin, before confronting Men'Thor and his son again. Blind, self-important fools. "Are you a complete imbecile, Radele? Every Word Winder has a retreat. He's just cast a winding to hide it."

"A winding!" Men'Thor whirled on Radele. "You didn't look for enchantments in the Vale?"

A properly stunned Radele hurried along beside me as I hurried out of the ruin. "Ah, my lord . . . I wasn't told . . . I didn't know . . ." Was it panic I detected in his voice? "Please, my lord, you must allow me to redeem this oversight. You and my father have fought these past days . . . the guesthouse is unharmed . . . you should rest . . ."

But I had no time to let a preening fool restore his honor. "I'll rest when my wife is secure."

I raced down the track into the Vale, while Men'Thor and Radele were yet calling for their mounts.

Sunbeams glared in my face as I came to the barriers, enchantments so subtle you wouldn't realize they existed unless you noticed how your eyes constantly strayed from the path. Your inclination was to veer off in any direction but straight ahead. And no sooner did you glimpse the white tower than your eyes slid off it and you forgot it existed . . . unless you had once been privileged to be a guest there . . . unless your dying wife was being held hostage by a man to whom you had bared your soul and a youth who held allegiance to your mortal enemy.

I pushed through the barrier, knowing the intrusion would warn Ven'Dar—if the man was indeed Ven'Dar and not my son destroying yet another of my friends. At the same time, I reached ahead with my thoughts, calling out the traitor. *Give them up, Ven'Dar, or I'll have your head even before I take the Destroyer's!*

When I rode into the tower clearing, a grave, unsmiling Ven'Dar stood waiting for me. His clothes were filthy, his graying hair damp and tousled. As I dismounted and approached the tower, he knelt. *"Ce'na davonet, Giré D'Arnath."*

I halted twenty paces from him and drew my sword. Love radiated from his posture and his words, telling me that he was indeed the Preceptor and not some depraved hybrid of my son's creation. But on this day I had no answer for his affection. My soul was barren, and I did not trust my hand. "I don't want your honor, Ven'Dar. I want my wife, and I want my prisoner."

Ven'Dar gazed up at me solemnly. "Come inside with me, my lord. We've precious little time." He got to his feet and motioned to the small doorway that led into the curved white wall.

I did not move. My senses roamed the simple structure and the soft green of the surrounding glade. I could

not feel her. Always I had been able to sense the exuberance of life that surrounded Seri, from the first time she
hurried into the drawing room at Windham, breathless,
flushed with youth and the evening wind, ready to argue
and tease and steal my heart. Even in these last months
when her mind was lost, I yet felt the air around her
golden . . . pulsing . . . her life ready to burst forth in a
ferocious embrace if I could but find the key to unlock
it. But not on this day. She was not here. "By every god
and demon in this universe, Ven'Dar, if you've harmed
her . . ."

"I beg you withhold judgment, sire. We must not be
out here when the others arrive. Please come up."
Ven'Dar turned his back and started up the curved stair
with no more concern than if I were a simple Reader
come calling to examine the enchantments on his rain
barrel, or a Glazier come to fill his empty windows with
colored glass to shape the sunbeams.

I would kill him. Abandoning the glade, I took the
steps three at a time, following him into a round, sunny
room that was just as I remembered it—unoccupied by
anyone save ourselves.

"You're a dead man, Ven'Dar." I raised my weapon.
"Tell me where she is in two heartbeats, or you'll never
see another sunrise."

"You're correct about the urgency, my lord." He gestured toward the window. "Men'Thor and Radele are on
their way. My enchantments will slow them, but we've a
quarter of an hour at best. Unless you can convince
them, firstly, that I am dead, and secondly, that I have
revealed nothing of importance, I fear that neither of us
may live another day unless it be in a prison cell or a
madhouse . . . unspeaking. They've gone too far. It is
your throne they want."

"You're already mad. Ustele's house is nothing if not
loyal. You accuse them to mask your own treachery."
Sunlight glinted on my sword, now hanging on a direct
line with his neck. "Where is my wife?"

"Your wife and young friend are safe for now, both
from your enemies and from you. Put away your

weapon, my lord. Trust me. If I can tell you nothing of interest, you will have ample opportunity to make an end of me."

Fool that he was, he walked right under my blade, laying a hand on my shoulder as he had so many times. And for the first time since Paulo had run away from Ven'Dar's tent, the rage drained out of me, leaving me hollow and dry and unimaginably tired. My tunic and breeches were rusty with blood. I smelled of it. It was under my fingernails, and in my pores, and I didn't think I could ever wash it away. I lowered my weapon, sank to the floor, and leaned my back against a crude wooden chair. "You cursed idiot of a sorcerer. What have you done?"

"Better you ask Men'Thor and his son what it is they fear about your wife."

"I'm too tired for riddles. You cannot convince me Seri's illness is Men'Thor's or Radele's doing. They have nothing to fear from me. I do exactly as they want—not because they say it, but because I have no choice."

"They are not convinced of your choice in the matter of your son, and to such men uncertainty is more dangerous than the evils they fight. It can lead them to violate the very law they profess to defend, to aid an enemy they would die to defeat."

"There is *no* uncertainty. I know what I have to do about Gerick. It is not what I want. And it's not because of what he did to Seri—only that what he did to Seri is proof of what he is. He is *not* my son, not since he stepped into the oculus in the halls of Zhev'Na. It doesn't matter that I won't remember that fact when I kill him, and it doesn't matter what will happen to me as a result. He has to die. There is no other answer."

Ven'Dar lifted a worn leather bag from a hook on the wall. Then he crouched beside a deep wooden chest and selected a few of his tools—a wooden mallet, a small steel-headed hammer, an adze, a drawknife—wrapping them in rags from a pile on the floor and packing them into the bottom of the bag, talking as he worked. "I cannot give you the answer you desire, my lord. But I can tell you this: Men'Thor and Radele have stolen your wife's mind and conspired to steal her life because they fear she can make you waver in your duty. As things stood one day ago, I would have judged them foolish to doubt your resolve; I believed you would indeed kill the boy. But today I can provide another view of your dilemma, one which may charge your heart to discover an alternative. If not, then we are no worse off than before. But before I present my case, I must know you will listen to Paulo's tale and my own with all of yourself—your true self."

"You know I can't control who I am. Not any more. The balance is lost. D'Natheil has won."

"But you, my good friend Karon, are still with us. I hear your voice even now." Retrieving a few books and scrolls from a small writing table, he slipped them carefully into the bag atop the tools.

I jumped to my feet again. "Then tell me why I had to leave Nentao six days ago because I was ready to torture Paulo until he told me what I have to know. Tell me why my hands, even now, demand to set this blade at your throat until you tell me what you've done with Seri. It's too far, Ven'Dar. All I can think of is death. I can't find my way back."

"Perhaps I can lead you back."

My fingers traced the vines engraved on my sword hilt. I could not allow myself to look at the man who had been my closest friend in this broken world until I was sure I could get through the next moment without taking his head off. My chest felt as if bands of molten steel constricted it, and my jaw like a locked cage, so that my voice came harsh and rasping. "I would pay handsomely for such a boon. But while you continue your fruitless speculation about what we have already determined to be irrevocable, *tell me* where are my wife and my prisoner!"

Ven'Dar remained unflustered. "As I said, they are out of harm's way for the moment. You cannot find them on your own. I sent them through a portal, destroying it behind them lest you be too hasty in your anger or Men'Thor too hasty in his ambition. Now, fair warning: I will speak no more of your wife or the boy until you can convince me you'll give fair hearing to young Paulo. And your word alone will not be enough."

"How dare you bargain with me?"

He tapped a finger on the pens that lay on the writing table and then made a small gesture of dismissal. Setting his bag on a windowsill, he began buckling the straps that would hold it closed. "How dare I? Because of who you are. I trust you, my lord, and all I ask in return is your trust."

"You ask the impossible."

He turned to me then, his face radiant, as if he were himself a winding, an enchantment of faith and hope set here in this tower to sap my strength and resolve. "But you see, my good friend, only this very morning have I discovered new evidence that the impossible is possible. Do not doubt. This is the chance you craved when you sat by Paulo's sickbed six days ago—yes, I saw it in you. Trust me. That's the first step. Then the rest will come as may be. . . ."

"I cannot allow my heart to get involved in this. I have responsibilities."

". . . I need you for three days . . ."

"Impossible."

". . . only a small delay in this pernicious war. You tell yourself you've committed so many sins; allow yourself this one more. One that might make a difference."

"The war—"

"—can proceed without you for three days. So . . . first, we'll need a little blood. . . ."

I raged and threatened, but he sighed and promised I would never see Seri again if I did not follow his direction. I spat and cursed, and he smiled and said mad fury was exactly what I needed. And he told me what I had to do. . . .

Trust him. When he would tell me nothing of importance. I was truly a madman.

"Burn this damnable place!" I yelled. "I want fire to break the stones, to scorch this patch of earth until it looks like the Wastes. Fail to do my will and you add your blood to that already on my hands."

I did not believe Ven'Dar about Men'Thor and Radele, but I left nothing to chance. As I emerged from the tower stair, I held my bloody sword and dripping dagger where they would shield the most vital parts of my anatomy. Yet, even if Men'Thor or his son meant me harm, I guessed that the agonized cries still lingering in the glade might distract them.

"My lord Prince, what's happened? Those screams . . ." Men'Thor stood at the bottom of the stair, complexion gray, eyes flicking from me to the tower and back again, weapons drawn but aimed in no particular direction. Radele moved in on my left quarter.

"Do not question me!" I spun around just enough to keep both men in front of me.

Mindless rage was all too easy. No contrivance made my hands grip the hilts of my weapons so firmly the mark of their engraving was etched into my flesh. "Burn this tower. I don't care how much power it requires. Everything of the traitor is to be destroyed along with him. It will be her pyre . . . ah, gods, if I could but kill him again! Every day remaining in this blighted life I would slay him again for my pleasure."

"My lord, tell us what's come about . . . the Preceptor . . . your wife . . . When we heard the shouts, we tried to come to your aid, but the villain had set impossible barriers on the stair." Radele was exceptionally pale, his speech halting . . . uncertain. It is no small thing to lose your sovereign's wife whom you were set to guard with your life, and to have your undefeatable prowess so easily dismissed by a quiet, gentle man older than your father. And I didn't know what else was making the young man so anxious, but I was going to find out.

"The Preceptor—Ven'Dar the traitor, the murderer— is dead. He tried to tell me some tale of enchantments and how he'd tried to bring Seri back to me by playing with words. He danced and dallied and promised to reveal secrets and betrayers. But when I forced him to still his prattling and give me my wife, he could show me only her corpse. Ah, cursed be his name forever! The traitorous servant of the Zhid has killed her."

I shoved my bloody hands in Men'Thor's face, and he
stepped back, his mouth hanging open, his eyes aghast.
"I opened his belly for it . . . slowly, a finger's breadth
at a time, so he would feel it. Now I want him to burn."

"Perhaps I should go up . . . to stand witness for you,
confirm his death and that of your lady . . ."

"You will not touch Seri. No one will lay eyes on her.
If you have no wish to burn with her, then let my will
be done this instant." I dropped to my knees, wrapped
my blood-soaked arms about my belly, and groaned.
"Help me, Men'Thor. I cannot grieve. I cannot follow
the Way until it's done." My weapons remained securely
in my grip.

Men'Thor's worried glance focused on the tower. A faint
trace of enchantment slithered through the noonday—he
would find no life remaining in P'Clor's Tower—and
then he nodded to Radele. The young man touched his
finger to every stone that formed the base of Ven'Dar's
tower and to the laurel and blueberry shrubs that
crowded close. Was the bastard an Effector like his mis-
begotten sire? I realized I didn't even know.

The heat grew quickly as Men'Thor hovered at my
shoulder. He crouched in front of me and laid a hand
on my arm. "My lord, this is grievous news. We have
differed on many things, but never would I wish—
Please, allow me to aid you in whatever wise possible,
grieve with you until the Way leads you past this sorrow.
But time and danger press . . . and I didn't understand
about the prisoner. Is he dead, too, then, or must I send
someone in pursuit?"

I spat. "The prisoner is a nobody, a stable boy, a messenger. Ven'Dar sent him back to his master—but I extracted his message from Ven'Dar before he died."

If I'd not been waiting for it, I might not have felt
Men'Thor hold his breath. "Then you know the location
of the Destroyer."

"Paulo was to arrange a meeting between my wife and
my son three days from this. Ven'Dar, in his arrogance
of power, promised Seri would be there. But I'll take
her place. The Destroyer's neck will meet my sword, and
his black heart will do no more murder."

With that, Men'Thor was satisfied. He offered again to stand vigil and grieve with me as was our custom. His hand was relaxed and kind as he lifted me to my feet and led me to a grassy hummock, making me sit down. He offered me water to clean my face and wine to soothe my thirst. In his vibrant baritone, he sang a chant of memory and acceptance, words so deep and heartfelt I could almost feel them myself.

But I pushed his hand away, and his cloth and his flask and his song. "Not yet, Men'Thor. I cannot. Not yet."

Ven'Dar had sworn to me that Seri yet breathed. I could not judge his truth, and, as I had witnessed for four months, breathing had little to do with life. To share a death chant might help me let go of her, but I could not accept her physical death yet, not even in sham.

We watched Ven'Dar's tower burn until nothing but a blackened ring of charred stones remained in the middle of the forest. The sun hung bloated and bloody on the western horizon as we rode down the Vale, past the smoldering rubble of Nentao, and on toward Avonar. I carried the image with me—the charred ugliness of something that had once existed in harmony with the world—and I believed it a reflection of myself. Ven'Dar had told me that I could rebuild what had been, that he would show me the way, but I could imagine no revelation that could change anything. I would go to the mysterious rendezvous he planned, but I would not listen to the voice of the Destroyer. Instead, I would kill my son, and I would be D'Natheil forever.

CHAPTER 25

"But, my lord Prince, how can we afford two more days of delay? What if another of the Vales is attacked? Only your presence rallied our warriors; only your power and your sword enabled us to take on so many."

"I have taken the life of a Dar'Nethi, N'Tien. I held Ven'Dar's bowels in my hand—an act of madness and revenge—and it matters not in the least that his execution was justified. The law is clear. I must be purified before I can act again as the Heir of D'Arnath. And on the day I confront the Destroyer, I must have all my rightful powers."

The slender Dar'Nethi chewed the end of his drooping moustache like a nervous schoolmaster. "But, my lord—"

"You will sit here and deploy our warriors as you see fit. You have a better head for it than anyone in Avonar, including me. Ce'Aret will govern in my stead. Ustele will hold the desert portals and Men'Thor the temporary command, as I've instructed him. Mem'Tara is new to the Preceptorate, but her experience in combat over the past fifteen years speaks for itself. With Ce'Aret's advisement, she will lead the defense of Avonar. I've charged Radele with the safety of the Vales."

The wizened old woman who sat behind the long table nodded and wagged a bony finger at N'Tien. "The Prince is correct. If the fiend Ziddari himself sat in this chamber or Parven or Notole had taken up residence in the Prince's palace, it would make no difference. The Heir cannot lead with Dar'Nethi blood on his hands. I would stick my knife in him myself before I would permit it."

Ce'Aret's words were as brittle as the bones beneath her dry skin. It was difficult to avoid peering under the long council table just to make sure her weapon was not already aimed at my spleen.

Earlier in the day, the old woman had interrogated me about Ven'Dar's death, battering me with her disbelief. The Heir was bound in service to the Preceptorate, so no privilege of my sovereignty could prevent her questioning. She had respected Ven'Dar immensely and could not easily accept the story of his rebellion and Seri's death in his care. Only the need for hasty resolution and my sworn word on the sword of D'Arnath had prevented her demanding a more thorough investigation. What was one more lie beside those already spoken? But Ce'Aret's hard gaze had never wavered all through the Preceptors' meeting. My skin felt bruised.

The ranks of my Preceptorate had become pitifully thin: Ce'Aret seated at the center of the long table, shriveled, bitter Ustele on her left, the dark-haired, large-boned Alchemist Mem'Tara on her right. Four empty chairs. N'Tien, my gloomy chief strategist, sat at one end of the table jotting notes on his list of deployments. A few chairs faced the Preceptors' table from the center of the chamber, available for petitioners or spectators. Men'Thor and Radele sat in two of them, exchanging sober whispers and passing messages to the three field commanders in attendance. D'Arnath's chair— a plain, high-backed wooden chair of great antiquity— faced the council table, offset slightly to one side so Avonar's prince could see and hear both Preceptors and spectators. I had been in and out of the chair all morning, too restless to sit still for long.

"So we are agreed, then?" I said.

Ustele hammered a stubby forefinger on the council table. "It is unforgivable to take time at this, our most desperate hour, to wallow in a discredited custom. No right-minded Dar'Nethi has undergone the Rite of Purification for seventy years; only the weak-willed seek it out. We should seal the caves with the cowards still inside."

"I cannot but agree with you, Master Ustele," I said,

"and I have a thousand things I would prefer to be about, but the law is clear. I'll not let a missed provision stand between me and my legitimate claims. Are you not the one who holds me to the law so strictly? I'd not give you arrows to loft back at me."

"Who will accompany you to the pools, my lord?" asked Mem'Tara quietly, as Ustele settled back in his chair with an expulsion of disgust. "It would have been Ven'Dar's office."

"Bareil will be my companion."

"A Dulcé," muttered Ustele, curling his lip. "I should have expected it. You have no taste for your own kind."

"A most unusual choice," said Mem'Tara. "Surely many Dar'Nethi would gladly serve you in this way."

"My madrissé has served the Preceptorate longer than anyone save Ce'Aret and Ustele. He bears the necessary knowledge and full respect for our customs. No sorcery is required of the companion."

They talked among themselves about the novel concept of a Dulcé taking a Dar'Nethi for purification. I half expected Men'Thor to volunteer Radele to supervise the rite, but he was too busy reveling in his new importance as the permanent commander of Ven'Dar's troops and temporary high commander, already writing lists and sending messages even as he listened to our debate. His son's appointment as a sector commander had almost set him crowing. The whisperings had already sped through the chamber and into the outer rooms. Everyone in Avonar would be expecting an quick appointment to the Preceptorate for one or both of them. I had best make certain Men'Thor's initiative was severely limited during my absence, or he would have us knocking at the gates of Zhev'Na before sundown.

"And so when will you begin the ordeal, my lord?" asked Ce'Aret.

"Within the hour," I said. "That's why I assembled the Preceptorate so early. You can be sure I'll make this business take as little time as possible. I've already sent my orders to those in the field, and you certainly have no need of my direction, Preceptor Ce'Aret. Avonar has never been out of your care. You can tell Mem'Tara all she needs to know."

"And the announcement of Ven'Dar's crimes and his death?"

"Nothing is to be said until I say it. We will leave the Destroyer in uncertainty. Tell Ven'Dar's troops he is on a mission for me. Say anything you choose save the despicable truth."

"So be it. Vasrin Shaper and Creator grant you balance, my lord Prince," said the old woman, echoed by Ustele and Mem'Tara. I rose to leave, and everyone in the room rose with me. I didn't look at any of them.

The Caves of Laennara were entered by a gated arch in a sheer limestone wall near the lower end of Kirith Vale, but their proximity to the city was in distance only. Every step along the steep, pebbled path that led from the road to the gate was an unfathomable separation from everyday life. The air became noticeably thinner, as if we had scaled one of the peaks that soared beyond the wall, and the normal sounds of the surrounding forest were muted: the rustle of the leaves soft, the darting movement of the rivulets of water that cut through the grass but a whisper, like exuberant children hushed by their mother.

The petitioner, the one who had come to cleanse himself of the burden of life-taking, kept silence on the road to the caves. You were supposed to gaze upon the forest, the sky, and the stream, the deer, the foxes, and the birds, taking their essence into your soul, building power for the ordeal ahead. Your companion walked ahead of you bearing a gold luminant, a small box of gold or brass with pierced sides, a lid, and a handle, designed to hold a living flame that would be used to light the lamps hung in each of the seven caves.

On the morning I left Avonar to begin my purification for taking Ven'Dar's life, I did as was required on the road, gathering power for what was to come. Of course, I had no intention of undergoing the purification rite. Unless something had gone dreadfully awry, Ven'Dar should have slipped safely out of his tower before the fire. He was to meet me in the first cave and lead me to Seri and Paulo and my son.

I almost regretted that I would have no time to try the Pools of Laennara. Though I'd not slain any loyal Dar'Nethi in anger—not yet—a great number had perished because of me. My guilt drew no distinction between warriors sent into battle by my command or enemies slain by my own weapons. Nor could I distinguish between Dar'Nethi blood and the blood of the Zhid. Zhid, too, were Dar'Nethi—changed, made soulless and cruel—but Dar'Nethi just the same. Was I the only one who had ever considered it? My soul could use a cleansing. Yet another death, my own son's death, was the only purpose in my journey to Laennara. Neither balance nor peace nor purification had anything to do with it.

I followed Bareil past the black latticework gate and through a narrow passage. The tiny flame peeked out of the sides and out from under the gold lid of the luminant, its gleam no bigger than a firefly, doing little to relieve the blackness as it led me onward and downward.

Seri would have hated that passage. A childhood mishap had left her with a terror of dark, confined spaces. Shamed by such "weakness," she had tried to hide her fear from me when we were first married, not understanding what joy it could give a lover to share such an intimate part of the other . . . and to be able to soothe it. *Ah, gods, Seri* . . . As always when I thought of her any more, rage boiled in my gut and pulsed in my arms, engulfing all other emotion. What could ever soothe the pain of her loss, her death in all but breathing?

Abruptly Bareil and his firefly were swallowed up by a more expansive darkness. I closed off all thought of Seri. I needed to remain clearheaded.

I followed the Dulcé into the larger space and felt his hand on my breast, signaling me to stop. The air was warm and heavy and damp, smelling of old stone with a trace of sulfur, while from somewhere to my right whispered a cool draft. The glimmering light moved to the left, stretching into a wavering beam as the Dulcé removed the lid of the luminant. Bareil, now a small figure sculpted of shadow and light, touched the flame to the wick of a diamond-paned lamp. Soft light reached out and pushed away the shadows just enough for me to view the cave and the Pool of Cleansing.

The cave walls were milky white and yellow, lumps and rills of weeping stone, pockmarked by holes and nooks and niches. Steam hung over the small pool, an irregularly shaped basin no more than twenty paces around. The draft from deep in the caves twined the mists among stalagmites as thick as my wrist.

Bareil awaited me beside the pool, his dark eyes filled with kindness and concern that had never flagged, though I had all but ignored him for three years. As D'Natheil had slowly encroached on my spirit and behavior, I had not bared my soul to Bareil as I had to Ven'Dar. Nor had I ever given the Dulcé permission to speak to the Preceptor on any personal matter. I could not abide the thought of the two discussing my "condition," so I had shut out my madrissé from all but his most ordinary service, and most especially from the easy intimacy we had shared after Dassine's death. But he knew more than anyone of the changes in me, and it had never altered his bearing in the slightest. I found that fact inexplicably infuriating.

He held out a folded robe of white wool. "I'll take your clothing, my lord. You'll need nothing but this."

I should have thought to have Bareil bring me a change of clothes, for I still wore the bloodstained shirt and breeches I'd had on for a week. It had seemed foolish to change them before trying to convince the Preceptors that I needed the Rite of Purification. They had examined the freshest stains and identified Ven'Dar's blood. The Preceptor had insisted on it, there in his tower, while weaving his mysterious plot—the gentlest of teachers, Ven'Dar, opening a vein to slather my knife and my shirt and my hands with his blood. I hadn't even been capable of closing the wound for him.

Bitterness welled up in my belly. "Put away the robe, Dulcé. You'll be happy to learn I need no purification rite as yet." Though it will be soon, I thought. Of their

own volition, my hands felt for my sword, and I growled
when I found the empty scabbard. Of course, Bareil had
carried my sword and knife into the caves, as ritual forbade me having them during the Rite of Purification.
"And you can give me back my weapons. We'll have to
enjoy these pleasantries another time."

The perplexed Bareil laid the white robe on the floor
beside the cloth-wrapped bundle that held my blades.
"As you wish, my lord," he said softly, untying the bundle and pulling away the wrappings. He kept his eyes on
his work.

"We're to meet someone here," I said. "That's all. I
expected he would be here when we arrived."

"And so I am." A figure robed in dark blue stepped
from out of the shadows.

"Master Ven'Dar!" Bareil's head popped up. The
newly unwrapped sword clanked on the stone floor.

"Indeed, Dulcé. I'm even more glad to be walking
about than for you to see me doing it."

The Dulcé's dark eyes flicked between Ven'Dar and
me, filled with unreasonable hopes.

"I've given the Preceptor a reprieve," I said. "Until
he proves to me that Seri is safe and Paulo ready to tell
me what I must hear from him. Now give me my weapons just in case he reneges on his bargain."

Better. The unreasonable hopes were gone again. I
gestured to Ven'Dar. "If you please, Preceptor . . ."

Mist swirled about Ven'Dar as he crossed the cavern
to stand close enough to fix his light blue eyes on my
own. "Ah, my lord, where are you? You are not the one
who must hear what is to be told."

"Do not toy with me, Ven'Dar. We've delayed long
enough."

"I'd hoped my choice as to our meeting ground was
unnecessary, but your eyes tell me otherwise. Your wife
and your young friend are indeed nearby, but I cannot
allow you to come to them except as your true self.
There is a healing to be done that only you can
attempt."

"Impossible. You know I can do nothing for anyone."

I grabbed his arm and exposed the angry wound he'd made in his tower. "I couldn't even heal this."

"Then you condemn us all."

"I never claimed to know how to stop this war! I never asked for this life. I was dead, and Dassine should have left me dead. But as long as I'm here and as long as I'm your prince, I will do what I have to do. And *you* will do as I command you. Take me to Seri and Paulo."

"I cannot, my good lord. Not until I know *you* will listen."

"Damn your eyes, Ven'Dar . . ." I felt like strangling him. He couldn't have stayed so calm if he'd known how thin the tether that restrained my hand.

But even as I railed, he spoke softly. "I trust you, my lord . . . I know it is difficult . . . I understand it is not a matter of will . . . that's why I brought you here."

By the time I really heard what he was saying, I felt as though I'd fought a match in the slave pens of Zhev'Na. My hands were shaking, and I'd thrown my weapons to the far side of the pool to avoid using them. "Stars of night, what do you want of me?"

"I want you to go through the rite."

"This?" Incredulous, I pointed to the steaming pool.

He raised his eyebrows and shrugged, rubbing his wounded arm gingerly.

I walked over to the pool and stared into the still, murky water of dark green. Steam wreathed my face, depositing a sheen of damp on my skin. "You are no saner than I."

He stood at my side and gazed into the pool, all his wry humor vanished. "The rite cannot change what is, my lord. You are and will ever be D'Natheil, as well as Karon. But for a thousand years we have used this rite to restore balance in lives skewed so far as to damage the things we love most. It is the only thing I can think of that might counter this anger that consumes you. Don't you see? If we could but provide you a brief interval of peace, would not that be the time to hear what Paulo has to tell? And perhaps, given that time and peace, you might be able to heal one who is dear to you.

If you, in that more equitable state of mind, are still convinced that your son's death is our only recourse, then at least you will have the comfort of knowing it was Karon who made the choice and not D'Natheil. It is all I can offer you, my lord. I profoundly wish it could be more."

"I should kill you and be done with it."

"That you have not is but support for my conviction. Most gratifying."

I wanted to be rid of D'Natheil. Fifty times over the past few years I had picked up Dassine's black crystal, the pyramid-shaped implement of my long imprisonment, the artifact that yet held my waiting death, and contemplated touching its smooth surface. Surely release from the prison of this body, this life, would free me from D'Natheil's unrelenting anger. I had never taken that final step. I had a wife, a son, responsibilities. But if I could ease the Dar'Nethi prince's influence over me, restore some balance . . .

"This is idiocy, Ven'Dar. You've taken my wife and my prisoner. Men'Thor is to meet me the moment I leave here to plan the assault on Zhev'Na. The fate of two worlds rests in my hand, and you want to give me a bath."

He held out his hand and smiled. "Seven baths, my lord. May your heart be eased."

Our histories say the seven pools have existed since the beginning of time, but that in the years leading up to the Catastrophe and the beginning of our terrible war they were rarely used. Their effects were too strange and unsettling. Only in D'Arnath's time, when the world was forever changed, did the Balancer Laennara discover the benefits of using the seven pools in turn and create the Rite of Purification. Life is, of all things, the most precious to the Dar'Nethi, and the taking of life throws our private worlds out of balance like a reflection of the great Catastrophe. We are very good at dealing with our joys and sorrows, but our guilts can be devastating.

Supposedly the rite was used quite often in D'Arnath's day, but as time passed and killing grew more common, the custom died away. Most of us dealt with our guilt in other ways. Only for the Heir was the rite ever required.

I knew it was not to be taken lightly. That was why the petitioner always brought a companion, lest the ordeal be too rigorous or too painful. I was a fool, I believed, as I stripped and gave Bareil my clothing, listening to Ven'Dar's instruction.

"Do not touch the water until you are ready. You must immerse yourself wholly in each pool and remain beneath the surface for at least a steady count of one hundred. The additional time you spend in each pool is your own choice, though I will bring you out if you stay beyond the point of safety. In some pools that is an hour, in some half a day."

"Half a—how in the name of all gods would I stay underwater for half a day? There is a small matter of breathing."

"My lord, you are Dar'Nethi, a born enchanter, and one of the most powerful of your race. You have lived beyond death; you can control the chaos between worlds; you can speak in the minds of others, heal broken limbs, torn flesh, and diseased tissue, and you can create light, that most basic wonder of the universe, from your hand. How can you doubt that you can survive a few hours underwater?"

I gave Bareil my undergarments. As the Dulcé bowed and withdrew, I felt naked far beyond the matter of my bare skin. How hot was water that could produce so much steam?

The Preceptor's hand rested on my shoulder. "Know that I will be within reach of your voice, or your mind's call, or a signal from your hand at every moment. I will not desert you, my lord. And I will be ready to guide you between the pools and tell you whatever is necessary for the next."

"And if I wish to end it?"

"You may end it at any time. Depending on how far you've gone, it might take some period of days for your mind to restore itself to something like its current state,

but it would do so. Better you should go to the end,
once you've begun."

"I will be quite vulnerable." *Stupid, stupid to do this.*

He stepped aside, leaving me alone at the brink of the
pool. "I've set the wards on the gate. And Bareil will
remain there to watch, as well. No one can enter the
caves without our leave."

I watched Ven'Dar's hands as he spoke, wondering if
he was casting some winding to convince me to do this
thing. But the short, capable fingers stayed still. "And
the Lords?" I said.

"We are always vulnerable to the Lords. I will be
vigilant."

"Then I—all of us—are in your hands."

"Trust me, my lord."

My last friend closed his eyes and whispered an invocation to Vasrin. As he spoke the last word, I filled my
lungs and stepped into the Pool of Cleansing.

Searing . . . scalding . . . torment . . . I would have
screamed, but the water was already well over my head.
I fought for the surface, but I'd plunged so deep . . . My
feet dragged me lower as if they were made of lead. My
flesh would be boiled away before I could reach the air.

"Count, my lord Prince! It has been thirteen, fourteen,
fifteen . . ." The muffled voice came from an immense
distance, but the cadence penetrated mind and body with
all the force of Ven'Dar's will.

A hundred counts. *Twenty-eight, twenty-nine . . .* Some
part of me began to count, while the rest of my resources
were devoted to controlling panic. *Others have done this.
If Ven'Dar wanted you dead, there are a thousand ways
he could have managed it. Don't fight . . . kick and glide
to the surface . . . fifty-three, fifty-four. . . .*

My chest was on fire inside as well as out. The bottom
of the pool was dark, but even hotter than at the surface.
As I swam toward the green light sparkling at the surface, trailing mosses of green and red floated from the
stony basin walls, brushing my skin. . . . *seventy-five,
seventy-six . . .*

*Almost done. There's nothing here. You should stop
this now . . . you've too much to do to waste time in self-*

*indulgent foolery. Ninety, ninety-one . . . only an arm's
reach from the air.*

My lungs strained to bursting. But as I stretched out
my hand in a last pull for the surface, the water around
it swirled dark, as if I were . . . bleeding. In horror and
disgust, I thrashed it away, only to have more of it leak
out of me. Soon blood flowed from my every pore, from
hands and arms and legs, from my eyes, my ears, my
nose, from under my fingernails.

I never knew when the count passed a hundred, or
when my body began using the scalding water instead of
air, for I was preoccupied with the dark exudation from
my flesh. So much blood . . . The water scalded my
throat and my gut, yet I wished it hotter so as to clean
all the blood away. I rubbed and scraped at my skin,
gouged my eyes and ears, and still it flowed. Instead of
reaching for the surface, I reversed course and swam
deeper.

At the bottom of the pool, moss-covered boulders of
all sizes lay in a jumble, radiating heat like a blacksmith's furnace. Soul-sick, weeping scalding tears, I huddled in the dark, mossy depths and prayed the cleansing
waters to boil the blood away.

An hour passed. Two. Eternity . . .

The distant surface of the water appeared as a patch
of pale green light. A shadow moved beyond the
surface . . . beckoning . . . Ven'Dar, reminding me of
the passing time. Reluctantly, I kicked from the bottom
of the pool. I would stay at the surface only a moment,
long enough to tell him how I had to go down again
until I was clean.

But as I rose to the top, the water around me bubbled
clear. My hand broke the surface, and a strong, cold
hand clasped it firmly and pulled me out.

My reddened skin protested the chill in the air as I
knelt on the uneven floor beside the pool and coughed
up a bucket of water. Someone dropped a robe of soft
wool over my shoulders. A hand on my elbow helped
me to my feet—not an easy task. Besides my violent
shivering, my legs were as limp as soggy bread.

"Only a short way, my lord. Breathe deeply and

slowly as we walk. The Pool of Truth lies just beyond the archway."

A short passage. Ven'Dar carried the luminant. A brief burst of fire and another diamond-paned lamp revealed a cavern rimed with frost and a long, narrow pool of deep blue. Jagged shards of ice protruded from the surface, knife edges glittering in the lamplight. The water could be nothing but glacial. It was all I could do to let Ven'Dar take the robe away. My fingers and toes were already numb.

"Ah, Ven'Dar, I don't know . . ." My throat was raw from the scalding water, my words little more than a rasping whisper.

"Deep breaths, my lord. Count. There are things far worse than the pain your body reports to you. Step in just here where the water is deep, and no ice can cut your skin. Don't hesitate. Don't think. Just do it."

I stepped forward. My nerves exploded in shock as the icy blue waters closed over my head.

"Count, my lord, one, two, three . . ."

. . . four, five, six . . . I sank into a blue-white sculpture garden, twisted frozen flowers, trees, gargoyles, every fancy of a demented artist who worked in ice rather than stone. . . . *twenty-five, twenty-six . . .* Why did they call this one the Pool of Truth? Pool of Ice would be better. Pool of Madness. Pool of Breathless Folly. . . . *fifty, fifty-one . . .* My head felt like to split with the cold. I was desperate for breath, my chest rigid, constricted. *. . . sixty . . . impossible . . .*

But as Ven'Dar had warned me, some things are worse than physical pain. Truth lay waiting for me in the frigid depths—the face of every person I had slain, every person I had sent into battle to die, every person I had failed to protect, to save, to heal, all of them depicted in unyielding ice, eyes cold and empty and accusing . . . Seri's face was there, so sad and alone, and beside her a newborn infant . . . Gerick, the child I had abandoned to his fate because I would not compromise my youthful ideals, because I would not fight . . . And Martin, Tanager, and Julia, our friends who had died for love of me. Dassine and Exeget, Jayereth and Gar'Dena. Gods, there were so many. . . .

Suspended in the frigid water, I drifted from one to the next and touched their cold faces, drowned in guilt and shame and grief. To take life . . . to be responsible . . . to throw it away carelessly in anger or vengeance or thoughtless, pious arrogance . . .

How long I faced my accusers, I could not have said. Long enough that my heart beat with the ponderous pace of a funeral dirge, and the blood in my veins was surely turned to slush. My extremities were dead, my face numb, my heart a lump of ice in my breast. And when the cold and the guilt and the grief became unbearable, and I reached my hand above the surface, I could feel neither the hands that helped me out nor the robe laid over my shoulders. I staggered through the next passage unspeaking, able to walk only from habit rather than from any sensation in legs or feet.

The black waters of the Pool of Darkness lay in perfect stillness, swathed in shadows the diamond-paned lamp could not penetrate. I did not fear it. Darkness was exactly what I wanted. I prayed it would blot out the images of truth frozen into my vision. The water was thick like honey, and I embraced its warmth. It would be easy to make it to the hundred, to force myself to relinquish air and swallow the dark water.

But as I sank into the depths of the pool, I lost myself. Blind in the blackness, I quickly lost track of which way was the surface and which way the bottom. The thick water formed a barrier about me, preventing any part of me from touching any other part. Nor could I feel where the water ended and my skin began. I might have been a loose mind floating in the emptiness of a universe before its creation, alone with myself—both selves—my thoughts and my fear. After a time, set free from any physical containment, thoughts and memories floated away, leaving only fear. And eventually fear, too, dissolved, and nothing at all remained.

Perhaps it was my total emptiness that allowed me to float to the top at last. Gentle hands pulled me out, wrapped me for a moment in dry softness, and led me blind and deaf to the next pool—the Pool of Oblivion. The wrapping was removed again. Warm water swallowed me. . . .

Gray light. A gentle rocking. Soft slurping sounds. Salt on lips and tongue. Throat, nose, eyes stinging . . .

"Come on, then. Half a day is the most allowed here, and you're already well beyond."

I knelt, pressing my head to the cool grit of stone, gagging and coughing weakly on the remnants of the salt water. The robe he laid over my back was damp and chilly now, making me shudder. Lethargy held me to the ground. So much water . . . such perishing thirst.

Hands grasped one shoulder. "Come, my lord, you mustn't stop here. It's farther to go back than to go forward, now. You'll like this one better—the Pool of Refreshment."

My companion dragged me to my feet and led me slowly toward the sound of splashing. Dull, mindless, I huddled in my robe, too weak to turn my head as he lit the lamp, illuminating a gigantic cavern with jeweled light. Greens, blues, purple, and silver were reflected from a pool of turbulent water. Water dribbled, dripped, trickled, and splashed on every side: seeping rivulets feeding the pool, a waterfall, its source lost in the heights, a sheer veil of shimmering drops whispering across a wall of green stone. I stood numbly at the pool's edge, my ears and eyes throbbing painfully with the sounds and colors.

Ven'Dar removed my robe. "Deep breath, my lord. Enjoy yourself."

He rotated me until my back was to the pool, and then gave me a gentle push. I toppled backward, the shock of the cold water forcing me to inhale just before the water closed over my head.

Through the brittle, shifting surface, I glimpsed a tired smile. "One, two, three . . . Count, if you remember how."

Cold. Drifting. . . . *seventeen, eighteen* . . . Something tickled my back . . . my feet. A school of brilliant red-

and-orange fish darted past my nose. A warm current bathed my legs and dragged me deeper. The water was so clear . . . water and light, swirling, teasing, caressing. . . . *thirty-one, thirty-two* . . .

Scarcely had the count passed a hundred and my body made the transition to breathing water when I was sucked into the vortex of the waterfall pool and swirled to the blue-green deeps, tumbled past smooth stones of purple and green, a lacework forest of sculpted stone, and a garden of sea flowers . . . a thousand vivid colors. An eddy tugged at my hair. From a crack in the rocks at the bottom of the pool a small geyser vented a pillar of bubbles that danced around me, as I floated in a hammock woven of lush fronds of water grass. The water that flowed through me bore the tang of new wine and commanded every nerve to wake up and live.

The pool must have extended half a league into the caves. By the time I reached its farthest limit I was swimming on my own, diving deep and rolling over like a dolphin just to feel the flow of the glorious water on my skin. I explored every crevice and eddy as I lazily paddled back to the beginning. There I arched my back and burst through the surface into the cascade, laughing aloud and blowing the water from my mouth in a fountain.

"You'll have to drag me from this one, my companion," I said, my voice crackling and strange, brittle like the clank of metal in the air after a storm. "Join me! While away the day."

Ven'Dar smiled regretfully. "Another day, my lord Prince. Come. Time to press on."

I practically dragged my weary friend through the passage to the Pool of Memory. "What's next?"

"Every petitioner I've taken through has gotten frisky after the Pool of Refreshment, just when the hours start to weigh on me," he grumbled as he held the luminant to the diamond-paned lamp. "I would order the pools a different way were I designing them. And I would vent this chamber much better."

None of the pools had looked so formidable as the Pool of Memory. Thick, yellow-green liquid bubbled in

the narrow basin, giving off an acrid yellow smoke that
made my eyes water.

"Are you sure of this?" I asked, my exuberance
quenched. "Others have entered? Submerged?"

Ven'Dar nodded without expression. "Be of good
heart, my lord. We are almost at an end."

The thought of swallowing the ghastly muck turned
my growling stomach. "I *was* of good heart until we
came here."

With the largest breath I could muster, and the vague
hope that my encounter with the Pool of Memory would
be exceptionally brief, I stepped from the edge and
dropped into the vile mess.

I could bear the heat—vicious, but not quite so fierce
as the Pool of Cleansing—but whatever substance gave
the water its putrid color and villainous smell caused
it to eat its way into the skin. Stinging, abrading like
acid in a wound. How could I possibly let it inside
me? My count reached eighty, and I had yet to open
my eyes.

It was time to end this exercise. Surely I'd gained
whatever benefit Ven'Dar required of me. I'd not felt
so near myself in at least a year. But I couldn't remember why . . . which must be why the Pool of Memory
followed the Pool of Refreshment. First reawaken life
and sensation, then reimpose the patterns of history. I
knew who I was . . . but why was I here?

So instead of following my instinct and my most profound desire to climb upward and out of the pool, curiosity held me to the count of one hundred. I released my
breath and let the foul mess flow into me. . . .

The yellow sludge ate its way through me, inside, outside, body and spirit, reawakening the tale of my life—
my lives—twenty-two years as D'Natheil, forty-two as
Karon, ten of those dead, a disembodied soul in Dassine's captivity, and almost six as this strange joining of
Prince and Healer. In a moment's passing all these times
were made clear to me, etched into my renewed soul,
all the deeds I had done—good and evil together—the
words I'd spoken, the faces I'd known, even my own

death and rebirth, all laid out in unfiltered clarity. Orderly. Unaltered.

Instinctively I curled into a ball, floating there in the vile yellow stink, as if I were trying to contain it all or prevent its escape . . . or perhaps protect myself from the intensity of feeling that must surely accompany such a panorama. But, for the moment, only the facts as they had happened floated there with me. In the hot, murky silence, I existed with my past until I uncurled and floated free.

Enough. I was becoming increasingly nauseated in this pool. I reached for the surface, but could not find it.

Relax . . . drift . . . make sure which way is up. Now, reach again. Still nothing. My heart beat faster. *Easy, easy. Ven'Dar is watching. You are not abandoned here to drown in the past.*

There was a pulse to the Pool of Memory, a throbbing life somewhere in its depths, faint when first I entered the pool, but growing in strength as I reached and strained to find my way out. The pulse drew me in a direction that every instinct screamed was wrong. Deeper. Panicked, I thrashed and struggled against the pull, opening my eyes to a dark blotch on a scaly yellow shelf of rock. Though my body cried out for air, I forced myself to keep drawing in the foul liquid. The blotch grew larger—a swirling vortex with a bottomless black center. I could not hold back, and inexorably the sluggish whirlpool swept me into its dark nexus, my head and feet in a tangle.

Some dense, fibrous, elastic material settled about my flailing limbs, squeezing tighter and tighter, until even the turgid yellow of the pool was lost in darkness. The pulsing continued, squeezing the yellow stuff from my body, but leaving me nothing at all to breathe.

In a single, stifling, choking instant of blind terror and despair, I was shot into a pool of cold, sparkling crystal. With my first desperate gulp of the waters of Rebirth came the emotions I had feared—a vast universe of feeling. Love, loneliness, grief, joy—so much joy I had known—all my anger, too, and hatred, and terror, but in proper balance and proportion. In the span of an hour I drowned in the feelings of two lifetimes, feeling them settle into their rightful positions like sand into the crevices of a stone path.

It is the gift of the Dar'Nethi to take in what is dealt by life and see it in its proper perspective against the glorious backdrop of the universe, accepting and savoring the good and bad alike. To view life without blinders can be difficult and fraught with pain, for you are left with no possibility of self-deception, but from the seeing comes our power.

Face down I rode the cool, gentle swells of the pool like flotsam in the tide, letting them carry me at will, forward and back, having no strength left to do otherwise, and no desire. After a while my toe scraped on a rock. I shifted slightly. My feet dragged the rocky bottom, and soon my knees, too. Only then did I crawl, exhausted, onto the pebbled shore.

I remained on all fours, coughing up the water, my arms scarcely able to hold me up, the chill of the cave quickly settling over me and into me. As before, the white robe was laid gently over my shoulders, and a hand reached out to help me to my feet. But the hand was not Ven'Dar's. It was slender and pale, with long, graceful fingers that looked strong and capable.

I touched the hand, ensuring it was real before I dared look further, but no watery fantasy could be so much of sweet flesh and blood. And so did I look up into the luminous countenance of my beloved Seri, and in weary grief did I weep for the pain I must bring to her beauteous eyes.

CHAPTER 26

Seri

"Watch for my signal: two flashes, a pause, and then one more. All will be well, my lady. You'll see." With a touch of my hand, Paulo vanished into the night. A very dark night.

The ruins of Calle Rein—the Lion's Grotto—lay like a smudge of soot on the black cloak of the desolate valley. Only a few stars glimmered in the enveloping midnight, the last outriders of the glittering heavens of Avonar, just as the ragged thornbushes and the gray, brittle grasses that braved the scree were the last remnants of life and growth that marked the border of the Wastes. Not a breath of wind stirred the chill air, and only the screech of a hunting owl, echoing from the barren cliff walls behind me, marred the heavy silence.

There . . . A pinprick of light flared briefly from the ruin, as if one of the lonely stars had given up its fight against the encroaching darkness and fallen into the valley. Had someone noted the dark figure so carefully picking his way down the rocky slope toward the light? Who was waiting inside the broken stone walls so far below me?

Foolish, all our precautions. If the one who awaited us in Calle Rein was not who he claimed to be, then the place would surely be surrounded with enchantments—wards to let him know his grand trap was sprung. But if he was only what he claimed, and he was alone, we had nothing to fear.

The excitement and anticipation that sharpened my

vision, pricked my ears, and made the hair rise on my neck at every whisper had no relation to the truth of the night's events. Such reactions must be a remnant of a primeval innocence, when life was a constant wonder, and survival depended on the scents and sounds carried on the night wind.

Dread was my proper companion as I hid in the rocks above Calle Rein, and her brother grief hovered on the dark horizon, for unless some miraculous circumstance intervened, my child would die before morning, and the true heart of my husband die with him. It was a mutual sacrifice of such unfathomable proportion that only the salvation of three worlds could demand it. And I—a woman of some experience, but not the least shred of power—was the only voice that dared cry out that the price was far too high. I could not allow it. Not if the Lords of Zhev'Na themselves were to die alongside my son at the hand of his father—not even for that could I permit it.

I had stayed with Karon all through the Rite of Purification, hiding in the shadows while he struggled with his demons. No reassurance of Ven'Dar's could alleviate my terror when he dropped below the surface of each pool and failed to emerge for hours at a time.

"Is it truly necessary to put him through this, Preceptor?" I said, after watching my love stagger blindly from the Pool of Darkness to the Pool of Oblivion. "If it won't reverse the change . . ."

"He is D'Natheil, my lady," said the Preceptor. "And while the essence you cherish is still part of him, it has become subservient to D'Natheil's passions. The rite can push one to the limits of endurance, but if anything can quiet the rage that consumes him, if anything can allow even a small part of what he was to emerge, it is this."

And so I wasn't sure what to expect when Karon crawled from the Pool of Rebirth, and I couldn't even attempt to interpret the tears that tempered his smile. But whatever the truth of the rite, I felt a lifetime of love in his fierce embrace.

"You didn't describe this part, Ven'Dar!" he said

hoarsely to the man who stood just behind me. "I'd never have dallied so long if I'd known a miracle was awaiting me."

"It's a benefit I've added just for you, my lord. But if you recall, I most certainly told you that your lady awaited you at the end of it."

"What winding have you cast to make this most magnificent of gifts possible?" His cold thumbs traced my cheeks, my neck, my lips, my brow.

"It was not my own doing, but that story will have to come with the rest. Right now, I'll look after our fire and our supper." The smiling Preceptor bowed and retreated into an adjoining chamber.

"A day of visions. If you're yet another, don't tell me," said Karon, burying his face in my hair, scarcely able to speak for his shivering.

"A day of enchantment," I said, kissing his shoulder and his neck. "More than a day, in fact. I've hurried the hours along, but now I don't want it to end."

He pulled away enough that I could see the cloud of sadness that crossed his brow. "Seri, I must tell you—"

I put my hand to his lips. "Not yet. The Preceptor has a fire ready in the next room. Much as I would love to tarry with you in this beautiful place, you're getting me dreadfully wet, and I'll soon be as cold as you are. Everything else must wait." The hard knot in my breast, loosened for a single moment, wrenched tight again.

Ven'Dar had not only a fire in the next room, but soup and tea and dry clothes . . . and Paulo. We had debated whether to have Paulo with us or not, and came to the conclusion that we gained nothing by waiting. Karon would be expecting him. And indeed when he caught sight of our young friend tending the fire, scarcely daring to peek out from under his shaggy hair, Karon gave Ven'Dar a curt nod.

For a while none of us spoke of anything save commonplace arrangements for food and fire and places to sit. The important things were too large and everything else trivial.

Karon relinquished my hand only long enough to pull on the breeches, shirt, leggings, and wool tunic Ven'Dar

gave him, and to tie back his wet hair with a leather
thong. But once we were seated beside each other on
the floor of the cavern, he twined my fingers in his cold
left hand as he used his right to drink three mugs of
steaming soup and three more of tea. When we'd finished our refreshment, however, he kissed my hand and
laid it carefully in my lap, leaned back against a block
of granite, and looked from one of us to the other like
a magistrate facing three pickpockets. "So, who is to
begin?"

Ven'Dar answered. "Young Paulo has the most fascinating story to tell, my lord. But I will begin with the
small part I have witnessed and my theories as to the
nature of our dilemma. I believe it casts a critical light
on Paulo's tale. Your wife is both our evidence and
our advocate."

"So you can speak to me now?" said Karon, cocking
an eyebrow at Paulo.

"It wasn't my choice, my lord. You'll see."

"Tell me your tales, then, all of you. I'm listening."

Ven'Dar began with the story of his imprisonment by
Radele, and his belief that Men'Thor and Radele intended to goad D'Natheil's anger to make Karon re-
ceptive to their beliefs about the conduct of the war.
The Preceptor then told of Radele's silencing enchantment and how Paulo had discovered the secret of the
list of the Hundred Talents that enabled Ven'Dar to set
us free.

"Men'Thor and Radele . . . and Ustele, no doubt. And
I never suspected," said Karon, his eyes stormy. "Naive
fool that I am. Though Men'Thor annoys me to distraction, I've always believed him a man of honor. He offered to grieve with me and seemed sincere . . ."

"He longs to be a Preceptor. His initiation robes have
been prepared for many years," said Ven'Dar.

"He can wear them in the Wastes after his banish-
ment! And it was all so pointless. Silencing Seri . . .
yes, it perhaps accelerated what was happening with me
anyway. But your story changes nothing of true importance: Jayereth, Gar'Dena, the betrayal, the initial attempt on Seri's life. Radele was searching the ruins of

the main house when she was stabbed; I saw his light moving through the windows. We were hunting Gerick, while Gerick was standing over Seri with a bloody knife in his hand. Paulo saw Gerick, not Radele, back away from her and bolt."

"Oh, but my tale does change matters, my lord," said Ven'Dar. "You've heard only the first hint of the true mystery. Leave off thoughts of Men'Thor and Radele, and hear my story again. How was I able to use Paulo's information when I could not so much as distinguish day from night? My thoughts were wholly out of my control. Something else . . . someone else . . . intervened . . ."

As Karon leaned forward, intently focused on the Preceptor and his story, Ven'Dar described the mysterious infusion of strength that enabled him to free himself and then me. ". . . No one imposed the list on my thoughts; the knowledge was my own, couched in the terms I have used for thirty-five years to articulate it. But I was provided with the strength, focus, and reason to use what I knew. The second hint of the truth came when your wife emerged from her captivity, looked into the eyes of this youth, and saw something she did not expect to see. And the third came when I awoke in my tower the next morning and found a letter from your son. . . ."

"I've never heard of a Soul Weaver."

Karon was visibly shaken by Gerick's letter. I felt his desire to believe in Ven'Dar's theory, to grasp some hope out of the tangle of revulsion and grief. But his responsibilities left him no such freedom as I had, to believe as soon as he heard, to accept without rational explanation.

"We've no written record of a proven Soul Weaver. Few believe such a profound talent could even exist. But my studies of the talents have allowed me to spend a great deal of time considering the legend of soul weaving." Ven'Dar's face was alight with discovery and wonder. "Unlike the ordinary Dar'Nethi who mind-speaks, reading or hearing the thoughts of another person, or the Healer, who can link his own mind with the body and mind of the other, seeing the damage done to him and sharing the pain of his injury or disease, a Soul Weaver actually becomes one with the other. The Soul Weaver leaves his own body behind and subjects himself to the physical dimensions of the receiver, taking or yielding control of the body and mind as he wishes or as need demands. Courage, skill, knowledge, will . . . all these things the Soul Weaver can offer or withhold, and then, when ready, relinquish the mind and body of the other, separate himself, leaving the other soul intact. Such acts would require a clear sense of self and monumental self-discipline. To subject oneself to the physical boundaries and mental confusions of another being, giving such help as I received, while resisting the temptations of control and exploitation would require an immense generosity of spirit. Easy to see why nature would make it so rare a gift."

Karon propped his elbows on his knees, his chin resting on his clenched fists. "But the Lords do this thing—possess. How can you know this is not just the manifestation of his true identity, dressed with an honest face for his own devious purpose?"

"Of course, I cannot. Yet, it's this ability of the Lords to possess another that's always made me believe that soul weaving was not just a myth. *Everything* the Lords do is a perversion of true talent. Think of their 'healing' that destroys one life while preserving another, and their mind-speaking that withers the soul, locking one being in subservience to another rather than enlarging the realm of understanding between the two. Even their Metalwrights devise such things as an oculus that allows them to draw on our worst parts—our hatreds, fears, our cruelties and despair—enhancing and growing their power. Is it not inevitable that the Lords' version of soul weaving would leave only death in its wake? The boy himself feared that he had killed Paulo the first time it happened. But Paulo lives, his mind free and undamaged."

"What the young master does isn't wicked, my lord," said Paulo, speaking up for the first time from his place in Ven'Dar's shadow. "My . . . thoughts . . . my feelings about things . . . get all mixed up with his. It's so big a thing going on inside me . . . I can't tell you how big it feels . . . but it isn't wicked. I would know."

"And what of Gar'Dena?" Karon remained the prosecutor, determined to squeeze the guilty truth from us. "When my trap was sprung, I probed Gar'Dena's mind to find out why he would betray us. But he was *not* Gar'Dena. I could not mistake Gerick. And when Gerick left him, Gar'Dena died. The boy so much as admits the deed in this letter. If this is his own gift, and not a perversion of the Lords, then why, in the name of all the stars, did he betray us?"

Karon crushed Gerick's letter in his hand and threw it at the little fire. It bounced to the side on the uneven floor, stirring up ash and sparks. Ven'Dar retrieved the letter before the floating sparks could settle on it, smoothing the crumpled paper against his knee.

"Read this again, my lord." The Preceptor's eagerness and wonder had dimmed, but not his urgency or conviction. "Your son neither denies that he did these things, nor does he supply any easy explanation. He understands it no more than we do. Less, in fact, because he has so little knowledge of Dar'Nethi talents. More is involved here than soul weaving, though I am convinced your son's talent is the mechanism by which these horrors are accomplished. Paulo, tell the Prince how young Gerick came to believe he was the betrayer, even though he has no remembrance of the deeds."

"To explain it, I got to tell you where we were, and what happened there . . ." Paulo told Karon of the strange land called the Bounded, and of the Singlars, the Guardian, the firestorms, and the Source, and of the day Gerick saved his life by taking over his body and then gave it back again.

"Is it not a marvel?" whispered Ven'Dar.

Karon did not answer, but motioned for Paulo to continue. And so he did, telling the story of Gerick's devastation when he saw the oculus in the cave of the Source and heard the revelation of his own crimes, and how he then made this desperate plan to arrange his death on his own terms.

Karon shook his head and scraped his fingers through

his hair. "I can't see beyond the Lords, Ven'Dar. I hear speculation and possibility and the faith of a true friend. But I hear nothing to prove that his connection to this new world is a result of Dar'Nethi talent and not the Lords taking control of the Breach as they have craved for a millennium. If I do as Gerick asks, link with his mind, only to find I have linked with the Lords . . ."

Ven'Dar nodded. "You have told me the story of your own coming to talent, my lord. Of how desperation to save your young brother's life forced you to take up the knife and recite the Healer's invocation. You've told me how only when you looked back through the years could you recognize the precursors of your talent: aversion to combat, fear of carrying a knife, a thirst to know how the human body worked . . .

"Now consider your son. He has told young Paulo here that he's been seeing visions of the past: his mother as a young woman, his friend Paulo as a crippled child, and his true father's face—your true face—that no portrait has ever shown him. And each of these visions occurred in the presence of the person most concerned. He has dreamed their dreams, felt their joy and shame, experienced the pain of a broken wrist that was his father's, not his own. I believe he has been slipping in and out of souls, uncontrolled.

"And even earlier, what do we see? What could be the trigger that charted his course? Desperation, just as you experienced. Four years ago, on your journey out of Zhev'Na, desperate to escape the pain of separation from the Lords, your son's soul fled his own body. Not understanding what was happening, unable to control his gift, he could not seek refuge in any of you three. That left him adrift in chaos . . . as if he were a part of the Breach itself. I believe that by his act, he imposed order upon the crippled bits of matter and sentience that existed there, forming a solid center . . . a source . . . from which a world has grown—immature, awkward, with all of the spotty wisdom and ignorance of a sixteen-year-old who has experienced too much and too little of living. He loaned a world his life."

"And that's why the firestorms come near killing him as they destroy the Bounded," said Paulo.

"And why the Source knew what he'd done, even though he didn't realize it himself," I said. "Because the Source is a reflection of himself."

"Yes," said the Preceptor. "And when this strange joining occurred as you traversed the Breach, he was still connected to the Lords . . ."

". . . through the jewels and the mask they had given him in Zhev'Na . . ." I said.

". . . and so the Lords indeed obtained their foothold in the Breach." Ven'Dar's conclusion dropped a pall of silence over us, so that Gerick's desperate plea echoed in that firelit cavern as if he stood before us. If it was possible for Gerick's link to the Bounded to be severed, a Healer of Karon's skill and power was the only one likely to accomplish it.

Karon stood up and walked away from the fire into the shadows. Only after a long time did he speak, his voice no more yielding than the stone walls of that cavern. "And so you agree that Lords are still part of him, that the oculus in the cave of the Source is the manifestation of his soul's link to them. Somehow, they can control him, just as he says, and make him do things he would not, even to attempting the life of his mother."

"Yes, my lord. This connection lay dormant for four years, manifest only in nightmares and the boy's unsettled nature. But I believe it was rekindled when you took him across the Bridge that night. Everything started after—"

"And have you even considered the rest of it? If all this is true—if he's been in the mundane world and the Breach and now here in Gondai—then he has taken his friend Paulo across the Breach unscathed, not with struggle and difficulty and expense of power as I do, but easily. Do you know what that means? Do you see the implication? The danger? The impossibility? It means he can transport Zhid between worlds."

"Indeed. It would seem so," said Ven'Dar, quietly. "My hope is that when you go to him knowing all of this, you and the boy together will discover how to resolve the problem. Your son needs to understand he is not evil, my lord. As do you. If nothing else, perhaps you will be able to do what he asks of you."

The knot around my heart drew tighter yet. Karon's resolve was written in his face. The rite . . . the revelations . . . had led us nowhere new.

"Where is he, Paulo?" Karon's words hung in the air like a headsman's ax.

"What will you do?" I blurted out before Paulo could answer.

"Tell me my choices, Seri."

"There's got to be another way, now we know he's not one of them. They're just using him."

"For now."

I stood up, too. Though I fought to stay calm and reasoned, my voice rose. "So what prevents the Lords from crushing Avonar right now? What prevents them controlling him all the time? There's something else at work here, and you can't stop looking for answers just because Gerick has. He doesn't understand what he is, so his solution may not be the only one. We just need time. . . ."

"Time is exactly what we don't have. If there is the smallest possibility that I can do what he asks, what Ven'Dar has tried to give me the chance to do, it must be now. The war won't wait. If the Lords come to this same conclusion, they won't wait. And D'Natheil won't wait." He turned his back on me. "Where is he, Paulo?"

"Half a day's ride, my lord. A ruin out at the edge of the Wastes near the place you found me. The young master said it must have once been a portal between worlds, like the one in Valleor where we went into the Bounded, as it was easy to find once he knew to look. I'll take you there."

"Perhaps I could make a portal to take us there, my lord," said Ven'Dar. "It would take me only an hour or two."

"No. No portal so close to Avonar. Not when we can't be sure—"

Not when he wasn't sure who would be waiting for us on the other side of it.

"I don't mind riding," I said.

"You're not going."

The ten paces between Karon and me stretched wider, across the cavern, across Paulo and Ven'Dar and the litter of packs and supplies and pulsing coals . . . across sixteen years of grief and anger and longing, of loneliness and pain.

"Gerick is our son, Karon. I *will not* abandon him."

The waves of the Pool of Rebirth, wreathed in mist beyond the shadowed arch, lapped softly.

"I will do what I have to do, Seri. I cannot say what that will be. But neither my own desires nor my feelings for you can weigh in my decision." He had not moved from the growing shadows, so I could not see his face, only the shape of his powerful body, taut and still.

"Then the Lady *must* go with you, my lord," said Ven'Dar quietly. "If she reminds you of the past with all its joys and guilts, then you are indeed the man who should be making these dreadful decisions. And truly, our Way says she must make her own choice as to the physical dangers, the risks to her heart, and the way she will endure what is to come."

Ven'Dar began wrapping a round of cheese in a piece of cloth, and soon it was as if time had taken up its path again. Uneasy, but moving forward.

"It has been three days since you slept, my lord," said the Preceptor. "And before that you were in combat for five more. You can scarcely stand. Even the urgency of your mission cannot preclude your need for rest. Any chance of success in whatever you attempt will require all your strength."

Karon's shoulders sagged a little. "Damnable body . . ." He came back to the smoldering fire, then, and sat heavily beside me, pressing the heels of his hands into his eyes.

Taking his shoulders, I pulled him sideways until his head rested in my lap.

"Three hours, Ven'Dar," he said, his command already slurred. "No more."

"Aye, my lord. Three hours it is."

I stroked his damp hair with my fingers as he dropped

instantly into profound sleep. His sword belt lay just
beside us, sword and dagger within easy reach of his
hand. D'Arnath's weapons. Some among the Dar'Nethi
believed these sacred talismans ensured that the city of
Avonar itself would never fall and had been willing to
sacrifice the incapable D'Natheil to the Lords to retrieve
them. Karon had laughed and said he was grateful that
our first venture to the Bridge had returned both Prince
and weapons safely to Avonar. The memory of his
laughter was a knife in my breast.

Ven'Dar had closed his eyes and sat motionless for a
moment. Now he blinked and gave me a sad smile. "I've
cast a winding to wake me in three hours, so I am going
to take the opportunity to sleep a bit myself." He bundled a cloak under his head and pulled a blanket up to
his chin, yawning. "You should do the same." He closed
his eyes and was instantly asleep.

My back rested on a protruding rock. My fingers
traced the wide brow and sculpted jaw, grizzled with
many days' growth of light hair . . . D'Natheil's face,
stern even in rest. I closed my eyes and tried to remember Karon's face, but for the first time since his death,
his features would not resolve clearly, as if we lay together in the darkness and I could catch only the shape
of his cheekbone or the line of his dark hair. I wished I
could sleep.

Paulo had sat quiet since giving his testimony, looking
soberly from one of us to the other. Now he, who could
usually sleep anytime and anywhere, sat staring into the
dying fire. After a while he muttered a quiet oath, jumped
up, and wandered restlessly back through the arch to the
Pool of Rebirth. Before very long, he was back.

He crouched beside the fire and poked it aimlessly.
Then, so quietly I almost missed it, he said, "If we was
to leave now, ride hard, you'd have three hours' head
start."

Three hours. To do what? Hold my son? Convince
him to run away? Find an answer?

"Not deceiving. You could leave the Prince a writing
to tell him we've just gone ahead. . . ."

*   *   *

And so, many hours later after our frantic ride from Avonar, I crouched behind the still-warm rocks and waited for the signal from Paulo that all was well. After an interminable, breathless time it came, two flares of light in quick succession—a pause—and the third.

I hurried down the barren slope toward the crumbling stone walls. A tall, lanky figure appeared against the lighted rectangle of the doorway. Paulo. And another, smaller person beside him. Not tall enough for Gerick. I hesitated, just outside the light that spilled from the doorway.

"Come, my lady. It's all right. I didn't mention we brought someone else with us when we come from the Bounded," said Paulo, as soon as I was within earshot. "I thought it best to leave her out of my story until I knew what was what. She's watched over the young master's body when he wasn't in it. Lady Seri, this is Princess Roxanne. I told her you know her da."

Evard's missing daughter! I'd not given the girl so much as a thought in the hours since my awakening. Fair like her mother and just as regal in her bearing. A pale, smooth complexion out of place amid the half collapsed walls and piles of windblown debris that shaped the little haven. Yet her sturdy brown shirt, tunic, and breeches looked strangely appropriate on her, and her father's sharply intelligent eyes flashed in the firelight as she sat on the cracked paving stones and watched over my sleeping son.

Gerick was curled up in a dusty cloak, his head pillowed on a small bundle. If I'd not laid my hand on him and felt the slow shallow breathing, I would have believed him dead already. He was as pale as starlight and dreadfully thin.

"Another day and the water will run out," said Roxanne, as she dripped a clear liquid from a tiny cup into Gerick's mouth. "He said he'd come back before the water was gone, but he's not moved so much as a finger since he put himself back to sleep three days ago."

"What do you mean, 'come back'? How is it you're here? It wasn't Gerick who abducted—"

"No. The confounded little Vroon and his friends took me to the Bounded by mistake. Gerick freed me from

their wretched prison, but he never really told me anything that was going on—not then—only that the place
we were was 'not Leire.' "

The girl's animated expression took fire in the firelight
as the torrent of words poured out of her. "Then, after
he almost goes crazy when he finds that ring spinning in
the cave, and just before he leaves for this cheery place,
he tells me he needs to sleep for a few days while Paulo
goes off to find his mother, and that he needs a friend—
a friend, he says—to come along and watch and make
sure he doesn't die—for heaven's sake—to make sure
he doesn't die by giving him water from the Source! I'm
not an idiot, and you couldn't be in the Bounded very
long without becoming accustomed to the fact that the
world isn't quite as you believed. But I'd never had anyone trust me like that. And I said that if we were truly
friends, then he needed to tell me what this was about.
Of course, he didn't tell me everything, not by a league
or ten. After we got here, he lay down and went away.
Gone. His body was here for me to keep alive, but he
was riding around with Paulo like a fat duchess in a
carriage to help him look for you, while hiding where
his enemies couldn't find him. Who could believe that?"

She slapped her palm on the stopper of the blue flask,
cramming it tight, then stuffed flask and cup back into
a worn gray rucksack.

"Three days ago, he came back," she continued.
"After ten dreary days with his mostly dead body, and
I thought I was going to be here forever and not even
know quite where, I wake up in the morning to find him
walking around like he'd just dozed off for an hour. He
ate half the food we had left and told me about what
had happened with Paulo and you and the list enchantment. He said we'd just have to wait to see what came
about next. But it wasn't two hours until he turned fifty
colors of white, and I thought we were dead, because it
was just the way he'd look when the firestorms came.
Those storms were the most terrifying things, as if the
world were shattering to bits. The poor Singlars would
get caught in them, and their towers disintegrate right
before your eyes, and one time I came near falling into

one of the rifts and a Singlar pulled me out. It was the worst fright I've ever had. With Gerick looking so pale and awful, I expected *this* place to split open and fall apart any moment, but he said it wouldn't happen here, and maybe it wouldn't happen back in the Bounded either, if he could just turn off his head for a while. He felt so responsible. He said the storms were his fault, though I'll never believe that. He almost died trying to stop them. Do you think I'll ever get used to this, Lady Seriana? Bodies lying around with no minds in them, bodies walking around with two—"

She paused in her breathless chatter, staring at the doorway behind me. I whirled about, and I couldn't tell whether the iron-visaged figure who stood there was Karon or D'Natheil.

"Karon!" I said, choosing that it be so.

Gently, but firmly he took my arm and raised me up, moving me to the corner of the little room. When he returned to Gerick and looked down at him, the world paused in its spinning path.

Only the princess refused to heed the dread of that moment. Glancing at me briefly, she took up her story once again, as if she'd never been interrupted. ". . . so, before I quite understood what he meant, he took himself off again. I don't know exactly where."

She wrinkled her straight nose and pursed her lips while shifting her unabashed stare to Karon. "And Gerick—my friend, Gerick—said to tell his father—I presume that's you—that he'd be waiting for you to fulfill your agreement. He didn't explain that part or anything about the enemies he was hiding from, and I find it quite annoying, as I've had all this time to think, and he didn't explain the most important part. 'Too complicated,' he'd say, which have to be the most exasperating words that can be spoken, and despite the fact that I'm almost two years older, and I helped him sort out all manner of things while he was being the king of the Bounded. He just said that if anyone could take care of the firestorms so the Singlars wouldn't suffer so from them, it was his father. The only thing he was afraid of was that Paulo wouldn't find you."

"It took a number of people to find me," said Karon, softly. "I thank you for your care for him, young lady. Now you'd best move closer to Seri. It will be safer. Or you might want to step outside."

"But you see, just as I've been telling the Lady, you don't have to pretend there's no sorcery involved here. I'm not afraid . . ." Roxanne's words limped into the void very quickly. She stood and backed away from Gerick and Karon, but only as far as my side. Her chin was still firm and high. Paulo, who had said nothing since Karon's arrival, stood behind us in the doorway.

Karon's hand was steady as he drew his silver dagger from its sheath. I wanted to stay his hand until I was sure of him, but terror robbed me of speech.

"Oh, demons, Gerick—" Roxanne gasped and lunged forward as Karon raised his glittering knife.

I grabbed her and drew her close, holding her tight and allowing her cry to loosen my own tongue. With all the hope I could muster, I said softly, "There are no demons here, Roxanne. No need to be afraid. This is Gerick's father, who cherished our son before he was even born, who led him out of the darkness once and will do so again. He's come here only to help him."

At the same moment, Karon raised his other hand, closed his eyes, and with a passion that was all of his life, spoke words that would forever summon visions of a rainy summer afternoon at Windham, a frost-rimed Vallorean bandit cave, and a towering wall of white fire, blazing joyfully in a mountain fortress. "Life, hold. Stay your hand. Halt your foot ere it lays another step along the Way. Grace your son once more with your voice that whispers in the deeps, with your spirit that sings in the wind, with the fire that blazes in your wondrous gifts of joy and sorrow. Fill my soul with light, and let the darkness make no stand in this place."

"It's all right. It's all right," I whispered to the terrified girl, as Karon's knife left its bloody track across Gerick's limp forearm and his own scarred left arm. And while the golden flames danced on the ancient walls, the blaze of Karon's enchantment embraced us all.

CHAPTER 27

We had basked in the warmth of Karon's magic no more than half an hour when Paulo slipped out of the ruin into the night. I thought nothing of it. There was too much else to consider, too much wondering at what was happening between the two who were bound together by a narrow strip of bloodstained linen. Such a monumental task as exploring the link that connected Gerick to the world he had created from the Breach . . . who knew if such a thing was even possible? And his connection to the Lords . . . I was all too aware that this blessed reprieve was only temporary. Judgment would come with Karon's withdrawal. I didn't want to hurry it, even if I could. Karon's work with Gerick after our return from Zhev'Na had taken as long as four or five hours each time, and I couldn't imagine this venture could take less.

So after Paulo's abrupt departure, I watched and continued whispering an explanation of Dar'Nethi healing to Roxanne.

But suddenly—far too soon—Karon's hand fumbled for his knife, and with a swift motion, he sliced through the strip of linen that bound his arm to Gerick's. He fell back on his heels, sweat beaded on his brow and soaking the tendrils of light hair dangling about his face, though our dying fire had invited the nighttime chill into our shelter. "Get out of here, Seri," he said harshly. "Take the girl and hide. Empty your minds. Someone will come for you."

Gerick was stirring, and I hesitated.

Karon waved his knife toward the door. "Go now! For everything—hurry!"

I jumped to my feet just as Paulo burst into the shelter. "Someone's coming. Horses beyond the ridge to the north."

Karon had hunched his shoulders and closed his eyes, grimacing and cradling his bleeding left arm in his right. His incision did not close if the enchantment was interrupted. "Hurry!" he gasped.

"We'll go south," I said, kicking dirt over the fire. Then I grabbed Roxanne's arm and pulled her out into the night. Halting abruptly in the deepest shadows next to the broken walls, I gave my eyes time to adjust to the dark, sacrificing the quick start for speedier going.

"What's happening?" demanded the princess, wresting her arm free. "What did he mean? What's he going to do?"

"I don't know. It didn't seem like the time to ask him. Now be quiet and come with me."

I took off across the cracked dry earth of the valley floor, the reluctant princess lagging behind me. *For everything—hurry!* The distance across the exposed valley stretched impossibly far, and before very long a stitch in my side protested my long idleness. But the echo of Karon's command drove me on until we had scrambled up the rocky incline at the southern edge of the valley. I had to trust him.

"Here," I said, collapsing behind the first boulder that commanded a view behind us. "I can't go any more just now."

"I couldn't go any more half an hour ago," said the panting girl. "What happened?"

"I don't know. Maybe something went wrong in the healing, or . . . I just don't know."

"Is the earth going to open up, something like that, like the firestorms in the Bounded? I've become accustomed to other things, but not that."

"I don't think so. But, Roxanne, if I tell you someone's coming, I want you to clear your mind of every thought. Focus your attention on a rock or the sky, but don't think of where you are or who you are or anyone or anything you know. No questions, no sounds or sensations, no fears. Make yourself empty. Do you understand me? Do you think you can do that?"

"Like 'think of yourself out'? I believe I'm beginning to speak your sorcerer's language."

"The less substantial your thoughts, the more difficult for anyone to locate you with sorcery. We'll hope we won't have to do it."

Across the dark valley, blurs of light moved rapidly down the slope where I had lain waiting such a short time ago. Riders carrying torches, at least ten horsemen. A few of them dismounted at the ruin, and light soon blazed from inside the walls as well as out. After a time, three men emerged from the ruin, leading someone who stumbled and fell. They dragged him up and placed him on the back of a horse, binding his hands to the saddle. Slender shoulders, long legs, dark hair . . . Gerick.

I half expected Karon to be brought out a prisoner also. But he strolled out in the company of two other men. After conferring with them for a moment, he walked over to Gerick and raised his arms. Bolts of white fire sparked from his hands. An agonized cry pierced the night, and Gerick slumped forward in the saddle.

"No!" I leaped to my feet, only to be dragged down instantly. I lay slumped in the dirt, my elbow and chin stinging after grazing the sandy boulder.

"This doesn't seem like the time, my lady." The girl's hands were steady as she brushed the grit from my face and helped me sit up again.

Roxanne crept upward to peer out at the valley across our sheltering boulder. But I drew my knees up tight and buried my head in my arms, trying to cry out the knots that choked off breath and tears, condemning me to dry shudders.

"They're riding back the way they came," said the girl, slipping down the rock face to sit beside me again. "His father leading." She laid her hand on my back. "They put one of the soldiers up behind him, as if to hold him in the saddle, so he's not dead. And another interesting thing. *Everyone* rode out. No horses left be-

hind. No guards posted. No torches left. But Paulo
wasn't with them. I'll be right back."

"Roxanne, wait! Don't . . ."

The stars wheeled slowly above me. The cold wind
blew off the desert. I could not bring myself to watch
whatever foolish mission the girl had contrived. If this
night demanded more grieving, it could not wrest it from
me. Eventually, plodding steps crunched and slid on the
steep gravel-strewn path.

"Whew!" A warm body flopped down at my side.
"Well, Paulo's not dead, either. He didn't go with them,
and he didn't stay behind, dead or alive, that I can see.
So he's either wandered out into the desert again or run
away somewhere—perhaps back to the Bounded the
way we came. That's a good sign, don't you think?"

Something in her question forced me to look outside
my private horror and glance over at her. Tears rolled
silently down her dusty cheeks, and her face was etched
with fear and grief and the yearning of a courageous
child who has been too long from home. I gathered her
in, and Evard's daughter and I held each other through
the long, cold night.

Sunrise brought searing heat. Roxanne and I kept
watch atop our boulder, taking turns once the shade
began to dwindle. As we waited, I told her about Radele
and Men'Thor and their plotting, about Karon and
D'Natheil and my fragile hopes, shattered so inexplicably last night. Near mid-morning, about the time doubts
began to sap my spirit along with the withering sun, I
spotted a lone traveler on the northern rim of the valley,
leading two riderless horses.

"Clear your mind as I told you," I said, shrinking
down beside the rock. "Think of the emptiest place you
know and erase each object and association you find
there."

I followed my own instructions, but kept my eyes
trained on the rider through a slot between our rock and
another. A needless precaution. As soon as the rider—
a slight figure that might have been a woman or a
youth—passed the ruin, he peered up at the rocks at our

end of the valley, shading his eyes with his hand. When he reached the base of our slope, he pulled off his hood, revealing olive skin, wiry black hair, and neatly trimmed beard, and eyes that, had they not been squinting, would have displayed the elongated oval shape of an almond. Quickly, I climbed onto our sheltering boulder and waved. "Up here, Bareil!"

Karon's Guide raised his hand in greeting and dismounted as Roxanne and I slipped and slithered down the graveled slope. "It is good to find you none the worse for your night in the open, my lady," said Bareil, bowing in the Dulcé fashion, one arm behind his back, the other extended.

"And it's very good to see you," I said. "It would have been a long dry day. Your Highness, this gentleman is Bareil of the Dulcé, my husband's friend and confidante. Bareil, Her Royal Highness Roxanne, Crown Princess of Leire."

The Dulcé repeated his bow and expressions of pleasure, though his demeanor was uncharacteristically somber. The formalities seemed surreal in the harsh surroundings. The girl and I were filthy and travel-worn, and, without regard for manners or breeding, we grasped the two waterskins Bareil detached from his saddle. And, of course, no protocol could keep the activities of the previous night at arm's length.

"What news, Bareil?" I said, as soon as I'd swallowed as much water as I could manage in one swig. "What's happened to Gerick? What did the Prince say? Why did he tell us to hide? Who were those men?"

Bareil's face was layered with care, his drawn brow and the creases about his mouth leading me, for the first time, to speculate about his age. "I am charged to bring you to the palace unobserved, my lady," he said. "The Prince offered me the strictest instructions for your safety and anonymity. Beyond that, I am privy to nothing about any of these matters. Indeed, it has been a long while since I have been my lord's confidante." He pulled two gauzy cloaks of light blue from a bag attached to his saddle, exchanging them for the half-drained waterskins.

"Then tell me, how did he appear? Was he all right? Was he . . . himself?"

"My lady . . ." Bareil's color deepened.

I bit my tongue in frustration. "I know. I know. It's improper for you to speak of him. Rude of me to ask. I'm sorry." A Dar'Nethi and his Guide—*madrisson* and *madrissé*, they called the pair—were linked by deep enchantment, the intricate workings of the Dulcé's astonishing mind available only at the Dar'Nethi's command. Such a relationship was only tenable if based on absolute trust: that the Dar'Nethi never abuse his ability to compel his madrissé's obedience and that the Dulcé never use the resulting intimacy to betray his madrisson's privacy.

"I am truly sorry, as well. If I could help you— It's just—" The worry etched about his almond eyes deepened. He shook his head and averted his gaze. "We must return to Avonar as swiftly as possible."

I touched his arm, clasped the blue cloak at my neck, and pulled up my hood. "Let's go then, and I'll ask the Prince myself. No protocol will stand in my way."

Leading the horses to a rock of convenient height, Bareil helped Roxanne mount a placid bay and, likewise, offered his hand to steady me onto a gray mare. We rode out at a moderate pace across the baked valley floor and upward, over the ridge to the road that would take us back to Avonar. The blustering wind that filled our eyes and mouths with dirt, and the burden of ominous events and forbidden topics, did not promote easy conversation. The sooner this journey was over the better. So I was somewhat surprised when we reached the top of the valley rim, our journey scarcely begun, and Bareil pulled up abruptly. Laying his small hand on his horse's mane, he did not shift his gaze from the road that stretched in front of us.

"You said you would get your answers from the Prince when you arrived in Avonar." He tossed out the remark carelessly, as if making casual conversation, as if we had stopped for some other reason. Perhaps pretending it was of little importance mitigated his breach of a Guide's protocol by speaking of his madrisson. "My lady . . . I must say . . . I don't know if you should depend on that."

The heat of the day vanished as if the sun had been blotted out.

"I am privy to nothing, my lady, as I said, and if I were, I could not share it unless the Prince permitted me, as you have remembered so well. But as I prepared to ride out from Avonar this morning, I obtained my horse from a public stable so as not to be remarked in the royal yards. As one will at any public place, I heard rumors . . . a great number of them . . . Some that might be of interest to you." He stroked his horse's mane slowly. Deliberately.

I forced myself to maintain his pretense, lest urgency force him back beyond the barriers of discretion. "Rumors are always interesting, Bareil, but rarely accurate."

"One says that the honorable Men'Thor is to be named to the Preceptorate this day."

"Such a rumor has been spread for months," I said, "probably by Men'Thor himself. The gossipmongers just don't know all the Prince has learned in these past days."

"So I believed also, my lady. But one of the men who spoke this rumor has a brother in service at the palace"—the words flowed faster now—"and he said that the Prince rode in before dawn this morning. My lord's first act was to summon Men'Thor from the Wastes and his son from the watch on the Vales. They were in consultation for a goodly time. When Men'Thor emerged, he sent my informant's brother to take a message to his own house—to set in motion a feast he had long planned and to make all in readiness for a momentous event. Another servant was sent to Radele's tailor to prepare ceremonial garb—on a scale far beyond anything he has ever requested."

"They're fools. They've misinterpreted." Why would Bareil be skirting his vows to repeat rumors? Why stop here in the wilderness to tell me this? "I don't understand, Bareil."

His gaze at last met my own. Unflinching, the Dulcé

continued as if I had made no comment. "I have heard another rumor, my lady."

"Which is?"

"The Prince is to name a new successor this night."

"Earth and sky! Let's ride!"

"I thought no city could rival Montevial," said Roxanne, craning her neck as we rode through the colossal bronze gates of Avonar. "But our cities are as far from this as the Bounded is from Leire."

I glanced at the stone pillars that supported the gates, columns higher than the towers of Comigor, sculpted into two long, slender bodies whose eyes gazed down benevolently on all who passed, creations of such delicate perfection that the robes of stone that draped the perfect naked forms were the image of windswept gauze. Vasrin Creator and Vasrin Shaper, the male and female expressions of a single god. The ancient gates themselves reached almost as high as the figures, and the bronze panels that sheathed the ancient wood depicted in intricate detail hundreds of scenes reflecting a Dar'Nethi life far removed from what we saw around us.

"Perhaps we would be equally capable of such beauty if we'd only allow ourselves to learn it," I said. "But we've always chosen to fight wars instead. After so many years of their own war, Karon says the Dar'Nethi are losing their arts and becoming more like us all the time."

We had ridden hard for several hours across the sweeping borderlands, stopping only when we needed to rest and water the horses at the watercourses that flowed out of the city and the Vales. The rough dry borderlands and thready streamlets had yielded to healthier grasslands as we approached Avonar. Though ripe and fertile land for planting, these fields had been long abandoned, for it was across these rolling meadows that the tides of war ebbed and flowed. Here the armies of the Zhid would advance on the royal city, besieging the enchanted walls for months at a time. And when the Dar'Nethi shoved the Lords' forces back into the Wastes, grass and flowers would slowly recover the reeking ruin left behind, only to be crushed when the war tide flowed again.

Roxanne had spent our journey questioning me about Avonar and sorcery, about Karon and the succession, but mostly about the Lords and what they had done to Gerick, which neither he nor Paulo had fully explained. Only in the last few leagues had she fallen silent, either from exhaustion at keeping such a pace or the need to mull the complexities of all I had told her.

We left our horses at a stable near the gates and shaded our faces with the hooded robes and long scarves Bareil had supplied. The shadows were lengthening, but the normal activities one would expect in the wide streets of the royal city on a summer afternoon were nowhere in evidence. Instead of street vendors hawking sausages and magical trinkets, small groups of citizens stood on the street corners talking with great animation. Instead of children running and laughing at their games around the fountains of colored light beams or water sprays that shaped themselves into figures of horses and birds, twos and threes of women walked side by side in deep discussion, tugging bewildered little ones behind. Every shop door had a gathering in front of it, and every hostelry, bathhouse, and house of refreshment seemed overflowing with custom. Anticipation was as palpable as the late summer heat.

"We've made good time," said the Dulcé. "I'd not expected to make it back here before sunset."

All night and all day I had pondered what I might do to influence the next few hours—hours that meant life or death for those I loved most in the world. I had composed words of reason and logic to lay at Karon's feet, to shout at the Preceptors, at the Dar'Nethi, at the Lords themselves. After Bareil told me his "rumors," I had tried again and failed to come up with any plan worth the dust on my shoe. I didn't know enough. My feet slowed. "Tell me, Bareil, where are you taking us?"

"I was told to bring you to the palace discreetly. I am to settle you and the young lady in a suite of rooms in a private wing and see to your comfort until such time as the Prince commands me otherwise."

"And you have no further orders concerning me or the princess?"

"Only that I am to insist that you remain in hiding and hold communication with no one until you hear differently from the Prince. For your safety, he says."

"I see. He said nothing about when I might expect to speak to him again or to see my son?"

"No, my lady. Nothing."

I needed to understand what Karon was doing. If he wasn't going to tell me, I needed to seek answers elsewhere. And we were at least two hours earlier than Bareil had expected to get us here. Though Bareil fidgeted at the delay, I left the street and led the others into a lush green parkland in the shade of spreading trees, laden with fragrant pink blossoms. "Bareil, do you know where I might find Ven'Dar?"

Bareil glanced anxiously in every direction and dropped his voice so that a bird on my shoulder couldn't have heard him. "I've not seen him since I left him with the Prince at the caves, but I am certain he is still in hiding. His 'death' has not been publicly reported, but the rumor of it has spread throughout the city and the Vales."

"Help me find him, Bareil. I must speak with him."

The Dulcé's face crumpled. "Ah, my lady, that would be far too dangerous. He might be hidden anywhere."

"No, he'll be somewhere close. Even if Karon ordered him away, I don't believe he would go. Does he have a house in the city or family, someone trustworthy, somewhere he might be able to remain hidden?"

"His only family is a sister who lives in Lyrrathe Vale. When not at Nentao or at the battlefront, he resides in the palace to be close to the Prince. But, of course"— Bareil scratched his short beard thoughtfully—"in his student days, Master Ven'Dar had rooms in Master Exeget's old house, the Precept House. That was many years ago, of course, but Exeget took no other students, except for the Prince himself. Master Ven'Dar might have kept the rooms. Few people would know of them. And with so few members of the Preceptorate any more, the chance of discovery would be small. Close to the Prince. Private. Yes, if the Preceptor is to be found anywhere in the city, I would guess he might be there."

"All right. Stay out of sight and keep Roxanne safe.
I'll meet you back here as close to sunset as I can
manage."

"My lady, please—"

"I remember the way to the Precept House, and yes,
I will be very careful. No one is expecting us so early.
We'll be safely stowed in the palace before anyone even
suspects we're in the city. Though if I can't find
Ven'Dar, perhaps I'll go looking for Men'Thor and have
a talk with him."

I hadn't thought a Dulcé could go so pale. His complexion looked like soured milk. "Madam, you *must* not!
To risk anyone seeing you, especially Men'Thor . . . My
lady, you are the key to the Prince's reason."

"But that doesn't seem to have done much good, does
it?" I said, loosing far more anger than I should have
directed toward the kindly Dulcé. "Men'Thor and Radele will *not* destroy my family. The Lords of Zhev'Na
will *not* destroy my family. I can't depend on the Prince's
reason, and I can't depend on any of these Dar'Nethi
who believe that my son is a devil and that I am somehow less worthy of their concern because I do no magic.
I have to do something."

"We should go with you," said Roxanne, who had
been uncharacteristically quiet as we walked through the
dappled parkland. "This fellow is right. It's foolish for
you to risk encountering these sorcerers who've come
near murdering you. But I understand you have to do
it. So Bareil and I will stay close and be ready to rescue
you or distract them, if need be. My presence could present them a mystery! As Gerick could tell you, I am quite
accomplished at intrigues and deceptions."

Knowing how I would bridle at such insinuations myself, I resisted the temptation to ask her if she was sure
she wished to put herself at such risk. She was not a
stupid girl. Gerick had trusted her with his life. "All
right then. Come along."

Roxanne jerked her head in satisfaction, and while
Bareil spluttered and moaned, we pulled our scarves
down low about our faces and merged with the preoccupied traffic in the streets.

CHAPTER 28

The city bristled with gossip about Men'Thor and Ven'Dar and what was to happen that night. Among the other opinions and speculations, tossed through the streets from person to person like a child's ball, was certainty that the mysterious boy, the Prince's son, who had not been seen since he was acknowledged before the Preceptorate, was to be disinherited. Perhaps the youth was dead, the rumors speculated, a victim of the same villains who had murdered the Preceptor Jayereth and the Circle. Perhaps he was truly corrupted by the Lords, as rumor had had it four years ago. That must be why he had never been brought to Avonar. No one even knew the boy's name. The Prince had claimed that the secrecy was for his son's protection, but now . . .

Unease pricked at me like thorns in my clothes as we hurried through the crowded streets.

The Precept House of the Dar'Nethi stood behind tall gray walls. Though I had seen it only once before, I could not mistake the formidable house where the child D'Natheil had been tested by the demanding Exeget and found wanting in all but the skills of war. In this same house Karon had finally recovered the full memory of his lost life and terrible death. And in the vast meeting chamber on its lower level, Gerick had been brought from Zhev'Na and acknowledged as Karon's son and successor before the Preceptorate and Darzid/Ziddari, the Third Lord of Zhev'Na.

The blocky edifice was altogether ordinary in appearance for a house that had seen events of such extraordinary strangeness and significance: three stories of rough

blue-gray stonework and many tall glass windows as
were common throughout Avonar, but none of the
graceful galleries or fountains, wide porches, or romantic, cloistered gardens the Dar'Nethi loved. Perhaps its
severity was intended to be a reminder of its more serious purpose, as a meeting place for the Preceptorate and
the residence of its head.

We slipped through the stable, a discreet entry at the
back of the gardens that Paulo had discovered years ago.
Bareil led us quickly across the manicured grounds, over
a low, ivy-covered wall, and across a grassy nook to a
side door. Our luck held. The door was unlocked, left
so quite often, so Bareil said, for Preceptors who needed
to take a breath of air during an extended debate.

The Dulcé led us through a tangle of dim passages to
the marble-floored foyer, where a broad staircase led
downward to the council chamber. We planned to slip
around the corner and up the narrower steps that led to
the third floor. There, at the back of the house, Bareil
had said I would find Ven'Dar's old rooms. While I
sought out the Preceptor, Bareil would keep Roxanne
safely out of sight.

Just as we were ready to step from the passage, someone came up the stairs from the council chamber.
". . . called in every commander for new orders," said a
male voice. "It's going to be all or nothing, I think.
Ce'Aret is about crazy with it. I heard her tell Preceptor
Mem'Tara that"—the voice dropped to a whisper as the
speaker stepped into the echoing foyer—"he's gone off
his head since his lady died. He can't grieve for her. He
can't follow the Way."

"It's as Men'Thor says," said a much older man,
wheezing slightly. "It's no good when we get mixed up
with mundanes. They're not like us."

We held back in the dim passageway. The unseen
speakers could be no more than twenty paces from us.

"When the Prince first came back from Zhev'Na, all
of us in Terrison could see how he followed the Way.
So much hardship . . . so much pain and grief . . . but
it had made him stronger . . . kinder . . . and such
power . . . Just to watch him work a healing filled my

heart with peace. It's what made me come to serve him here, so maybe I could learn how it was done."

"It ate away at him, though," said the second man, "the other world . . . the woman . . . the boy that was snatched by the Lords and rescued. I've heard he keeps traveling across the Bridge to that place. The Bridge wasn't meant to be crossed. Who knows what harm might come from such doings?"

"But—"

"Hsst! Someone comes."

A tall, large-boned woman with a long dark braid strode past not five paces from me, emerging from the very stair that was my goal. "F'Lyr! Kry'Star!"

"Yes, Preceptor?" Two men in light blue robes stepped into view at the top of the Chamber steps.

So the woman was Mem'Tara, the Alchemist Karon had named the newest Preceptor. I could see only her back. She wore a dark green robe of the formal style that the Dar'Nethi Preceptors wore on solemn occasions, draped gracefully about her large frame and belted with a silken cord.

"Please send word to Men'Thor that his steward may inspect the residence on the day after tomorrow. The Prince wants everything in Master Exeget's library moved to the storage room nearest his apartments in the palace. Bareil will know where to put it all. Beyond that, my lord says that everything in Exeget's workroom and apartments can be burned for all he cares."

"Yes, ma'am. As you say. Is the Prince coming down to speak with Ce'Aret? She awaits him in the council chamber."

"The Prince has already returned to the palace. He said"—the tall woman hesitated—"to inform Ce'Aret he has nothing to say to her at present. The Preceptorate convenes at sixth hour, and she may voice her opinions then." Shaking her head, she added, "Offer my apologies to Preceptor Ce'Aret."

The two men bowed again, and the older one followed Mem'Tara out of my sight in the direction of the front door. The younger man adjusted his robes and hurried down the wide marble steps.

I peeked carefully from my hiding place, whispering over my shoulder to Bareil. "No one there." Only the mask of the god Vasrin that hung high over the downward stair, the two perfect faces serenely unaware of the apprehension choking the city.

We hurried around the corner and up the stairs. Though the first and second floors of the Precept House were quiet at the moment, they looked well used. Open doors gave glimpses of furnishings and rugs. Closed doors were well polished and marked with symbols I didn't know. Books were stacked on narrow tables that lined the passages, alongside carafes and teapots, rolled maps and pens and inkwells. These rooms would be the studies and workrooms of the Preceptors and those who worked for them overseeing the training and practice of sorcery throughout Gondai.

At the second landing, Bareil pressed my arm, pointed to the first door in the passage, and then motioned me to continue upward. The Dulcé guided Roxanne through the door and closed it behind her. He snatched a book from one of the tables and leaned casually against the door, ready to watch the stair behind me.

I tiptoed around the corner, up the last stair, and down the passage. The wood floor of the third-level passage was thick with dust, unmarked by footprints. The dim sunlight from a grimy round window at the far end of the passage revealed no furnishings but a scuffed leather trunk shoved to one side, its brass fittings tarnished to the color of iron, and two broken chairs, shoved into one corner. Open doors revealed a series of small, unfurnished rooms. Closed doors were plain and unmarked. Storage rooms and student rooms, Bareil had said.

The last door on the right appeared to have been attacked by an army of small boys. Dents, gouges, and scorch marks marred its plain surface. A closer look revealed the traces of a large, flamboyant *V* that had been boldly incised into the door panel and then painstakingly scraped away.

Carefully I pressed the latch and swung the door inward. Unlike the other rooms I had glimpsed off this passage, this chamber was large and bright. Its furnishings were simple—little more than bed, table, two chairs, well stocked bookshelf, and a patterned rug of green and yellow. But its grace was a ceiling-high window that overlooked a sparkling lake surrounded by green hills, a living landscape that, as it happened, existed nowhere near this particular room . . . this sorcerer's room. Ven'Dar stood gazing out of the magical window, his hand stroking his short beard. The afternoon light bathed him in a golden glow, restoring his graying hair to its youthful coloring. He did not move when I stepped into the room.

"Master Ven'Dar," I said.

He jerked and spun about. "Lady Seriana! What are you doing here? How did you find me?"

"A friend's surmise."

"Bareil . . . He shouldn't have. You ought to be at the palace."

I closed the door behind me and walked as far as the patterned rug. "Why should I? Explain it to me."

He turned to the window again. "You haven't spoken with him?"

"Not since he told me to run from Calle Rein and hide. I don't even know from what or whom I was hiding."

"The Prince had informed Men'Thor and Radele that he would meet with his son on the third day from my 'death.' The two of them came to the caves, hoping to meet with him as soon as the rite was completed. To ensure his resolve had not wavered, of course. The Prince managed to evade them when he set out after you, but he commanded Bareil to leave the caves at the expected time and reveal his destination. He could not give the Preceptorate reason to doubt either his loyalty or his intent. Not until he knew more. He just didn't expect them to catch up with him so quickly."

"What have they done with Gerick? What's Karon's plan?"

"My lady, I—" Ven'Dar had been so much at peace, so sure of himself in his tower and in the Caves of Laennara, but now his quiet was the uneasy stillness of a summer afternoon with thunderheads looming black on the horizon. He tugged at his beard, and his gaze flicked from me to the window and back again. "Your son is in the palace. Many years ago a cell was built there for Dar'Nethi who must be held . . . powerless."

"He is imprisoned, then."

With a slight movement of shoulder and hand, Ven'Dar acknowledged it.

"What's to happen to him? I know Karon was here not an hour past. What did he say?"

Ven'Dar grimaced. "I can tell you nothing more."

"You cannot or will not?"

He shook his head and pointed to a chair. "Sit down with me. We'll have a glass of wine and talk for a while. Perhaps I can help you understand."

I remained standing. "Gerick is my son. I have a right to know what's going to happen to him."

"My lady," he said, "please do not ask me questions I cannot answer."

Karon believed Ven'Dar to be a man who prized keeping faith with the Way of the Dar'Nethi above safety, above comfort, above everything else he valued. A man supremely honest. Even in our short acquaintance, I had seen enough to confirm that opinion. No amount of sarcasm or fury, wheedling or tears, was going to get me anywhere Ven'Dar wasn't prepared to take me. "Then tell me this, Preceptor. Who swore you to this oath? Was it Karon or was it D'Natheil?"

He flinched as if I'd slapped him. Then, sighing heavily, he looked me full in the eye. "I don't know. I hope. I've gambled . . . heavily . . . on the answer. But I don't know."

I walked over to his window and glared at the pastoral landscape. Ven'Dar wisely kept his peace until I spoke again. Only one other person might know what was happening. In only one place might I be able to do something. "I must see Gerick," I said at last.

Ven'Dar rubbed the back of his neck, grimacing and nodding. "I agree. You should."

I was so prepared for a refusal or some further claim of ignorance or oath-swearing that I was left stammering. "But— Well, then. Will you take me?"

"The Prince will have my head for it, if I'm not careful. And we'd best go now. The sooner the better, I think. But I beg of you, my lady . . . afterward . . . do as the Prince asks you. Our only hope is in his wisdom and in the work we've done to bring him to this point with his true heart. You must stay hidden until he is ready to reveal his purpose. His enemies must believe you are dead."

"I'll think about it after I've seen Gerick."

I didn't see Bareil as we crept down the stairs, and I dared not delay to search for him lest Ven'Dar change his mind. The Dulcé would figure out what had happened.

We left the Precept House grounds by way of a tree-shaded path and a small gate, hidden in a tangle of overgrown ivy that seemed to grow back thicker than before as soon as we tore our way through it. Ven'Dar led me through the city, pausing at each turning of the way to move his hand as if brushing sand from the path in front of us. No gaze settled on us all the way to the palace.

Soon Ven'Dar was leading me down a long sloping passageway through the heart of the fortress of the Princes of Avonar. Lamps mounted along the polished gray walls of the passage flared into life as we approached and faded again when we were well past, a small wonder in a city of wonders. In another life I would have asked Ven'Dar how such things fit with the science and nature I knew. In another life, I could imagine Ven'Dar joining the stimulating company at Windham, jousting with my cousin Martin over the proper uses of magic and the comparative delights of conversation and mind-speaking. That would not have been the life where my son was the prisoner of my husband.

When we came to a metal-banded door at the end of the passage, the Preceptor pressed a finger to his lips. Then he closed into himself for a moment, so clearly removing himself from the existence I shared that I half expected him to vanish. But, instead, he spread his upturned hands slightly apart as if strewing a handful of seeds for a flock of birds. When his eyes blinked open, he pressed a finger to his lips yet again and cautiously pulled the huge door open.

Across an empty, windowless room of massive stone, four guards, two with pikes, two with drawn swords, barred access to an iron gate. But as Ven'Dar took my hand and led me across the chamber, their eyes did not move in the slightest. We slipped around behind them and through the gate without challenge. Yet, in the instant we latched the iron gate behind us, one of the four hurried across the room and slammed his open palm against the outer door, peering into the outer passage and yelling, "Who's there?"

Ven'Dar shoved me into the deepest shadow behind the gate. One of the jutting stone columns that supported the gate protruded from the passage wall just enough to hide us. There, like rabbits caught in the open meadow, we held motionless, our backs flattened against the stone wall.

"I'd swear to my own mother I heard steps out there," said the guard, scratching his head and retaking his position beside his three comrades. "Guess I was wrong."

"We're all skittish," said one of the guards—a woman. "What if the Three come to free their Fourth? And what would our people say if they knew he was here? We don't know if the cell can even hold the power of a Lord."

"Not sure I believe one of the cursed ones is here. Not after so long. He doesn't have the look I expected of a Lord. I'd heard they've metal faces with jewels for their eyes."

Signaling me to remain still, Ven'Dar slipped farther down the passage that would take us deeper into the bowels of the palace. The guards' backs formed a solid wall on the other side of the gate.

"They can change their appearance at will," said the woman. "Take anyone's body they want and use it till it's dead. It's why you're not to look on him. Not ever."

"He ought to be dead," spoke up the largest of the four, a barrel-chested man who was closest to me. His

thick jaw was pulsing, and he flexed thick fingers on the
pike-shaped weapon that glowed blue in the dim light.
"After finding my two brothers spitted like suckling pigs
two years ago . . . still warm they were, with those collars
grown into their flesh . . . Eyes of darkness! It makes
me want to slit this prisoner's throat. I never felt that
way before—*wanting* somebody to die by my own hand.
I can't see why the Prince would keep a Lord alive."

The man standing next to the speaker laid a hairy
hand on his comrade's shoulder. "He won't be much
longer. . . ."

A hand touched my own sleeve. I jumped, grazing an
elbow on the column. Ven'Dar led me down another
sloping passage, past another quartet of paralyzed
guards, and into a dimly lit chamber, bare of any furnish-
ing save a wooden bench pushed against one wall and a
narrow, raised stone platform or table in the center. Eyebolts had been seated in the corners of the stone table.
The only break in the gray stone walls was a rectangular
gate of narrowly spaced bars that shone silver in the
light of a single small lamp. The air was thick with enchantment, heavy, dreadful, weighing on my spirit like a
mountain of lead. I shuddered.

"We've only a few moments," whispered the Preceptor, as he closed the heavy door softly behind us. "A
Dar'Nethi Watcher has already detected my winding and
will be here very quickly to investigate. Not a subtle
enchantment, but the only way to get us in."

Ven'Dar motioned me to the bars, standing close behind me as I peered through. The cell was dark. The
weak gleam of the guardroom lamp reached through the
bars only far enough to illuminate the wooden bowl,
filled with meat and bread, and the full mug that sat just
inside the enclosure.

A light flared at my shoulder, casting a sharp, barred
shadow deep into the cell. The prisoner was sitting on
the floor in the corner, and when he held up his hands
to ward off the new brightness, silver bands about his
wrists glinted in the light. More of the shining metal
bound his ankles and linked him to ring bolts on the

wall. The bands and chains and the silver strips embedded in the walls and ceiling would hold the enchantments that kept him powerless, if such was possible. Two blankets lay crumpled on the floor beside him.

"If you've come to gloat, get it over and go away. I prefer the dark and would as soon not look on you."

"Gerick, dear one, are you all right?"

"Mother!" Squinting into the brightness, he jumped up and moved toward the bars the few steps his restraints would allow. "What are you— Mother, you must get away from here!"

"I can't believe this. I thought he'd at least—"

"How did you get here? He would never have brought you into so much danger." Gerick wasn't even listening to me.

"I brought her," said my companion. "Ven'Dar is the name. We've already met, I believe. You remember— the list."

"You're a fool, sir. Take her away from here." Frost edged his words. "Mother, please go. Hide yourself away where you can't be found. There's nothing to be done here."

"I won't let him hurt you."

"He'll do what he has to do. But you mustn't be anywhere near me. Things could happen. . . . You don't understand how much they hate you—the Three."

Ven'Dar clamped a hand on my shoulder. "Time for a discreet exit, my lady. I'm sorry."

Though I, too, heard the shouts and running footsteps from the passageway, I had no intention of leaving. But Ven'Dar closed his eyes and spread his hands again and was soon tugging insistently on my arm. "We must trust the Prince. And that means you must do as I tell you."

"Gerick, you are not what you think," I said, as Ven'Dar gently, but insistently, pried my hands from the bars and dragged me across the room. "Remember everything I've told you. The Lords do not create. They only destroy, and they care for no one but themselves. You are not one of them. I still believe it. I'll always believe it."

The enchanted light illuminated the face of my beautiful son, who smiled at me with a sweet, sad radiance. "I
am what I am. I'm sorry."

Sorry . . . as if sixteen years of horror inflicted on an
innocent child were his fault. I wanted to scream out
the injustice.

"Absolute silence, madam," whispered Ven'Dar, his
powerful arm crushing my back against the gray stone
beside the door to the passageway. "You are a wall. Act
like it."

The guardroom door burst open, and eight armed men
hurried into the chamber, followed by Karon, Men'Thor,
and a stooped man in gray. Radele trailed behind, remaining in the open doorway, watching the others as if
he were only an observer, not one of their party. Not
the slimmest shadow remained in the room once they'd
brought their torches inside, but to my mystification, no
one remarked Ven'Dar and me. Deciding to take
Ven'Dar's odd suggestion as legitimate, I emptied my
mind, and tried to think like a wall: flat, silent, so ordinary as to be unnoticeable.

"What foolishness is this, Ben'Shar?" Karon snapped.
His hard gaze whipped about the room, passing over
Ven'Dar and me without a moment's pause. "I see no
intruder. These 'rumblings' you noted must have come
from your own belly. Was I dragged from a Preceptorate
meeting because you failed to digest your lunch?"

"But, my lord, it was a powerful enchantment—a
winding, I'm sure of it," said the stooped man, scratching
his chest as his eyes darted about the room. "This prison
block is a snarl of windings. I'm never wrong about
these things."

"Perhaps the prisoner himself has a rumbling belly,"
said Men'Thor, peering through the bars. "Clearly he
hungers, and there's not enough pain and fear in Avonar
on which to gorge himself. Perhaps he summons his dark
brethren to feed him."

"Their need is their weakness," said Radele, softly.
No one could have heard him save Ven'Dar and me,
who were but a handsbreadth from his back.

"You have no idea of what my 'dark brethren' are

capable," said the voice from behind the bars—a voice so cold, so alien to the sweet vision that still hung in my memory, that I wondered if I'd missed seeing some other prisoner locked in with my son. "These pitiful bands you use to detain me are but sand to the hurricane of their power. They'll devour you, and you can't even see it coming. Touch my mind. Open the door you find there, and you'll see what your Prince has seen. You'll understand how they appreciate mind-stealing murderers like you and your son."

"Silence!" roared Karon, slamming his hands into the bars. "You will not speak, Dieste . . . Destroyer. For four years you've twisted words, twisted lives, befouled the world with your deceptions. No more. Tomorrow you will show what you really are. Let your putrid brethren come when you cry out to them, and I'll put an end to them, too." Karon raised his fist toward the cell, and the bars began to glow, first silvery blue, and then yellow. And when they flared a brilliant white that seared my eyes, from behind them came a scream of such mortal agony that the Dar'Nethi warriors shrank from it, and the old man Ben'Shar covered his ears. Ven'Dar pressed his hand to my mouth, but he could stop neither my tears nor his own.

Once the interminable cry had died away, a stone-faced Karon pushed past his companions and the guards and vanished into the outer passage. The shaken soldiers stood aside to let a somber Men'Thor and the stooped Watcher pass, but Radele did not accompany them.

After the last guards had left the chamber, Radele stepped up to the wall of fading fire and peered into the dark silence beyond it. "He'll speak no vileness for a while," he said to no one, as he stroked the bars with his fingertips. "A taste of the Heir's power looks to be quite effective. It would finish the devils forever if wielded properly."

His face fierce and determined, Radele spun on his heel and followed the others into the passage.

When all was quiet and dim once again, Ven'Dar, still pressing me tightly to the wall, spoke in a quiet voice that I thought might bore a hole in my skull. "Your son lives. There is nothing to be done for him, except what he and his father ask of you. Hide yourself away until the time is right. Hold him in your heart . . . and the Prince also."

When the Preceptor released me I hurried to the cell and fell to my knees, gripping the still-warm bars. Gerick sprawled facedown on the stone floor. Unmoving. On his arms were long, angry scratches as if he'd tried to claw the manacles away. I had no talent to tell me he lived, and saw no other sign of it, so I had to take Ven'Dar's word. "This is not over, dear one," I said to him, as the Preceptor drew me away.

Like shadows we passed through the guard posts once again, and into a maze of deserted back stairs, dusty storage rooms, and passageways long unused. Dusk lingered in a weed-grown courtyard. I followed Ven'Dar without question. It was as well Gerick had lain unhearing, for my brave words had no more substance than a single raindrop in the desert. It mattered not in the least what I did. I put no faith in Ven'Dar's hopeful intimation that there was some underlying purpose in what I had just witnessed.

Up three flights of stairs. At the end of a long, unlit passage hung with cobwebs and faded tapestries—a passage that looked as if D'Arnath himself had been the last Dar'Nethi to walk it—the Preceptor pulled open a wide, plain door and ushered me into a beautifully appointed room, a softly lit haven of comfortable couches, deep carpets, and shelves of finely bound books. A fire popped and crackled in a brick fireplace, and on a small table next to it, ivory and jade chessmen stood ready on an onyx chessboard. Everywhere were small things—a watercolor of a lighthouse, an ivory horse, a needlework cushion—unmatched in the grace and loveliness of their working.

Yet the place might as well have been my hovel at Dunfarrie. Numb, heartsick, I sank into a fat, cushioned chair and laid my useless hands in my lap.

Ven'Dar pulled a footstool close to my chair and sat on it. His gray-blue eyes were troubled. "I cannot stay, my lady. Only a little while longer and my own hiding must end. I understand your grief, but I did not take you there to hasten it, magnify it, or resign you to it. I took you there to remind you of your power. Do not forget what you saw. Who you saw. Do not forget what you've given him all these years. Hold fast. The Lords of Zhev'Na hate you as they have hated no one since D'Arnath himself. Here at the culmination of their thousand-year war, you, a seemingly powerless woman, have denied them their prize twice over. You must not falter in this third challenge."

He enfolded my cold hands in his warm ones. "Tonight, at one hour past moonrise, the Prince will speak to the people of Avonar from the balcony you can see from that window over there. Even now his messengers summon the Dar'Nethi from the Vales, from the borderlands, from the Wastes, from the city—at least one person from every family. Whatever may be the result of my lord's words, know that you bear my deepest regard, and that in any way that may be possible, I will be forever at your service."

He lifted my limp hand and kissed it, and then he rose and left me there alone.

CHAPTER 29

For an hour after Ven'Dar left I sat in my chair and indulged in self-pity, an exercise at which I began to think I could become quite expert. Why had they bothered to bring me out of my living death, if only to witness horror? Why open my ears, if they were only to hear my husband in mad rage and my child in agony, and no explanation for any of it? What had gone wrong at Calle Rein just when I believed Karon had put D'Natheil in his place?

But an hour was enough. Self-pity would change nothing, and I had never been able to abide unanswerable questions. I forced myself to get up and walk about the room, hoping the activity might stimulate some semblance of purposeful thought. Carafes of wine and water stood on a sideboard, alongside one of the marvelous Dar'Nethi ceramic teapots that stayed constantly warm. I poured myself tea and then abandoned the cup on the oaken table when I wandered over to one of the windows draped in gauzy fabric the color of jade.

The window looked out over the grand command and parkland that fronted the palace. No sign yet of the rising moon, so Ven'Dar's mystery would have to wait. The evening was quiet in the city, only a few people hurrying past. Where were Bareil and Roxanne? Surely the Dulcé would bring the princess to safety when it became clear I had left the Precept House by another way.

Absentmindedly I moved to the bookshelves and brushed my fingers over one of the leather-bound books, noting to my surprise that its title was in Leiran. The next also, and the next—and all of them familiar. On the shelf was a book of Isker poetry, and beside it a book of Vallorean folktales—very like one I had cherished long ago. I looked about the room again, wondering at it. Everything was just on the edge of familiarity. Nothing mysterious, nothing of magical design save the teapot. A burnished brass lectern stood by the windowed wall, positioned to take advantage of the light. A suspicious guess as to what I might find there was proved right when I found a silver flute lying on a sheet of music that had been transcribed in a fine hand.

"It is a lovely room, is it not?"

A tall young woman in a gown of deep green stood just inside the door, holding a tray of fruit, cheese, and fragrant pastries. "You must pardon my entrance without knocking, my lady, but I must keep my hands where they are. I can be rather clumsy, if I'm not careful." She set the tray on a low table between two comfortable chairs, and something about the way she slid her hand along the edge of the table as she placed the tray, and the way she turned exactly half a revolution to face me told me she was blind. My guess was confirmed when her blue eyes failed to settle on my own.

"You're Aimee . . ."

"Indeed, my lady." She extended her hands, palms up, and dipped her knee.

". . . Gar'Dena's daughter, to whom he promised to bring a rinoceroos."

The girl had a smile that could melt snow. She'd been no more than thirteen when I'd met her at the giant Gem Worker's house—his beloved youngest daughter, now a graceful young woman with hair like curls of sunlight held off her face by an amber comb. Pleasure and animation brought a flush to her fair cheeks, her brows rising and eyes sparkling.

"He did it, you know. For my fifteenth birthday, just after the Prince's return from Zhev'Na. Three of the great beasts right in our house. We had to rebuild half the main floor and hire thirty Gardeners and Tree Delvers to replant our gardens. But no girl ever had such a birthday."

"I'm so sorry about your father, Aimee. He was a wonderful friend and a good man."

Her smile softened, but did not dim. " 'A glorious man of great appetites,' as he would say. My sisters and I were blessed to have him." She motioned to the food she'd brought. "It is such a dear pleasure to have you well again, my lady. Come, you must be hungry."

The border between hunger and nausea can be very fine. I invited Aimee to sit and share the fruit and pastries that looked and smelled so delicious. But one small bite of cheese came near gagging me. "Tell me, Aimee, how did you come to be charged with my care?"

She held a ripe strawberry she had been on the verge of popping into her mouth. "The Prince summoned me to the palace early this morning and said he had a great secret and needed my help. He asked me if I would please to come here and keep you company, assisting you in any way possible. Only a few people know of these rooms: myself and Bareil; Papa did, of course, and . . . the Preceptor Ven'Dar . . ." She frowned as she mentioned Ven'Dar. "My lady, do you know—" She stopped short and ate her strawberry.

"How is it that you were privy to such a great secret as these rooms?" So many uncertainties. Perhaps she was privy to other secrets.

Her flush deepened as she blotted her lips with a square of linen. "Because I made them."

Avonar was truly full of wonders.

"Two years ago the Prince asked if I would help him prepare a suite of rooms for you—where you might feel at home were you to come here to live. He knew that Avonar, for all its beauties, would be strange and unfamiliar—the palace, especially."

"But how did you know all this? The paintings, the flute . . ." I was willing to accept that a blind Dar'Nethi sorceress could conjure books and furniture, but everything was so perfectly right.

"The Prince would describe to me each piece he wanted. My talent is in Imaging, creating an exact depiction of objects in my thoughts. I would then have the piece made to match the image I had created, using my skill and my hands to judge. When I thought it was ready, the Prince would tell me if I'd got it right or not. It was a great pleasure to him. He took to coming here himself to sit and work almost every day. I think it made him feel close to you."

I pressed a hand to my mouth and took a moment to shut off the welling tears. No time for them. No use in them. "You did well, Aimee. Very well indeed."

"Thank you, my lady. Tell me . . . was there not to be another lady with you this night?"

"Yes, but we became separated on our way. Bareil should be bringing her very soon."

"Then she's quite safe, I'm sure. Bareil is very wise."

"Yes." I picked at the nut-filled pastry on my plate. "So, Aimee, the Prince knows I'm here?"

"Oh, yes. It's how I knew when to come just now, for he sent me a message that you had arrived. He says no one else is to have the least inkling that the grievous reports of your death are false."

"But he said nothing of when he might come here."

"No, my lady. I'm sorry. Nothing."

Karon, what are you doing? Why won't you tell me?

As Aimee and I set the plates and bowls back on her tray, a soft knock on the outer door announced Bareil. "My lady, what a relief to find you here safely. And Mistress Aimee, a pleasure, as always."

"I'm sorry we were separated," I said. "I was brought here by the gentleman. . . ." Gods, I hated all these secrets.

"I understand, madam." He closed the door carefully.

"Bareil, where's the princess?"

"That's what I've come to tell you, my lady. Unfortunately Ce'Aret's aide, F'Lyr, saw me in the passage outside the Masters' Waiting Chamber, the room where I had hidden the young lady, and insisted I speak with the Preceptor Ce'Aret. No insistence that I was on the Prince's business would satisfy him, so I had to go, lest Ce'Aret herself come up to fetch me and discover the princess. I told the young lady to remain quietly hidden until I could return for her. Though I apologized for abandoning her, she did not seem frightened. She seems . . . uh . . ."

". . . a very resilient young lady," I said.

"Indeed. Before I could return to her, the Prince arrived for the Preceptorate meeting. He asked me only if you were safe, and I said you were, but I didn't tell him that the princess was not yet here"—he swallowed hard and glanced up—"and I do most sincerely fear his wrath if he discovers it. Even worse, when I slipped up the stairs to fetch her, Radele was entering the Masters' Waiting Chamber! The girl must have hidden herself or gone elsewhere, for I heard no evidence of discovery. The Prince was waiting for me, so I could not stay long. Now I am commanded to return to him immediately, so I've no assurance as to when I'll be free to retrieve the young lady."

"I can find the way there and back," I said, standing up. "I'll go for her myself." Roxanne was sensible. She would not let herself get caught. She would remember how to keep herself empty . . . surely she would remember.

"You must not leave the palace, my lady," said Aimee, frowning. "The Prince was most emphatic about that. Perhaps I could retrieve the young lady. No one will remark me."

"But how—" I almost bit my tongue.

Aimee's laugh chimed like silver. "If you or the good Dulcé will permit me to know her through your eyes, I'll be able to recognize her."

"It would be a great service," I said, unsure what she meant.

"Of course, I can't go just now. Everyone is gathering to hear the Prince speak, and so many people abroad will confuse my ability to travel. But the Precept House will be deserted, and that will keep her safe. Later, when the crowds thin out a bit, I should be able to find her quite easily. I'll go the moment the Prince is finished speaking."

A relieved Bareil said he would be happy for Aimee to take an image of Roxanne from his thoughts. While

they discussed descriptions, images, and the most discreet routes by which to bring Roxanne into the palace,
a low hum from outside drew me to back to the window.

This apartment lay on the inner face of the curved
north wing of the palace, so the cushioned window seat
had an excellent view of the broad front steps and the
royal balcony above them, as well as the commard and
parkland below and beyond. As the filmy draperies
shifted in the breeze, I settled there and watched a
crowd grow, pouring from every street, carrying candles
and lanterns and magical lights of all kinds, until the city
looked like rivers of fireflies replenishing a jeweled sea.
Beyond them all, low in the east over the mountains,
hung the huge silver crescent of the moon.

The parapet of the wide royal balcony had been
carved with the arch and stars and rampant lions of
D'Arnath. On tall posts at its corners hung lamps shining
with pure white light, their fiery brilliance reflected and
multiplied a hundredfold by the tall, many-paned windows behind the balcony.

Three people in the formal robes of the Preceptors
filed out and took seats on the balcony. My vantage was
close enough that I could recognize them: tall Mem'Tara
whose long, bony face and heavy braid I had glimpsed
earlier in the Precept House, the fiery little Ce'Aret, and
the stoop-shouldered Ustele who crouched low in his
chair. Radele, attired in magnificent robes of green,
trimmed in gold and gems, followed the Preceptors. The
imposing older man that accompanied him could be
none but his father Men'Thor, even more resplendent
in red. I had met Men'Thor, they had told me, but not
in any state where I could remember him.

"The Prince comes," said Aimee from behind me.
"His presence fills the city."

The Preceptors stood and the crowd hushed when
Karon stepped onto the balcony from the doorway and
walked to the center. The night wind gently shifted his
plain silk robe of dark blue, so that the narrow silver
trim at its hem and sleeves glinted in the lamplight. In
the traditional fashion for a Dar'Nethi Healer, a silver
band bound up his left sleeve, exposing the scars on his

arm. The open front of the robe revealed the sword and dagger of D'Arnath sheathed at his waist.

"People of Avonar, brave warriors, defenders of the Vales, of the city, of the last hope of the worlds, I have called you here in grief and in hope, to tell you of great changes in the world."

The hair rose on the back of my neck. Though his speech was not shouted in the usual harshness of public oratory, I could hear him as clearly as if he stood three paces from my seat.

"Four years ago I swore an oath to break the bonds of terror forged by those who rule in Zhev'Na. I promised to serve you in the ways laid down for D'Arnath's Heirs, to heal the wounds of war, and to nurture my son to follow after me, so that life could thrive in all the worlds that have been given into our care. In all of these things I have failed."

No breath, no cry, no whisper of sound muted the stark clarity of his judgment.

"Every man and woman within sound of my voice has lost someone to the evil that is Zhev'Na; you have seen your sons and daughters, your parents, brothers, sisters, and cousins enslaved, tortured, driven mad, or slain. You know that my family has suffered alongside yours, and that only by the talent and skill of your Preceptors do I live to walk the beauteous hills of Avonar. Tonight I have come to tell you that with me, the line of D'Arnath will end."

My body, mind, and spirit turned to stone, while throughout the command the long-held breath of rumor and speculation was released at last. From here and there a mournful wail arose, only to be quickly hushed when Karon began to speak again.

"My son, who was acknowledged five years ago before the Preceptors of the Dar'Nethi, has been corrupted by the Lords of Zhev'Na. By his own hand was his mother, my beloved wife, struck down, and by his acts were the Preceptors Jayereth and Gar'Dena and the Circle of our most brilliant Talents destroyed. His guilt is clear, his subjugation to the Lords indisputable, and at one hour past dawn tomorrow, he will die for these acts. My own hand must accomplish this terrible deed, for only the Heir of D'Arnath can judge a Dar'Nethi life too evil, too dangerous, too broken to continue. This is a bitter sorrow for Gondai as well as for me, and I will need all of your strength to enable me to encompass such grief.

"But you must not lose heart, for the crooked paths take us to the most unexpected places, places beyond our dreaming, and for those who follow the Way, our sorrows bring us power. In the choosing of my new successor have I been forced to give thought to all our troubles, our life, our history, our strengths, our failures, all that I—and you—have become in this interminable war, and I have come to the conviction that the changes thrust upon us by these dread events will be the key to our future. For too long I have been so absorbed in my own distress, in my anger, and in my determination to right every evil according to my own lights that I lost sight of the Way, lost the clear vision that it offers us. Many of us have lost the Way over the past thousand years. It is the greatest evil the Lords have done to us— to make us destroy our best selves.

"The Preceptor Ce'Aret has taught me how the Heir can name a successor not of his own blood, and at dawn tomorrow so I will do. Avonar is graced by a community of worthy men and women, every one of whom has the welfare of our people at heart, every one of whom is unyielding in vigilance against the depredations of Zhev'Na, every one of whom is undisputed in courage and devotion. But only one man's vision has allowed him to see the true threat and to hold steadfast through slander and dishonor and false accusations to prove his mettle. He it is whom I have judged most worthy of D'Arnath's legacy."

Those seated on the balcony had been nodding solemnly all during Karon's words, but now several of them began to shift uneasily. Old Ustele leaned toward Men'Thor, poking at his son's chest while he whispered in his ear. But Men'Thor pushed the old man's hand away and arranged his robes to his liking once again, looking as if he were already breathing the rarefied air of royalty.

Karon took no note of those behind him. "When my day is over and a new Heir must take my place, his hand will guide you with wisdom and serve you with grace, and he will lead you to the renewal, not only of the Wastes, but of yourselves. Thus from all of us, not from the Heir alone, will come the power to maintain D'Arnath's Bridge and restore our world. From midnight tonight will my successor stand alone in vigil at the Bridge, and at dawn tomorrow will he be invested with the knowledge of the Heir, to hold in trust until such time as I can no longer serve. On this night, in the presence of the host of Avonar, do I, D'Natheil, the only legitimate Heir of the mighty D'Arnath, name as my successor Ven'Dar yn Cyran. *Ce'na davonet, Ven'Dar, teca Giré D'Arnath!*"

From the crowd swelled murmurs of wonder, of disbelief, of confusion and dismay that the Prince had gone mad to name one that two days of rumors had claimed dead or disgraced. But when Ven'Dar stepped through the door at the back of the balcony, opened his palms, and knelt to Karon, the murmurs erupted into cries of joy and approval, of hope long held close and faith renewed, until the sound rolled through the city like a hurricane. Discontent rumbled beneath the wind, not a few jeers and shouts of anger invoking the name of Men'Thor. But when Karon raised up Ven'Dar and embraced him, the roar from the people came almost as one, *"Ce'na davonet, Ven'Dar, teca Giré D'Arnath!"* *All honor to you, Ven'Dar, next Heir of D'Arnath.* "Ven'Dar! Ven'Dar!"

Mem'Tara rose immediately and bent her knee to Ven'Dar, and Ce'Aret, after a stunned moment, embraced the Word Winder as if he were one of her long-lost sons. But Ustele folded his arms and maintained his seat, while Men'Thor and Radele and two or three others abruptly disappeared from the balcony through the doors at the back.

"He's killed him," I said to no one and everyone.

"Did he not say tomorrow?" said Bareil, softly, from behind me.

"No, not Gerick—not yet—but Ven'Dar. He has purposely humiliated Men'Thor before the host of Avonar. He cannot believe Men'Thor will accept it. Ven'Dar's life is at terrible risk."

"Surely then, the Prince will watch."

Surely . . . Of course. Enrage Men'Thor so he'll make a mistake. Remove his threat by catching him in undeniable treachery. And name Ven'Dar as the successor, so that when Gerick is dead . . .

As thunder follows the lightning flash, I saw the truth at last. I did not know Karon's plan, but I knew what was to be its result. He was going to die, too—and not just the part of him that was my husband. At some time in the past hours, he had decided he was not going to leave D'Natheil behind to destroy Avonar.

"My lady, I must . . . are you all right? You look unwell."

Wordless, I waved off Bareil's hand. I was very much not all right.

"I must go to the Prince, my lady, as I was commanded. Is there a message I could carry for you?"

There was far too much, even for a Dulcé, who could bear the knowledge of a hundred libraries at once. What could be said?

"Just tell him . . . I understand the implications of his choice."

And at last I also understood why it was so important that I remain hidden. I was evidence against Men'Thor. If Men'Thor detected Karon's trap or decided to bide his time, Karon needed evidence to indict him anyway. He would want to leave Ven'Dar free to teach and to guide the people of Avonar without the threat of Men'Thor's meddling. And I had left Roxanne in the Precept House, carrying the knowledge of my existence and my whereabouts. *Fool of a woman, why didn't you think?*

And in all my newfound understanding, I found no hope for Gerick. In his attempt at Calle Rein, Karon had discovered something that precipitated this convoluted strategy, and I could unravel no twisting of plot and no cleverness of words that was going to keep Gerick alive. Vaguely I considered making my way down to his prison

again, but his cell had no visible lock, and I had no shred
of power. I had come to the limits of my abilities and
understanding.

So I did nothing. As the excited crowds wandered
back to public salons or their homes, I sat in the window
seat, still envisioning Karon on the deserted balcony, the
wind caressing his long hair like a lover's hand. Gentle
Aimee brought me a shawl and a cup of tea, thinking to
quiet my shivering, but though the nights of the waning
summer were indeed growing cool, a blanket of goose
down would not have warmed me. So the girl led me to
the candlelit bedchamber and took off my shoes and
covered me with the soft blankets she had chosen just
for me. "Try to sleep, my lady, while I fetch the princess.
I'll wake you before dawn."

Curled up in the dark nest of the great bed, I had no
choice but to let go of everything. I couldn't think any
more, for there was nothing I could bear to think on.

Sometime deep in the night, long after the vigil candle
had burned itself out, I was roused from my exhausted
half-sleep. A wide hand lay on my cheek, gently brushing away my dreamer's tears. "Do not weep, beloved,"
came a voice in the dark. "All that can be done, I will
do. Listen carefully to me. You must not give up, even
in the depths of sorrow. I need you to play the part that
only you have ever been able to play. Follow the Way,
my love, and know that you will be with me forever."

Before I could shake off the heaviness of sleep or
open my eyes to see his face, he kissed my eyelids softly,
and I sank into a peaceful, embracing slumber. When
Aimee shook me awake in the dark hour before dawn
to report Roxanne still missing, I might have thought it
was all a dream, save for the rose of blazing scarlet that
bloomed at my bedside.

CHAPTER 30

Karon

D'Natheil hated waiting. His irritation would begin as a tightness in the jaw, proceed through nervous chewing of lips and fingers, leak out into restless movements of increasingly destructive tendency, and finally explode in some verbal or physical violence that served no purpose but to grow the dark and bitter core of anger that lived inside him. Inside me.

There had once lived a Gardener in Avonar, my lost Avonar, who enchanted the city gardens to bloom for one day longer each year, so that after thirty years the city was known for its marvelous climate that allowed flowers to bloom a full month longer than others. His was a story told to J'Ettanni children to teach them patience. In a life where any oddity could get you burned alive, and among a people where the savoring of every moment, every sensation, resulted in an increase of the glorious power at the root of being, patience was very near the pinnacle of the pyramid of virtue.

The necessity for patience was one of the fundamental conflicts between D'Natheil and me, the reason he had never been able to summon the power he wanted to wield, the reason I could no longer heal, and the reason I would never be able to lead the Dar'Nethi as they needed. This was, perhaps, the hardest truth revealed by the Rite of Purification. I had emerged from the Pool of Rebirth renewed in spirit and found Seri living and herself again, the most precious gift I had begged from life standing before me, yet I could not savor the moment

for needing . . . wanting . . . craving to get on with the
business of executing my son. I was as much myself as
I could ever be, and it was not enough.

So, as I lay hidden just beyond the Gate of D'Arnath's
Bridge, watching through the wall of white fire as my
friend Ven'Dar knelt in serene meditation waiting for
someone to murder him, I found myself with jaws
clenched, plunging my dagger over and over again into
the cold mud in front of my face. Cold mud was the
current aspect of the small island of stability I could
create from the constantly shifting chaos behind the
Gate. After today . . . no more. No more blood on my
sword. No more feeling the exhilarating surge of enchantment when I slipped through the roaring Gate fire.
No more of this unending dispute between the man I
was and the man I wanted to be. No more of anything,
if all went as I planned. As I ground my dagger into the
gritty slop, I almost laughed aloud at the word. *Planned.*
A comet streaking through a conjunction of the planets
was more under my control than the hours to come.

Ven'Dar had been kneeling on the pearl-gray stone
for hours, motionless, his arms outstretched to embrace
D'Arnath's fire. He was most likely freezing. His white
robe was thin, and the chamber of the Gate was chilly,
the Gate fire a manifestation of enchantment rather than
flame. But the cold, and the creeping dread of a knife
in the back, and the nagging anxiety as to whether his
friend, the Prince of Avonar, was still there behind the
roaring curtain, still awake, still watching, still sane, had
been stitched with patience into the tapestry of Ven'Dar's
life as he took his next step along the Way. I envied
Ven'Dar his patience and his cold and his fear. D'Natheil didn't understand the Way and did his best to keep
me from feeling anything but his anger.

*Think. Use this time. Plan. What if Men'Thor doesn't
take the bait? What if dawn comes and Ven'Dar is unthreat-
ened? You'll have one hour to take Seri and Ven'Dar and
Paulo before the Preceptors, confirm Ven'Dar as the successor, and convince the Preceptors that Men'Thor and his son
are murderers. Risky. Uncertain.*

A weapon snatched from an assailant's hand, imprinted with his will to do murder, would be so much better. Even Ustele would not be able to argue with it. Then I'd have done all I could do for my people's future, and I could safely move on to the day's other matters: my son and the Lords of Zhev'Na and dying.

You could have left yourself more time. Yes, speed was necessary to keep them off balance, but so many things could go wrong. I had just wanted it done.

To my relief, it was only a short time later that the door to the chamber of the Gate—purposely and publicly left unwarded as Ven'Dar began his vigil—swung open. Men'Thor, still arrayed in his elaborate finery, strode through. I wiped the mud from my dagger, drew my sword, and crouched low, ready to spring. Timing would be everything. Ven'Dar's life and Men'Thor's guilt must both be preserved. I felt neither satisfaction nor fear, only the urgency to get on with it.

Men'Thor was alone and his hands were empty as he stood glaring down at my friend like a stern father ready to mete out judgment to an errant child. "What winding did you cast to place the ruin of Avonar in your hand, Ven'Dar? What enchantment did you conjure to force the mad Prince to waste this magnificence—D'Arnath's holy fire—and leave it blazing at the feet of a minor magician?"

I could scarcely hear the brittle words, squeezed through Men'Thor's icy composure. Ven'Dar, lost in his meditation, showed no awareness of his companion.

"Of all the obstacles in my path, I never thought *you* would be the one to cause me to stumble. I never gave you credit for artifice. Why aren't you dead?" He walked around Ven'Dar like a disdainful tailor inspecting his client's worn apparel. "And now what am I to do with you? Will we be forced to make do with our mad Prince, and have you constantly at his ear encouraging his unhealthy yearning for these mundanes? At least you are one of us . . ."

If sound had any meaning behind the roaring Gate fire, Men'Thor would have heard my sigh when he pulled the dagger from beneath his gem-studded belt. Soon . . . soon it would be done.

". . . but you're a coward, aren't you?" He waved the knife before the Preceptor's unseeing eyes. "You and your discredited philosophies that have left us at the mercy of our enemies, denied us the advantages of our power, reduced us to tricksters, hardly better than these shallow, ignorant creatures from the other world. I'll not have it. Do you hear me? I'll fight you with every voice and heart I can muster to my cause."

"Voices and hearts are not enough, Father. We need more forceful, more visible weapons in this particular war."

I'd been so intent on watching Men'Thor's knife that I'd not seen Radele appear in the doorway. He leaned against the wall with his arms folded across his breast, smiling. "Even now the witnesses gather to watch the Prince invest his successor, but how much faster would they come and how many more of them, if they knew they were to witness our first true victory over the Lords. At last they'll see what viper has been nurtured in their midst and how close we've been to a second Catastrophe, a final Catastrophe. Then shall the people of Avonar decide who is to bear D'Arnath's sword."

"What do you mean?"

"You'll see. You will have everything you deserve, Father, and more."

The smiling son gave an exaggerated bow and held the door for his father. His laughter echoed across the Gate fire as he followed Men'Thor from the chamber. Men'Thor's knife was safely—annoyingly—back in its sheath.

No sooner had they gone than somewhere beyond the palace walls the sun broached the horizon. I knew the time, for Ven'Dar's arms fell heavily to his sides, and he began to stretch the cramps from his neck and shoulders, easing himself off the floor.

"I gather I'm still alive," he said, grimacing as he rubbed his knees, while at the same time trying to huddle his arms into his thin robe. "Though I'm cold enough to be a corpse, I don't think a dead man's knees would ache so much. Did our honey catch any flies?"

I stepped through the Gate fire, sheathing my dagger with such force that I split the leather. "My plotting's been no more successful than anything else. But it's not over. They're up to something. Come. Paulo is to meet us at the council chamber, and I'll send Bareil for Seri."

I started for the door, but Ven'Dar lingered, letting his gaze dwell on the towering wall of white fire, its full extent unseeable in the brilliance far above our heads. "It is magnificent, is it not? Such purity. Such power. I close my eyes and see it still; everything I look on is made more than it was. To have it be a part of me . . . it's as if I've been given new eyes. Is it that way for you?"

"Now is perhaps not a good time to ask me," I said and slammed my palm against the door, careful to watch for any ambush along our way.

As I had commanded him, Bareil was waiting for us in the small, book-lined anteroom off the council chamber. Ven'Dar sank into one of the enveloping chairs and dived most appreciatively into the steaming saffria and crusty bread Bareil set out for him. I had no time for such—and no need.

"Paulo?" I asked.

"Asleep in your private chamber, my lord," said the Dulcé. "He arrived two hours ago."

"And his report?"

"He said to tell you that all went just as planned and to wake him if you needed to know more. The lad was asleep on his feet."

One success. Good to know that something had gone right.

I nodded toward the door of the council chamber. "Is everyone present?"

"The Preceptors, the Archivists, Master Men'Thor, your commanders, the witnesses from ten families as Mistress Ce'Aret specified—all are present," said the Dulcé. "She says that when you are ready to proceed, each Preceptor will take an imprint of Master Ven'Dar, then lay hands on you for acknowledgement, much like the test of parentage."

"I remember it." An adoption rite, in essence.

"A quarter of an hour—no more—and it will be done."

"Good"—I lowered my voice—"and have you brought what I told you?"

The Dulcé looked at me solemnly and matched his tone to mine. "Yes, my lord, but—"

"You will speak of it to no one. No one. Do you understand me, Dulcé?"

"Of course, my lord." He dropped his eyes.

"So, give it to me." Into my hand Bareil slipped a red silk bag about the size of my fist. "Now you must fetch Seri. Keep her in here until I call for her."

"As you wish, my lord." He bowed very low, and turned to go without looking at me again.

I laid a hand on his arm. "There are not thanks enough for all your good service, madrissé, nor for your kindness and care that the madris cannot compel. You've never failed me. It is I who lost my way, not my Guide."

Silent, eyes averted, Bareil kissed my hand and hurried away. Ven'Dar raised his eyebrows, but I left him ignorant and shoved the small heavy bag into the leather pouch I had fastened to my belt that morning. Already in the bag was a second object, retrieved from the vault in my bedchamber last night, where it had lain for the past four years, an artifact of the Lords that made my soul shrivel to touch it. I was as prepared as I could be for the eventualities of the morning. Laying my hand on the latch of the council-chamber door, I said, "Shall we see what surprises our friends have readied for us?"

The three members of the Preceptorate were seated at the long table on a raised dais at the far end of the huge windowless room. It might have been a winter's night instead of a summer morning, for the lamps were lit and a fire crackled in the wide hearth behind the Preceptors' table, burning off the chill of the eternal stone. My stomach never failed to give me a twinge when I walked into this room. The first time I'd sat in the Prince's chair facing the dais was the day I'd stuck a knife in my gut to convince the Lords of Zhev'Na I was mad. On that day death had been but a painful feint. The paths of life were uncompromising.

"Ce'na davonet, Giré D'Arnath," intoned Ce'Aret as I entered. The greeting was echoed by the others in the room, and I extended my hands, palms up, as ritual demanded.

The air of the room was thick with anticipation. Perhaps fifty people, dressed in their finest and fully aware of their privilege, were in attendance. Their eyes were wide and alert for the least nuance of expression from the principal players, ears pricked, shoulders straight, voices kept low. Every whisper was cause for excitement; every sound quickly hushed lest it distract from full perception of the historic event.

The old woman spoke with the authority of age and righteous power. "What business have you with your Preceptorate this day, my lord Prince?"

"I bring my chosen successor, Ven'Dar yn Cyran, to be acknowledged before the Preceptorate. As you have instructed me, I have taken him onto D'Arnath's Bridge and touched his mind with my own, imprinting him with my family's patterns of thought and all that I know of the Bridge and the Gates. Then did he open himself to the Gate fire for the time allotted to attune his power to the Gate and the Bridge. I have judged him worthy and capable, and as the Preceptorate witnesses my choice, so shall the secrets and the power of D'Arnath be unlocked in him, ready for his anointing."

"Why such hurry, my lord?" asked Ce'Aret. "Is it not a risk for the successor to be privy to all the Heir's lore so soon after his accession?"

"Our times are dangerous, Preceptor, and the deeds I must do today and in the days to come carry risks that are unknown. Ven'Dar is not a child to be protected and nurtured before he can shoulder his responsibilities."

"Reasonable, I suppose. Yes. Very wise. Please be seated, and we will proceed."

I settled in the Prince's chair, facing the Preceptors. Ven'Dar took a position somewhere out of sight behind me. Ce'Aret spoke to the assembly to explain the ritual.

The most difficult part had already been accomplished, she said, and the acknowledgment was little more than a formality, a key to unlock the knowledge that had already been passed along to the chosen.

While the Preceptor droned on about my family and my unique inheritance of D'Arnath's chair, I kept thinking of Seri. She would be watching from the anteroom through a myscal—an enchanted glass. It was all I could do to keep from looking up, from trying to express . . . something . . . of what I felt for her. But I had already slipped once. I had not intended to go to her in the night. She would do what was necessary, no matter if I told her or not, and if the Lords caught the least hint of my intent, we would fail. But I had not been able to leave her without a word or a touch. She was my foundation. My fortress keep. To share such a life as hers was a grace few men were given. And no man but I bore such hatred for the Lords of Zhev'Na, who had forced me to this day. Ah, gods, I would crush their bones in my teeth if I could.

Ce'Aret finished her recitation, stepping from the dais with the brisk movements of one half her age and disappearing behind me. She would be standing before Ven'Dar, splaying her fingers across his face, using her power to carve an image of his soul upon her mind. And soon after, she would transfer that image to me. An intrusive rite for the one whose image was being taken, exposing emotions and convictions one might prefer remain private. I was happy she was not probing *my* soul at the moment. All I had to do was read what she gave me and reflect my response to it. I shoved my murderous cravings aside and tried to unclench my fingers, which threatened to break the ancient wood of my chair, and focus on the rite.

Small hard hands settled on my shoulders. In an instant, I was infused with the image of Ven'Dar, not merely his physical aspect, but his essence: the joy that permeated every moment of his life, his love for our Way, for our land, for me.

"Is this the one you have named, D'Natheil?" Ce'Aret's voice was as clear as a brass trumpet. "The one who will follow your steps onto D'Arnath's Bridge, whose hands shall serve the people of Avonar and all of Gondai, leading us and guarding us with their skill and power?"

"This is Ven'Dar, my friend, my mentor, my heir," I said.

Ce'Aret removed her hands, and the image dissolved.

Mem'Tara brought me another image of Ven'Dar, this time the sounds of his voice, rich and clear in its timbre, honest and gentle in its tenor, powerful in its articulation of the words that were his life. She gave me the image of his eyes that could see so far beyond the moment and so deep into the past, and his hands that had calmed my anger as skillfully as they smoothed and shaped rough bits of wood into articles of use and beauty. She brought me his laughter, and his raucous baritone, singing a bawdy song. "Is this the one you have named, D'Natheil? The one who shall assume your place in the life of this world when your span of days is complete?"

"This is Ven'Dar, my friend, my comforter, my heir."

Then it was Ustele's turn. Slowly, leaning on a wildwood cane, he hobbled from the dais and passed by me without meeting my gaze. I wasn't worried about Ustele. The ritual was strict. He could refuse to participate, and I would remove him from the Preceptorate, appointing another person of my choosing to his place. But if he wished to retain his position as my counselor, he could only do as the ritual prescribed, take the image and present it to me.

My bones ached. A chill draft made me shudder. When had I last slept? My gritty eyes stung, and I rubbed them, causing a moment's shift in the light, smearing faces and colors . . . red . . . green. The hour was speeding by. I flinched when Ustele laid his cold, bony fingers on my head.

"Is this the one you have named, D'Natheil?" The old sorcerer's voice quavered in my ear, filled with bitterness. "The one who shall wield the sword and the power of D'Arnath and be privy to the innermost secrets of the Dar'Nethi? Is this the man to whom you would entrust the fate of the worlds? Consider well, for with your word will your successor be proved."

Even dull-witted with exhaustion, I knew this one thing was sure and right. "This is Ven'Dar, my friend, my brother, my heir."

But no sooner had I spoken, delivering the future of Gondai and the Bridge into his hands, than I glimpsed the flaw in the image that lingered in my mind. Ven'Dar, yes, his courage in battle, his unyielding devotion to justice and truth. In all things honorable. Yet, behind the image, lurking in the midst of everything I expected to see . . . what was it? A shadow. A scar. Alien. A flash of gold, a glimmer of ruby, of amethyst, of blue-white diamond . . . and familiar horror . . .

"No!" I slapped Ustele's hand away and burst from the chair, whirling about to see Ven'Dar's eyes grow cold and his smile harden.

"First friend, then brother, then heir. I'm dizzy from coming full circle—for I believed myself to be your heir to begin with. Family, yes, but not brother. And never friend. Most confusing. And even more so for these others who cannot see what you see or know what you know. Tell them who I am, my lord Prince. Tell them who will reign in Avonar in three heartbeats from this moment, when their mad Prince lies dead on the floor. Say my name, and let them shudder and curse your failure."

It was impossible, but there was no mistake. "Gerick!"

"No, no, good Father. Call me Dieste."

CHAPTER 31

Seri

Bareil had given me a square of glass through which, by some magical mechanism, I could view the morning's events while remaining hidden myself. I'd watched the ritual in the same state of heightened expectation I'd experienced since waking to see Karon's rose.

Play the part that only you have ever been able to play. Follow the Way . . . What did he mean? He thought I'd understand. He had been rushed, pressed for time. But my message had told him that I knew what he was planning, at least the result of it, and he had come to tell me . . . what? Fragile hope held my soul together, but despair picked and jabbed relentlessly.

The sole bright spot of the morning had been finding Paulo in the antechamber. But before he could tell me where he'd been since Calle Rein, Paulo had raced off in search of the missing Roxanne, hoping that she was only hiding and would emerge if she saw his familiar face.

And then the ritual fell apart. . . .

"No!" Karon's cry of outrage pulled me to my feet, the magical glass held even closer to my face. But it was impossible to see anything once chaos erupted in the council chamber.

How could Gerick be here?

Shouts and curses. The unmistakable sliding clangor of swords engaged. As I strained to see, the door of the antechamber burst open, and several of the Dar'Nethi

poured through it, reminding me that the chaos was only
steps away.

"Cover your face, my lady," whispered Bareil as the
first rush of refugees fled through the outer door and
others began to crowd in from the council chamber.
"Perhaps we should withdraw."

Play the part . . . Follow the Way . . .

To follow the Way meant to accept whatever came
and fit it into the larger context of the universe. But I
had never been able to accept whatever came, not until
I understood the truth of it. That took time, and everything was happening too fast. But, of course, Karon had
even less time than I to unravel the truth of these events,
and he couldn't always control his reactions, not with
D'Natheil's emotions confused with his own. Was that
what he wanted from me? To stay close to him through
everything? To watch and listen no matter how painful
the event? To look for the truth and hold onto it?

"No, Bareil. I think I need to be here."

I shoved my way through the fearful crowd into the
council chamber. By the time I stepped past the door
only a few observers remained in the room: the three
Preceptors, the enigmatic Men'Thor, and four or five
stalwarts in sober military garb, who I guessed were Karon's field commanders, bound by honor and duty to stay
beside their prince. Gerick was nowhere in sight. But
Karon and Ven'Dar were engaged, swords in hand,
Ven'Dar's sleeve already bloodied from their first closing. Now I understood. . . .

"Stay back!" shouted Karon to one of the Dar'Nethi
who stepped forward, sword drawn, ready to enter the
fight. "He's mine!"

He didn't need help. He already had Ven'Dar in a
steady retreat. Karon—D'Natheil—was an incomparable
swordsman. And Gerick . . . though it had been his childhood ambition to excel at sword combat, and he'd
trained ferociously under the most skilled masters in
Zhev'Na, he'd not touched a weapon in four years.

Ven'Dar pivoted and delivered a powerful counter to
Karon's thrust. Karon's feet did not budge. Ven'Dar delivered another blow. And another. But Karon might

have been waiting for an annoying fly to settle so he could swat it with his hand.

I wanted to scream out my confusion. If Gerick truly had control of Ven'Dar's body and forced Karon into killing the Preceptor, then the god Vasrin himself could not keep our son alive. If Gerick left Ven'Dar's body before it was dead, Karon would fly down to the palace dungeon and slaughter him. If he did not leave Ven'Dar's body in time, then he would be trapped and die with the Preceptor. Why would Gerick challenge Karon this way, knowing it was a sure route to his own death? Surely the Lords were controlling him. But to what purpose?

If the Lords' intent was merely to prevent anyone other than Gerick from inheriting the powers of D'Arnath, then why had they not forced Gerick to kill Karon at Calle Rein when they were linked and he was most vulnerable? Gerick had been Karon's acknowledged successor for four years. The power the Lords wanted was within their grasp, and it made no sense that they would put Gerick, their prize, at further risk of Karon's wrath. So, why this masquerade? All that was likely to happen from this futile exercise was that everyone would end up dead—Gerick and Ven'Dar and Karon, too, of course. Once he finished killing his dearest friend and executing his son he would be soul-dead, at the least. What would it benefit anyone . . . ?

Frantically I scanned the onlookers and confirmed that the face every instinct insisted should be present was missing from the crowd. Earth and sky, I knew!

I shoved my way past the remaining observers, until I was so close to the combatants that I could feel the rush of air as their swords sliced the air. "Karon! Stop! This is not Gerick's doing!"

Relentless, unbending, unheeding, Karon pressed the sneering Ven'Dar to the dais, laying blow after ringing blow on his opponent's sword, his powerful arms unwavering, his face like iron. Mortal enchantments flew with every strike. Ven'Dar seemed scarcely able to parry, much less mount an attack of his own. The end could be only moments away.

"Get away from here, Seri!" I heard nothing of Karon in the command, only cold fury and death. He never took his eyes from his objective. Ven'Dar's cold gaze never wavered from his Prince's face. He showed no fear. No concern. No hatred. No interest in me. Only singular determination. I knew I was right. I just didn't know how it was possible, even for a sorcerer of exceptional talent.

"I don't care what you see, Karon. I don't care what you feel. This is not Gerick. Stop and listen to me. For everything, listen to me." I switched from the language of Avonar to the language of Leire, the language Karon and I had shared.

Ven'Dar let loose a powerful offensive that engaged Karon's full attention, then dodged a deadly stroke that split the ancient Preceptors' table with a flash of blue fire. One of the Dar'Nethi observers grabbed my arms from behind and tried to drag me away, but I shook loose and stayed close.

"Think, Karon! Someone wants Gerick dead, and Ven'Dar dead, and wants you to be responsible—for then you'll be as good as dead, too."

Another blow and Ven'Dar staggered backward. Karon wiped the sweat from his face with a bloody sleeve, and walked slowly around the table. "The Destroyer will not escape me this time. Not like the day he murdered Gar'Dena."

Another blow and Ven'Dar's sword clattered across the floor, and Karon had the Preceptor backed up to a toppled half of the long table. His sword point rested at the older man's heart vein. "Not this time, Dieste."

"Do it, D'Natheil—Father," said Gerick's voice from Ven'Dar's lips, cold, unconcerned. "It's what you've wanted for four years. She can't see what you see. You know who I am because you've been closer to me than any mundane woman, even my mother, could ever be. If you don't do it, then you'll see all of them dead, including this pitiful relic you've chosen to lick your boots."

I would not *allow* this. "Listen to me, Karon. Once, very long ago in Martin's drawing room, you swore that you'd never seen my match when it came to solving puzzles, and that if ever you were to wager your life on a riddle, you would ask me to solve it. So. The time has come. Place your wager."

Karon's body was alive with rage, and no more than the weight of a hair would press his sword point into Ven'Dar's flesh. But he held back.

I forced everything I believed about our son into my words . . . everything I believed about Karon's true heart . . . about our love, our family, our history . . . everything and anything that might reach him through the armor of D'Natheil's anger. "That day at the Ravien Bathhouse, why did Gar'Dena turn the knife on himself once Gerick left him? How was it even possible? Those the Lords possess are left mindless. You have seen it in Zhev'Na and here in Avonar. They can't eat; they can't pull on a boot; they can't breathe. They die. You told me the vessel died because once the Lords had used them they didn't know how to live any more. So how was Gar'Dena able to turn his knife on himself? And why would he need to do so if the very act of Gerick's withdrawal was his doom? What if Gar'Dena was not possessed by a Lord, but controlled by some other power? What would you have seen when that illusion was done? You would have seen Gar'Dena as himself again, not mindless at all, not dead, and you would have known the truth. And so Gar'Dena had to die. By the Lords will, certainly. Using Gerick's soul weaving, yes."

I pressed harder. "Is this not the same thing over again? The one who controls Ven'Dar will make sure you've killed your dearest friend. But this time, something is different. As surely as the sun rises, you will also kill your son, the Soul Weaver, and your own true heart will be destroyed. And who benefits? Not Gerick. Not you. Not even the Lords who intend for Gerick to inherit your power. Before you kill this man," I said, "ask Men'Thor, Where is his son? *Ny vah mordeste, es Men'Thor yanevo Radele?*"

Infuriated, Men'Thor lunged forward, restrained only by two of the commanders. "How dare you—?"

But Karon was not swayed. "Impossible! Radele has

no skill to possess a man or to create the seeming of
another soul. Only the Lords have that kind of power."
Karon's words dripped with loathing. He snarled and his
shoulders tensed. Blood seeped from Ven'Dar's neck,
and I had no answer but faith.

"Wait! Radele *does* have the power!" A young woman's breathless voice came from the doorway. The remaining Dar'Nethi turned as one, parting enough that I
could see a disheveled Roxanne who stood panting as if
she'd run a race. "The same power he used to ensorcel
the King of Leire!"

Paulo stood beside her, gulping and heaving. "It's one
of the rings, my lord. Roxanne says that Radele has got
one of the magical rings that spins, like the one in the
cave of the Source, an oculus like the ones the Lords
use in Zhev'Na, but small so's it'll fit in your hand. Radele must be controlling everything."

Before I could quite comprehend their meaning,
Ven'Dar growled and twisted out from under Karon's
sword, lunging for his own dropped weapon that lay but
an arm's reach away. Karon was quicker. He slammed
his boot into Ven'Dar's middle. When the Preceptor
curled into a ball, Karon dropped his sword and grabbed
the Preceptor's arms, calling two of his warriors to aid
him. The Preceptor writhed and fought and spewed foam
and spittle from his mouth.

"Hold him," shouted Karon. "Ward him with the
strongest bonds you can manage. No one—*no one*—is
to touch his mind. And on your lives let him touch no
weapon. Seri, with me!"

He ran from the room, and as I followed him, Ce'Aret
and Mem'Tara rushed to Ven'Dar, who fell limp in his
warders' arms.

Men'Thor had been restrained by two warriors. He
squirmed and shouted, "Madman! How dare you accuse
my son—?"

With a barked command, Karon called up the portal
in the anteroom and vanished through it. I stepped after
him, Paulo and Roxanne on my heels. Thunder exploded
behind us. Over my shoulder, I glimpsed Men'Thor
strike down his captors with a flash of fire.

I cried out a warning, but Karon was far ahead, already disappearing down a long stairway. Through galleries we sped, down wide staircases, past astonished servants, and into the warren of sloping, narrow passageways that looked increasingly familiar . . . the steel-banded doors . . . past four fallen warriors . . . through the iron gate and the second guardroom where other warriors lay still in pools of blood . . . From the prison chamber ahead came a scream . . . as if the victim's heart was being torn out. *Gerick.*

I stood at the door of the prison chamber gaping in wonder and horror. The walls had vanished, replaced by fathomless darkness, riven by bolts of blue-and-white fire. Hanging in the center of all was a pulsing orb of lurid light, created by a small brass ring, spinning so fast that it swept every mote of light from the room and wove the light into a palm-sized universe of blinding yellow-streaked purple and gold. A particularly potent burst of lightning illuminated Radele's smiling face. The spinning ring hovered above his palm.

Another burst of blue and white shattered the darkness and struck the orb of light. At the moment of impact, Gerick jerked and screamed again. He knelt on the stone platform in the center of the guardroom, curled in a knot, his pale, trembling fingers interlaced and cradling his head. Silver bands at his neck, wrists, and ankles were chained to the eyebolts at the corners of the platform.

"Come no closer, my lord," said the smirking Radele. "I require you to stay where you are while we work out a settlement."

Karon was just inside the door, trying to move closer to the stone platform. But his every forward movement caused another streak of blue lightning and another scream. Finally, with a curse, he stepped back, and the storm was stilled. "I make no settlements with the Lords of Zhev'Na or their servants."

Gerick collapsed on the platform, shaking, his face buried in his arms.

"Oh, come now, I'm not one of the Lords. This"— Radele pointed to the magical orb spinning in his left hand—"is only a temporary device, made necessary by your infernal stubbornness. It will help us accomplish what is needed, and then . . ." He shrugged.

"You think they'll let you sever your partnership?" said Karon. "Or perhaps you believe you're more powerful than the Lords? Or more clever? Yes, that's it, isn't it? So you're a fool as well as a traitor."

"Once the sword of D'Arnath rests in the proper hand, the opinions of those in Zhev'Na will have no more weight than the opinions of a fly . . . or the opinions of a dead coward of a prince or his demon spawn."

"And whose hand would be the proper one to hold D'Arnath's sword?" said a calm, equable voice from behind me. A firm hand moved me aside, and a straight-backed figure in red robes strode into the room. Men'Thor—his legendary composure regained.

Radele smiled triumphantly, straightened his own back, and gave a deep bow. "Yours, of course, my father. And after yours, mine."

Men'Thor walked slowly past Karon, assuming, correctly it seemed, that Radele would allow him to pass his barriers. When the man in red stood next to his son, he examined the spinning ring for a goodly time.

"You have made alliance with the Lords of Zhev'Na in order to make me the Heir of D'Arnath?" he said at last. He might have been discussing a gift of a new pair of boots or the talents of an untried sweeping girl.

"It was the only way. If you had seen it, Father . . . the madman Prince brought the boy sneaking across the Bridge in the middle of the night, as if to show his demon spawn the prizes awaiting him! How could I permit it? I was appalled. Furious. It happened that one of the Lords came to me that same night in the guise of a Zhid defector, thinking I was some weak-minded fool who would not recognize one of them. He said the boy was just biding his time, hoping to learn Avonar's secrets before rejoining the Lords. I could see they feared the boy would supplant them and take the powers of the Heir for himself alone. But for the time our purposes were the same, and I allowed them to think they had deceived me. That's when I bargained with them and obtained this device."

"And today you were able, using this Zhev'Na device—this oculus—to displace Ven'Dar's soul with that of the boy?"

"The Lords own this creature's mind. They taught me how to use the oculus to reach into his corrupted soul and command him, so that he would not even remember his own deeds. And though he is no longer an immortal Lord, his soul has this ability to move into other bodies. Ask our Prince. He recognized the boy. It was no illusion."

"But it was you all the time, controlling him, putting the words in his mouth and wielding the weapons in his hand."

"I could not allow Ven'Dar to be named successor. He's weak. Just as you said, Father. If the Prince had only named you instead, Ven'Dar would never—"

"And in the Preceptor Gar'Dena, too, you did this thing?"

"I used the oculus to discover what secrets the Prince told the boy that night and learned of the information cache at the bathhouse. If the Prince had named you to the Preceptorate, as he should have, nothing would ever have happened to it. But we had to control the knowledge of mordemar. If the people thought the Prince could prevent enslavement, it would take them another thousand years to listen to our reasoning. It was unfortunate that Jayereth and Gar'Dena had to die."

"And the Circle . . ."

Although there had been not the slightest change in Men'Thor's demeanor, Radele's grin began to fade. "Yes, yes. When Grandfather Ustele told you of the Circle, you said such a flimsy enchantment so close to our borders would ensure the destruction of Avonar. You said they should all be executed for treachery. So I used the oculus to learn the disposition of the Circle from the boy. I pretended to be horrified at the result. The Lords never knew the destruction of the Circle served our own purpose more than theirs. And then

Grandfather said that the best thing that could possibly happen would be an attack on the Vales, to make the people wake up to their folly, to make the Prince forget the mundanes and concentrate on our own people. You agreed. So I probed the boy to see what he knew of the Vale Watch and told the Lords of it, too. You said the woman had to be silenced, to free the Prince from his bondage to the mundanes, and I knew there must be no question of the boy's succession.

"I did everything you wanted, Father, and now we've won. The people have seen the Lords in their midst and witnessed the power of evil. They will follow us anywhere we wish to take them. With the mad Prince and his demon son dead, and the puling Ven'Dar out of the way, no one can hold us back. We will lead the host against Zhev'Na and we will prevail. What is it, Father? What's wrong? Everything is accomplished just as you wish."

Men'Thor spun on his heels, and with a formality that seemed ridiculously out of place, he bowed to Karon, spreading his hands, palms up. "My lord Prince," he said softly, "words cannot express my humiliation, my disgust, my dishonor at the despicable deeds of this traitorous fool I have sired. I accept full responsibility for his crimes, and may my actions, in some small part, remedy the damage he has wrought. *Ce'na davonet, Giré D'Arnath!*"

And before the red-faced Radele could digest the significance of his father's speech, Men'Thor straightened his back, drew his knife, and buried it in the belly of his son. With a twist and a jerk, the bloody implement was withdrawn and turned on its wielder, and before anyone could move, an ashen Men'Thor gave a single agonized sob and caught the slumping Radele. The two collapsed to the floor in a mortal embrace.

Horror robbed me of breath. Dread weighted my bones . . . my spirit . . . my soul. The spinning ring did not fall, but hung suspended in the air, pulsing and whirling in an obscene dance. Like a swelling bruise, it grew larger, a bilious swirl of purple and red and green. A cold wind swept through the guardroom, bearing the stench of old stone and foul smoke and such despair as would cause the bravest warrior to turn his weapon on himself.

"They come." Gerick, still shackled to the table, struggled to his knees and raised dark, haunted eyes to Karon. "Father . . ."

Karon turned away. Crouching down beside Radele and Men'Thor, he felt their wrists for signs of life, closed their eyes, and murmured words of Dar'Nethi peace sending, as if no one else was in the room.

Gerick wrenched his gaze from Karon's forbidding back and looked about the room, bewildered. When his gaze fell on me, he shuddered, looking gray and sick. Then, taking a deep breath, he closed his eyes and lifted his head until the light of the orb lay full on his face.

The pulse of the swelling orb increased until it set my teeth on edge and skin aflame, forcing my very heartbeat to throb in time with it.

"They come." Gerick's words were almost inaudible now, his eyes haunted. Hopeless. Lifeless. "Father, help me."

This time Karon rose and turned to the stone platform. Grim and merciless, he drew his sword and stood waiting.

From out of the bitter wind and the whirl of the oculus rose whisperings to paralyze the blood, voices that grew louder and easier to distinguish one from the other, weaving their wickedness through the thick air like writhing snakes.

"You called us, Dieste?" As the voice sighed and slithered through the air, I envisioned Notole the Loremaster, the gray-haired hag whose face was of beaten gold and whose eyes were emeralds.

"Your acceptance of your destiny gives us great pleasure, little brother." So spoke the wide-browed Parven, the Warmaster, he of the amethyst eyes.

"We had almost despaired of you, young Lord," said Ziddari, so clearly present that I imagined his ruby eyes gleaming in the shadows beyond the orb, his voice still that of Darzid, my brother's lieutenant who had once been my friend and confided in me of his terrifying dreams. "We feel your craving, and desire nothing but to fill you as you ask. Let us remove your bonds, so that as we share this body, we can wield our power as one. Power is your birthright."

Karon made no move to stop what was happening. Gerick lifted his hands to the orb, and the manacles snapped and fell away. He kicked the broken shackles from his ankles, then took another deep, shaking breath. "I've been powerless too long," he said. He looked as fragile as winter moonlight. Yet with a flick of his index finger Karon's sword flew out of his hand, clattering against the far wall. "No need for ugly blades. My execution has been stayed."

"And so you show yourself at last, Dieste," said Karon. "All pretense stripped away. Radele didn't know that his maneuvering was unnecessary. You would have done everything he wanted without the oculus. You were looking for a way to go back all the time, weren't you? Is that why you carried this with you from one world to the next, awaiting the opportunity to make amends to your fellows, once you'd done all the damage you could do?"

From a leather bag at his waist, Karon pulled something that flashed gold in the strange light. He threw it onto the platform in front of Gerick. Gerick turned deathly white, then slowly extended his hand and picked up his mask, the Lords' gold mask with the diamond eyes that had been molded to his flesh when he became Dieste the Destroyer.

I wanted to scream. What was Karon doing? I was not wrong about Gerick. I was not. Why would Karon drive him back to the horror he had rejected?

Karon did not take his eyes from Gerick. He didn't even blink.

"I hunger!" cried my son, a spasm racking his slender frame, drawn from the very depths of despair. "Notole, help me! Ziddari . . . Parven . . . join with me . . . fill me!"

As his white fingers gripped the mask and lifted it to his face, he groaned with the animal hunger of a starving man who sees his first bread. Lust distorted his features, as his eyes darkened until they became pits of unending blackness. A blast of winter cut through my flesh, infusing me with the revolting pleasure of the Lords. They had him.

"Gerick! Dearest child, don't do it!" The cry burst from my lips and heart and soul all at once. "I know your true heart! You do not belong with the Lords!"

Gerick paused, and Karon moved at last, not with any weapon, but only his hand, holding it out where Gerick could not fail to see. "Come into me, my son," he said softly. "My dear and beloved son."

For one brief instant Gerick's bottomless eyes met my own and then shifted, coming to rest on his father. The world, the stars, the mighty universe held its breath along with me. And then Gerick reached for Karon's outstretched hand.

At their touch, thunder shook the foundations of Avonar. The Lords' unholy pleasure, their depraved satisfaction and unmuted lust were shattered by shock and dismay, as first Gerick and then Karon collapsed to the unyielding gray stone. For one instant, a hellish symphony of pain and terror and screeching disbelief rattled my bones . . .

. . . and then absolute silence fell upon the world.

As the light of the spinning orb winked out, I glimpsed the oculus and the gold mask fallen to the floor, sagging into a pool of molten metal, the two diamonds floating in it like sparkling eggs. Gerick lay crumpled on the stone platform. Karon sprawled across the edge of it, one hand still clasped in Gerick's. In my husband's other hand lay a small pyramid of polished black—Dassine's crystal where Karon's soul had been bound for ten dark years, the stone that held his long-postponed death.

I sank to my knees beside the two of them, and in the darkness that fell on me like a woolen blanket came a soft breath on my wet cheeks, an invisible touch that bore a lifetime of love and reassurance. Karon had taken Gerick to the only place he could be free of the Lords, a bittersweet gift from father to son, swift passage beyond the Verges to L'Tiere, the following life.

And what of the Lords?

CHAPTER 32

Paulo brought the light. I sat on the stone platform where Karon and Gerick lay pale and still, feeling them grow cold even as I willed them not. Roxanne sat beside me, her head on my breast, weeping silently. As I stroked her hair, a certain calm settled over me, even as my own tears flowed unchecked.

"I had to go all the way back to the first guardroom to find this," said Paulo, setting a small, sputtering torch in a bracket on the wall, revealing the devastation around us in ghastly clarity. "Nobody was about. Don't understand it." He gazed down at Gerick. His voice was husky. "I guess he's free of 'em now. Don't seem fair. The Singlars are going to be torn up real bad."

"I don't think Karon was able to save them," I said. "If Gerick was right, then they're all destroyed."

"The Bounded may be gone, ma'am . . . I don't know. But the Singlars are safe . . . well, as safe as anyone could be in Valleor."

"You did it," said Roxanne, lifting her head. "Just as we planned."

"What are you talking about?" I said.

"Paulo took the Singlars out of the Bounded," said Roxanne. "We planned it before we came here, gathering all the Singlars we could find into the Tower City and telling them to be ready to leave at a moment's notice. If it looked as if Gerick were going to die without a . . . solution . . . Paulo was to go back to the Bounded and take them out. Gerick believed that as long as he was alive the Singlars should be able to move through the passage up near this sheepherder's place in northern Valleor."

"You really did such a thing?" I said to Paulo.

He nodded. "After the Prince sent you away the other night, knowing he had to kill the young master." Tears filled Paulo's eyes. "They both knew it. So they sent me back. Wasn't nothing I could do here."

I gathered Paulo into my arms, and we both wept for a while.

Roxanne decided when it had been enough. "Don't you think we should tell someone what's happened? They need to know about the Prince and all. And if I'm to get back home to see to the Singlars . . ."

"I'll go," said Paulo, dabbing his face with his sleeve. "Nothing better to be at."

Paulo returned to the dungeon inside the hour. He had found a troop of terrified warriors at the far end of the passage and asked to be taken to the Preceptors. "They stayed back from me, like maybe they wasn't sure whether I might be one of the Lords myself," he reported.

But whatever the warriors had thought, they had taken Paulo to the council chamber where Mem'Tara and Ce'Aret were standing watch on Ven'Dar. "I told them what happened as best I could, and they said to come right back and tell you not to touch nor move anything, and not to let nobody come here. Wait for them, they said."

The wait was not long. Ce'Aret arrived first. The old woman knelt alongside Karon and laid her hand on his forehead, closing her eyes. I could tell by her slow rocking when she began to grieve. After a while, she stood up and nodded her head to me. "The Prince's lady . . . here. Alive. Your presence tells me that the mysteries I feel and see are a more complex weaving of joy and sorrow than imagining can tell." Her withered hand gently stroked Karon's hair. "It will take a very long time indeed to take in this sorrow."

"Yes." The world, the conversation, the stone, and

the torchlight might have been illusion. I could not feel any of them.

"And the prisoner . . . the Fourth . . . lies dead as well . . ."

I nodded, and she shook her head sadly. "A Soul Weaver, the Prince told me. Corrupted before we could know him." She paused for a while, as if to ponder her own assessment. "I've no wish to intrude on your grieving, lady, but as you well know, these events are of such significance to our world . . . and your own, as well . . . I must summon the others."

I had no strength to explain that Gerick was innocent. What would it matter? "Do as you need. As long as I can stay with them for a while."

She nodded, then took on the slightly vague expression of a Dar'Nethi who was speaking in someone else's mind. When she was finished, I asked her about Ven'Dar.

"He collapsed once the Prince left the council chamber," she said. "He lives, but has not regained his senses. We continue to hope."

A short time later, Mem'Tara swept into the room, followed by a hobbling Ustele. Once she'd paid her respects to Karon, Mem'Tara began to examine the room, from every finger's breadth of the walls and floor to the oily stain where the oculus, the mask, and the diamonds had vanished. Ce'Aret saw to old Ustele, who knelt hard-faced beside his son and grandson, laying his hand on the knife, perhaps to gain some understanding of the circumstances of its use. I believed it would tell him that Men'Thor had done the terrible deed, but I didn't think it would tell him why or the part he himself had played in it. Even if it did so, I wasn't sure that he would understand it. Who would mourn Men'Thor properly? Who would judge his place in Dar'Nethi history? Before very long, the old man shoved Ce'Aret aside and hobbled out of the room.

I watched all these activities with no more involvement than a star observing the actions of those of us who crept about on the world's surface—until Mem'Tara, examining Karon's body, reached out for the black pyramid. "No!"

I said, surprised at the strength of my own voice. "Don't touch it."

The dark-haired sorceress raised her eyebrows in question.

"I just—" It was too personal. Too intimate. As if she were reaching out for Karon's soul. I would not have him violated in such a way, even by someone well-intentioned. How could I explain it? *Follow the Way . . .* "Isn't it true that the dead should not be moved for several hours? Isn't that your custom?"

Mem'Tara nodded. "Why yes, that's usual. So that the soul will have crossed the Verges and will not need to find its way back to this life. I was only going to examine the device, but if it concerns you, I'll leave it for a while. But the Prince caused his own death. . . ."

Dar'Nethi history and custom were very clear. No Healer would attempt to revive one who had caused his own death, especially a soul who had been returned to life once before. And no Healer in all of Gondai would touch Gerick.

My heart constricted, laboring to pump blood through my dry veins. "Thank you, Mem'Tara. That would be better."

The tall woman moved on to other matters.

Roxanne began talking, then, allowing the safe solidity of speech to soothe her. She told me the story of her rescue from the Guardian's dungeon, and how she had tried to order Gerick around and hurt him and humiliate him . . . and how she had never imagined that she could find friendship in that strange land. And then she told me then how Radele had come into the Masters' Chamber at the Precept House while she was hiding there, waiting for Bareil. . . .

"When he pulled out the ring and started it spinning, I knew it was wicked. Gerick was so horrified by the one in the cave of the Source, though he wouldn't tell me what it was. But you had told me how he became a Lord and that the spinning ring was the Lords' tool. Just seeing it made me feel sick. As the ring spun, this Radele began to speak, and I recognized his voice. He was the man I heard taunting my father on the night he was

enchanted, the one touching him. If I'd had a weapon,
I'd have killed him. Then I heard these other dreadful
voices . . . horrid . . . just like here . . . though no one
was in the room. As soon as Radele left, I ran out of
the house. But I got lost and there were so many people
around, and no one understood me. I thought that once
it was daylight I could find my way. I've never been so
glad to see anyone as I was when Paulo came running
down the street, calling my name. But now—" Tears
dripped from the end of her nose. "By the Holy Twins,
what manner of weakling queen will I be? I can't stop
talking. Can't stop thinking."

"You did the world a great service, Roxanne." I put
my arm around her and laid my cheek on her tousled
hair. "This is just very hard."

Ce'Aret offered one of her aides to attend us, so I sent
Paulo and Roxanne with the woman to find something to
eat. They needed something to do, while I, though I had
no purpose in mind, had no desire but to stay exactly
where I was. To leave was simply unthinkable.

I sat with my arms wrapped about my knees and
began telling Karon and Gerick how desperately I would
miss them. I crafted the words carefully in my mind as
Karon had taught me to do so long ago. "It makes my
head hurt when I have to sort out one of your thoughts
from another," he would say. "You always have fifteen
ideas popping up at once, and very noisy opinions on
all of them." Ce'Aret and Mem'Tara must surely have
believed I'd lost my mind to see me sitting by my dead
family, smiling at the sweet remembrance. Or perhaps
not. Finding joy, even in such overwhelming grief, was
the very essence of the Dar'Nethi Way.

"Ah, Vasrin!" The exclamation came from behind me,
startling me out of my drowsy contemplation.

"Ven'Dar!" The two Preceptors and I voiced our astonishment as one.

"A considerable delight to see you so quickly recovered, my lord," said Ce'Aret, opening her palms and
genuflecting. "We hoped."

The Word Winder greeted the two women, and then
his firm, warm hands enfolded my own, his kind eyes

searching my face as if he could read the story of the
battle from my grief. Though I welcomed the comfort
and strength he offered, I knew what he needed to be
doing. After only a moment, I gently pushed him away.
He moved on to the two who lay beside me.

Standing beside the stone table, he swept his eyes over
Karon. "Ah, my friend," he whispered, laying a gentle
hand on Karon's brow, "what sorrow can compare with
this, unless it is that you'll never know what you've
done? You never spoke of L'Tiere. Too close, you said.
You had seen the Verges, and the desire would be too
strong if you were to dwell on the memory. You wanted
to give yourself to life. And so you did. But if there is
knowledge of this life in the one that follows, then know
this, my Prince, a message has already come to Avonar
that rain falls in the Wastes. I cannot but think it is
your doing."

He took Karon's hand and sat down beside him. Dar'-
Nethi leave-taking could extend a very long time, Karon
had told me, but it always began this way, a little conversation, quiet meditation, embracing with eyes and heart
the evidence of one's loss. I did not disturb Ven'Dar.
His presence was a comfort.

After a while he shook off his silence, came around
the table and took my hand once more. "There are no
words sufficient to this day, my lady, even for one so
comfortable with words as myself. The event is too complex for 'I'm sorry,' and 'thank you' is far too ordinary."

"To hear your hopeful news and to see you living is
thanks enough. You will be D'Arnath's Heir as my husband intended. I wish you a path of great beauty."

He eased himself onto the stone platform beside me.
"Would it pain you to tell me what happened? I've
heard only bits and pieces since I've come back to my
senses."

"I believe it went very much as Karon had planned,
even after he understood about Radele and the oculus.
You probably know more than I do."

"Not at all. He told me nothing of his plan save my
own part: I was to be named his successor because it
wasn't possible for his son to serve, as the boy's mind

was still linked to the Lords. My first duty as his successor would be to bait the trap for Men'Thor with myself.
Yes, you were to be his witness to tell the Preceptorate
of Men'Thor's treachery if it came necessary. That's all
I knew."

When I had told the full story, he punctuated it with
a puff of amazement. "Vasrin's Hand! If this is true . . .
if the Lords were fully joined with the boy at the moment of his death . . . Well, we shall see what results
from it. Your son was blessed that you were here to
remind him of his own goodness before the end. It
sounds as if you did exactly what was needed."

"Play the part. Follow the Way," I murmured. Somewhere beyond the outer guardroom a door opened and
banged shut again, causing a slight movement in the air.
The torchlight flickered.

"What's that?"

I told Ven'Dar of Karon's nighttime visit and the
words that had echoed in my head all day. He looked
bemused. "He told you not to give up even in the depths
of sorrow and also to follow the Way—contradictory ad-
monitions, for, of course, following the Way could be
said to be 'giving up,' relinquishing our desires to change
what is."

Like a bubble rising to the surface of a pond, words
welled out of my grief. "If he would just have told us
more of his intent. Gerick was in such pain, such despair,
and Karon offered him nothing until he was almost lost.
I didn't understand it. I still don't." It didn't seem right I
should be saying such a thing, but I couldn't stop myself.

"Think, dear lady. He planned to rob the Lords of
their prize by an extraordinary means. And if the Lords
took possession of the boy, both living in his body and
linked to his soul at the moment of his soul weaving . . .
his transference into his father . . . his death . . . perhaps
the Lords would die, too. But if Gerick, or any of us,
had the least suspicion of what was to occur . . ."

". . . the Lords might never have come."

"In order to make their sacrifice meaningful, the
Prince had to proceed alone, to relinquish the very com-

fort for the boy and for himself and for you that might
have made it bearable."

"So we're left with his words. 'Follow the Way. You
must not give up . . .' Give up what? It's been three
hours; they're beyond the Verges. I should let Mem'Tara
have her way with them, and go find Paulo and Roxanne."

"Mem'Tara?"

"She wanted to take the pyramid stone. I couldn't
bear the thought of her touching it, so I reminded her
that the bodies shouldn't be moved for half a day."

"Follow the Way . . . must not give up . . . play the
part . . ." Ven'Dar's calm voice took on an edge of
excitement. "Tell me, my lady, have you—please, don't
think me foolish or rude—*spoken* to your son or the
Prince as you stood vigil with them here?"

Ven'Dar wouldn't pry without reason. Politeness and
embarrassment were trivialities. "So much never gets
said, and we'd been apart so long. In a way I've been
speaking to them since it happened, but—"

"And before the Prince touched the crystal?"

"Yes."

"As you did in Zhev'Na when the boy was transformed?"

"I suppose it's much the same. Why?"

The Preceptor—no, he was the Prince of Avonar
now—jumped up and went to the other side of the platform, where he closed his eyes and placed his hands
on Gerick's breast. After several suspended moments,
Ven'Dar sighed deeply and shook his head. "I thought
perhaps— Paulo told us that when your son first entered
him, he unlocked his own cell door and pulled his own
body, still breathing, from confinement. To take young
Gerick with him beyond the Verges, the Prince would
have had the boy come into him—perform his soul
weaving. Only then could the stone have released them
both. Your bond with your son was strong enough to
survive his transformation into a Lord of Zhev'Na; with
the thread of love and words, you led him out of that
darkness. And so I had a brief hope. . . ."

"But he does not breathe."

"No. His heart is still."

You must not give up hope. . . .

Red-clad guards from Ustele's house carried Men'Thor and Radele away on velvet-draped litters, and Ce'Aret and Mem'Tara finished their examination of the room. "We should go now, my lord," they said to Ven'Dar. "The people are afraid and hear only one rumor more dreadful than the next. When word goes out with Men'Thor's and Radele's bodies, it will be worse. They need reassurance from their Prince."

Ven'Dar shook his head. "As most senior Preceptor, Ce'Aret, it is your place to inform the people of Gondai that Prince D'Natheil is dead. Do so, and tell them I stand vigil with him as our Way prescribes. I would ask them to do the same—to hold the Prince and his beloved son in their thoughts as a lighthouse shines its brilliance into the tempest, so that wherever they journey, they may find the Way."

The two women bowed and left us there, Ven'Dar and me, sitting together with Karon and Gerick. After a while Paulo's torch guttered out, leaving us in the dark, but Ven'Dar made no move to create another light. Instead he held my hand in quiet companionship, and I felt his gentle thoughts of Karon entwine with my own. As it had been sixteen years before on a bitter day in Leire, I was left to mourn, only this time, I was not alone.

And so it was in the darkness of the silent guardroom, as I drowsed against Ven'Dar's shoulder, trying to maintain my one-sided conversation with Karon and Gerick, that I felt the first tug on the other end of the lifeline. . . .

CHAPTER 33

Gerick

It was a long wicked time from the moment I possessed my father's body until I realized we were dead. The last true physical sensation was the touch of my father's hand. He gripped it firmly . . . *I* gripped it firmly, for I was both of us. And more. I was not only Gerick, not only Karon, not only some intrusive scrap of D'Natheil, but I was also the Three, the vile, immortal, all-powerful Lords of Zhev'Na, who believed their day of victory was come after a thousand years of devouring desire. I could scarcely hold a single thought together, and if I'd waked in the madhouse in Montevial, it wouldn't have surprised me at all.

I suspected my father had done something extraordinary when I looked down to see our bodies draped across the palace guardroom . . . or perhaps I was traveling with the Lords again, on my way to call down lightning over the Wastes. But I'd never felt sorrow when I traveled with the Lords, not like that which overwhelmed me when I saw my mother kneel weeping at our sides just before the darkness fell. And the Lords and I had never reached out to comfort one who wept at our passing as my father reached out for my mother with his body's last breath.

With the darkness came the fire . . . fire that drove me to the edge of reason . . . that set my blood boiling in my veins. Choking, acrid smoke scorched my lungs, all the more horror because it smelled of my own seared flesh. My vision failed as my eyes charred in their sockets.

The fire set the Three howling. They had felt no pain since they were transformed, but had only consumed it, lusted after it, for it fed their power. But this fire was their pain, as it was mine, as it was my father's. Neither true flesh, nor blood, nor eyes were necessary, for all of the horror was in the memory of my father, at last made real for the ones who had caused it, and for me, because I had to be there to bring the Lords.

Hold, my son. I will not pass it over. . . . Whatever comes, the Three must have a taste of what they've wrought in the world.

Ten years my father had lived with his death fire fixed in his conscious mind. I'd never really understood.

It had been the most difficult thing I'd ever done to take my father's hand, more difficult than leaving Zhev'Na, more difficult than enduring the firestorms in the Bounded or D'Arnath's fire in my prison cell, more difficult even than allowing Notole, Parven, and Ziddari to enter my body and mind again. Once they were inside me, choking off every sensation of life, devouring every shred of humanity I'd regained, my craving for power was magnified a thousandfold. To touch my father's hand would be to give it up all over again. And who knew what else I might be letting myself in for. His sword was out of the way, but his enchantments had come near killing me fifty times already. Though I'd spent a great deal of effort trying to convince myself that my father's silence had been intended to prevent the Lords' learning of his plans from me, it was almost impossible to relinquish the Lords' cold comfort for something I couldn't imagine. I had to trust him, and I wasn't even sure who he was.

He had made his decision on the night at the Lion's Grotto, when he linked our minds together with his healing magic. His voice had been gentle at first, just as I remembered him, my true father. He told me of Ven'Dar's belief that I was a Soul Weaver, so that what I'd done to Paulo and Ven'Dar had been no more a sign of my corruption than Ven'Dar's word windings or his own healings. Though I was glad to hear him say such things, instead of how vile I was or how much he wanted me dead, I didn't believe their theories. I knew what I was.

As he explored what I knew and believed of the Bounded, and the story of my dreams and all my confusions, he was appalled at what he considered his failure with me. *Unforgivable that I couldn't see,* he said. *That I let it come to this pass. I should have been at Verdillon more often, and perhaps I could have come to understand what happened—and what was happening—to you.*

Whenever he grew angry, I had to distract him, for his touch became less sure, and his presence less substantial, and I very much wanted his help. But he came very quickly to the conclusion that there was no way to detach me from the Bounded. His first slight attempt at separation seemed to leave a gaping hole in my memory where someone named Ob was concerned, and my father said there would be nothing left of me if he proceeded, with no accompanying assurance that the Lords couldn't use me anyway.

Then Paulo must go back to the Bounded, and lead the Singlars through the portal to Valleor, I said. *I prepared them before I left. They just await my word.*

It would give King Evard a greater mystery than he's ever known, but unfortunately, I doubt these Singlars will fare better in the Four Realms than to chance their fate with you. That was my father speaking, so I knew he was still with me.

Roxanne will see to them, I said.

You care for these people a great deal.

I just . . . I would not have them die because of me. They're not evil.

Neither are you, Gerick. You never were. If this new world is a reflection of you, then you must see that it is not just the oculus that defines what you are, but the goodness and strength and resilience of the Bounded, as well. This ocean of light . . . what a wonder . . . that, too, is a part of you.

It was then he told me he needed to learn more of how the Lords controlled me. Perhaps something other

than my death could disrupt their attachment. He asked
me to open the door in my mind.

I didn't want him to see. If he could be D'Natheil
while he looked, instead of my father, perhaps I
wouldn't care. *There's nothing you can do,* I said. *Just
give Paulo a day, then do what you have to do. It'll be
too dangerous if you start poking around in my head.
They'll know.*

But he told me how important it was to him and to
my mother that we look for every possible solution. And
if we were to find another answer, he needed to know
everything—what I was and what I had been. What I
had always been.

*If I allow it . . . you won't tell her? I don't want her
to know.*

*I promise. She knows your true heart, Gerick. She's
always known, and nothing will ever change her mind.
No one in any world can match your mother for stubbornness. But there's no need for her to know everything
that's been done to you. Whatever is between us here, will
stay between us.*

All the words were very nice. He seemed to mean
them. But I had no illusions about what would happen
when I opened the door and introduced him to Dieste.

Indeed, it was all he could do to stay with me. Rage
and revulsion threatened to destroy my father and leave
only D'Natheil, who very much wanted to stick a knife
in my gut. Instead, he withdrew from my thoughts for
what seemed like a very long time. When he spoke
again, his inner voice was cold and hard, and I could
hear only words, nothing of his intent or his true feelings
any longer. *You were right all along. You have to die.
There is no other course.* Nothing more about me not
being evil. He had seen the truth—why I would rather
die than go back.

There's always satisfaction in having your judgment
confirmed by those deemed wiser than yourself, and to
have the decision made was a relief. But I had thought
he might tell me how he would go about it . . . or that
he'd make it fast . . . perhaps even what it was like . . .

after. As it was, he did not speak again before withdrawing from me completely.

I opened my eyes to see him wrapping a rag around his bleeding arm. Paulo stood in the doorway of the ruin looking worried, and Roxanne was nowhere in sight.

Events moved very quickly after that. I told Paulo he had to go back to the Bounded. He knew what that meant, and he promised to "see to things back there." The Prince had taken his place by the door and stood looking out, as if we weren't even there.

Paulo squatted beside me, tracing a finger in the dirt. "It don't seem fair," he said, quietly. "I never thought he'd do it. Never."

I glanced at my father's motionless back. "He tried to find another way. Honestly, he did. Take care of yourself, Paulo."

I appreciated that Paulo didn't try to convince me to run away. We had already discussed this back in the Bounded. Though he didn't want me to die, he had no alternatives to offer. But he shook his head. "It's not over yet. Don't you think it. The Lady'll have a say about this."

"Where is she? Is she all right?"

"She's—"

"Get out of here, Paulo!" The Prince moved quickly, yanked on Paulo's arm, and shoved him away from me. "One instant more and you'll reveal your passage to our guests."

Pounding hooves from across the valley announced rapidly approaching riders. Ten or more.

Raising a hand in farewell, Paulo passed through the portal again—little more than "thinking himself through" the protrusion of rock in the heart of the ruin. I'd forgotten to ask him about Roxanne.

My father did not speak to me as we waited for the riders to arrive. Knowing what he had seen inside me— and knowing what was going to happen a day from now—I didn't know what to say to him, either. Certainly nothing I said was going to change his mind about what he had to do. So I just sat in the corner and waited, wondering who was coming, wondering whether he would give Paulo the time he needed to save the Singlars, wondering whether he would use his sword or his knife or some enchantment to kill me.

The "guests," Radele and his father Men'Thor and some of their men, were all for executing me right there in the ruins, and from the way the Prince talked, I thought he was going to do it. But then he told them that he was planning to make a public show of naming a successor and executing me, so that the Dar'Nethi would see clearly what was happening. So, they made me a prisoner instead, putting me in restraints that would prevent me using power.

When I thought of all those I'd sealed into slave collars, I couldn't complain about their bindings. The spell-ridden silver manacles that made it feel as if bars of red-hot iron had replaced the bones in my arms and back weren't half so bad as the slave collars. But I thought it strange that my father would do such a thing to me, when I'd freed him from his collar in Zhev'Na. That irony must have been on his mind as well, for when I was tied to the horse, and he came up to put his own seal on the magic, he wouldn't look me in the eye. And at the very moment his enchantment ripped through my mind and body like a flaming ax, I would have sworn I heard him whisper, "Forgive me." But I was screaming, and after that I couldn't think of anything for a long time.

Over the next day and night I kept telling myself I was a fool even to think about my father any more, much less believe he had some plan that might keep me alive. Yet those two words kept popping into my head every time I saw him. He brought one group of blood-thirsty, superior Dar'Nethi after another to gawk at me, and he'd tell them how corrupt I was, and how I'd tried to murder my mother. But then he'd call up D'Arnath's magic again, the white fire that made me want to crawl out of my own skin, and I couldn't put two sensible thoughts together.

The interesting thing was that he never told the damnable gawkers the real evils he'd seen in me, only the things they already believed. And he would always finish with the same speech. "When the time comes for his execution, he'll call on the Lords to come for him. It doesn't matter what he claims now, but when the moment arrives, he'll do it. That will demonstrate what he really is. If, at that moment, I were to reach out my hand and offer him freedom from his depravity, what would you wager that he'd take it?"

He would never answer his own question, and just about the time I would begin to think that perhaps he was trying to tell me something, he'd slam me with the fire again. After ten times or twenty on that endless day, I believed that the only thing he was telling me was that I was going to be dead sooner rather than later. And I didn't care in the least.

But, of course, when the time came, after Radele and Men'Thor were dead, and I was chained to a stone, trying to make sure my skull hadn't actually cracked in two as it felt, I remembered what he'd said all those times. If he wanted me to summon the Lords, using the oculus would be the way to do it. I could tell the Three I was desperate, that I was ready to surrender, that I would do anything for power and to escape my father's sword. It wouldn't be hard to be convincing. But I dared not take too long to decide; the Lords would feel my doubts and know it was a trick.

When I could move my head without passing out, I looked at the Prince for some signal that would tell me what he wanted me to do, but he showed no interest. I warned him, and he turned his back on me. But behind him . . . behind him was my mother, and if he'd brought my mother, then he cared very much about what was going to happen. I had to trust him.

So I reached into the orb and called on the Lords to come and save me. They came. In the instant they joined with me, I felt as if I were back in Zhev'Na, bursting with all those things I'd hidden and ignored and buried in myself for so long: the smell of the blood I had taken, the taste of the pain I had inflicted, the intoxication of causing horror to feed my pleasure and my power. Though the remembrance disgusted me, though I loathed

what I had been and had tried everything I could to
leave it behind, I hungered for more. My hands quivered
with the desire for power, and my soul craved the emptiness the Lords had given me, the freedom from confusion and pain and fear. I'd had more than my fill of pain
and confusion.

No more of it! I flicked away my father's sword and
ignored his accusations. Why should I die? I was what
I was. Better to live with power . . . The Lords were
congratulating me, welcoming me back, drowning me in
their lusts and hatreds, and my four years of denial were
erased in the first instant of my listening. When my father threw the mask in front of me, I remembered nothing of duplicity, nothing of an imagined plan, nothing of
deception. My body begged for the touch of gold, for
the vile ecstasy as the mask embedded itself in my flesh.
My feeble human eyes burned for their diamonds that
would see everything and nothing.

Yet even as my hand raised the mask to my face, my
mother took up the tether that bound me to her. She
called my name as if to remind me who I was. "I know
your true heart! You do not belong with the Lords!"

I almost spat it back at her. *If not in Zhev'Na, then
where do I belong?*

But no sooner had I voiced the question, than I realized that, for the first time in my life, I knew the answer.
I know your true heart. . . . Everything my parents had
tried to tell me suddenly made sense. Everything I had
learned and felt in the past months settled into place. I
belonged in the Bounded, where my broken people were
just learning how to live. I was one of them, broken,
too. And if this was so, then perhaps, like them, I was
not evil.

For that one astonishing moment, this novel possibility
quieted my pain and hunger and the enticements of the
Lords. Thus, when my father whispered, "Come into
me," I heard his voice. When he said, "My dear and
beloved son," I believed him. And though it was one of
the hardest things I'd ever done, when he reached out
his hand, I took it.

*   *   *

Only after the pain of the fire began to recede did the Lords begin to bargain. They writhed and squirmed within our shared mind like snakes in a kettle, but I drew up power as they themselves had taught me and held them still.

"Young Lord," wheedled Notole. "I have nurtured you in the ways of power. All this"—I could envision her hand waving across the black velvet landscape revealed by the waning flames—"is but more food for your talent. You will be the greatest of the Lords, feared and worshiped in every world, able to take any soul at your whim, to eat or use as you desire. You will stand with one foot in one world, and one foot in another, and laugh while Parven and Ziddari grovel for your favors. Release me, and I will draw you back to Zhev'Na to take your rightful place."

We were one—my father, the Lords, and I—a single vessel passing through this midnight realm toward a horizon alive with streams and veils of colored light. Strange that I could see, though I had no eyes, and I could walk . . . or fly or move somehow . . . though I had no limbs, no physical substance at all. My senses were all blurred together, so that I tasted the rich darkness and heard the song of the light.

"I will not bargain," I said. Not if this strange venture would destroy the Lords. Soon, surely, my father would tell me where we were and what we were doing.

"Crush this mortal being who dares contain you," growled Parven. "No more should a cavern contain the sky, than this pitiful D'Natheil imprison the Destroyer. There is still time to cast him off. Let him pursue dissolution if such is his wish, but the Four of Zhev'Na are at the brink of triumph. We made you what you are—strong and powerful and ruthless—now we call in our debt. You swore an oath never to oppose us. Cast him off! Travel the winds of the world with us."

"I have no wish for your companionship," I said. "And I've not taken up arms against you. You chose to come at my call. But I am a Soul Weaver, and I control this place where you reside. I yield my father the choice of destination, not you."

"But you don't even know where that is, do you, boy?" snarled Ziddari. "Tell him, D'Natheil. Tell your son where he and his futile hopes are bound."

My father took a long time to answer. He seemed very distant, though I had given him control of our shared mind. "I take him to the only place he can be free of you. I take you where you can no longer destroy what is beautiful."

His thoughts trailed away. The geysers of colored fire—closer now—shattered at their peak into cascades of music and color that aroused such deep and fundamental longing that every past desire, even my craving for power, paled in comparison. What was this place?

"He's killed you, young Lord," said Ziddari, his voice as cool and mocking as it had ever been. "When we pass that barrier, there is no going back. Never again. No wind on your face, no solid horseflesh powering you across the earth, no exploring the wonders of the world at your will. No chance to do those things you've never done. You've never sailed on the ocean, never scaled a mountain peak. You've never even had a woman. Shall I tell you of these things, quickly, before they're lost forever? Quickly, before your body rots, forfeit to D'Arnath's revenge? Shall I show you what you've chosen to leave behind?"

Into our mind came one vision after another: women, riches, sailing and adventure, wine, food, and every pleasure, commonplace or exotic, that a physical being could enjoy. Each one was replete with sounds and smells, and tastes, and sensations, and it was true, I'd never experienced even a tenth of it. I was only sixteen, and I was dead.

"Now tell me why your father has murdered you. He should have made this journey before you were born. This yearning you feel is his, for he is tired of existing where he doesn't belong. But you, young Lord, have not even begun to know what is to be found in the world . . ."

And then he bombarded me with another round of visions, this time of his own pleasures, corrupt, brilliant, loathsome, depraved, exciting, a world of power and enchantment where I could do anything I wanted—and never to end, for I would be immune from ordinary death.

"Now tell him, D'Natheil. Tell him why he has to die. Tell him why he cannot live forever."

"Tell me," I whispered, suddenly confused. My progress toward the barrier of light slowed, and the fading visions of warmth and pleasure left me cold and empty. Alone. Dead. A shudder of terror swept through me. "Father . . ."

It took even longer for the answer to come back this time, as if my father had to gather himself up from the shimmering fragments of light that showered down on us.

"Because Gerick is not one of you. He is loved and cherished by uncounted souls, who even now bear him in their hearts with reverence. He does not live for the pain of others, but for their benefit. Despite all you've done to him . . . all I've done to him . . . Gerick owns his soul and has used it to choose his Way. His long journey has led him here . . . to his freedom." We moved forward again. Faster now. Upward.

"Words. Lies." Ziddari's voice rose. Louder. Tighter. Tinged with fear. "You murder him at the very threshold of manhood, just as you abandoned him to murder on the day of his birth. *I* am the one who saved him on that day, and I am the one who will save him on this day. The only freedom you offer is oblivion."

"Ah, but you see, Ziddari, unlike myself, and unlike the Lords of Zhev'Na, my son will not die on this day. For all your wisdom, all your years, all your magics, you have no true power. True power lies in the hands of those like my wife, who has no talent for sorcery yet changes the course of the world with her passionate heart, and Ven'Dar, who witnesses to the glory of history and fate, and my friend Paulo, who cannot even read yet hears the quiet pulse of life and sustains it with his faithfulness. You've never understood. While Gerick lives out his future free of you, you will have ample time to consider your lacks."

Light and shadow traveled on the warm wind that

swirled around me. Through me. As we climbed the
ridge of light, music took shape around us. Haunting
blues and greens, frothing like ocean waves. A swelling
wall of purple-and-violet melody, a mountaintop of singing rose and white . . .

"Betrayer!" bellowed Ziddari. "Weakling!"

The taunts did not touch me. I thought of my mother
and Paulo and knew that what my father said about
them was true. My whole being smiled as I remembered them.

The Three went wild, then, and I thought my mind
would distingrate. Red-hot claws of fury, frustration, and
terror rent my mind and soul into shreds of words and
images. They lashed me with the fullness of their power,
blinding me with pain and hatred, slashing, ripping, tearing at my reason.

"Heed my last word, Destroyer." The venomous voice
penetrated the hurricane of madness, as if the ruby-eyed
Ziddari had bent down to whisper in my ear alone. "You
will never be free of us. No matter in what realm we
exist at the end of this day, you will not escape the
destiny we designed for you. You are our instrument. Our
Fourth. Every human soul—mundane or Dar'Nethi—will
curse the day you first drew breath."

The storm closed in again. I held against them, trying
to stanch the spreading poison of despair, trying to
shield my father's fragile spirit, until I could no longer
think of my own name, could not fit two thoughts together, could not exist . . . I needed breath. I needed
life. Screaming, I fell back. . . .

"Gerick, hold on . . . just a little farther. I know it is
so hard . . . but you are stronger than all of us. . . . My
father's voice was distant, but filled with everything he
believed about life, and the reasons he had been willing
to take this path to preserve the worlds. His will—not
at all fragile—held me together, pulled me forward.
"Stay with me . . . ah, gods, it comes. Quickly, my
son . . . trust me. . . ."

On the brink of madness, I took one more step. Then,
with a long sigh, we began to separate, my father and I
and the Lords. The Lords' curses disintegrated rapidly

into unintelligible ravings, cries that existed apart from and not inside me, and then, after a final, horrifying crescendo of terror, the Three fell silent . . . and I was free.

All that was left was the music, haunted, wandering music, just on the edge of beauty, yet just on the edge of dissonance. Streams of light and music bathed us like sparkling wine. The doors of my mind were flung open, and the melodies drifted through them, sweeping away the lingering shadows and cobwebs, and I felt my father's joy untouched by any trace of anger. We had crossed the Verges, and he, too, was free.

Vague forms began to take shape in the distance, and I strained to see what they were, but my father took hold of me again, closing off my vision as if he had brushed my eyelids shut to make me sleep. *Submerge now . . . go deep. You must not see. I believe your gift can take you back into your body, but only if you don't see. To know L'Tiere would be . . . unbearable . . . for a living man, I think. Go deep and wait for your mother's call to lead you. She'll find a way. I know it. She has always been able to learn what she needs.*

But what of you, Father?

Ah, I wish so very much— But my span of years was done long ago. Dassine gave me the chance to know you, to know of my people and our world that no Exile could remember, and to embrace my Seri once again. How could I ask for more? An eternity of sadness tinged his words.

But what of D'Natheil? His time was not yet. One of you should still be alive.

D'Natheil has not enough mind to go back alone. So much was destroyed by the Bridge when he was young. The rest, when Dassine displaced his soul with mine.

Another burst of color and the music splashed about us. My father's presence was a lacework of frost, thinning in the blaze of winter sunlight.

Quickly, son. I will hold here at the Verges for as long as I can. Tell your mother that she crossed with me as I told her she would. Live with joy, and with all my love.

And as if he were pushing me under the water to

teach me to swim, he forced me deep into his mind, leaving me only enough awareness that I might hear the call that would draw me back to life.

But I was a Soul Weaver, and I reached for my father as he had reached for me, and I drew him in beside me to wait. . . .

CHAPTER 34

Seri

If it had been daytime, or I'd been more awake, or the room had been filled with light and activity, I would never have sensed it. It was no more than the glimmer of a forgotten inspiration, or a feather out of place in your pillow, or the earliest stirring of a child in the womb, but it jolted me awake and I listened until I thought my inner ears might bleed. There. Again . . .

Gerick, child, is it you? Is it true what Ven'Dar said, that you can find your way back? Follow my voice, dear one. I shaped each word carefully.

At the end of half an hour the touch was stronger, still faint, still very far away, but I refused to believe it was some midnight fantasy of a tired and grieving widow. A lamp flared from the doorway, searing my eyes and rousing Ven'Dar, who also had dozed off.

"I was just—" said Paulo, but I held up my hand for quiet.

Mother. The call, the touch, had come again.

"Vasrin's hand," whispered Ven'Dar, watching as I focused my attention inward. The sorcerer slipped off the edge of the table, and hurried around to where he could touch Gerick's body.

Words poured from me into the night, like a river gathering its power and leaping from a cliff into a bottomless gorge below. Some of the words made sense, some didn't. Anyone would have called me a fool, but I'd come so far from logic and rational expectations in the years of my life that nothing was beyond the realm of possibility. My husband had once come back from the dead. Why not again? Why not my son?

I heard a harsh intake of breath from across the stone table where Ven'Dar hovered over Gerick. Then the sorcerer, in muted excitement, said, "Continue, my lady. Don't let go."

I couldn't even move to look. I couldn't do anything lest the fragile connection be lost.

Listen to my voice, Gerick. Find your way. Come back and live.

Can't . . . The stone . . .

The black stone pyramid was still clutched in Karon's cold hand. Dared I move it?

Hurry . . .

With a glance at Ven'Dar, I pulled the smooth stone from the linked hands and set it aside.

"By the holy Way, you've done it!" said Ven'Dar.

I scrambled across the platform until I was kneeling at Gerick's side with my hands on his face. A tinge of color graced his pale cheeks, and a faint breath passed his pale lips. I rubbed his hands, speaking aloud now, talking, weeping, laughing, babbling, coaxing him back to the world.

Ven'Dar put his arm around my shoulders and laughed until tears came. "You can rest now, my lady. He's here. You don't want to drive him away. Give him a little time."

So I sat back, and instead of Gerick's warm hand, I held Karon's cold one, and watched my son wake up. It was gradual at first. His color improved; his breathing deepened; his hands and eyelids began to twitch. Then somewhere in his journey, he crossed a dramatic threshold that caused him to sit bolt upright, gasping for breath, his eyes wide, seeing things that were not in the room with us.

". . . got to come . . . not finished . . ." He swallowed and breathed. ". . . oh, yes, you can. You must . . ."

It may have been the sound of his own voice that brought him to awareness, or perhaps the shattering of glass when Paulo dropped his lamp. But, whatever the reason, Gerick squeezed his eyes tightly shut and then opened them to look straight at me.

"Welcome back," I said, throwing my arms around him, trying to warm him, to quiet his shivering. He held me tight, but clearly his mind was on something else. When I drew back a bit to look at his face, his eyes were on Karon's body.

"I tried to bring him back with me." He touched Karon's lifeless hand. "I thought . . ."

"It's all right," I said, laughing and weeping all at once. "I'm sure it's all right."

"Tell us, young Gerick . . . Please. About the Lords," said Ven'Dar, anxiously. "We've seen signs . . . I'm sorry. I can't wait for the proper time to ask. I must know."

"They didn't come back with me," said Gerick. "I don't know if that means they're dead, but we separated from them beyond the Verges, and they're not in me any longer." And he told us all that had happened when he touched Karon's outstretched hand.

". . . and so I thought it wasn't fair. Imprisoned so horribly for ten years, and then trapped with D'Natheil for the rest of it. A slave in Zhev'Na for over a year. He had so much life left in him, and I thought it was because only one of them was supposed to be dead, and it had to be D'Natheil because D'Natheil couldn't come back. I guess I was wrong, and that's why it didn't work."

"He made his choice," I said. "He did exactly what he wanted—set you free. And Avonar. And all of us."

"He was free, too," said Gerick. "By the end, there was no more D'Natheil."

"I'm glad to hear it."

"But I wanted him to live."

We sat together at Karon's side. I was too wrung out to say much of anything. Yet the passions of a sixteen-year-old are not easily dulled. Gerick kept his hand on Karon's unmoving chest. "He's close, Mother. He wants so much to be here with us."

It must have been near midnight when we finally persuaded Gerick, half sick with exhaustion, to go back to my apartments with Paulo to eat and sleep for a while. I promised that Karon would not be left alone and that one of us would continue talking to him. Paulo laid Ven'Dar's hooded cloak over Gerick's shoulders to protect my son from curious eyes. Gerick was still condemned and feared, and it would take a while for the Dar'Nethi—and all of us—to understand what had really taken place that day.

As soon as the boys had gone, Ven'Dar summoned Bareil to prepare Karon's body for his funeral rites. "The people will need to see him laid out. You understand. So they can believe and accept."

"Of course I understand."

"You should go with your sons, lady. I'll wait here, keep our promise to Gerick, until Bareil arrives to take care of the Prince. You've had a day such as no one should ever have, and tomorrow will have its own burdens. We have a number of decisions to make, and perhaps some journeying to do."

"And what of you, Ven'Dar? Tomorrow you will be anointed Heir of D'Arnath, and face the task of rebuilding a world. Perhaps you're the one who needs to take a few hours of sleep."

"Another hour of peace here would probably benefit me more. I have a great deal to consider." He looked at me quizzically. "Will your son have regrets, do you think, when he looks back to know he might have been the Heir of D'Arnath?"

"No. I don't think he'd ever feel like he belonged here. Karon knew exactly what he was doing, and Gerick has so much as told you the same. Even if he still had any legitimate claim, he wouldn't press it. You are the only living Heir."

"And if so, I certainly need to meditate for a little longer. I've summoned a guide who awaits you in the first guardroom. Good night, dear lady. I promise you, the Prince will not be left alone tonight." He smiled and touched my hand. "I've a few things more I need to tell him."

And so I left him in the prison block and found Aimee

waiting in the guardroom to guide me back to my apartments. Gerick and Paulo were sprawled out on the carpets when I arrived, and Roxanne curled up on the couch, all of them sound asleep. I smiled through my tears at the sweetness of life and youth, and fell into my own bed. Karon's rose still bloomed beside me.

Neither dreams nor true sleep came to me that night. Rather I drifted in some half waking, at peace save for the ponderous grief that wrapped heart and body in a blanket of lead. My long farewell continued through the dark, quiet hours.

But for one more night, my rest was destined for interruption. "Madam, please . . . wake up. My lady, come quickly." Two almond-shaped eyes shone in the gray light. It was Bareil.

"What is it?" I whispered, instantly afraid for Gerick, for Roxanne, for Paulo. The Lords were back. The world ending . . .

But he just shook his head and urged me up.

I threw on a gown over my shift. Avonar, exhausted with its emotions, lay quiet in the faint light outside my window. Even the birds were hushed as if in respect for the weary populace. Paulo and Roxanne still lay wrapped in their dreams and Aimee's blankets, and Aimee herself dozed in the chair by the door, waiting until her charges might awake. Morning lay over them like a soft gray mantle. But Gerick wasn't with them.

Once Bareil and I were in the passage, I tried again. "What is it?" But he only shook his head and hurried me through the wide galleries and down a graceful curved staircase, through the formal public rooms of the palace. "Where's Gerick?"

Two huge doors of carved walnut swung open at our approach, and we entered a long room with high arched ceilings. The dawn light tinged with rose angled sharply through the tall windows, making an enchanted mist of the dust motes floating in the air. Halfway down the length of the vast, empty room sat a simple bier of polished walnut, surrounded by hundreds of candles in crystal bowls. That's where they would lay him.

Bareil didn't pause by the empty bier, but led me to

a side door, a very plain door. "This is the preparation room, my lady."

Where they took their dead princes to enchant their wounds away, I thought, to bathe them and array them in whatever attire was deemed suitable for burial—to hide the terrible truths of death. Oh, gods, why had he brought me here?

The room was small and businesslike, with a marble table at its center, clearly the resting place for the honored dead, though it, too, remained vacant. Waiting. At one side of the room was a rack with silk robes of various colors, and on the other, rows of glass shelves containing vials of oils and perfumes, boxes of candles, scrolls, small velvet-lined boxes of leather and wood that contained jewelry and gemstones. Across the room were several cushioned mourners' benches, flanking an open doorway. The room had no windows, but opened onto a small garden, a gentle reminder of life in a room devoted to the service of death. A very Dar'Nethi arrangement.

Gerick sat on the mourner's bench, his head resting in his hands.

I crossed the room and laid a hand on his hair. "Are you all right, dear one?"

"I couldn't sleep," he said, without looking up. "I'll be all right."

Ven'Dar appeared in the arched doorway from the garden. "Good morning, my lady," he said, somberly. "My apologies for waking you so early, but a matter of some urgency has arisen with regard to the Prince's funeral rites. Your son and I believe that only you can resolve it."

"But I know very little of your customs . . ." I began.

"The one who is concerned will explain the difficulty. It is very complicated, but I believe your knowledge will be sufficient. If you would step into the garden . . ."

Exasperated with the Dar'Nethi and their incessant ritual, I hurried through the door into the garden. In a corner that the early sun had not yet touched, someone in silk robes of dark blue was bending over a bed of miniature roses.

"Excuse me, sir," I said. "I understand you've discovered a problem with the Prince's funeral arrangements. Please explain what is so urgent that it must be settled before the birds leave their nests. Funeral rites rarely require such haste."

The man's back was toward me, and the sun was in my eyes, and even when he straightened up, I thought, for a long moment, that he wasn't going to say anything. The dawn breeze wafted a hundred scents about my head until I felt almost giddy. Was that what made the hairs on my arms prickle—or was it the breadth of his shoulders or the color of his hair bound with a clip that glinted silver in the sunbeams . . .

"The problem, my lady, is with the subject of these rites. He just doesn't seem to be dead."

And so in the gentle dawn did my love turn and greet me in such fashion as to leave no mistake as to his condition of life or death. In his unshadowed blue eyes was reflected the soul of my Karon, and in his smile was all the joy of the universe.

EPILOGUE

I had given up too soon in my waiting, back in the prison block at the palace. Karon had so much farther to come back than Gerick, and it was so much more difficult, for he believed himself properly dead. Yet Gerick's plea had held him at the Verges, and he could not dismiss our son's belief that only one life need be forfeit—that of the incapable D'Natheil.

Gerick claims to have felt a "stirring" in his mind as he fell asleep. Perhaps. For whatever reason, he went back to sit with his father through the night and found Bareil bathing Karon in preparation for his funeral. Gerick has never told me what he did as Bareil went about his work. The Dulcé says Gerick sat in the shadows and went to sleep. But I've surmised that Gerick entered the dark, cold shell of his father's body and kept it living, allowing Karon time to use our lifeline and find his way back. Perhaps the bathing water was a bit cool, the Dulcé confessed sheepishly, but he never thought it cold enough to wake the dead.

Together Karon and Ven'Dar decided that the Dar'-Nethi would not be told that the man they knew as Prince D'Natheil had survived his last battle with the Lords. Though his body yet housed Karon's soul, in truth, the sad and angry D'Natheil was dead. His passions no longer influenced Karon, and Karon no longer held any of the Heir's power. Likewise, D'Natheil's corrupted son would remain dead, executed by his father's hand. Gerick had no interest in helping Ven'Dar explain how the Fourth Lord of Zhev'Na had been willing to give his life to defeat his corruptors and protect the

poorest of worlds. The people of Gondai had been confused for too long. They needed to move forward and
to heal.

And so later that day, as soon as the newly anointed
Ven'Dar could shake off his aides and well-wishers to
take us across D'Arnath's Bridge, we slipped quietly out
of Gondai with only Aimee and Bareil to bid us farewell.
The Prince deposited us in a place I selected—a quiet
lane in Montevial—with a promise to visit us at Verdil-
lion as soon as he could find the time.

We returned Roxanne to her home that same evening,
using the opal brooch her mother had given me to gain
unnoted access to the palace. As we suspected, Radele
had silenced Evard with the same enchantment used on
me. We could only speculate as to reasons. Karon maintained that Radele had merely thought to scare us back
to Verdillon where he could control Gerick more easily.
Ever more cynical than my husband, I believed that Radele wanted to provoke chaos in the mundane world
to further justify his family's contention that we were
unworthy of Dar'Nethi concern. When we pressed Gerick for his opinion, he surmised that Radele was beginning to enjoy the power the Lords had given him with
the oculus, toying with the most powerful of mundane
rulers as a child torments ants and beetles.

On that night Karon and Gerick together released the
King of Leire from his months of silence, and we saw
our old enemy embraced with love and relief by his
clear-eyed wife and daughter. We did not linger to answer his befuddled questions or hear his thanks. Even
for Karon, there were limits to compassion.

Roxanne sent us on our way with money, horses,
promises, and every gift we would accept. She kissed an
astonished Paulo on the forehead with an offer of her
friendship if ever he required it, and then she clasped
Gerick's hands, studying him as if to press his image into
her memory. "You're going back, aren't you?"

Gerick nodded, flicking his eyes our way. "I'll see
them to our friend's house in Valleor first."

Roxanne nodded, as if she expected nothing else.
"You'll miss my help."

Gerick laughed a bit. "Indeed I will."

Roxanne didn't laugh, but squeezed his hands until her knuckles went white. "You'll find many people willing to help you. But sometimes you need to ask. Don't forget that." Then she released him and shoved him toward his horse. As Gerick mounted up, she strode back under the torchlit gate tower, and the portcullis clanged shut behind her.

Mere days after reestablishing the reign so tenaciously and skillfully perserved by his queen, King Evard promulgated two decrees that would have been unheard of a few years earlier. Sorcery, in and of itself, was no longer a crime, for sorcerers had worked closely with the king to end the strange disturbances of the previous year. The second decree, that women could own property and inherit the titles of their fathers, needed no explanation.

Of less interest to the people of Leire, but of some significance to Karon and me, was an envelope that followed us to Verdillon, where Karon and I planned to stay with Tennice awhile. In it were the deeds to Windham and the Gault titles that had been vacant for sixteen years. Though sorely tempted by the opportunity to care for Martin's home, we were inclined to refuse anything from Evard's hand. What decided the question was the simple note that accompanied the documents. It said only, *From a grateful father and mother.* In that spirit we accepted.

Gerick remained with us only long enough to make sure we understood how his life was changed, so we shouldn't worry about him too much when he and Paulo headed off to northern Valleor, where rumor had it that a tribe of barbarians had invaded the Four Realms. If the portal still existed, he told us, he would take the Singlars back to the Bounded and stay as long as they seemed to need him. He promised to send word as soon as he knew anything to tell.

Long anxious weeks passed until a weary rider showed up at the door with a crumpled paper, saying it had been left at a tavern in northern Valleor with the promise of a gold coin for the man who would deliver it to us. I paid the man and tore open the letter.

Dearest Mother and Father,

This is the first moment I've had to write. I found the Singlars in good health, thanks to the preparation Paulo gave them before we left the Bounded. The Vallorean villagers had not welcomed them, but had not harmed them, either, as there were so many, and some of them so fierce in appearance. We've left a tale for many an inn's common room, I think. But now I've taken them home, and they've set to work rebuilding their fastnesses and starting up their markets and trades again. Few of our fastnesses survived, including very little of my own residence, so things are very hard right now. We have to work long hours just to get everyone fed. But no firestorms assault them and no terrified Valloreans growl at them or chase them away, so no one complains about the price. We don't know as yet whether the wild folk we left here survived. We have reinstated our watch until we are sure there is no need for it.

The biggest news of this week is that one of the Singlar girls is with child—a first. Paulo may have to find a midwife on his next journey to Valleor, I suppose, and persuade her to come back with him. This is a great mystery to the Singlars, and I'm not exactly experienced with it either. They think I know everything!

The Source has maintained throughout all. I understand now that she knows no more than I, but she helps me think clearly, and question myself, so that I believe I come up with decent judgments and reasonable rules.

Paulo will be going back and forth a good deal, I think. He says he needs a touch of sun and a taste of jack fairly often or he'll get testy. Though we use the portal to Valleor frequently, the portal to Avonar has completely vanished; I suppose because I am no long the son of D'Arnath's Heir. Paulo thinks it's

*too bad, but I can't say I'm sorry. I've no wish to
set foot in Gondai ever again.*

*When we get a little more settled, I hope you will
come visit here. I know you each could give me lots
of good advice. I'm not fool enough to think I know
all I need to be a good ruler, but I can't quit and
apprentice for ten years to learn it. They have no one
else. Luckily, they have no expectations, so we suit
very well. This is where I belong.*

*Know that you are both in my thoughts every day.
It makes no difference what worlds we walk, I feel
your presence and your faith in me, and it gives me
strength to do whatever needs to be done. It will take
me a while to come to terms with what I am and
what I have been. To know how close I was to going
back leaves me wary.*

*But no oculus hangs in the cave of the Source any
longer. A wall of solid rock stands where it was. And
from a crevice in the rock has sprouted a tree, little
more than a stick as yet, too small to reveal its variety. I like to think it is a sign of the life you've given
me. I promise I'll do my best to nurture it.*

> *Your loving son,*
> *Gerick*

Karon has begun to write a history of his people in
our world, a project he has dreamed about since he first
went to the University. And he has begun to heal again,
quietly until we are sure of Evard's new law. We live in
the Windham gatehouse, as the main house is too ruined
to rebuild. I am working to restore Martin's gardens.

Gerick's infrequent letters tell of Singlars and sunrocks and towers that grow, and of the small victories
and immense frustrations of responsibility, but very little
of himself. Nothing of the scars that I fear go far deeper
than those on his hands. *Wary.* I, too, feel wary. Karon
told me of Ziddari's final curse: *You are our instrument . . .*

Are the Lords truly dead? Gerick and Karon believe
it. Ven'Dar, too. On a visit this month, the Prince reported how the society grown up about constant war in
Gondai has begun to crumble, just as the towers of

Zhev'Na collapsed to rubble at the moment of Karon's and Gerick's victory. But though I rejoice each morning when I wake with Karon beside me, I cling to him fiercely each night when the inevitable darkness comes.

ABOUT THE AUTHOR

Though **Carol Berg** calls Colorado her home, her roots
are in Texas, in a family of teachers, musicians, and rail-
road men. She has a degree in mathematics from Rice
University and one in computer science from the University of Colorado, but managed to squeeze in minors
in English and art history along the way. She has combined a career as a software engineer with her writing,
while also raising three sons. She lives with her husband
at the foot of the Colorado mountains.